GOLDEN REFLECTIONS
STORIES OF THE MASK

Baen Books by Fred Saberhagen

Of Berserkers, Swords & Vampires
Berserker Man (omnibus)
Rogue Berserker (omnibus)
Berserker Death (omnibus)
The Dracula Tape
Vlad Tapes
Pilgrim
The Black Throne (with Roger Zelazny)

Author's Note
For more information about Fred Saberhagen
and this series, see:
www.berserker.com

GOLDEN REFLECTIONS
STORIES OF THE MASK

FRED SABERHAGEN
et al.

A Baen Book Original

Baen Publishing Enterprises
P.O. Box 1403
Riverdale, NY 10471
www.baen.com

ISBN 13: 978-1-4391-3415-3

Cover art by Bob Eggleton

First Baen printing, February 2011

Distributed by Simon & Schuster
1230 Avenue of the Americas
New York, NY 10020

Printed in the United States of America

10 9 8 7 6 5 4 3 2 1

CONTENTS

GOLDEN REFLECTIONS

Additional Copyright Information

Golden Reflections in the Maelstrom
by
Robert E. Vardeman

The world is in the throes of change as we shift into the Digital Age from technology that has changed little since Gutenberg. This is no less profound than when the Industrial Revolution forever gave societies new ways to prosper. The Internet is scarcely fifty years old, and the World Wide Web only twenty, so the full impact of what it means to have all information—and entertainment —available through a handheld device is still murky.

The publishing industry is caught up in this maelstrom and still not sure which way to turn. One word pops to the surface of any conversation about print vs. e-books, libraries vs. online wikis, newspapers vs. blogs—and that word is *content*. No matter the medium, print or digital, content is king. If the reader doesn't want to see it, what's the use?

Fred Saberhagen began his career in print and immediately delivered exciting content through his wild, weird, innovative stories of Berserkers and Empires of the East and Swords and Greek gods and falling veils and, as this volume celebrates, *Mask of the Sun*. Most science fiction time travel stories are rooted in the same Eurocentric milieu, but Fred ventured out and posited an unexpected future, a different reason for a time war, with antagonists that should have been familiar but were not. Those struggling for timeline supremacy are the Aztecs and the Incas, masters of the twenty-third century and would-be masters of all time.

This shift from European to Mesoamerican protagonists was not enough for him. Thrown into the time war was a more mysterious artifact. The Mask. Look through it and see . . . what? Your own destiny? What you desired most or what the Mask somehow wanted to happen? Who created it and for what purpose? The intricacies of time travel allow for one Mask to be in multiple timelines and eras. Does the Mask follow rules or does it make them?

As Joan Saberhagen has pointed out in her introduction, the possibilities suggested by this time war, those fighting it and their methods, and the Mask itself, became endless. David Weber and Jane Lindskold bubbled with ideas as different as the American Revolution is from the Pueblo Revolt. When we cast outward for other authors, their responses were similarly enthusiastic. But simply doing an anthology—strictly a print anthology—was not all that Fred would have considered. Where was the innovation? He would have sought out the different to elevate the work above the herd.

The usual approach would have been to invite twenty or so writers to contribute 5,000 word stories. But novelette and novella lengths are the ginger-haired orphans of the field and deserve better than they get. Joan and I decided to limit the number of authors but allow them more room to roam through the timeworlds of the Mask. We have six novelettes and a novella in this volume to allow top-of-the-field authors ample room to explore their ideas and alternate histories. And they have.

But still, an anthology of longer works cried out for something more. Why not reprint the novel that sparked all the enthusiasm, as well? For those readers unfamiliar with one of the finest time-travel novels in the field, *Mask of the Sun* is part of the volume. Seven substantial new stories *and* their inspiration? Only in *Golden Reflections*.

Baen Books is a pioneer in moving beyond the print medium and is sure to do well with online electronic sampling from this print volume. It seems only fitting that Fred Saberhagen's work will be part of the forefront of a change in presentation of solid entertainment—with content that transcends its medium of presentation.

Golden Reflections Origins
by
Joan Spicci Saberhagen

The origin of *Golden Reflections*—A Group Story

In 2008, about a year after Fred had passed, I attended Albuquerque's annual science fiction convention, Bubonicon. A small
group of us, David and Sharon Weber, Jane Lindskold and her
husband, Jim Moore, and I and my grandnephew John Goldberger
took a break from convention activities and went out to dinner.
Over some delicious barbeque we began to discuss Fred's works.
Dave and Jane strongly voiced their love of Fred's short novel
Mask of the Sun. As we batted around the main points of the book,
Dave suggested that I might want to put together an anthology of
stories set in the world of *Mask*. Jane chimed in that she'd like to
try her hand at a story in this world. Of course, the fact that Jim
is an archeologist probably adds to Jane's fascination with *Mask*.
Dave, too, thought the world of *Mask* would be a fun place to play.

So was born the concept of the *Mask* anthology.

I asked my good friend, Robert E. Vardeman, if he would be
willing to help with the editorial chores. Bob is a well-published
author with quite a few anthologies to his credit. Also, he has been
teaching writing for some time. In addition to the fact that Bob is
a well-qualified professional, he has been a friend of Fred and

3

mine for over twenty years, and, not to be overlooked, he lives nearby, so we could consult over stories and the project's general progress face-to-face.

Dave approached Toni Weisskoff at Baen Books with the idea. She was willing to look at a proposal. And she agreed to support the project.

Authors were lined up. As story ideas were presented to us, Bob and I soon realized that our original requirements were a bit too narrow for the wonderfully fertile imaginations of our contributors. So, we held to the minimum requirements: use of the Mask and a background setting of future struggles between the Inca and Aztec empires.

The authors did themselves proud. To our amazement many of the stories dovetailed, leading naturally from one to the next.

Hope you are as entertained and delighted by the imaginings from a fine group of authors as we are!

The origin of *Mask of the Sun*—A Personal Story

Fred became interested in the Inca and Aztec cultures as a result of the sheer number of books and memorabilia brought to our joint home way back in the late '60s when we married. In the two years prior to our marriage, I had spent extended vacations in Mexico and Peru. So there were books, brochures, toy llamas, Bolivian wooden plaques, et cetera all around our home. About five years (and three children) into our marriage, we spent a summer in Key West. All these experiences mixed with Fred's diligent research and fertile imagination to produce *Mask of the Sun*. Please enjoy.

Mask of the Sun
by
Fred Saberhagen
1. The Raising

Key West, 1975

It didn't pay to reach too fast for gold.

Better to savor the still-possible dream for a few moments longer . . .

At low tide in this part of the Gulf, the white sand bottom was nowhere more than about ten feet below the surface. A snorkeler could let his finned feet trail and for a moment imagine himself a soaring bird, looking down on an unpeopled world and letting his thoughts roam as wild and fantastic as he liked. When Tom Gabrieli's eye caught a single faint golden gleam from the trough of one winding sand-ripple, hardly more than arm's length below, old habit made him slow his gliding progress to a halt, savoring the dream still possible, before it turned out to be a yellow metal beer can dropped last Tuesday.

Then he reached down—the water was little more than four feet deep just here, and you could hardly call the requisite maneuver a dive—and brushed away the sand. His fingers touched smooth, rounded hardness that somehow, before he even tried to move the thing, gave an impression of substantial weight. Throat muscles spasmed on his held breath when the first golden surface, broad and curved as a cheekbone, came into view.

A moment later, he was standing chest deep in water, his snorkeling mask already pulled off and tossed into the nearby boat. What he held in his shaking hands was a different kind of mask, of thick, solid gold, with inlaid squares of ceramic decoration here and there. Realistic enough to be a life-sized portrait, with the cheekbones broad and high, and the mouth curved in a subtle, lordly smile that might have been meant to express hauteur and hatred instead of joy. The nose was hooked and decidedly masculine; the nostrils, like the mouth, were closed as solidly as a statue's. The inlaid eyes, of some white stone or glass, were a little more prominent than life beneath the heavy ridge of brow. At each temple, and again in the center of the upper forehead, were golden flanges pierced with holes, through which straps or thongs might have been strung—

With a surging splash, Sally came up on the other side of the boat and clung there to the gunwale. Her own snorkeling mask was held in one hand, her blond hair coming out from under its cap, strong sunbrowned arms and shoulders agleam with water above a yellow bikini top. Tom glanced at her, then brought his eyes back to scan the golden mask held in his hands. His senses registered that Sally was calling something to him, but he could not really hear a single word.

. . . the mask he held would not be wearable, not with those opaque eyes. Why, then, the places to secure a strap? Of course it might be funerary; meant to cover eyes no longer seeing, a face no longer fit for others' sight.

On impulse, he lifted the gold face to his own and found his chin fitting neatly into an interior hollow while the side flanges gently clasped his temples. And at once he discovered that the eyes were not truly opaque. Darkly translucent, they transmitted a shimmer of faint rainbow light. He vaguely supposed this must be some result of the sun on the miles of little waves that danced around him out to the horizon . . .

"Tom? What in the *hell*? Tom—?"

This time he heard her plainly. And at the same moment it flashed on him that someone else, in some distant boat or aircraft, might be able to see him, too—might just possibly be scanning with binoculars or telephoto lens. He snatched the mask down from his face and plunged it into concealing water. Holding it submerged, he turned to scan the horizon.

There were some clouds, and sun-hazed sky, and a million gentle waves upon the shallow waters. To the east, the nearest of the Keys made a green smear along the boundary of sea and sky. Green would be the mangroves along the water's edge, screening the buildings and other vegetation behind them.

"I found this, Sal." Reluctantly he brought it up again, held it above the water long enough for her to see.

"Oh, my God!" Sal had climbed into the boat and was now leaning out of it on his side to look. Her blue eyes were wide, and she had pulled off her cap, making her head a blond explosion. "Is it gold?"

"Just like that . . . ten times as much as I ever found when I was in the business. A hundred times. Sure, it's gold. Unless they're buried deep in the bottom, damn few things'll last submerged in seawater for any length of time. Pure gold is one."

He kept turning and turning it over in his hands, held just below the water's surface. Almost unconsciously, he had turned his body so that the mask would be between him and the boat, thus providing the maximum degree of shelter from any prying eyes. Of course he knew it was unlikely that anyone was really watching him with a telescope. But still.

Tom said, "There'll be a couple of pounds of gold in this. A few thousand bucks just for the metal. But the thing itself . . . it'll be worth a fortune."

"What're you going to do with it?" Sal's voice was quieter than before.

"Right now, put it away." He moved against the boat, snatched up a towel lying inside, wrapped the mask quickly, and shoved it under a thwart. Again he looked around, unable to shake the feeling that the state tax agents—or somebody—were already cruising toward him to take away his treasure. But there was no one. No vehicle approached.

He quickly put his snorkeling mask back on and began to swim around the boat in an ever-widening search pattern, scanning the bottom as he had never scanned before. Nothing. Back at the very spot where he had found the mask, he tore into the sand with hands and feet. Nothing.

At last he gave up and clung to the side of the boat. He said, "You look as if we just lost a fortune overboard instead of bringing one up."

"Tom. If it's real, wouldn't there be a . . . a chest, or something? The wreckage of a ship?"

"No. No, not likely." He levered himself up into the boat, felt once of the hardness wrapped in the towel below the thwart, and then started to take off his fins. "That's got to be from some Spanish treasure ship. And it was four hundred years ago when they came up this way from Mexico and Peru. By now, any wood is gone, completely rotted away."

"Peru's on the Pacific."

He got the impression that she *wanted* his find to be unreal. "Sure it is. But they brought the stuff in ships up to the isthmus of Panama and lugged it across, then put it in different ships on the Atlantic side. Then up this way, hugging the coast all around the Gulf. That was the easiest route then. But what with war and pirates and storms, a good part of their loot never made it back to Spain." Black-haired, black-bearded, his chest hair a dark mat slow-drying even in the sun, he worked with practiced hands at getting the boat ready to head home.

Meanwhile the girl sat there holding her bathing cap and looking under the thwart.

He paused. "Look, Sal, I'm gonna split this right down the middle with you. And it can be worth a fortune. For your part, what you've got to do is keep this *absolutely* quiet. I know how these things work. If we're good little citizens and tell everybody what we've found, the state government steps in, and they'll rip us off for more than half. And it might be years before we get what little we're allowed to keep."

Sal had nothing to say, and she maintained her silence until the boat was moving and the Keys were noticeably closer. Then she suddenly said: "I don't know if I want half."

Tom looked at her. "Sure you do. Later you will, if not right now. Look, I'm going to handle all the business. All you have to do is keep quiet. If anyone should ever ask you, all we did today was swim and snorkel and mess around. The subject of treasure never came up."

He swept his eyes hurriedly once more round the horizon, then bent and with one hand unrolled the towel and lifted out his find.

His fingers held it. Incredible. Wanting to get Sal more involved in this thing, he asked, "You want to try it on?"

She had pulled her sunburned feet back as if to keep them away from the towel when it was being opened. She didn't answer. But her body was tilting forward slightly, as if being drawn; her eyes were fascinated.

Before handing it over, he raised it to his own face once again, seeing the watery light-ripples float in through its eyes. Seeing—

He jerked the mask down from his face and sat there blinking at it in his lap. He rubbed his eyes.

"What's wrong, Tom?"

"Nothing." He gave the yellow weight to her. "It was like I thought I could see through the eyes. And there was . . . "

"What?"

"Like a couple of men." He cut short his answer abruptly. When he looked up again from tending the boat, Sal was sitting there holding the thing in both hands, her eyes wide and face solemn, a little pale around the lips. He wasn't sure whether she had tried it on or not.

"Tom."

"What?"

"You're gonna want to kill me, but I wish you'd throw it overboard again."

"What?"

"All right, all right. But at least don't wear it anymore. I don't like the way it looks. And I don't care if I get any money or not."

He reached for the thing, smiling with one side of his mouth, and repeated, "You will, later on." He wrapped the golden weight and tucked it far back under the thwart; a casual glance would not even notice the towel.

Now some detail could be seen in the rim of vegetation ahead on the horizon. A couple of other islands in the staggering chain were visible, along with the white tracery of the connecting highway bridges. On an island to the south he could see a high-rise going up, looking as out of place as it would have at the North Pole.

He had to say something about it, thought he really didn't want to: "I thought I saw my brother Mike, as if he was sitting right there beside you . . . " He let his voice trail off. It had been too crazy. A white-haired man's figure near Mike, and somewhere in the air behind them a huge golden sun-disc, and stylized red daggers or lightning bolts in a circular pattern.

Sal took his revelation with surprising—no, disturbing—calm. She said, "I saw—myself, throwing the thing overboard." She wasn't joking in the least, or even smiling. "Maybe that's just what I should have done. You could have found it again if you'd tried hard enough. And that way you'd have believed me—that I don't want the money. And you'd have kept me out of all of it from here on."

Tom shook his head. He had read somewhere that certain psychic disturbances could be contagious. There had been epidemics of people thinking themselves possessed by demons. He said aloud, "Out of all what? There's not gonna be any trouble, just some money. The light must come through in some funny way, and you saw what you were thinking about anyway, something like looking into a fire. You'll take money when the time comes, kid. You'll be willing."

After that they were quiet for what seemed a long time, riding the light chop between infinite sky and sea. Only when they were actually coming into the harbor did he speak again.

"I'm going to find a good place to hide it, to begin with. And I damn sure don't mean to give it away."

"Why don't you call your brother about it?" Sal suggested after a moment's silence, sending prickles down his spine through the July heat. He was certain he had said nothing to her about Mike's holding a telephone in his vision.

"Why do you say that?" he asked. "You haven't even met him."

"Just the way you talk about him sometimes. He sounds—I don't know. Smart. Competent." She still hadn't found the exact word for what she meant.

Tom smiled faintly. "He's lucky, is what he is. And if you think I have a mean streak, you should see him sometimes."

"He doesn't sound *mean*, the way you talk about him."

"All right, he's not mean. Basically." And with that he had to get busy docking. As he worked, he could catch glimpses of the masts of the treasure-hunting company's vessels, moored not far away. If *they* ever learned of his find, they would think it was something he had located while working for them and had somehow managed to keep for himself till now. They would be putting in a claim. If that happened, Sally could testify . . . but once the legal wrangling started, most of the money would be lost to him, one way or another.

No, he was going to think positive. This time, for a change, he was going to screw the world. Maybe in a secret sale he could get fifty thousand dollars for this thing. Then, even allowing for a split with Sal—say he gave her fifteen, twenty thousand, that would be enough, more might scare her too much—he would have a stake big enough to give him a fighting chance against the world. To get somewhere and be somebody.

· But maybe he could sell a thing like this for as much as a hundred thousand. To do that would for damn sure take some hard bargaining. Nobody gave away that kind of bread. But he knew for a fact, from stories heard when he worked for the treasure hunters, there were wealthy art dealers and collectors willing to pay such sums and ask no questions beyond authenticating whatever they bought.

In silence he and Sal left the rented boat at the dock and went to unchain their bicycles from the uncrowded rack. One thing about the Keys in summer—you rarely had to wait in line for anything. And once you got through the bottleneck of the single connecting highway, heavy traffic was six cars coming along without a break.

Tom had stuffed the wrapped mask along with other odds and ends into his habitual backpack. Sal still in her bikini, himself in trunks and T-shirt—sweat-soaked the moment he put it on—they pedaled through the humid heat, past weather-beaten houses, oleander, cheap bars, breadfruit, old and new motels, palm trees, uncrowded beaches, bougainvillea, tourist-trade shops, royal poinciana, open-air laundromats. An active little city, you could usually find what you wanted in it. The trouble was, despite all the underground stories and rumors he heard when he was in the diving game, he had no names of any of these wealthy and unscrupulous collectors, nor any way of getting in contact with them, in New York or Chicago or wherever in hell they lived.

He could start trying to make contact by talking to some shady people he knew. He had in mind one sometime drug dealer that he thought he could find, here on the Keys or in Miami Beach. Of course he wouldn't trust that cat for a moment. And meanwhile, where was he going to hide the thing?

Following Sal, Tom climbed the narrow stair to her small apartment over a Spanish grocery store. As expected, her roommate was out at work. Tom slipped off his backpack and stood there swinging the promising weight of it by a strap while she closed the door and peeled off her bra and stood luxuriating in the cool wash from a window air conditioner that had been left running.

Maybe two pounds of gold. He had to get it stowed away somewhere, then do some thinking. "I'll see you later, Sal."

Today was not the day to change his routine, and Tom went as usual to the book-and-record store, in the new shopping center, where for a couple of months now he had been working evenings as a clerk. He would call Mike, he thought. After work tonight . . .

Business was slow. The Chevrolet crowd of summer tourists didn't buy as much as the Cadillac people who came in winter, so he had time this evening to sit behind his counter and think. The break was welcome. From a display table he picked up a gift volume, *Central American Art*. It proved to be full of beautiful color plates, though short on the hard information he was seeking.

He felt sure the mask was Indian—pre-Columbian—though he wasn't an expert and couldn't begin to pin it down any closer than that without help. He wanted to identify it before he went to anyone. If he didn't sound stupid, they wouldn't try to cheat him so badly. Tomorrow he would try the library.

. . . Jesus, it had been weird. In the background, red daggers and a great golden disc. Up front, apparently right in the boat, Mike, holding a phone, plain as day. Certainly Mike, though near as Tom could remember, the face had looked sort of like a drawing rather than an image from memory. Some psychologist could explain it, sure. But meanwhile he wasn't going to put that thing on again—

The shop's door chime signaled a customer. Tom looked up at the approaching white-haired man, whose face might be taken for young or old—a strange face that would be hard to forget.

Tom had never met the man before. But he had seen him. Just today.

2. The First Giving

Lake Texcoco, Mexico, 1325

Amid tall shoreline reeds, under a blaze of stars that spanned a moonless midnight sky, Cimatl waited, standing almost motionless on a small flat rock at the lake's very edge. He shivered slightly and continuously in the chill that had come with night in this tropical high valley. To his ears that listened persistently for the strange sounds of certain gods, there came now only the cries of nightbirds, croaking of amphibians, an occasional splash of a jumping fish. But Cimatl did not falter on this third night of his vigil. Last night at midnight, when the Sun's great jealous eye was farthest from the world, he had been briefly, tantalizingly rewarded by the rush of great wings overhead, and for one moment he had seen a shape far larger than any bird pass swift against the stars.

This vigil by night was necessary because their age-long and faithful worship of the Sun had not saved Cimatl's people from the terrible dangers that now seemed certain to overwhelm them. Two generations past, their long flight from the north had ended in this land—ended in sheer exhaustion, not success. Except for this stretch of swampy lakeshore, disdained by other nearby tribes, they were still landless. New persecutions threatened, as terrible as those that had driven their grandfathers from the north, and there seemed no place left to flee. The Tenocha had been unable even to attach themselves as vassals to a stronger tribe, and thus gain some measure of protection.

By day, Cimatl and the other priests of the Tenocha continued to beseech the Sun for help; but by night Cimatl, fasting and desperate, had as a last resort begun this other, secret worship.

Here amid tall reeds, the darkness of midnight seemed the deepest. And now, as on the two previous nights, Cimatl began to chant a litany to the gods of darkness whose names were terrible to speak. As his voice rose up, he heard, as on the preceding midnight, wings that could not be those of any ordinary bird beating at some great distance—beating so fast they made a steady roaring, like the wind in great tree branches.

Cimatl threw back his head and saw a looming shape too large for any bird. Amid a sudden rush of air that rattled reeds about him on all sides, he stumbled in his chant. When unexpected light stabbed down, it was so violent against the entrenched darkness that Cimatl was completely blinded at first. The terrible idea smote him that this might be the very eye of the Sun, returned in midnight anger at his servant's faithlessness, and his heart failed him momentarily. But even as he cowered against the burning wrath to come, the light dimmed. His eyes could start to see again, and no, this small light was not the Sun. It seemed to issue from the belly of some hovering god of eagles, from whose belly also there was being let down some kind of a large burden on a string or cord.

Around Cimatl, a mad pattern of reed shadows danced. His vision gradually gained strength against the artificial glare. The light was strongest directly beneath the hovering eagle-god, where it shone full upon another flat rock. On this a huge snake coiled, drawn perhaps from mud and water by some faint sun-warmth still lingering in the stone.

Cimatl saw that the burden being lowered on a cord, directly above the snake, was of the size and shape of man, but garbed like no man he had ever seen, in a peculiar suit that covered nearly all the skin. In one gloved hand of the suspended figure, a short lance flared once with orange fire. On the rock below, the snake's head vanished with a puff of steam and stringy splattering. The serpent's body, thick as an arm, writhed there until the man-shape stood beside it and with one booted foot shoved it away into the reeds and water.

In the air above, the roar of wings held steady. The man-shape raised its face and looked toward the medicine man. Long hair of black, with golden ornaments. Red daggers drawn on its chest. "Cimatl!"

The priest bent down and hid his eyes in awe.

"Cimatl, the favor you have asked the gods of night is granted you. Greatness shall be your people's lot, from this night forward."

After the voice had been silent for a few moments, Cimatl dared to squint timidly toward the speaker. In one gloved hand, the god was holding something out to him. Cimatl eagerly plunged off his own rock into the shallows. A stump of broken reed stabbed into his foot, but he did not yet feel the wound. Something dying thrashed in mud; the Snake of Time was still alive, but with its head had gone its power to strike. Meanwhile, in droning triumph, the Eagle of the Night maintained its place above. In his exaltation, Cimatl strove to miss not a symbol, not a nuance, of this mighty vision. One quick glance upward against the light showed him a symbolic dagger, red as blood, limned on a smooth gray flank.

Then he held his eyes downcast, for he was standing now before the man-shaped god, who still held something out for him to take. Groping at the edge of his averted vision, the priest carefully received in both hands a small weight of metal.

The son of the Night-Eagle was speaking to him again: "With this gift you shall become a mighty nation. See that you keep it hidden. Let only your First Speaker dare to put it on his face, and that in secrecy. Do not mention it in your songs, when you shall come to sing them, or show it in your sculptures when you come to carve. Let no one know of it except your inner priesthood."

Cimatl wanted to speak his transcendent gratitude, but could not find his voice. He managed to make a violent gesture of assent, both his hands locked on the gods' gift as if they might crush it in their zeal. Abruptly, then, the almost-blinding lights were gone. A few words were spoken nearby, in some inhuman-sounding tongue, as if the visiting deities exchanged banal comments between themselves. Then suddenly the wings were beating louder, casting down a gale. Cimatl was left in darkness, temporarily blind again, able only to listen until the rush of wings had receded, vanished into the sky.

Cimatl turned away then from the lake. Trying to chant his gratitude, he staggered amid unseen obstacles toward the distant fire-specks marking the Tenocha camp. His eyes gradually retuned themselves once more to starlight and he began to see his way. He felt pain now from his injured foot, but pain did not matter. Nothing mattered, save the gift he held in his hands.

He could see now that it was of metal and crystal, a leather thong strung through holes in its outer flanges. *Let only your First Speaker dare to put it on his face . . . with this gift you shall become a mighty nation . . .* Not a word of that solemn charge would Cimatl ever forget.

The Mask now in his hands had no high cheekbones, nor mouth or chin, nor was it gold. It was not much more than a large pair of goggles. A century would pass before the Mixtec slaves encased it in a gold model of a smiling face. They were to work for the secret pleasure of Cimatl's successor as First Speaker of the Aztec-Tenocha, who by then had become the lords of most of Mexico.

3. The Finding

After a morning flight down from Atlanta, Mike Gabrieli spent the middle part of his day in Miami Beach, talking fruitlessly to police and to people at the hotel where Tom had been registered when he disappeared, leaving a suitcase, some clothes, and an unpaid bill. Then Mike got on the late-afternoon flight from Miami to Key West.

He had never been south of Miami before, and found the look of the Keys pleasantly surprising. Unwalled by hotels, and stitched by the slender thread of US1, an immensity of blue-green water embraced near-tropic islands. Near the end of the brief flight he tried to catch a glimpse of Cuba, which was now closer than Miami, but he could see only August clouds massed on the south horizon.

From the air, Key West looked more built up than he had expected. Still, the airport was far from busy. Actually it seemed almost deserted. The next flight back to Miami—there were apparently no scheduled flights at all to anywhere else—might be planned for next month instead of tomorrow morning.

One cab was still waiting after his few fellow passengers had vanished into the sullen heat. Mike got into it without hurrying, sport shirt already sticking to his ribs, and dropped his little traveling bag at his feet. He gave the driver the address of Aunt Tessie's house, and hoped silently that the air conditioners there were working as well as the cab's was.

The cab left him on a corner in what might have been a lower-middle-class suburb, except that at least two of Aunt Tessie's neighbors were building large boats in their backyards. A dog barked someplace, and another answered. The vegetation looked tropical, all of it different from what was common anywhere north of Florida.

Feeling in his pocket for the key, Mike hefted his little bag and strode down the narrow walk toward the little white stucco house. Palms in the front yard, and in the back what looked like a tall banana tree. He had seen family snapshots of the place; a number of relatives had stayed here at one time or another. Tessie also let the house out frequently through a temporary rental service, so the utilities were kept turned on. He had heard there were two bedrooms.

Looking into a screened-in front porch, he saw some heavy wooden lawn chairs, stained redwood not long ago. He walked on. His key was for the side door, which he entered from the carport.

The carport was empty—completely empty—and Mike stood there for a moment making a teeth-baring grimace. The Humphrey Bogart look, Tom used to say. It was no doubt the dumb little bastard's own fault, whatever had happened to him. Mike could only pray that he was still in one piece, somewhere . . .

A four-inch green lizard sat on a boundary wall of open-work masonry and looked impassively back at Mike. Tom had lived in this house for a while when he first came down to the Keys, a year and a half ago, to work as a diver for the treasure hunters and to try to get his head together, as he had put it. Then came the Great Pot Party, infamous in the annals of the Gabrieli family. Police cars right here in Aunt Tessie's driveway, and all hell broken loose with the old folks. Although the cops had never convicted him formally of anything, Tom had been firmly requested to move out. Now, since his disappearance, Tessie seemed to be having guilt feelings, as if her eviction notice had contributed to some ultimate downfall.

Mike unlocked the side door and went in, to find all serene. Inside was no hotter than outside—it was evidently impossible to close the louvered doors and windows tightly. After he got the three window air-conditioners going, Mike looked around.

Inside the doors of kitchen cabinets were notes, informing all tenants where the household goods and fuses could be found, when they could pick the two kinds of limes from the trees in the backyard, how to obtain good plumbers, electricians, babysitters. Tessie had renting down to a science. She admonished tenants to keep their foodstuffs tightly sealed against tropical insects and to bring all lawn furniture indoors if they left during hurricane season, August through November.

The phone, like everything else, was working. But the first time Mike tried the number that he had brought along, there was no answer. After ten rings, he hung up and went to inspect the refrigerator. Two cans of beer and a bottle and a half of pop. He again consulted the kitchen-cabinet notes, then found the key to the tool shed just where it was supposed to be, on a small brass hook just inside the door leading to the carport. He went outside.

The grass was only a couple of inches long; somebody must be mowing it regularly. The tool shed was a small metal structure set against the back wall of the house. When he took off the padlock and swung the creaking door, he was observed by a solemn frog who looked up blinking like a long-term prisoner, but made no break for freedom. Maybe he could squeeze in and out under the loose door. Maybe enough bugs came in to keep him happy

As Aunt Tessie had said, there was a bicycle in the shed, amid a miscellany of tools and junk. He dragged the power mower aside and got it out.

After a quick trip to a nearby grocery, Mike popped open a soft-drink can and tried Sally Zimmerman's number again.

"Hello?" The tone of the girl's voice answering told him nothing. "Sally?"

"Yes, who's this?"

"I'm Mike Gabrieli. Tom's brother." He let silence grow for a few seconds before he went on. "I'm in town right now, and I'd like very much to talk to you."

It took a few moments before she said, "All right. Is there any word yet on Tom?"

"No, that's why I'm down here. Listen, it's six o'clock. Have you made any arrangements for dinner? If not, I'll take you out somewhere—your choice, I don't know my way around."

"All right—thank you, that would be fine." Yet something in her voice was holding back. "Where are you staying?"

They traded information. Sally volunteered to borrow her room-mate's car and pick him up. It sounded as if she hadn't been to the house before.

By dusk, the two of them were seated in a cool restaurant, looking out through a wide, sealed window at sunset gulls, and a moored rank of what Mike supposed were commercial fishing boats.

" . . . so when your father called me, I felt so sorry. I wished I could do something to help him. He sounded like such a nice old man."

"He is." Mike considered. "See, he and Mom are both getting up there. Tom's being what they call a little bit wild has just gotten to them more and more of late. He was arrested last year in some marijuana-smoking deal down here. Probably you heard about that."

Her tanned fingers broke a dinner roll and started to butter it. She was wearing a pink top that left her midriff bare, and it wasn't hard to see why Tom had kept a more-or-less steady thing going with her. She said, "I heard about that incident from Tom—I wasn't there. I gather it was at your aunt's house."

"Yeah. So. I want to ask if you have some clue to what's happened to him. Maybe there's something you didn't want to worry nice old Dad Gabrieli with, but you wouldn't mind telling me."

"Like I say, I wish I could." Sal took a neat but good-sized bite of roll. "The police were asking, too. But I couldn't help them out."

"He told you he was going up to Miami Beach?"

"Yes, but not why. You and he look quite a bit alike." She studied his face almost impersonally. "He used to say you were a little bigger and meaner. Enough alike so I have no doubt you're really his brother."

"Why should you have any doubt about that? I mean, why would I say so if I wasn't?"

It looked as if she hadn't heard the question. Very much in control right now, this girl.

Mike asked, "Excuse me if I get personal. Tom talked as if you and he were—very close. Is that the way it was?"

She gave him a harder look than any yet. "If you mean did we live in the same room and fight over closet space, no. Neither of us wanted that. If you mean did we spend a lot of time in bed together, yes."

"So he just said, I'm going up to Miami Beach and never gave you a reason, and you never asked him why."

"That's right. Well, here comes the real food at last." But when the red snapper was put in front of her, she didn't really attack it seriously.

Mike let her nibble a little before he said, "You know, Tom phoned me in Atlanta, a couple of nights before he went up to Miami Beach."

"Your father said."

"But there's a thing or two my father doesn't know because I've never told him. Things Tom told me on the phone. I was the only one at home that night he called." He took a mouthful of his own fish and chewed it stolidly. Delicious. Well, he thought, here goes. "About the whereabouts of a certain object."

He had been wondering if she might drop her fork, but it just stayed there in her hand. She looked across at Mike, then down at her plate, then out the window. She put the fork down finally, picked up a roll and looked at that, and settled at last for a cigarette, which she took from a metal case like one a soldier might carry.

"Oh, damn it," she said. Her voice sounded softer and younger than before. "Just damn it all anyway."

"Now, I 'm going to have to dig into that, Sally. Maybe I'll have to get the cops to help me. See, I don't care one way or the other about this package itself, or who else might get into trouble or might not. All I care about is finding Tom—finding what's happened to him."

She fidgeted with the metal case. "You smoke?"

"No. Not even tobacco."

"He wasn't into the—drug thing, anymore, if he ever was. I told you, that famous pot-smoking party was a couple of months before I knew him."

"Good." Mike waited.

Sal glared at him awhile and finally had to speak. "Is this—thing—wherever he said it would be?"

"It's supposed to be somewhere around Aunt Tessie's house. I figure Tom kept a key to the place even after she officially threw him out . . . as soon as we finish dinner, I'm going back and do a thorough search. You want to be there when I find it?"

A violent headshake. "I want nothing whatever to do with it."

"If you're so sure as all that, you must know exactly what it is."

She wouldn't answer. Puffed out smoke. Wished with all her power (he was certain) that the airplane that brought him down had crashed on landing, killing all aboard.

"Things are getting awfully goddamned serious, Sally." His voice was low and slow. "My brother might be dead. If you're really his friend, I want what's good for you as well as him. If not . . . " She closed her eyes. "I'll drive you over there."

Night had come down fast. The Datsun's headlights pulling into the carport lit up the red metal cabinet like a warning barricade. It sat right at the carport's rear, just next to where the backyard's grass began, where nothing had been before. Sally parked a yard from the cabinet, and Mike got out of the car and stood there looking down at it. Its doors were hooked closed with a small, unlocked padlock. The cabinet was about a foot deep, two feet wide, three high.

" 'Evenin'."

The southern accent came from just beyond the nearby wall of openwork masonry that edged the yard and carport. In the next yard, the lights from the next house filtering through shrubbery behind him, a tallish man, gray-haired but hale, stood leaning on the wall.

"Hello," said Mike.

The neighbor smiled. "Saw y'all were stayin' here now, so I brought the little cabinet back. Miz Gabrieli keeps the gasoline in there for the power mower—I figured you might be wantin' it. Last tenants just left it sittin' out in the carport when they left. Then a couple weeks ago we had a hurricane watch, kinda early for the season. So I took it in. Back in '62 when she blew, I got a picnic table from the yard on t' other side right through the wall o' my house. Don't pay t' leave stuff sittin' round the yard if she's gonna blow."

"Thank you," said Mike.

"Hope y'all don't mind my takin' it in. But it's safer when she's gonna blow."

"Quite all right."

Mike unlocked the side door and ushered Sally inside. After turning on a light in the living room, he stationed himself beside a kitchen window where he could look out into the carport and keep an eye on the red cabinet and also on the yard next door. He said, "Whyn't you get us two beers out of the refrigerator? Or if you'd like something else, I think there's bourbon and vodka above the sink."

"You said you were going to search for—something."

He got a beer for himself, tasted it, continued looking out.

"Where's it supposed to be hidden?"

"Right in that little cabinet the kindly neighbor just brought back."

"Tom said he put it *there*? Do you suppose it's still—?"

"I don't know. I'm waiting for that man to go inside before I go out again to take a look. He's still goofing around in his yard. What is it, Sally? What did Tom hide?"

"You mean he didn't tell you that?"

"The way you say that means he did tell you." Mike sipped his beer again. "Whyn't you tell me about it now?" She was quiet and he shrugged. "I'd mix you a drink, but I don't want to leave my post just now. Why don't you help yourself?"

After a while, she did.

At last a porch light went out, over on the other side of the masonry wall, and a screen door swung and banged. Dogs barked peevishly, as if bored with their own routine. Eventually all was quiet.

"All right," said Mike. On the kitchen floor he spread old news-papers someone had left beneath the sink. Then he went out into the dark carport, picked up the little cabinet—it felt promisingly heavy—and carried it in. He closed the blinds on the kitchen windows. Half an eye on Sally, who was hovering a few feet away, he lifted the padlock from the metal doors and opened them.

Inside was about what he might expect—flammables that good safety practice forbade storing inside a house or even in an attached shed. First a red safety can marked Gasoline, on the cabinet's top shelf. Mike sniffed at it, shook it, and put it aside. No doubt it was mixed with a little motor oil to fuel the mower's tiny engine.

On the bottom shelf were a roachlike thing that scuttled away rapidly into the woodwork, a small can of paint thinner, a mined brush, and a large paint can, its cover pressed down solidly upon a hardened rim of redwood stain that would match the chairs on the front porch. Mike got out a pocketknife and with its stubbiest blade pried up the lid. Paint filled the can nearly to the top.

Sally let out breath almost explosively and relaxed into a chair. Mike sat back on his heels and bared his teeth. "Get me an empty jar," he said. "I think there's a big one in the cabinet under the sink." There shouldn't be so much paint left in the damn can—not with all those drippings down its sides.

Sal hesitated, but in a moment brought the glass jar. He took off its lid, and carefully started pouring paint. With most of the liquid out of the way, he looked into the can, grunted with satisfaction, and used more newspaper as a crude glove to extract from it something heavy and crinkly that occupied most of its remaining space. A plastic bag, bound tight with rubber bands around some-thing irregular and hard. Heavy enough to be a gun, but the shape seemed wrong. He had been half-expecting, fearing, dope, which he visualized as small packets of white powder. But this . . .

Mike worked methodically, getting only a little paint on his fin-gers. And then, feeling emptied by astonishment, he was holding in his hands the golden face. A little paint had gotten on its chin, and he wiped it off mechanically.

Sally waited in her chair. Her face showed fear, he thought, but no surprise.

"Stolen?" he asked.

She sighed and got out another cigarette. "No. Tom just found it, snorkeling, one day . . . I was along. He was determined he was going to keep it, not tell any authorities. Some crazy tax laws or something they have here—the state winds up owning most of the treasure if you just tell what you've got. Anyway. He wanted to sell it secretly and keep the money for himself. That's all I know."

"So. And he went up to Miami Beach trying to make some kind of deal?"

"I suppose so. Yes, yes, it was that."

A length of plastic clothesline, which looked as if it would match that strung in the back yard, had been tied into the holes in the mask's flanges.

"Did Tom walk around wearing this? Don't tell me he found it in the ocean with this cord in place."

"No, it had no cords tied on it then. I told him not to wear it—I don't know. It had no cord, the one time that I saw it."

He started to reach for his beer, and then forgot about it. In a way, he could almost wish he had found heroin. That could have been flushed down the toilet, and no one the wiser. No one would know that Tom had been mixed up in such a thing, and there would have been no evidence left to hang a rap on him if he was still alive. But this. You couldn't simply throw away a thing like this.

Mike asked, "You told him not to wear it? Why?"

It was a few seconds before she answered. "I just told him not to get me involved in anything. I didn't want any share. Mike, just keep me out of this. That's all I ask."

He stood up, holding the mask carefully. "Is my brother still alive?"

"How should I know?" Real-sounding anguish in the voice. Ragged draw on the cigarette. "Oh, God, I hope he is . . . Now you know as much as I do about it all."

"Who was he going to see? Who was he talking to, to make this deal?"

"Mike, I'll tell you absolutely the last thing I know about it, and then you can do what you like. I'm finished—I've had it—call in the cops or not."

"All right, all right, what's this last thing?"

Sally choked on smoke, then seemed to pull herself together. "Tom was seeing a man called Esperanza about something, I suppose about the mask. I heard Tom talking to him on the phone

one day. Then several times he asked if Esperanza had called for him. One night when I was staying at Tom's place. And then a day or two after that, I saw Tom meeting this old man out on the street, and they ducked in like they were trying to hide. Rather a big old guy—I say old, because his hair was white, you know? But he might have been, what do you call it—platinum blond, except his complexion was darker than Tom's or yours . . . Indian-looking, or maybe Bahamian. You see a lot of people from the Bahamas here in the Keys. And he had kind of a big hooked nose."

The sinister foreigner. It sounded just a little peculiar. Nursing suspicious thoughts about Sally, Mike raised the gold weight in his hands and started to fit his chin into the accommodating hollow—

"Don't!" She rose from her chair, gesticulating.

He jerked his hands down, the thought half-formed that she must have seen some poisonous tropical vermin on the mask. Or there was something about the thing itself . . . "What?"

She stood there awkwardly, as if frightened despite being ashamed to be frightened over something so foolish. She blurted out: "You can see funny things that way."

"Huh?" His vague suspicions of some kind of drugs involved came back. Scowling, he sniffed at the mask, looked at it closely from every angle. Then, while Sally remained silent, he slowly pulled it on, this time all the way, setting the clothesline strap around his head. He would hear Sally if she moved, though now he couldn't see what she was doing. He could see *something*, though. Just some kind of light-specks, racing in the translucent white stones that made the eyes.

The light that did come through seemed to form patterns, hinting at the familiar. It was probably like holding a seashell to your ear, and hearing patterns—in that case, voices—in the random rushing of the molecules of air.

But he had no time now to play. He pulled the mask off and, holding it in one hand, went to the phone in the living room. He looked up a number in the thin local book and started dialing.

"Mike, please. I don't want the police on me again." Her tone seemed to imply that something could be given in exchange. She stood in the kitchen doorway, smiling hopefully.

He bared his teeth at her briefly and said into the phone, "What time does the next plane for Miami leave? Thank you." He hung up. "Not until morning."

Sally leaned against the wall, relieved.

Now he was sure there were going to be legal complications. The only dependable legal help he felt sure of was back home in Atlanta. Maybe he would be committing some kind of technical crime by taking this thing across a state line, but Tom had left it for him—left it in his trust, though vaguely—and now it looked like something finally had happened to the crazy little bastard.

He should have come down weeks ago, maybe. But he hadn't. You always expected that Tom would stay out of any real trouble, would turn up smiling somehow . . . Thinking dark thoughts, Mike went into the bedroom he had been going to occupy, picked up his still-packed bag, came out, and dropped it on a kitchen chair. He started stuffing paint-smeared newspapers into a plastic garbage bag. "What's chances of driving me up to Miami?" he asked.

A complex of emotions danced across Sal's face. "It's about a hundred and fifty miles. My girlfriend will be wondering about her car."

"See if you can call her, arrange to borrow it."

She hesitated for a moment, then went into the living room, where he could hear her dialing. He kept on cleaning up the mess of paint and papers. The mask was on the table where he could keep an eye on it. Now Sal was talking on the phone; he couldn't quite hear what she was saying, but she seemed to be making no effort to keep her voice low, so he didn't try very hard.

He had finished the hasty clean-up job before she got through with her call. Standing in the kitchen, he heard her quick footsteps coming back. She started to say, "She doesn't—" and then her voice broke off with a quick catch of breath when she saw what he was doing. The small sound seemed to modulate the storm of light-flecks that the mask's translucent eyes were passing on to his.

He started to ask, "Did you ever try this—" He let the question die, with the discovery that he could now see her, the kitchen around, the living room behind her. The eyepieces were growing quite transparent. Did the warmth of the wearer's body somehow—

Through what might have been glass, he beheld Sally standing in the doorway leading to the living room, one hand raised to protest what he was doing, her blue eyes wider than he had seen them yet. And simultaneously and without confusion, he saw something else. The new scene occupied the same space, as if it were superimposed by half-reflection on a glass window. He could see the outside of the front of the house in which he stood. It was dark night out there, yet he could see it clearly. A car was just easing to a stop before the house, its movement and its braking done with the utter soundlessness of silent film.

"The eyes have gone transparent," he reported steadily to Sally, meanwhile watching three dark-haired men in sports shirts get out of the car.

"It works that way," she said unsteadily. She still held one hand up, a warding-off of something. "From the outside they still look white, but you can see—oh, take it off. Oh, I should have thrown it away, the way it warned me that first day."

Two of the phantom men were coming down the front walk with rapid strides, entering the enclosed porch where the redwood chairs were stacked. The third was moving even more quickly to take up a position in the carport. Except, of course, none of them were really there. No screen door, no footsteps could be heard.

"It warned you?"

"To throw it back into the ocean. Why? What are you seeing?"

His point of vision was now abruptly back at his true location. He watched while his image, ghost, something, looking like a line drawing of himself done by computer, separated itself from his body and moved to the front door, as if to answer the knocking that had not sounded. In its right hand, his image swung an image of the mask.

His image turned the knob, and abruptly an image of the door—not the real door, he could be quite sanely sure of that—swung in, so violently that his ghostly double recoiled. The two men who had come down the walk burst in, strange-looking weapons flaring in their hands. Mike's doppelganger fell; one of the two men snatched the image of the mask from his imaged hand. The whole incredible scene was frozen at that point—at the instant at which the telephone began to ring.

Mike took the mask off while it rang again. Sally looked at his face, muttered something frightened, and sat down.

He moved to the phone, while his ears kept listening for the sound of that car coming to a stop outside.

"Mike Gabrieli?" It might be an actor's voice, so resonant and precise.

"Yes."

"This is Esperanza. Quickest way I could get in touch with you was by phone. Tell me what you are going to do with the Mask." Somehow the capitalization seemed audible. There was no doubt about which mask he meant.

Mike held the phone in one hand, Mask in the other, looking back and forth between them. Then he put the receiver to his ear again. "What in hell you talking about?"

A hissing, rapid chuckle. "Tough guy, huh? Good, that'll be needed. Look, I don't want to get it away from you. I'd rather you wore it. If it warns you about something, better pay attention. Your brother wore it some, but not enough to save his skin. But tell me your plans. What do you want?"

"What do you know about my brother?" For a moment, he thought Esperanza had hung up, but then he realized that the phone had gone dead. He hung it up and instinctively raised the gold face to fit his own once more. Sally was saying something that he ignored.

The eyes were still clear, and he could see the same sequence starting over. The car stopped and the same three men got out of it and approached the house, one at the side, two from the front. But this time the brakes and doors and feet were audible. This time the pounding on the door boomed loudly.

"Police officers! Open up!" The voice was vibrant with authority. Again Mike's image separated from himself. But this time it darted across the living room, moved a floor lamp two feet west, a coffee table one foot north, and came back to stand at his side, facing the door, which now an image of Sally moved to open. This time the Mike-image wore its Mask. As Sal's spectral hand touched the doorknob, the scene faded, though the Mask's eyes remained transparent for its wearer.

"Open the door or we're gonna break it down!"

Mike drew a breath, and moved. People said he was lucky, but it was really a lifelong feeling for when to move, when not. He quickly shifted the floor lamp two feet, coffee table one, and came back to where he had been standing. "Sally, get the door."

Her eyes kept marveling at his Masked face. "Hadn't you better take that thing—?" She was puzzled by his shuffling the furniture, and she was scared, though a long way from hysterical; she thought they really were policemen at the door.

"Just open it," he said from inside gold, as he pulled the strap a little tighter above his ears. He knew they had the side door to the carport covered. With metal louvers on all the windows, there was no way of getting out.

4. The Second Giving

Tenochtitlan, Mexico, 1519

It was broad day when the high priest arrived at the First Speaker's palace, but the fine cotton shades that had been drawn at all the windows made it quite dim and almost cool inside, in the inner room where Montezuma waited alone, seated on a low chair.

"Lord, lord my great lord!" growled the high priest in deep reverence, entering barefoot and crouching. His gaze was lowered to the floor. The article he had brought—a small oaken chest—he carried as a symbolic burden upon his back.

"Get up and open the *petaca*," ordered Montezuma. From an arrow's flight outside the room's white, dim walls came priestly voices chanting. They were preparing human sacrifice at the great altar of Huichilobos, god of death and war.

The high priest set down the chest and opened it. What it contained he handed to the First Speaker, who sat upon his little stool and looked steadily for some time upon that familiar and yet, to him, enigmatic golden smile.

Thongs of leather made from human skin were tied now between the flange-holes. A great drum boomed outside. Montezuma suddenly hooked his thumbs inside the straps and raised the Mask and put it on. The high priest, who had dared to rise halfway, once more shrank down.

The Mask's eyes cleared for Montezuma, and he could see a small lizard looking down at him from a high corner of the room. Then the vision came.

Today the vision did not last long, and the First Speaker soon took off the Mask again. He said: "Quetzalcoatl and the other white-skinned, bearded gods are coming, as has been long foretold. The Gift of the Dark Gods we will no longer need." And he held out the Mask.

The priest took it back, restored its wrapping of soft cloth, and stowed it back in the small chest and closed the lid. He said nothing. There was subtle disapproval in his bearing.

"Is it in your mind," Montezuma asked him, "that this stranger from the sea is not Quetzalcoatl after all? That he and his companions, who come in floating houses from the direction of the sunrise, are only men? I tell you, I see through the Mask their leader's face, and I know in my heart who he is—Quetzalcoatl the divine. The god for whose return I long have yearned with all my strength. Of course he is a man. A god may be a man, too, may he not? Even as it is with the First Speaker who now sits before you?"

The high priest had fallen to his lowest crouch. A verbal answer was now required. "It must be as my great lord says."

Montezuma rose to his feet. "I tell you, Quetzalcoatl returns from the sea to rule his people, as the Gift of the Dark Gods long ago foretold. So take it to him now, along with the rest of the gold that we are sending him—what further need will I have of its help, when he for whom we yearn is here? But see that the Mask is given to him secretly, for his use alone; that he may know that I have recognized him from afar."

The high priest did not speak again, but trembled as he backed away.

5. The Wearing

The door seemed to burst inward at Sally's mere touch upon the knob, and two sport-shirted men, solidly real this time, bulled in. Both had straight, dark hair. Their faces looked vaguely Indian or Oriental. At sight of the handguns they were leveling, Sally cried out and backed away, arms wrapped about herself as if for protection.

The men paid her no attention; their eyes froze on Mike's Masked face the moment they beheld him. For a long instant he had the feeling that he was the armed man, and his two enemies, despite their pistols, all but defenseless.

Still backing away, Sally bumped into a chair and then into the coffee table. She tripped and started an awkward fall. The two men did not turn. It was Mike that they were after. Their weapons were aiming at him, and he could see his death in the peculiar, off-round holes that marked the ends of the blunt barrels. The Mask forgotten, along with the momentary feeling of power that it had brought, he turned and ran. Even as he did so, he saw his own Mask-projected image running on ahead.

And from the corner of his eye he saw the floor lamp, now toppling in some chain reaction set off by Sally's accident. The metal shaft of it was swinging down with what seemed glacial slowness toward one gunman's outstretched arm. In danger's terrible time-elongation, Mike heard gunfire crackle behind him, saw something almost invisible—no ordinary bullet, he had time to realize—drill into the wall beside his moving head. The impact left no mark upon the wall.

His image ran before him into the kitchen, where it grabbed up, in passing, an image of his traveling bag. Half a second later, his own hand took the real bag from the kitchen chair. Guidance was being given him, and he was following it on instinct. Thought could come later.

With his free hand, Mike straight-armed open the door leading to the carport. Outside, he caught one passing glimpse of a man sprawling on the concrete beside the Datsun, gun lying near his open fingers. If the shot fired back in the living room had passed clear through the house wall, it would have emerged in just this direction . . .

Two running strides behind the uncatchable image of himself, Mike continued his unthinking imitation of its movements, tossed his bag over the masonry wall, and followed it with a lunging climb and a broad jump from the wall's top into darkness. The air around him sang as again gunfire crackled—no common pops or bangs—somewhere behind. He landed on his feet and running.

Another fence to climb, and then another. Amid an uproar of awakened dogs, Mike crashed his way through neighbors' yards. Racing always ahead through the deep gloom, his own likeness in the form of a luminous line-drawing led him through another carport, crossed a deserted street, then dove once more into shadow amid the rough trunks of tall palms.

Just beyond the palms, his doppelganger stopped abruptly, crouching amid bushes. When Mike dropped down beside it, it blinked out like a light.

What now? Back in the direction of Aunt Tessie's house, men's voices sounded, low and purposeful. Now he should run and get the cops, of course. And then explain to them about the Mask . . . At the moment, the Mask was giving him no help, though its eyes remained perfectly transparent, and a quick test showed that his night vision was as good with it on as with it off.

What about Sally? Well, it was too bad if something had happened to her. But the men hadn't been out to do her harm. They had been after him.

And they still were. About ten yards away, the two of them were coming with guns drawn, openly prowling the middle of the otherwise deserted street. As boldly as if in the middle of a desert, they brandished their weapons and looked about. In the distance, a dog was going frantic. Here at hand, there was no sound or sight of any human being other than his pursuers. Houses showed lights, but no one was looking out to see what was going on. And the silence, from the houses, when he noticed it, seemed hardly natural . . .

Call for the cops. But he had the irrational feeling that it might not be that simple.

The two men in the street exchanged carelessly loud comments in some unknown language. Then they separated, one going back toward Aunt Tessie's while the other continued to stand there, boldly as before, holding his strange pistol but otherwise with an air of carelessness. After a minute, this man also walked on, poking into the bushes on the other side of the street. He approached a house and opened a door, peered in. Peering past him from a distance, Mike could see in the lighted interior two children at a table, blond heads slumped down amid stacked books as if they napped. Shortly the armed hunter let the door close, walked away from the house, and around a corner.

As soon as he was out of sight, Mike's doppelganger reappeared, to lead him across more fences and then across another street. Sometimes, for no reason he could see, the course he was set doubled back. Sometimes the image he followed moved on at a run. Again, it crouched immobile in deep shadows for long moments.

Despite the numerous detours, delays, and switchbacks, as if invisible hunters were to be avoided, Mike was being led gradually east. The one automobile he saw on any of the streets he crossed was sitting lightless and motionless, its engine dead, right in the middle of its traffic lane. But of course there was no traffic. None at all. No more than there were any people walking, or people's voices to be heard from any of the houses where the lights still burned. Only the dogs, one in this block, another in the next, more of them farther off, were active. Their voices grew more and more frantic as they realized that things in their portion of the world had gone unprecedentedly wrong . . .

There were a man and woman in the car, both in the front seat. Both with their heads slumped unmoving on their chests, though the man's hands still gripped the driver's wheel. The car windows were open, and Mike could hear them breathe, as if they slept. He wanted to touch them, try to rouse them, but the spectral figure that led him paced on without a pause, looking like something from the dream of an electronics engineer.

Suddenly from a block ahead there came a familiar hiss of tires. A street light there shone with joyful banality upon a trickle of live traffic; first one car and then another traversed the intersection, crossing the street of silence on which Mike walked. From a house on the corner ahead, a man's voice burst into laughter. Mike's throat formed small sounds of relief.

Standing under that corner light, trying to make himself believe that he was back in a sanely human world again, Mike lifted his Mask momentarily from his face—partly to wipe away sweat, partly with the idea of getting the treasure back into hiding, partly, good God, not to look foolish in the eyes of normal people when he wore it. And when he looked back without the Mask along the way that he had come, the stopped car he had just passed disappeared, and normal traffic seemed to come into existence at the next intersection back. Mask on, the zone of silence and strange sleep, in which some awful interdiction had effectively closed down human activity, was perceptible. Mask off, he saw instead a semblance of normality.

Mask on, he trotted quickly after his guiding image, which was getting away from him toward the east. The idea of looking for a police car, that had returned once more, departed. He did not know what powers were ranged against him, but to look for normal human help seemed certain to be futile.

Moving now within a normal region of the city, he passed people who turned to stare after his Mask. He would take it off as soon as he dared. But not just yet.

Adjust the lamp's position by a foot, so it will stand where Sal will cause it to fall down across the gunman's arm and deflect his shot into the carport, felling his accomplice there and leaving the way open for escape—God, he didn't know what powers were *helping* him, either, but in some ways they seemed almost more frightening.

The voice on the phone, calling itself Esperanza, had said that Tom didn't wear the Mask enough to save his skin. That sounded bad. He had to find Tom somewhere, or find out just what had happened to him. Then, get this Mask back wherever it belonged. Meanwhile he would help Sal if he could. But first—right now—survival.

Mike walked east, with now and then a passerby turning to look after him. A block ahead, the street he was on sprouted a stop sign and ended in a transverse highway where traffic was comparatively heavy. Beyond the highway, a dim palm or two, then darkness that must hide the ocean.

His guide led him in a brisk trot across the highway, inviting him to take what looked like a dangerous chance in front of a fast-moving sedan whose driver was fortunately alert enough to use both brakes and steering wheel adroitly. A roared obscenity came hard after the passing sound of rending rubber; but with that recent crackling gunfire still fresh on the eardrums, a few bad words made no impact at all.

On the ocean side of the highway, overlooking a warm but unpopulated beach, his image stopped and turned to face the northeast-bound traffic—as if waiting to be picked up, not hitch-hiking, for he wasn't directed by example to gesture with his thumb.

Then, after a score of cars had been allowed to pass unchallenged, his transparent mentor surprised him after all by raising a hitching arm, with thumb neatly pointed as if the technique were one long practiced. Mike imitated the motion, while some part of his brain thought madly: Have you room for two? See, my friend here is invisible—maybe he can sit on my lap—

He had hardly raised his arm before brakes squealed again. A large, middle-aged white convertible, driven with its top down, dragged to a halt a few yards from where he stood. A woman alone in the car turned her face back, smiling gleefully. As he trotted closer, he saw she was a well-worn forty-plus. Her lean cheeks looked somewhat overrouged, though her dress and makeup otherwise were conservative. His Mask, far from intimidating her, evidently provoked an arch enthusiasm.

"Going to a masquerade?" Her voice was ready to join in the fun if he could offer any. She had the door open for him before he could reach the handle. His image hopped in and vanished to his sight even as he landed right in its unsubstantial lap.

"Something like that. Thanks for stopping."

She slid back to the controls—none of your nonsense about seat belts—and blasted the car fatalistically out into traffic. "Well, here I am." Giggle. "If you're going to attack me, get it over with. My friends are always haranguing me not to take the chances that I do, picking up strangers."

"Oh, you're safe with me. Don't worry." His fingers went up to ease the weight on forehead and cheekbones. How did the wearer know when it was safe to take the damn thing off? Or was it ever, once he had put it on?

"Knew I would be." The woman was speaking loudly now, over a noisy muffler, and driving rather fast. "I've never had any really bad experiences, all the people I've picked up. There was that stranded circus act I picked up one time in Alabama. That was the trip when I met the Saucerians." (The what?) "Yes, I'm one of the few people who've ever really ridden on a flying saucer. And I had a witch once. Said she was one, anyway. On her way to a science fiction convention in Washington, D. C."

"I guess you do carry some strange riders."

"Yes, and it was a strange ride that the Saucerians gave me in their craft. Flew low over my car in Tennessee and stalled all its electrical systems completely . . . but the stranger *my* prospective riders look, the safer I think I am. No clean-cut young men holding up neat lettered signs, no, sir. Them I won't touch. How far are you traveling for your masquerade?"

Through the Mask's eyes, Mike suddenly saw the image of a highway sign flying a few feet above the shoulder of the road on his side, keeping pace with the car. "Marathon," he read aloud and wondered if he was asking for somewhere off in Greece.

"Well, I can drop you there. I'm going up to Key Largo." They took the bridge out of Key West, going north and east on US1. They had been going half an hour or so, driving, it seemed, more on bridges than on solid land, Mike mostly listening and trying to make sense, when he saw the solid sign his latest vision had foreshadowed: Marathon. Followed in a moment by broken railing, tow trucks, and police cars blocking half the narrow bridge.

Bystanders in shorts and beach attire gathered, gaping down. The woman driving, silent in the required concentration, slowed down and followed police arm signals through the jam around the accident. Looking out on his side, Mike whipped off the Mask while the police seemed to be looking. He caught one glimpse of a white car, open-topped, being raised dripping within a spiderweb of winch-connected cables and the stare of emergency spotlights. The car was badly smashed.

Gapers and constriction left behind, they picked up speed again. Mike eased his Mask back on. At once a new image was before him—that of the very car in which he rode. This image moved on steadily ahead, in the same lane. He might have taken it for a real car outlined in reflective tape were it not for certain unnerving moments when real cars passed briefly through the same space.

"You can turn off here, if you would," he told his chauffeur suddenly. Ahead, the convertible's phantasm had begun to flash its turn signal on the right. The driver of the real vehicle eschewed such frills, but made the turn. Her conversation was picking up speed again, reviewing some masquerade that she had once attended in New Orleans. The next passenger would hear the incredible story of the man with the golden head.

"Right down this lane," he instructed. Now some kind of a canal had appeared, running parallel to the dimly lighted residential street they had got onto. The houses here were big and expensive, with large lots abutting on the channel. Step out your back door into your luxurious cabin cruiser—that was the idea.

Ahead, the image-car stopped right in the semicircular driveway of a large house in which no lights were showing. The image-Mike got out, glowing against the night.

"This house right here."

"Looks like nobody's home."

"I might be just a little early, but that's all right. Thanks a lot for the lift."

When he had got out and the car was gone, the quiet, near-tropic night closed down. The street lights here appeared to be two blocks apart. There was a racketing as of exotic creepy-crawlies on all sides.

His silent, computer-drawn guide was standing waiting for him, looking at the house where they had stopped. For the first time, he paused to take a calm look at the details of the image. The face was not only recognizably, but indisputably his own: a portrait—not a caricature—done by a drawing-master.

Now suddenly it moved before him, toward the front door of the house. He followed it, his feet crunching on the short walk of crumbled shells.

There was a large, open porch, roofed but, like the rest of the house, unlighted. Mike let his own hand follow the ghostly one and was guided to touch the doorbell. Now, if only he knew what he was going to say when someone—

With horror he realized that his doppelganger had taken off its Mask and was stowing it inside its traveling bag. Mike had only just time to do the same before the house door opened, into darkness.

"You're late." It was a youngish woman's voice; it took him a moment or two to see her figure even in outline. "We expected you a couple of hours ago."

"There was a traffic tie-up on the bridge," he improvised after an awkward moment.

"Any sign of enemy action?" Then, as if she noticed his hesitancy, she added: "All right, don't talk to us about anything if they've briefed you not to. Let's get going."

The woman locked the front door up when he was in the house, then moved ahead to lead. From somewhere upstairs, enough light filtered down to let him find his way through the large rooms that they traversed from front to rear. In one there was a man—a thin, vague figure in the gloom, who seemed to be gathering up things as he moved about.

The woman brought Mike straight through the house to a rear door, and out again onto a patio. Three more steps and he was on a dock where a large boat was moored. He followed her aboard, feeling the unfamiliar slow shifting of a deck beneath his feet. Then down through a cramped companionway and into a darkened little cabin. When she flicked on lights, he saw that the port was covered with a shade. There was one little bunk.

Leaving the cabin door ajar, the woman went above again. There were jumbled footsteps overhead, and her voice saying something to the man, his answering. Soon the boat's engine coughed loudly into life. And shortly after that, Mike could feel that they were getting under way.

He closed his cabin door and leaned his back against it to block any surprise entry. Then he unzipped his bag and looked into the

Mask again. Its eyes were now opaque, just barely flecked with sparks. He put it away.

When waves began to come beneath the hull with solid impact, he judged that they had found the ocean. No one had told him to stay below, so he decided to go up. After a brief hesitation, he left his bag there on the cabin floor, went out and up the short companionway.

In a glow from the instruments, dim and indirect, he could see the man's and woman's faces, both young and intense. The man glanced up at Mike but then turned back, preoccupied, to navigate. On the nocturnal ocean all around, a few small lights looked lost in starlike distances.

The woman now looked up. "Why don't you just go down and rest? I'll bring you some food in a while. It'll be a long night." Her tone was friendly but impersonal, that of a stewardess.

After a moment, Mike turned and went below, entered the small head next to his cabin. He knew next to nothing about ships or boats, but he thought the pace of the regular hammering of waves beneath the hull indicated an unusual speed. Still, the ride was not uncomfortably rough.

Traveling bag clutched in one hand, he was starting to doze off in his cabin's chair when the woman came tapping at the door. She handed him a couple of sandwiches wrapped in plastic bags and a small Thermos full of what proved to be hot tea.

Left alone, he discovered that he was in fact hungry. And after he had eaten, sleepiness returned. It had been a day . . . of madness, of course. He should have gone to the police in Marathon, if not in Key West. He wondered if the citizens back there had all revived, with none the wiser. But no way to do a thing like that, unless you could play tricks with time . . . should have gone to someone . . . He woke up with a small psychic jolt, wondering if they had drugged his tea. But that would have been superfluous, Watson, after a day like this one . . . He was going to have to stretch out in the bunk, or sleep sitting in the chair . . .

He awoke to the unchanging hammering of waves beneath the flying hull, and gray daylight coming in around the shade. The bag had fallen away from him, but a quick inspection showed that the Mask was still inside. A brief trial showed that it had no visions for him at the moment. And a look out through the port showed him nothing but ocean, vast tree-trunks of sunlight marching on it in the distance, reaching to the broken clouds.

His watch, with calm irrelevance, showed a little after seven o'clock. He guessed that the boat had been traveling at a constant speed all through the night. He would guess, also, from the angle of those slanting shafts of sunlight in the distance, that they were heading approximately east. To the Bahamas? But he had the feeling in his gut that land was far away.

A tap came at his door. He stowed the Mask away and zipped the bag, and called out to come in.

The woman entered, with her impersonal smile, a stewardess in slacks and denim shirt. Last night she had been wearing something different. "Good morning. Here's some coffee and donuts. I've got a box lunch up there, too, for you to take along."

Take along? "Thank you."

She went right out and closed the door. All was business around here. What business, he was getting afraid to try to think. But the coffee in this second Thermos proved to be hot and tasty; there were six donuts left, reasonably fresh, in a slightly crumpled bag that might once have held a dozen.

Mike finished his breakfast, visited the head, thought about trying to shave, but didn't. He was wondering what to do next when the man called down the companionway: "You can come up anytime now. Pickup should be in ten or fifteen minutes."

That sounded like he was going to switch boats. He got his bag and went abovedecks. Something about his appearance must have struck the man, who looked at him closely and inquired: "They briefed you well enough on the pickup?"

Mike managed a grin, or maybe it was only a baring of his teeth. "If not, I expect it's too late now."

"Actually, I suppose it hardly matters." The man scanned the empty horizon, then looked round him at his instruments, of which it seemed to Mike he had an inordinate number. "Things are pretty automatic, I understand, from here on in."

The woman reached over to hand Mike a small lunchbox. It was something he might have carried to the third grade, with a painted clown on one side and an elephant on the other. "This has a handle," she offered, somewhat apologetically. "I thought it might be easier for you to hold on to."

"Thanks. Anyway, maybe I can put it in here." And with a little squeezing he managed to get it into his bag, along with the spare shoes and the clean shirts and socks and underwear. And something else.

Ahead, clouds seemed to have sunk onto the ocean and in the form of billows of fog were coming on to cut the visibility. The man throttled back his engines. The craft began to bob and wallow in the sea rather than merely slapping and skimming over it.

From the low clouds ahead and close above there came a muffled, whirring roar. The man and woman looked up tensely, then relaxed when the helicopter appeared. Maybe they hadn't come so far from land as Mike had thought.

There was a clammy touch of fog upon his skin through his light shirt. Now here came down a sort of chair, descending from the hovering aircraft on a cable. There was something almost eerie in the way it came down straight to him, without much sway, as if he were pulling on a cord to guide it. The chair, complex of wood and metal, had a big hook under each arm, and he slung his bag from one of these. With a sort of Disneyland feeling, Mike swung himself in and fastened the obvious safety belt. As the catch snapped, he was at once hauled aloft. The chair whirled as it rose, and he got only one more quick look at the boat, now tiny and already blurred by fog, before the thick clouds took him in. The roar from above had deepened, and he thought the helicopter must be climbing even as it reeled him in.

Now metal loomed right above him. A hatch gaped open, and in a moment he was swallowed as metal jaws snapped shut beneath his feet. His chair had lurched to a stop inside a cabin that was half metal, half plastic or glass, with gray cloud showing on every side and clear blue sky above, beyond a blur of rotor. The apparatus that had hoisted his chair now held it silently in place.

The cabin was very quiet. There were no other passengers in sight, nor any crew. Beside the hoisting-chair, there were three others, in Spartan-airline style, that took up most of the space. Solid bulkheads and closed doors sealed off the cabin front and rear.

The clouds were falling rapidly below, though another layer was mobilized above and well ahead. These higher clouds were coming on at what seemed a fantastic speed for a mere copter to achieve. Not that he was any great expert on aircraft, but . . .

Despite its evident speed, this craft felt even steadier than the boat, and Mike was grateful. There seemed to be no need to remain strapped into his chair, and after a while he got out of it and went to gently try the forward door. Locked. Through the inset of a small glass panel, he could glimpse what looked like smooth machinery and another spot of sky. Nothing that might be the back of a pilot's head.

Behind the door in the rear bulkhead were a washbasin with a prosaic rack of plastic cups, a somewhat peculiar-looking toilet, and what must be a waste-disposal bin or chute. To try and establish some control of the environment, he had a drink. The water tasted a little strange, but not bad. In tiny lettering on the bottom of his plastic cup was what might be a trademark notice. It was not in English, and he could not identify the language.

After he had tapped in vain on the door to the forward compartment, and studied it as well as he could through the little transparent panel, he began to think it probable that there was no one in there. He was alone on board. There came to mind the automated-airline joke: Passengers file into a cabin and take seats, obey flashed signs to fasten up their belts, and listen to recorded announcements. Only after they are airborne does the recorded shocker come:

" . . . historic event in which you are privileged to take part. The plane is fully automated and needs no human pilot or other crew. You are absolutely safe, because nothing can go wrong—go wrong—go wrong—go wrong—"

The glass and metal pill in which he rode was swallowed suddenly by a dense cloud. The flight went on unperturbedly. Mike sat down in one of the chairs, got out his Mask, and looked into its eyes. There were a few sparks there, nothing more.

The growing need to try to do something drove him to looking out of all the available windows at every possible angle. Forcing his vision down as closely as he could along the slight bulge of hull below the starboard glass, he could just make out an insignia of some sort—what seemed to be a golden sunburst. He hadn't noticed it from the boat. There was some large lettering there, too, though the extreme angle at which he saw the letters made them impossible to read. He strained to see more, cheek against the clear glass or plastic, which now felt freezing cold, though the cabin temperature had not altered from comfort. At what altitude was he now flying? With nothing but ocean to be seen below, it was impossible to guess . . . nothing can go wrong, go wrong, go wrong . . .

He sat in a chair again, not knowing whether to laugh, or beat on the doors and scream. One would probably be about as helpful as the other. The conviction was growing that he was in fact alone on board. Did they brief you well enough? Things were pretty much automatic from here on in.

The chair was comfortable. Later on he would open his lunch box with the clown and elephant, and then he would give the Mask another try. He looked at the hands of his watch, but could extract no meaning from them. "What are your plans?" the voice on the telephone had asked him.

The muted drone of flight machinery began to overcome him. His sleep aboard the boat had not been deep or restful. The helicopter lurched once, though not enough to make him open his eyes fully. Soon he must try again to see . . .

A golden lance of sun woke him, striking down into his face from a high purple sky. Mike raised his head on a stiff neck and tried to organize his thoughts.

At first he thought there was still nothing to be seen outside but sky and clouds. The clouds were mostly far below. And far ahead—

He slid from his chair to press his face incredulously against the glass. Clouds at his own level—great rolls of ragged cotton—ripped past before he could see plainly.

An awesome range of jagged, snowcapped, barren mountains marched toward him beyond a few miles of flatland bordering the shore of a great, calm sea. Even the highest peaks ahead fell short of his present altitude, but already he could feel that the vast curve of his flight was tending down.

6. The Third Giving

Seville, Spain, 1528

On an upper floor of the Alcazar, not a gem's throw from the apartments recently occupied by His Catholic Majesty Charles the Fifth, Most Holy Roman Emperor and also King of Spain, a soldier was following a priest through chamber after chamber of candlelight and tapestried elegance. The priest, a Mercedarian friar, was practically anonymous in his plain robe. The soldier, Francisco Pizarro, fifty-three years old, wearing faded clothing barely adequate as court finery, had the look of Toledo steel inside a leather sheath of skin. His spare body had been toughened and worn and wounded in campaigns from Italy to Colombia.

In the yellow bloom of candles, his face was set, gray beard jutting, thin lips compressed. He was not a man to be easily awed, but his audience with the Emperor, scheduled in a few days, worried him. So much was going to depend on it. So it was with gratitude, anticipating an offer of some kind of help, that Pizarro was responding tonight to the message just brought him from his cousin, Hernando Cortés.

The Mercedarian tapped on a door, then opened it and eased himself away discreetly. Pizarro went in, to firelight and more candles, and the door closed tight behind him with the good sound of solid oak. Cortés, who was nine years younger than his cousin and somewhat fuller of face, but otherwise bore him a good resemblance, arose from behind a writing table. He greeted Pizarro warmly and offered him wine. This drink Cortés poured himself. It seemed they were to be unattended.

When the two men were seated, however, cups in hand, and had exchanged the expected courtesies, Cortés seemed momentarily at a loss at getting to whatever point this meeting had.

Pizarro offered: "I am glad that you were successful with the Emperor: created Marques de Valle and confirmed as Captain General of Mexico! I expect to catch up with him at Toledo, and I admit that I would rather face a rank of charging savages alone. But there is nothing to be done but see him, if I am to have the men and money I need to reach Peru with an effective force. There is vast wealth to be won there—I know it . . . Have you any advice for me, cousin?"

Cortés nodded. "I know how you feel. Advice? Well, as for matters of soldiering, you must know all that as well as I. Better, perhaps."

Pizarro muttered a pro forma protest.

Cortés's gaze wandered to the fire. "As for how to best approach the Emperor . . . and other difficult matters . . . "

There was a pause that seemed long to Pizarro. "Yes?" he at last prompted gently.

The eyes of the conqueror of Mexico flicked at him and away. Cortés seemed to be nerving himself for something. "There is the necessary help of prayer, of course. And . . . "

And? Pizarro waited, wondering.

Tension built visibly in Cortes until it burst out in a handslap on the table. "To conquer an empire, cousin, as I have done and you may hope to do, it is necessary to take help where and when one can find it. To win a million souls for Christ *cannot* be an evil work. And when effective help is given toward that end, there is no need to fear that help comes from the Devil."

Pizarro leaned forward in his chair and uttered a short laugh. "I am quite willing to take help. So long as I am in command. As for the Evil One, with the Virgin and St. James to help me, I will look him in the eye and even twist his beard if necessary. I pray you, cousin, if you can offer me any effective help, or point out where I may obtain it, do so. My gratitude will be undying."

"Very well. There is—something." But still Cortés, with surprising indecision, dallied a few moments more. Then, sighing, he reached down for a large leather bag beside his chair. From it he raised an oaken chest, small and finely wrought, of a size that might have held a crown. With a key that hung around his neck inside his clothes, he opened up the chest and took out as its entire contents a weighty velvet bag

Balancing the bag in one hand, he told Pizarro: "I had this as a private gift from Montezuma—our Blessed Lord alone knows why. Later I was encouraged to turn it to matters treasonous. But I refused."

Encouraged by whom? Pizarro pondered. But he was not about to ask.

"Also I have considered making a present of this to the Emperor. But right now he and I are on good terms anyway. And I do not wish to stay in Spain, at court, however high my place might be. Rather would I leave well enough alone here and go back peacefully to New Spain, to enjoy the harvest that my sword has cut. This in the bag is a gift of power, not of peace. Where should it be, but in the hands of an honest, simple soldier, who will use it to win souls for God, gold for his Emperor, and estates and riches for himself and all his worthy men?"

Out of the soft bag he slid the heavy golden Mask. A cord of braided silver wire now ran between the flange holes at the temples and the crown.

Silently impressed, Pizarro understood only that he did not yet understand.

"Yes, cousin, it is gold." Cortés slid it toward him with a finger. "But do not take it as mere wealth and melt it down. Look through the eyes."

"The eyes?" He took the weight into his hands.

"Yes, and follow what it shows you. As I have, many times, beginning before I had even entered the City of Mexico. Without this, I doubt that I could have won its wealth." Pizarro was still turning it cautiously in his fingers, and Cortes went on: "Oh, fear not; I have had it immersed in holy water and prayed over much by a priest who is just sensibly cautious in such matters. Though of course I should not mention the existence of this object to the Inquisitors, or even let my own men know that it exists. Such secrecy out in the field may not be easy, but the results are worth a hundred times the trouble. And the Mask itself can help you find ways to keep it hidden."

"My gratitude, cousin." Pizarro's uncertain hands still held it on the table. " . . . look through the eyes?"

"At first you will probably see nothing much. But wait."

7. The Four Quarters of the World

His flight was going to end, it seemed, somewhere among the sharp and icy summits that grew higher and more forbidding with every moment that he hurtled toward them. Far down their great slopes, green hills tumbled. Mike could see a single river twisting between the mountains' feet, escaping them to reach the sea. On the horizon to the left, well inland, a tall plume of smoke trailed motionlessly into the upper air. Beneath the plume sat a white mountain cone with a truncated top.

With fumbling fingers, he got out the Mask again. Its eyes were still opaquely dead. He pushed it down again into the bottom of his bag and crouched by one of the windows, marveling.

Where in the hell *was* he? The Rockies? The Andes? Another planet? How could he have traveled in a single night, by boat and helicopter, from the Florida Keys to this? He tried to map the hemisphere in his mind, but got no help from the exercise. Had he really been drugged, and hours or days thus taken from him? Who would expend such effort on him, and why? This, he thought, is what paranoia feels like.

The mountains were closing at something more than jetliner speed, and he had to fight down the helpless fear that he would necessarily be smashed flat on one of them. Now the ocean and the strip of flatland were already miles behind, and on both sides some of the taller peaks were at his level and rising. One way or another, he decided, he would soon be down. He began strapping himself into a seat, bag tucked underneath it.

Craning his neck to see ahead as well as possible, Mike finally, and with considerable relief, caught sight of what might be a reasonable landing place. Almost at the peak of a tall mountain, a natural craterlike depression cupped a small round pillbox of a building. The curving, gray-white wall blended with the trackless snow and roadless rock surrounding it on all sides. Held like a dull jewel in a rough setting, the building must be completely invisible from any inhabited portions of the land below, hard to see even from the surrounding summits. Mike might easily have missed it from the air were it not right at the end of his apparent trajectory.

Deceleration came, pressing him hard forward in his seat's harness and confirming the happy prospect of a normal landing. The building was already much closer, and he could see that it was larger than he had thought at first. As his vehicle slowed steadily until it was merely hovering above the structure, he judged that it was perhaps forty yards in diameter and three or four stories high. Its topmost level was only a circular rim, some six or seven yards wide, around the flat roof of the next level down, which evidently served as landing deck. Several other helicopters—their rotors, at rest, looked like those of no other copters Mike had ever seen, but what else could you call them?—were already parked there. On their flanks, the golden sunburst was also visible.

From the broad rim made by the building's upper story there rose several gray, featureless turrets. No doors or windows broke the surface of the building's outer wall, but from the upper story a good many faced inward on the deck. A powdering of dry snow on the deck exploded outward in the rotor blast as his aircraft lowered itself, then set him down without a jar. The muted noises of machinery ceased, and he could begin to hear the whine of wind that rocked the landed craft beneath its slowing rotor.

All around, the doors and windows stared at him. Then there came movement to his left. A door had opened there and a figure hooded in a gray parka was trudging across the deck toward his

copter. The man—the figure looked big, and its walk was masculine
—reached up a gloved hand when he arrived. There came a clack
of mechanism and a simultaneous hiss of air. Mike's ears felt pressure drop, and almost in the same instant bone-chilling cold came
eddying in.

Still almost completely masked inside his fur-trimmed hood, the
man below was looking up expectantly. Mike drew in what his
lungs could still find of warm air, dropped his bag down through
the hatch, then swung himself down to the concrete deck. Almost
before his upper body had cleared the hatch, his legs in their thin
trousers felt numbed by arctic wind.

From inside the parka's hood, words in a Middle Western accent
fought out through the gusts. "Boy, they sure didn't dress you for
this job. Better get inside before you freeze your ass."

The danger to all parts of the anatomy seemed real enough, and
Mike was already running toward the door from which the man
had emerged. Its heavy glass swung wide at his gasping approach
—lungs seemed to be working on nothing here—and closed again
as soon as he and the other, who trotted after him, were both
inside. At once another door, a couple of paces inside the first,
swung back. The air that flowed from inside was healingly warm,
and dense enough to make Mike's ears twinge in reverse.

The room inside the double doors suggested a waiting lounge
at some small airport, with lockers and chairs set about in it, and
a window looking out onto the flight deck.

His escort pulled back his hood and started to take off his parka,
showing a youngish face, roughly rimmed by dark hair and beard,
above a thickly muscled neck. "Welcome aboard. M' name's
Gunner—not the Swedish kind, the shootin' kind. Don't tell me
your name until they pick out a new one for you here. Hell, they
prob'ly briefed you on all that back Stateside."

Mike shook the offered hand. "Glad to meet you."

Gunner began to throw parka, fur-lined flight boots, and gloves
into a locker, retaining a turtleneck shirt and trousers in different
shades of gray, and black military-looking boots. "C'mon along. I'll
show you your room, and you can get measured for some clothes.
Then you've gotta see Boss."

Boss? All right. There had to come a showdown sometime. Bag
in hand, Mike followed, through another door beyond which the
air pressure was greater yet.

Hotel? Military installation? Deluxe prison, maybe, if such were built. Soft light came from glowing panels in the ceiling, and an occasional lamp. Chairs and tables, as in a modern hotel lobby. Now and then a window looked out, but only onto the flight deck with its lashing snow and ranked machines. Then Gunner led him down a stair, and windows disappeared altogether, though the lighting remained cheerful and the furnishings offered comfort. The floors, brown or gray, were everywhere as smooth as tile, yet sank in slightly underfoot. Walls varied in color and texture, and there were panels of translucent colored glass. They traveled a hallway along which most of the doors were closed.

Mike heard male voices debating once behind a door, but otherwise the place was quiet. The room whose door Gunner finally pushed open fit the expensive-hotel hypothesis, except it had no windows.

"Here y'are. That rubber-suit thing over there on the chair is what measures you for clothes. Directions on the box. I'll be back in fifteen, twenty minutes, and we'll go see Boss." Gunner had the door pulled almost shut before he paused. " 'Scuse me for lockin' you in, but it's orders for all new arrivals, until Boss has a chance to brief you."

For half a minute after being left alone, Mike stood still in the center of the floor. The walls were patterned and colored to make the room seem bigger than it was. The lighting was bright but indirect. He tossed his bag onto the bed and tried exploring.

The door to the hallway was indeed locked. Another door led to an ordinary closet, empty and capacious; after a brief hesitation, he put his bag inside. The last available door led to a bathroom, almost disappointingly ordinary.

He was supposed to be somehow measuring himself for clothes, so he read the directions on the indicated box, then pulled out the gray rubbery suit that it contained. With the feeling that a fraternity initiation was well under way, with himself as victim, he followed instructions and stripped to the skin. The suit resembled long underwear with attached head and gloves, and was surprisingly easy to pull on. The main frontal zipper ended in a heavy catch at the throat. As the printed directions indicated, he walked about with the suit on, lay down, rolled over, got up, tried a somersault, feeling completely foolish all the while. The nagging sensation that someone was spying on his performance kept him from chucking it and trying the Mask again.

Gunner was back a little sooner than promised, entering without a knock to dump a fat armload of clothing onto the bed. "Put on some o' this here stuff. Any clothes you brought have gotta stay put away." In the pile on the bed were knit trousers and pullovers like Gunner's, along with boots, low-cut black shoes, sandals, and a fair assortment of other accessories, including socks and under-wear. As Mike changed again, he realized that everything was a perfect fit.

"I put your parka and boots and stuff in a locker topside, next to the flight deck." Gunner leaned against a wall, arms folded. "You'll need 'em every time you go out. Never gets any warmer at this altitude, so they tell me."

Just where in hell am I? But the simple question was not one he dared to ask. He must be expected to know that much.

He was dressed in a minute, and Gunner led him out again and down the hallway. His room was left unlocked this time. Well, if anyone was going to come in and search his room, they were going to—that's all. Then what? He hadn't the faintest idea.

Back on the upper level, Gunner tapped at a door and pushed it open when a man's voice within called out something. "See you later," said Gunner cheerfully, standing aside for Mike to enter.

The big room—office or study—struck Mike at once as military, probably because of the maps that dominated its walls. And there was a vaguely military look about the sturdy, middle-sized man with the clipped dark moustache who came forward saying heartily, "Welcome aboard!" and holding out his hand. He was wearing the same issue of gray pullover and knit trousers, and three people in that garb made it undoubtedly some kind of uniform.

Mike clasped a firm and energetic hand. "Thank you—Boss? That's what I'm supposed to call you? Glad to be here." And he was, since the main alternatives perhaps were to be found shot dead by mysterious weaponry in Key West, or spattered all over one of these mountains during the trip on Automated Airways.

"Yes, 'Boss' is right. You'll get used to the cover names quickly. Come, have a chair. How would you like 'Rocky' as your own name? Unless you have some strenuous objections—? Good, then I think we'll use it." He made a notation inside a folder on his desk.

"And now, with your arrival, we're up to full strength here—eight people—and we can get on with the job of serious training."

On the verge of beaming, Boss had seated himself behind his vast and ultramodern desk, after waving Mike/Rocky to one of the visitors' chairs in front of it. This room, too, was windowless, though on the flight deck's level. Besides humdrum cabinets and tables it contained other devices that did not look like standard office machinery. And that vast map that spread across the widest wall . . .

"Well, then, Rocky, there are a few simple rules we must insist on here, beyond the normal military or quasi-military rules of discipline. Violation of any of these extra rules must be considered extremely serious and will mean automatic termination of your employment here, and also revocation of the benefits you hope to derive from it, with respect to those you left at home." Boss was suddenly almost embarrassed. "Don't like to have to threaten such a thing, but it's life or death for all of us, and for uncounted others, too."

"Um."

Boss brightened. "I'm glad you understand. These extra rules really boil down to one, and it can be put very simply: we never under any circumstances talk to one another about our backgrounds in the States. Of course the Directors in Cuzco have all our personal information on file, and I as field commander know a good part of the background of everyone who's here. Clear?"

Mike cleared his throat. "I'm not to tell anyone where I come from. Or my real name."

"Right. But it goes a little further than that. We're all eight of us twentieth-century Americans—in the jargon, people from US-20. The Directors recruited that way believing we'd work better together if we shared a common cultural background. The temptation may sometimes be strong to reminisce about the sidewalks of New York, or growing up on the prairies of Nebraska, or whatever. Forget it. Don't mention anything from your home life, don't mention any twentieth-century events at all. Strictly forbidden. The reason is this: suppose you come from the 1990s and Lola, say, is from 1910. You mention that home electronic computers, for example, are quite prevalent in your time, and she takes that knowledge with her when she goes home. The disruptive results could be incalculable. A gross example, of course, but it gives you the idea." Boss paused expectantly.

"Good to know we're all Americans," Mike finally got out, baring his teeth. He was getting the idea, all right. The only question was, how had the inmates here managed to lock up the keepers? Unless there was more to the fraternity-initiation theory than seemed reasonable.

"Actually, the things we must especially watch for are much more subtle. None of us are really as far apart as 1910 and 1990."

"Oh." That sounded like good news, though why it should . . . Mike tried to draw some comfort from the fact that Gunner had seemed quite happy and healthy enough to be pumping gas somewhere on the prairies of Nebraska.

" . . . you may detect a British flavor in my own speech now and then, but I'm an American for all that. Also, Americans of our period are reputedly good at improvising, overcoming unexpected obstacles, getting things done. On this job there'll be plenty that's new and unexpected. Look over here."

Boss had got up from behind his desk and was now standing beside the largest map, which showed the northern two-thirds of South America. The continent's shape was unmistakable. And there were the Andes, modeled in exaggerated relief; and there, drawn in blue lines, the great tree of the Amazon with its uncounted branches.

But the political boundaries—if such they were supposed to be—and the names of the cities, if that was what the named spots were, looked totally wrong. Mike would not have been able to draw many of them in properly—his preference in history and geography had always been Europe—but these seemed completely unfamiliar.

Wait, not quite. There was Cuzco, where he had just heard that the Directors dwelt, whoever in hell they were. Cuzco perched in the Andes just about where he thought it should be, and was named in letters larger than those of any other city on the map. But where was Lima? Wrong, too, was the language, both in the place names and in the legend printed at eye level. It wasn't English, as might have been expected for the convenience of an all-American crew, and it didn't look properly Spanish or Portuguese. Where were all the *Sans* and *Saos*?

Brazil was not even named or outlined. Most of the eastern part of the continent was pretty barren of any kind of symbol, whereas the west was thick with them. The Pacific coast was almost entirely occupied by a solid block of light tan shading whose irregular border defined a territory that extended inland for hundreds of miles, engulfing the entire Andes and spilling over into the Amazon basin. Where were Bolivia, Peru, Ecuador, Colombia? What had he forgotten, Venezuela? It, too, should be here somewhere . . . and what was this tan territory?

He saw its meaningless name at last, stretched out in the large letters that were sometimes the most easily missed on maps. Its name was Tawantinsuyu.

"Now here *we* are, where it says *pokara*." Boss had picked up a pointer and now tapped with it in the midst of Tawantinsuyu, near Cuzco, where the Andean highlands rose in a central topographic node. "Means 'fort' in Quechua. In the next three months, Rocky, you're going to learn that language pretty well, along with a lot of other things. Tell me, what do you know about the Spanish conquest of the empire of the Incas?"

Mike shook his head.

Boss smiled pleasantly. "Like most of the rest of us when we arrived here. Well, as I said, we have about three months to train before the action starts, and the history of this part of the world, especially those branches where the Conquest happens, is one of the things we have to study."

Maybe these could be crazed revolutionaries of some kind, utterly freaked out on the dialectics of struggle against colonial repression. On the other hand, suppose it to be no more than some incredibly complex and expensive game . . .

Boss looked at his wristwatch—all right, normal enough—but then like a lunatic he accompanied the gesture with the remark: "It's now August first, 1532. Francisco Pizarro and about a hundred and sixty men are now up here"—tap with the pointer—"making their way slowly down the northwest coast. This invasion displays an incredibly perfect timing—I'll go into the explanation for that in a moment. At present they're about twelve hundred kilometers from where we stand; that's roughly seven hundred fifty miles. If you're like most of us in the Fort, you'll have to learn the metric system. Not difficult."

Francisco Pizarro. Of course, he was the one who extorted from the Indians the famous roomful of gold. The Inca's ransom that the Spaniards had got out of the poor bastard before they killed him anyway.

"Okay." Mike nodded agreeably. He had entered the room ready for a showdown, but not looking forward to it by any means. He clung to the thought, or hope, that he had just been invited to *suppose* that today really was August first of 1532, and that Pizarro was really on his way . . . It was just vaguely unsettling, and somehow not at all funny, that Boss had looked at his watch as if checking a real date.

" . . . on 16 November, Pizarro and his tiny invasion force will ambush and capture the Inca Atahualpa *here*, at the town of Cajamarca. From that moment Pizarro will have a grip on the whole empire of Tawantinsuyu—the Four Quarters of the World, as it translates. As many people as his own Spain, more land than Italy, France, Switzerland, and the Low Countries all put together. Four times as big as ancient Egypt in its days of greatest glory." Boss shot him a keen look. "Of course Pizarro could never have done it without help. I mean, an invasion force of a mere hundred and sixty men, against an empire!"

Mike seemed to remember that Cortés had done something comparable in Mexico, without help—indeed, in the face of active opposition from other Spaniards. Why not argue a little and see what happened? "What about Cortés?" he offered.

Boss only flashed his pleasant smile. "He had the same help. By help, I mean of course some very advanced technology from another epoch. Which we must nullify. You see, if Pizarro wins in this branch of history, then modern Tawantinsuyu must fall. By the twentieth century, in this branch, it has become one of the major powers of the earth, and continues as such for some time beyond the twenty-third century, where the Directors have their base—how far into the future I don't know. Now the Directors are prevented by some of the inherent paradoxes of time travel from going back in time to mend their own history themselves. They can't even feed information back here directly. So they have recruited us from another branch to fight for them. Follow?"

"I . . . " The trouble was, the man was so damn straight-faced and earnest. No, the trouble really wasn't that at all.

"Well, don't fret if you don't grasp all the details now. Our job is to preserve the Inca empire from the Spaniards. Sounds like a terribly large order for eight foreign mercenaries, I know, but it comes down to simply frustrating Pizarro's attempt to kidnap Atahualpa."

Sooner or later, Mike thought, he was going to have to decide whether to play this game wholeheartedly or not. All right, he would. They hadn't even asked him who he was, but told him. "Well. In our branch of history, as you put it, Pizarro is *supposed* to win, isn't he?"

Boss nodded energetically. "Of course. He does. He always will. In our branch, the enemy were stopped at a later point, and nothing done in this branch is going to upset things for you and me at home. When we return Stateside, it'll be to the same world—the same people—that we left. As I say, don't worry if you don't understand it all. Like trying to make common sense out of the theory of relativity. Waste of time for most of us to even try." Boss's face now wore a little self-deprecating grimace, and he gave a snorty laugh showing that he understood perfectly how crazy it all sounded. Mike felt a chill. *This* was the trouble, really. The voice of the woman who had given him the ride to Marathon had been unshakably calm, had carried total conviction, while discussing her ride on a flying saucer.

Putting down his pointer, Boss came back to his desk. "I know they try to start explaining these things to you when you're originally recruited. But somehow it never really sinks in. I suppose it can't. The last lingering doubts didn't leave *me*, I suppose, until the Directors took me to twenty-third-century Cuzco. Capital of a great nation. And even then there's still an Inca, and he's more than a figurehead, though the government's basically parliamentary.

"Anyway. In Cuzco I had time to look around, visit the universities, talk with people pretty much as I wished. I think the twenty-third-century Inca society is one well worth fighting for, if one values human freedom. Especially when you consider the alternative —I mean the world their enemies are trying to stretch across all the branches. Bah, twentieth-century English isn't designed for discussing any kind of time travel or branching. Anyway, I had the horror films all ready here to show you, but I don't know that I'll bother. They're so bad they look like something faked." Boss sighed lightly. "Well, we'd better do just one, anyway."

He moved a hand at the side of his desk, and the wall opposite the enormous map abruptly dissolved its collection of charts and diagrams and blurred into a blankness that was in turn replaced by a three-dimensional-looking color picture of—the surface of the Moon? No. From cratered and fissured flatlands there protruded stumps of what might once have been modern buildings.

"New York City." Boss's voice was flat.

"Good God!" said Mike, in banal reaction. But Boss was right—the scene did look fake, like something from a disaster movie of a year or so ago. Play the game, he reminded himself. "Atomic bombing? And is that the New York in *this* branch, or—?"

"It's not in ours. But it could be, if the war's lost." Boss's voice for the first time took on homiletic tones. "There's a war raging, Rocky, a world war the like of which you and I have never seen or imagined. Through branch after branch of human history, and up and down tile centuries. In the far future, they're fighting it in ways we can't begin to understand. This scene on the wall is not the result of anything as simple as nuclear bombing. Plate tectonics engineering, rather. Controlling the movement of the great plates of rock on which the continents float. Earthquakes, volcanoes can be brought about." His expression properly keen and grim, Boss gazed a moment longer at the scene of devastation, then switched it off.

"What . . . why is this world war being fought?"

"For survival, on our side. For conquest, I suppose, on the part of the enemy. The Tenocha—or sometimes we call them Aztecs, though neither name is strictly accurate—in *their* twenty-third-century territory, maintain a ritual cannibalism of captured enemies, along with a very advanced technology."

He was looking at Mike closely. "Too much here for you to take in all at once, of course. I'll let you go for the time being, after touching on one more essential subject. I told you Pizarro has help, in the form of very advanced technology. The weapon in question is potentially more dangerous even than plate-tectonics engineering."

Boss reached out a hand, spun a small pivoted wire cage that contained a pair of dice. Mike had been vaguely aware of the cage as an oddity on the big desk. The dice came up seven, and Boss frowned at them thoughtfully. He said, "You're probably not conversant with the theory of seriality? Few Americans of our branch and century have ever heard of it."

Mike shook his head.

"Today let me just say, oversimplifying, that it has to do with what are called coincidences. Actually, with laws of nature that work rather at right angles to the laws—gravity and so forth, that you've already heard about."

"You mean laws of statistics or probability?"

"Not exactly. Statisticians can give you the number of traffic accidents to be expected next week, or they can tell you the odds against one man's being in three accidents on three consecutive days. The laws of seriality might let you discover just which man, if any, was going to have such lousy luck, and where and when the accidents would be. In effect, Pizarro's weapon does this. It's the product of a technology so advanced that even the twenty-third century can hardly think of it as anything but magic. It was conceived and built at some great distance in the future and carried back through time to be dropped in the fourteenth century and eventually find its way into Pizarro's hands. It's very easy to use—it plots out coincidences, chance events of all kinds going on around its operator, and lets him take advantage of them—sometimes helps create them—to get exactly what he wants."

Someone was tapping at the door, but Boss chose to ignore the distraction for the moment. He was bending over to rummage in one of his desk's lower drawers. "Here's a copy—fortunately not a working model. If you should ever see Pizarro, or anyone else, with a thing like this in his possession, shoot the son of a bitch on sight. If possible. Ask questions later. Come in!"

Boss's hand made a casual tossing motion. With a thud whose heaviness seemed to define finality, an object landed on the desktop, to regard Mike with a familiar and suddenly terrible golden smile.

A girl's voice came from the direction of the door, and at last he was able to pay heed. He saw dark hair drawn smoothly back from a high forehead, blue eyes, a mouth a little too big to be pretty but still too smilingly mobile to be unattractive. She, too, was wearing the uniform.

Boss was saying to her, "Well, come in, Doc, meet the new man. Rocky, this is Doc, our local medic. Of course, like the rest of us, she pitches in to do chores outside her specialty; so I'm going to let her take you along now, and give you the tour. After that you'll be pretty much on your own for the rest of the day. There'll be a copy of tomorrow's schedule in your room by this time, I should think."

"Hi." Tall Doc offered her hand as Mike got up. Her eye-corners crinkled nicely when her large mouth smiled. Was she thirty? Probably not quite.

"Hi."

Her gaze fell momentarily to the golden Mask. In this version, the flanges were laced with braided golden cord. "Pretty. I always think I'd like to have one. The real one naturally."

Boss was not amused. "Shouldn't advise any joking, even, along those lines."

Some of the liveliness left Doc's face. "All right. C'mon, Rocky. I'll show you what you've gotten yourself into."

The first stop on the tour, a couple of levels below the flight deck, was a dining room just the right size for its massive table and eight modern chairs. Around three of the windowless walls ran a mural of what suggested the New York skyline circa 1930. A serving counter and cabinets lined the fourth wall, where passthroughs gave glimpses of a supermodern kitchen.

Doc paused. "I suppose Boss told you, we take turns on what little KP there is. Except for him. Rank has its privileges, as Gunner says. Anyway, with all these automated kitchen gizmos, the duty amounts to little more than pressing buttons . . . see, you're already down for the day after tomorrow."

She went on, showing him the kitchen machines and how they worked, and all the while his mind was chewing away on: Shoot the son of a bitch on sight, ask questions later. God.

He wasn't going to pursue the subject of the Mask just yet—with anyone. Instead, while their heads were stuck side by side into a cavernous locker nearly filled with frozen food, he asked, "How do people here make small talk if there's no discussing backgrounds?"

Her smile returned. "Can't talk much about the weather, either, since it seldom changes up here on the mountain. Oh, we do the best we can. No mention of home, though. Boss and the Directors are very serious about that."

"Oh, yeah, the Directors. Where are they, anyway?"

"In Cuzco, usually. And usually six or seven hundred years in the future, though only about a hundred kilometers off in space." Her manner was matter-of-fact. "So we don't see much of them. They've visited the Fort just once in the few weeks I've been here. Three of them came. Indian-type men, as you might imagine."

He let the game go for the time being and concentrated on what he could see. Shortly they were spiraling down a narrow stair to what must be the lowest level of the Fort. Down here it looked less like a luxury hotel and more like what Mike imagined the hold of a ship should be, with functional lights, hard surfaces, steel structural members constricting passage space, and a background hum of power.

"Generators for heat and light, they tell me." Doc indicated some devices behind a glass partition, looking not much like any generators Mike had ever seen. "And the Fort has defensive weapons that are driven from down here, too, or so Boss says."

"Then someone is likely to attack it?"

"It's a war." She gave him a doubtful look. "They didn't bring us here just to play around."

"No, I suppose not."

She pulled her eyes away from his. "They say the Fort draws its power somehow from the internal movements of the earth. Now, down this way's our shooting gallery."

He could see no weapons in it yet, but quite possibly it was intended as some kind of firing range: a long, barren room with devices that might be spotlights or projectors mounted in the rear corners, and a rough blank wall at the far end.

Doc shook her head. "Don't ask me what kind of guns we're supposed to shoot. That'll be your department, I expect. Once fighting starts, I expect I'll be busy taking care of casualties."

"My department? I'm a lover, not a fighter." He tried a mild leer.

Doc smiled, with a touch of wickedness. "Not a whole lot of loving goes on here, in the sexual sense. It seems inhibitors are put into our food and water."

It sounded like the hoary old army rumor about saltpeter. He didn't know how serious she was, and was still mulling the subject over when Doc left him at the door of his own room. Her parting injunction was to come to the dining room a little early for the evening meal.

"It's the best chance to catch the whole company together. You'll get to meet all the rest of them at once."

"I'll do that."

Once inside his room, with the door latched, Mike made straight for the closet and got the Mask out of his bag. He might as well use it for all it was worth, if they were going to shoot him on sight for just having the bloody thing. After what had happened on Key West, he trusted its powers far more than he had begun to trust either Boss or the unknown Directors.

Why had it brought him here?

. . . only darkness at first, then his eyes were sprayed with light-quanta in a hundred colors. *A technology so advanced that even the twenty-third century can hardly think of it as anything but magic.* And now the eyes of the Mask were suddenly turning clear . . .

Against the blank background of his room's wall there suddenly appeared a circular mandala-like design, abstract and intricate. The shape of its violent colors suggested nothing so much as several green snakes being shredded by crimson lightning-bolts. The pattern held steady for perhaps a quarter of a minute before being replaced by the realistic vision of a green metallic-looking door, standing ajar in a vague hallway, with a blur of light spilling out into the hall from the room behind the door. In a matter of seconds, this picture, too, had faded, and Mike was looking at an unfamiliar sort of instrument panel. One small projecting stud or button on this panel rapidly grew larger, while the rest of it faded into an obscure background. Again, the vision briefly held, then vanished.

The eyes of the Mask had gone opaque again. Mike waited for a moment, and the show started over with the mandala. Was it showing him things here inside the Fort? But no part of the vision matched anything he could remember from his tour with Doc.

After seeing the show start for the third time, Mike took off the Mask. It hadn't offered him any better idea on its own hiding place, so he simply put it into the bag again and shoved the bag to the rear of his closet, where he now began to dispose his issue of new clothing.

So there were two Masks, one in his hands, one out there with Pizarro. If Pizarro—

Oh, come on, goddamn it . . . in Pizarro's hands. Francisco Pizarro, sure, and this no doubt was really 1532.

At dinner, surrounded by the painted towers of old New York, Mike got to meet the other members of the company, as Doc had promised. Of the two girls he hadn't seen before, Lola was heavy and pleasant, and Rusty was really something to look at. It wasn't Rusty's face or figure, really, it was the fact that her curly red hair was showing straight and black for about an inch of its latest growth above her scalp.

She smiled, being determinedly a good sport about his stare. "The bright part's the real me," she said, and curled some copper round her finger. "But Boss says that in three months we've all got to have black hair or bust, so I get these little pills to take every day. My eyes are darkening, too, but the change there doesn't show up so plainly."

Which made Mike look around him and realize for the first time that everyone in the company was white, or Caucasian, or whatever the hell the type should be called these days, and everyone but Rusty had hair of very dark brown or black.

Sparks, the smaller of the two men he met for the first time at dinner, was quiet and plain-faced and not very big, a man who would be easy to lose in a crowd. Samson was the biggest man present, though he didn't look to be the athletic type, as Gunner did and Mike himself did to a lesser degree. Samson had thin legs and small feet beneath a massive torso. His hands were uncalloused and his manner retiring; like most of the others, he looked about thirty. Boss might be ten years older.

Somehow the atmosphere at table seemed to Mike more relaxed than it ought to be, everyone at ease but himself. There was quality in the food, whether or not it was dosed with anaphrodisiacs. Along the wall next to the kitchen, a serving table held corn, potatoes, fowl the size of Rock Cornish hens, and some fresh green vegetable that Mike could not at once identify, along with miscellaneous condiments and utensils.

"Chicha?" Boss was offering him a drink, holding a carafe filled with what looked like slightly cloudy water. "Good idea to start getting used to it."

"In that case." Mike held out a glass.

"One o' th' harder requirements of this job," Gunner joked, swirling his own glass. "Naw, hell, it ain't that bad."

Chitchat at the table went on about some card game adjourned on the previous evening. Gunner possibly excepted, the company gave no impression of being hard-bitten professional adventurers.

The grayish stuff in his glass tasted like slightly stale beer, which meant it tasted better than it looked. Now conversation had switched to some kind of model that most of the people had evidently been working on building for most of the day. It must be the model of a town, if it contained all the different walls and buildings that they mentioned. The voices in their only slightly varied accents were all so damned cheerful. These people were obviously here willingly.

Something about the scene was naggingly familiar, and on his second glass of chicha Mike made the identification: those war movies of the 1940s, where the clean-cut white American cast tended to bear names like Sparks and Gunner, and they all just got on great together even if one came from Brooklyn and there were misunderstandings, the team working like clockwork to destroy the lousy Japs or Nazis.

The comparison wasn't particularly reassuring. The Mask in his baggage represented more than a little misunderstanding, and what in hell *did* make these people so content in this peculiar place?

. . . also revocation of the benefits you expect to derive from it, with respect to those you left at home. Don't like to have to threaten such a thing . . .

Honestly pleading tiredness, Mike went back to his room without waiting for dessert. He latched his door and sat through the Mask-show once again: red-slashed mandala, green door, stud rising from a complex panel. He was sure he would know the real objects when fate brought them before him . . . as he was sure it would. Meanwhile, he was indeed fantastically tired . . .

A musically insistent chiming roused him, and to his fogged brain the notes seemed to have been sounding for a year before he got his hand over to the communicator at bedside and managed to shut it off. Some kind of centrally controlled alarm-clock function, evidently. He looked at his newly issued calendar watch (0702 hours, 2 Aug 1532; God, even the millennium number looked capable of changing) and at the day's schedule in printout form, which had emerged from a slot in the top of his bedside table. He gradually got himself collected, shaking off the dreamy feeling that he was about to be late for his first day of high school.

As matters turned out, the feeling was not far wrong. After a brisk breakfast in communal style, Boss repaired to his office, and the seven trainees went docilely to sit in a small room equipped with desk-armed chairs, where the printed schedule called for them to start the workday by hearing a formal orientation lecture.

Precisely timed, a three-dimensional image turned itself on behind a lectern. It was of an Indian-looking man with a professorial manner.

"Welcome to Tawantinsuyu. You have come to play a vital role in a great struggle on behalf of all humanity . . . we are fighting not against a race or nation, but against a way of thought and a way of life, the creed that the individual exists chiefly if not entirely to serve the state . . ."

The mercenaries were listening intently at the start, but in five minutes, most of them had begun to doodle on the pads provided. The abrupt cutoff of the lecture in midsentence, its deliverer disappearing like a djinn, snapped their attention back. They were just beginning to ask each other questions when another voice, this one faceless, came into the room.

"Attention, please. This is Boss. I'd like you all up on the operations deck right away. This is not a combat emergency, but something's come up that I think is of greater importance than those lectures."

On the stairs they trotted along joking, like kids elated to be let out of class. In a machine-filled room just off the flight deck, Boss sat before a huge television screen showing a mountainside that looked like one of those nearby, all sharp gray rocks lashed by thin whips of snow. Near the center of the screen, six spots of varicolored brightness made a small, nearly vertical string; it took Mike a moment to realize that the spots were climbers in bright garments.

"They're on the next mountain to the west," Boss informed his assembled crew. "Our defense system picked up motion there."

"Who are they?" Samson asked.

Boss fiddled with some adjustment. "There's a shrine to the sun god, Inti, on that peak, and probably those people are paying it a visit . . . Gunner, are our flyers ready to go?"

"Sure. I finished that checkout you wanted yesterday."

"Good. Why don't you warm up Number Three, then? That's best equipped for a rescue operation."

"Yessir." As if he knew what it was all about—maybe he did—Gunner went out. Through the doorway Mike could see him at his locker, getting his heavy outer clothing on.

On the screen the distant figures, like ants about to be blown off the side of a building, were proceeding upward with infinitesimal struggling steps. Mike remembered his own brief gasping dash of yesterday across the level deck outside. "How high is that mountain?" he asked the company in general.

Boss glanced back at him. "About the same as the one we're on. Around 18,000 feet, say 6,000 meters, at the peak. At that height, a lot of people need supplementary oxygen just to be able to sit up straight. Whereas the Incas built some of their stone walls and shrines above 22,000 feet. At one shrine they backpacked about a hundred tons of earth up to 20,000 feet from a deep valley. They're rather well adapted to altitude, the Andean natives. Lola, you already know how to work this console; come take over for a while, will you?"

As she replaced him, Boss stood up, smiling and rubbing his hands together briskly. "One more thing we're doing over the next three months is gradually lowering the air pressure here inside the Fort. It's kept at about 2,700 meters effective pressure now, and we're going to adjust to about 3,500 or even higher; so if and when we have to take the field at that level we'll be able to function. The Spaniards had to get used to it, you know; so can we."

"The shrine's on the eastern face, isn't it?" Lola asked. "Yes, I can see it now. I'm sure that's where they must be heading."

"Good!" A figure of controlled energy, Boss turned for a quick look at the screen, then spun away again. "I see Gunner's getting our flyer ready. Doc, I want you . . . and you, Rocky, to get on your outdoor gear. We're going to assume that's a sacrificial delegation going to the shrine, and that one of their number is going to be left there as a sacrifice to the sun. If so, we can pick that person up and bring him or her in here without interfering at all with the normal flow of history here; that person's life will already be over in this branch and century. We'll save a life, and we might just tap into a gold mine of information. The Directors have sent us a lot of data, of course, on the current local language and customs, but an independent native source could be invaluable."

Doc went to gather a medical kit, and Mike to his locker, to get into his parka, boots, and gloves. Then he trotted out into the frigid, thin air of the deck to join Gunner in the warmed and pressurized cabin of the flyer. It was a smaller and less complex vehicle than the one he had arrived in yesterday.

Gunner at once began to show him the workings of some of the machinery aboard, including a small hoist used in rescue operations.

"How d'ya like the job here so far, Gunner?"

"Hell, man, I'd do more than this for these people, after all they done for me. Shit, no need t' talk about it. I guess we were all of us signed up more or less the same way."

Mike doubted that enormously. He was still wondering how to fish for more information when Doc and Boss, in outdoor clothing, came out. Mike opened the hatch and took Doc's bag, then gave her a hand up. Boss came right after her, tugging the hatch shut energetically, then settling himself into the pilot's seat. Doc took the other forward place, while Mike and Gunner got their seat belts fastened in the rear.

"The climbers have reached the shrine," Boss remarked and switched on a small-screen color monitor inset among controls in front of him. The picture now showed a trapezoidal doorway in a wall of gray, regularly coursed stones. There didn't seem to be quite room enough inside the little structure for all six Andeans at once; various backs and legs, wrapped in bright garments, kept protruding into the blasting wind. "I want to be able to hop in there and extract the victim as soon as the others start down. Here we go."

Liftoff was quiet. As in yesterday's flight, some superb system of stabilization made the machine actually feel steadier after it had mounted into the air than when it rested, swaying in the wind, upon the deck.

"They're coming out now, Boss," Lola's radio voice reported excitedly. "Only five of them, I think . . . Yes, now they're starting down. Only five."

"Great! With that big screen, you can see better than we can, so keep the commentary coming." The flyer shot forward, barely clearing first a gray turret on the wheel-rim of the building's upper story, and then the surrounding gray rocks. Boss evidently meant to keep the aircraft low, as if to minimize the chance that anyone on the ground might see it.

Either he was a superb pilot, or a reckless one—or there were safety systems built into the controls that made the trip less hazardous than it appeared. Mike's fingers dug hard into his plastic seat-arms as the flyer skimmed vertiginously down the gray flank of the Fort's mountain.

A mile below their starting point, they scraped through a barren high-altitude valley. Boss flew steadily within a man's height of the ground, and fast. Mike saw Gunner laughing at him silently and was reassured enough to make himself relax a little. Now abruptly the landscape beneath the flyer fell utterly away, into a gorge still sheltered by its depth from morning sun. Down there a river that looked small wound tortuously between banks thick with greenery. Now Boss pulled back on a control and the flyer climbed, almost sliding its way up another mountainside of jagged rock and wind-lashed snow.

The peak was near when Boss eased the aircraft to a hovering stop. After a moment Mike saw the shrine, a little stone building stuck there almost as if clinging to a wall.

"Inca party's still going down," said Lola over the radio. "They're out of line-of-sight with the shrine right now, but moving fast. They may be back in view of it again in a few minutes."

"We'll risk that," Boss announced. "Whoever they left inside is not going to have very long." As he spoke, he kept easing the flyer a little closer to the rocks, almost at the very summit. A tiny level ledge, whose clearing and partial leveling with masonry must have taken unimaginable labor, supported the small roofless shrine against the mountain. The remaining open area of the ledge would be okay to land on. No, it wouldn't. There was not quite enough room for the overhead blur of rotor to avoid the mountainside above the ledge.

Boss gained a little altitude. Now he could get right over the ledge, and did so, meanwhile motioning Mike to open the hatch. Following Gunner's earlier instructions, Mike first secured himself with a safety line, then released the door. Swallowing with the sudden decompression in his ears, he let the ladder down.

Gunner gulped a little oxygen from a tube, then started down the swinging steps. Mike noticed now that he wore a sidearm strapped on one hip. Next Doc, her medical kit now in a small backpack, reached for the ladder. Gunner steadied it from below until she was down. Then both of them were moving toward the shrine and into it. Boss tuned his controls and held position, the rotor blurring within inches of a rocky face.

Less than a minute passed before Doc was back in sight, following Gunner. He bore in his arms a sizable burden: a human shape wrapped in a survival blanket with gray camouflage side turned outward. Mike had the hoist line lowered before they got back to the ladder. The line carried a hammock-like attachment into which Gunner quickly slung his burden, then gave the lifting signal with a wave. Mike started the hoist, then moved a step down the ladder to grab the rising load and swing it safely inboard.

Then, breathing like a tired runner, Mike leaned down to grasp Doc by her gloved hand as she came up the ladder and help her through the hatch. Gunner was right behind her and pulled the hatch shut as he got in. Boss gave them barely time to strap in before they were swooping once more down the mountainside.

Doc quickly began to unwrap her patient, who was lying in the narrow space between the seats. Framed in the bright inner orange of the opened blanket appeared silver ornaments and feathers patterned in black and white, all entwined in the intricately braided hair of a brown-faced child who seemed to be in peaceful sleep.

"Get her arm out of the blanket for me," Doc ordered Mike, while she prepared a hypodermic. "That's it. They had stones piled over her already. Drugged and entombed and left to freeze. But I've got a heartbeat."

Boss was concentrating on his flying. Gunner watched the medical efforts, twisting his head around.

"They probably gave her coca," Doc muttered, needling the little girl's bared arm. "What's in that little pouch beside her there?"

Mike dug into a small white woolen bag attached to a leather belt. "Looks like . . . teeth? Baby teeth, I guess. And this. Crumbs or flakes of something."

Boss took a moment from his harrowing exploits to glance back at their work. "Teeth and fingernail parings, sent along so the kid wouldn't miss them in the next world. Little girl, hey? Looks very much upper class—fine hands and fancy clothes."

"They sacrificed their own kids?" Gunner was quietly outraged.

"On special occasions." Boss had faced forward again. "Weren't very big on human sacrifice in general. Not like the Aztecs."

Still searching about the girl, Mike came up with another woolen pouch. In this was a whitish powder. For a moment he saw in memory a small kitchen, red cabinet, red paint.

Doc sniffed at a little of the powder held out in his hand. "That's it, coca. You know, what cocaine comes from. She's doped up to feel no pain or cold. All right, we're going to take care of that." She started to get another needle ready.

Looking out of the flyer, Mike caught a glimpse of distant western ocean, right opposite the morning sun. Then the bit of flat blue horizon was gone behind a peak. He brought his eyes back to the peaceful child's face. She might have been twelve.

The trouble with her face was that it wasn't born yet. Didn't exist. Couldn't. Not in the same world with Mike Gabrieli. About four hundred years before he was born, this kid had died . . . My God, they'd really left her there to die!

The timelessness of the scenery here on this ridgepole of the world had somewhat masked the truth. But now it was beginning to sink in. In Europe, Henry VIII, no joke at all, would be replacing Chancellor Thomas More with Thomas Cromwell about this time— perhaps this very day of northern summer. Leonardo da Vinci was dead only a few years, Copernicus still very much alive. In Rome, young Michelangelo was preparing his *Last Judgment*. Galileo and Shakespeare were not yet born.

The year of 1532. Now it was sinking in, and his hands began to shake with it, as if truth were the cold of the high Andes, penetrating to settle in his bones.

8. The Branching of the World

On a September morning—September here was Coya Raymi, the month named for the Festival of the Queen—Mike was working alone in the model shop, correcting some details of the toy-sized walls of Cajamarca to fit photographs of the town made on the latest high-altitude recon flights. He heard the door behind him open, but then no one spoke or entered. He turned to see little Cori standing there.

In the weeks since they had pulled her from her tomb, the Inca girl had made a complete physical recovery. Mike had grown used to seeing her, in gray sweater and trousers, sitting at a ninth chair squeezed in at the dining table, or walking quietly through the

Fort's endless circular hallways. She would cast timid eyes about her at the magical technology, then sometimes stop to stare for long minutes across the windswept flight deck toward the unchanged peaks that she must have known all her short lifetime. Her face was sometimes troubled, more often solemn and unreadable, rarely and only fleetingly showed a smile. She answered all the mercenaries' well-meant, gentle, but persistent questions with a nod or a word, very rarely with more words than three or four.

The questions stayed within limits. No one yet pushed Cori to tell how she had come to be given to the Sun, or how it had felt to wake up here in an alien bed instead of the expected house of Inti. The Fort must be unlike any heaven or earth she could ever have imagined. She was being altered rapidly to fit into her new world. The women had stripped her black hair of its feathers, cleansed it of the oil and urine used to set it in its braids. It now fell about her shoulders, free but for a single one of her silver ornaments. Her name meant "gold," though copper would have been closer to the color of her skin.

Looking across the model, which filled a mammoth tabletop, Mike winked and smiled at the girl, and practiced a Quechua greeting. Cori didn't answer right away, but something in her face suggested that she was ready for communication.

He set down the detail he happened to have in his hand—a scale figure of a mounted conquistador, ready to ride *a la jineta* with the lance—and waved a hand in a gesture that included the whole model.

"Cajamarca," he said. If she had been there she should recognize the place, and in any case she ought to know the name. The town was bigger than most others of the vast Inca empire, but otherwise not untypical. The recon photos showed stone and clay walls, thatched roofs, and a small stone fortress on a small elevation near the town's western edge. The place had a few thousand population. The central square of Cajamarca, in the fateful November of 1532, would impress the soldiers from Castilian cities with its size, as well as offering them a providentially suitable place in which to spring their ambush on the Inca. Pizarro's Mask, of course, would guide the conqueror to the perfect place for that, upon the perfect day.

"Yes!" Cori agreed suddenly, in Quechua, looking at the model. She came to stand beside Mike at the table. "And what is this?"

she asked, one slender finger almost touching the little horseman with his lance.

"*Wirakoka*, creator god," Mike answered, bilingually. He wanted to see her reaction to the name some Indians would give to the conquistadors—not for long thinking them truly gods, but still crediting their noble mounts and bright strong metal and their mysterious firepower.

Cori laughed at him, with him, as silently as Gunner sometimes did. She had taken his answer for a joke, and was still waiting for an honest one.

"*Suncasapa*, Bearded One," he said, pointing again to the small mounted figure. This was the name by which most of Cori's people would first know the Spaniards. And to an Indian hearing it for the first time, the name must suggest a man contemptible, ridiculous, a clown or jester, maybe. What warrior would cultivate a beard?

Still smiling, Cori shook her head, a gesture she had picked up from the others at the Fort. No, Mike, stop teasing me, it seemed to mean. But she was obviously still interested in going on with the conversation.

"*Cancha*," Mike said, using one finger to outline a walled space in the model. He wanted to see if he had the pronunciation right.

"*Cancha*." She nodded, but the word for "enclosure" sounded a little different in her mouth. He tried again with *cancha*, and then with *llama* and with the words for "house" and "town" and "street."

From the corner of his eye, he noted someone else coming into the open doorway, and glanced up to see Doc's pleased face. The woman was standing there silently observing the girl, evidently happy that her youngest patient was starting to communicate. Doc was a good-looking woman, and after some weeks in the Fort, Mike felt as fond of her as he might of a newly discovered sister. She hadn't been joking a bit when she told him that anaphrodisiacs were being put into their food. Which, he had to admit, was probably all for the best.

"*Pokara*," said Mike to Cori, meanwhile gesturing at the small fortress that overlooked the model town.

"Yes," Cori said in English, and nodded her head, black tresses jiggling. Her curious eyes kept coming back to the little Spaniard, and now with a glance at Mike she picked him up and set him on her palm. He wore a silvery breastplate and silvery morion helmet, and paint suggested a black bush of beard upon his chin. The human portion of the figure was melded with that of an animal having four towering hoofed legs. The Andeans had never seen a horse before the Spaniards came, and their llama were too small for practical riding. The toy Conquistador must be the most intriguing monster that young Cori had ever seen. "But what?" she persisted. "Who? Not *wirakoka*."

Abruptly all the fun went out of the game for Mike. "No, not a god. Only a man. A man who is coming to Tawantinsuyu."

And this time Cori's laughter struck out golden chimes, for that was the funniest thing she had heard since coming to the Fort.

November here was Ayamarka, the month named for its Procession of the Dead, and among the more minor things nagging Mike was a gloomy sense of aptness in the name. The month brought such spring as came to the Andean highlands, mainly a foretaste of the seasonal rains that would begin next month in earnest. At 18,000 feet there was no noticeable change in weather, but clouds were thicker on the lower slopes, where summer greening would soon follow.

By November the mercenaries all looked like Indians, or at least a good deal more like Indians than they had upon arrival. Pills had altered skin color to hues that ranged from coppery to chocolate. Gunner's beard was gone, and Rusty's hair had grown straight and black to an acceptable length. Operating in a surgery that looked more convincingly ultramodern than anything else about the Fort, Doc had pierced all the men's earlobes, stretching the holes enough to accommodate the weighty golden ornaments of the *pakoyoc*—men of the Inca nobility—those whom the Spaniards would come to call the Big Ears, *orejones*.

On the night the troops shipped out, Doc stayed behind in the Fort, getting her marvelous surgery quietly set up to handle casualties. Cori, a noticeably bigger girl than she had been three months ago in August, stood by, a nurses' aide in training. Rusty was in the pilot's seat of a troop-carrying flyer, and Lola took off alone in a faster craft laden with missiles and beam-weapons, flying cover for the coming operation on the ground.

In the middle of the night, the five men of the Fort boarded Rusty's flyer. Over long shirts of plastic chain mail, presumably proof against Castilian sword or lance, they wore capes and tunics of soft llama wool. On their feet were sandals of fine leather. Radios nestled in their golden ear-ornaments. Their axes and maces of bronze, too small to be anything but ceremonial, concealed weaponry enormously more advanced.

The two aircraft left the Fort sometime after midnight. Their flight beneath the incredible spread of morning stars was planned to take them 600 miles to the northwest in about an hour.

Mike rode in a rear seat, looking out at darkness that concealed far below some of the roughest and most spectacular landscape in the world. Before his eyes imagination and memory painted a mandala, and a green door, and a complex control panel with one button emphasized—the only things that his Mask had shown him in the last three months of almost daily secret viewings. Still, he would have tried to bring the Mask along tonight if he had been able to think of any way to conceal it from Boss's careful final inspections of clothing and equipment. In fact, it still rested in the bottom of his bag in the back of his closet.

They were going to frustrate Pizarro, to save the Inca power. In a few months, the unthinkable, incredible, became not only routine but almost boring except for the danger—now around him in the flyer the others were telling feeble jokes, making small talk, little bursts of technical conversation as afterthoughts about details of the job came up. Mike, too, would say something if an idea occurred to him. Most of the time, it now seemed to him that he really did belong here, that sometime, somewhere, he had really signed on the dotted line for some mysterious recruiting sergeant. His name was Rocky, now, and that was it. At times he nursed the fantasy that all the other mercenaries, maybe even Boss, were all here as a result of surprising journeys as unintended as his had been, that in the closets of all their rooms were hidden Masks, like secret vices . . . That this fantasy might be anything more than fantasy he had not the smallest shred of evidence.

The flyer bore on through the night. He had his eyes shut now, as if he were dozing, but his mouth was dry and he was frightened. All the mercenaries knew that they were going to have to fight against Pizarro's Mask, and their training and indoctrination had included numerous vague assurances that its powers could be overcome. But it seemed to Mike that only he among them could understand how hard that fight was likely to be. Were his own Mask's repeated cryptic visions somehow to guide him through it?

At this late date he couldn't see what connection there might be . . .

His three months of training had brought him a little more information on Pizarro's Mask. Through a chain of events that probably sounded incredible to his fellow trainees, who had not seen in their own lives what a Mask could do, it had come to Pizarro from Cortés, who had it directly from Montezuma of the Aztecs. In that tribe it had been for some centuries the secret property of a series of their First Speakers, and as such it had enabled them to extend their dominion across Mexico. It had come to the Aztecs of the fourteenth century probably from their own far future, in some way that even the twenty-third-century Directors seemed to find mysterious, and which Mike could not begin to really grasp.

There was of course one aspect of the matter that he dared not discuss with his fellow trainees, on which he could not formulate questions, for the Fort's sophisticated teaching machines. Privately he theorized that Pizarro, in at least one branch of history, had decided for some reason to ship his Mask back to Spain; then the ship bringing it north from Panama had gone down in the Gulf. Tides and currents and the slow movements of the sea bottom had had their way, and then four hundred years later Tom Gabrieli just happened to come by snorkeling. If anything just happened . . .

Mike's mouth was drier than ever. "Got Cajamarca on the radar now," Rusty remarked to her passengers, and Mike opened his eyes to note with great surprise that almost an hour had gone by since takeoff. Looking over Rusty's square shoulder at the pilot's panel, he could see on her screen the unusually flat valley, almost 9,000 feet above sea level, in which the familiar shape of the town's walls made their bright green reflected lines.

"Look there," said Samson, his face turned out to the speeding night. Orange sparks as numerous as stars were coming into view upon the otherwise invisible mountain slopes surrounding Caja-marca. Everyone in the flyer knew what they were—the campfires of the Inca Atahualpa's army, just victorious over that of his brother, Huascar, after five years of bloody civil war. On the way to reclaim his capital of Cuzco after monumental struggles, Atahu-alpa was pausing here, where hot springs made a royal spa, to rest and luxuriate in triumph before he faced the great task of welding a riven empire back together. Also, the Inca wished to amuse himself by taking a quick look at the handful of peculiar strangers who had evidently washed up somehow on a beach, and had somehow managed to bring their strange, huge, silver-footed animals this far inland and over the mountain passes, treading the fine pavements of the royal roads uninvited. These bearded, white-skinned aliens had already in passing abused some of the Inca's secluded holy women, and had stolen gold. For these misdeeds they would have to answer. But first it should prove interesting to talk to them in their unspoiled state, and observe something of their oddities.

Atahualpa's veteran army, tens of thousands strong, surrounded the town where Pizarro waited with his hundred and sixty men. Looking at the cookfires, Gunner shook his head. "If I was one o' them Spaniards, I'da shit my iron britches long ago."

"Their morale is certainly sagging somewhat at this point," Boss commented dryly. He chronically disapproved of what he called Gunner's strong language in mixed company, but made no issue of it because the Directors had laid down no regulations on the point and none of the women seemed to pay much attention anyway. "But consider their situation. They really have nowhere to go but forward, no choice but some kind of aggressive action. If Pizarro should try to retreat to the coast now, the Inca could raise a finger and destroy him—catch the Spaniards strung out and all but helpless in the passes. Some of those roads there are nothing but narrow stairways—sheer cliff going up on one side, down on the other. And Atahualpa would probably do just that. You know he says later, or he's quoted as saying, that he thought to save only a few of the invaders as castrated helpers in his harem."

Sparks spoke up, expressing doubt that the Inca had ever said any such thing—not that the brutality of it would have been out of character for him, who was like his ancestors a ruthless conqueror. After three months' schooling, all the mercenaries had their opinions on the subject, and a desultory argument began. Mike took no part. He only stared at the innumerable campfires and wondered at his fate, while Rusty slowed the flyer and began a cautious descent toward the chosen landing place in some high barren hills.

Circling and observing in her escort ship above, keeping guard against any unexpected Tenocha interference, Lola reported on radio now that she had nothing extraordinary to report, and it seemed the Directors had been right: probably the twenty-third-century Aztec-Tenocha were aware of this move by the mercenaries of the twenty-third-century Incas, but the Aztecs had elected not to try to interfere directly. Perhaps, as the Directors said, because such interference would let the Directors send their modern Inca legions into their own past to fight for it; perhaps, Mike thought, because the Aztecs knew a Mask was on Pizarro's side and no help would be needed.

. . . so Tom had quote just happened unquote to find the Mask, but then had rejected the warning visions it must have given him. Maybe he had enough experience with drugs—or with drug users—to make him very suspicious of visions of any kind. Anyway, he had simply planned and tried to sell the thing, without for a moment coming near to understanding just what kind of business he had been plunged into. Maybe the same gunmen who had come to Aunt Tessie's house for Mike had come there earlier for his brother. Then maybe they had come back to get the Mask, when they knew where he had hidden it, but meanwhile the neighbor with his hurricane precautions had moved it, hiding place and all. Then the neighbor brought it back, just in time for Mike . . .

It was chilling to suspect that maybe the Mask made its own plans, chose its own masters, let them think that they were using it, while it or its ultimate controller used them . . .

And Mike wondered, from time to time, what had happened to the girl. Sally, yes, that was her name. He hoped she had waked up safely on the morning after, tucked in her own bed. The rest of the town had, maybe, but in her case he wouldn't want to bet on it.

There was no end of questions fit for fruitless pondering. If the gunmen at the door were of the Aztec-Tenocha faction, as seemed likely, who then was Esperanza? If he was of the Inca faction, then why didn't the Directors know who Mike Gabrieli was when he arrived at the Fort? And if . . .

Landing skids crunched down on sandy soil, and Gunner opened the hatch to matching air pressure outside. Mike was the second man to tumble out, and as in the numerous rehearsals, he scrambled at once to take up his proper defensive position. His small bronze ceremonial mace with its concealed stun-maser was in his hands. His mouth was dry as long-dead bones.

Anyway, there was no need for defensive action. The hillside around the landed flyer was all serene, and very dark. A rack of clouds was beginning to shut off the marvelous Andean stars. Tomorrow here would be wet, and tomorrow night would be foggy, hard to find one's way about in. Sparks was already burying the small radio beacon that would allow the infantry to find their way back to this precise spot for recovery rendezvous.

After exchanging a few final words with Boss, Rusty wound up her rotor and took off. She and Lola would now head back to the Fort until time for rendezvous; if all went well, their ability to pass as Indians would never be tested; but Boss, if not the Directors, seemed to hold it as an article of faith that in matters of this kind all could never go well.

The sound of the flyer dwindled and was gone. Eyes grown accustomed to the darkness, the five men assembled and then set off downhill in single file. Gunner led; Mike came second; Boss brought up the rear. Their progress down the rugged slope was slow, involving much doubling back and subdued cursing. Before they came in sight of the town and the encampments surrounding it, a drizzle had set in, and most of the army's fires were out. Invisible in the darkness were the small buildings where the Inca and his personal escort rested: a stone complex at some hot springs two or three miles from the town.

Despite the drizzle, the air was gradually growing brighter, by a clouded process too indefinite to give the feel of dawn. Where the hills flattened down into the valley floor enough to let them begin walking freely, the five men found their way crossed by a level, stone-paved road, twenty feet broad and smooth as a modern street. From this point on, they would probably be under frequent observation by the Inca's soldiers, and Boss signaled to change the order of march from single file to a loose, informal grouping. Then they moved on, at a moderate walk, toward the center of the valley.

The hard and mostly barren ground crunched and scraped beneath Mike's sandals. Now, in the growing light, he could make out a vast number of pottery shards that were mixed in with the soil. These must be relics of a people far older than the Inca. And following that insight came a vision of the immensity of even human time, a vision lasting only a moment, but clear and intense enough so that he almost stumbled, almost forgot what he was doing here.

Gunner had an arm raised, pointing silently off to their right. Another road looped there, and on it there moved a supply train of llamas, gray and ghostly in the early light. There might be a hundred of the long-necked animals in the caravan, each no doubt bearing sixty or seventy pounds of food for the enormous army. The Inca supply system was functioning with the smoothness needed by successful empire-builders. At intervals along the train walked half a dozen herders in tight-fitting caps, clucking and tugging at the animals from time to time.

Ahead, the miles of valley floor, still vague and dim. Mike looked off to the left, where water tumbled from the hills to rush between high banks. Where the land broke again in a small shelf, a little waterfall fell. At a greater distance in that direction, a company of ghosts marched through a patch of fog—Inca soldiery in short white tunics, marching in loose order.

Mike's mouth was still dry. On impulse, he turned away from the four he traveled with and walked toward the stream. Below the waterfall its banks were gently sloped. He slowed his pace for a moment, as he caught sight of another lone figure, crouching at the water's edge on the far bank, but then he went on. A confrontation was going to have to come sooner or later, and he preferred to test his acceptability as an Indian on one man rather than a company.

Just as Mike reached the water the young man on the far side finished drinking, raised his head, and gave him an appraising look. By his dress and ornaments, Mike knew him for a junior officer, whose insignia of distinguished service, in the form of a bronze disc, swung against the chest of his cotton tunic.

"*Ama sua,*" the young man said. His eyes, not to mention his big nose, gave him something of the look of an eagle. "*Ama llulla, ama cheklla.*" Don't steal, don't lie, don't waste your time. It was something of a standard greeting among the Inca's subjects.

"*Kampas hinalatak.*" The same to you. Cori had at last approved his accent when he spoke the words, and now the young soldier accepted their sounds without any sign of suspicion. In Quechua, Mike went on: "And what do you expect the orders of the day will be?"

"Who can say?" The soldier shook cold water from his fingers. "The Lord Inca still warms his bones at the hot baths." With a little gesture, he stood up and went on his way; no doubt it was time that he saw how his men were doing.

Mike bent to drink. The men had been immunized against any infection or parasites they could pick up. The cold river seemed to flow into his blood, and he could feel it still with him when he stood up again. A connection with this high valley, with this whole world around him, had been sealed.

The others of his company were waiting for him in silence.

Among these Indians, the morning meal was often the biggest one of the day. With the sun well up though still invisible, the mercenaries stopped halfway across the valley to build a fire. They were somewhat away from the places where the smoke of others' cooking rose thickest. For fuel they selected the driest llama dung available along a nearby road. *Chuno*, dried potatoes, and *charqui*—jerky, or dried meat—came to life in the stewpot and made good food for Inca warriors.

As the five of them stood or squatted, munching food scooped up in fingers, Boss chose to attempt a final pep talk in low-voiced English: "I don't have to tell you men what we—each one of us—will be fighting for when we go in there today. At home, waiting for each one of us, is someone who . . . but I'd best say no more of that, even now." Deep emotions were threatening to come out in Boss's new Indian face. And one of his crew, at least, would have felt better if he had said more of that, even now; any information could be helpful. But no such luck. "Gunner, Rocky, you two as well as myself, of course, are the combat veterans here. The burden will be on us in a special way to make sure . . ."

Mike tuned out, having just heard convincing proof, if any were still needed, that Boss *didn't* know who Mike-Rocky was, had him irretrievably confused with someone else. Mike had been in the army, sure. Drafted, and then spent his hitch in California, punching a typewriter. But *who* did they think they had recruited as a desperado to help lead the charge? Tom? No, no combat for him, either, except in bars.

Gunner had probably tuned out the speech also, though he kept his Indian face impassively turned toward Boss. Sparks and Samson fidgeted. No one was eating very much. Boss soon ran out of attempted inspiration. The meal was concluded, or abandoned.

Boss gave the final signal, and the men, as often rehearsed, turned to move off in their separate ways.

For a little distance, Gunner kept pace at Mike's elbow. "Was afraid there for a while he was gonna say 'Good huntin'!' or 'Bring back their scalps!' or somethin'. Had a sumbitch of a lieutenant once who . . . well, never mind. See y' around." He strolled away on a slowly diverging course.

Mike waved to wish him well. All five men were to make their separate ways to the area of the Inca's lodgings. Around the royal headquarters, men from all parts of the empire would be mingling, coming and going on all sorts of business. There amid diversity, small oddities of speech or clothing seemed least likely to be noticed.

As expected, the population of *pakoyoc*, warriors, camp-following women, servants, and llamas grew ever denser around the stone buildings clustered where hot springs sent steam into the air. Messengers—*chasquichuna*—sped to and fro on foot, the knotted *quipus*, message cords, in hand or at their belts. Panpipes were tootling somewhere, and from inside a house there came a laugh as of a tickled concubine.

Mike approached the spa unhurriedly. He tried to look as if he were early for an appointment with some official—if the officials here had appointments—and was meanwhile pondering whatever weighty but not urgent business he had come upon. All this method acting seemed wasted. No one challenged him. People scarcely seemed to notice that he was around. All had enough business of their own.

The town whose white walls were visible a couple of miles away had been temporarily evacuated of its inhabitants by Atahualpa's order, and reserved for the Conquistadors' sole occupancy. For a full day now, the Spaniards in the town and the Inca encamped outside had been exchanging messages and small gifts. But not until late on this rainy afternoon was Atahualpa to decide to accept an earlier invitation and visit his treacherous enemies inside Caja-marca's walls. Lounging close outside the bathhouse, Mike saw the explosive flurry of activity that accompanied the announcement of this decision, and knew what it signified; he exchanged glances with Samson, who he had seen conversing casually with some Indi-ans in the middle distance, and who now had to get himself out of the way as the litter-bearers of the greatest lords came scrambling to lift their poles, the various teams jostling one another as if to win a more favored position for their masters in the line of march now forming.

Mike also backed away slightly. He kept watching, in an effort to see the Inca himself emerge from one of the buildings. But his view was blocked by a horde of menials in checkered livery who began to form squads in between. Chanting already in a thousand voices, they were beginning to sweep the ground free of debris before the Inca's progress. All the way to town they would precede the great mass of the Inca's ceremonial escort, none of whom bore any weapon much more formidable than a broom. That personal danger for him existed here, in the seat of his strength, was apparently too absurd an idea to have ever crossed Atahualpa's mind.

Once ordered, the royal progress formed and began to flow with practiced speed. Amid the wild profusion of costumes and insignias of the nobility and ranking soldiers, Mike attracted no particular attention. Beamed into his earplug radio came some unnecessary order from Boss, who sounded nervous. Mike caught sight first of Sparks, then Gunner, at a little distance in the milling crowd.

Now the crowd made way for the passage of the first of the great nobles' litters, several of which would follow Atahualpa's to the town square. And now, suddenly and almost unexpectedly, Mike caught sight of the Inca himself, borne aloft by scores of lords in livery of blue, in an enormous feather-roofed litter whose poles were covered in silver. Rattles whirled, the shrilling chanting of the royal sweepers rose, and Atahualpa passed. Mike got a perfectly clear look; the Inca was about thirty, stocky and well-made. The tassled *borla*—his unique sign of rank—hung on his forehead, and a thick rope of emeralds about his neck. Overhung by roofs of gaudy plumes, he sat on a small cushioned stool. Heads were bowed across the throng, like grass before the wind; the Inca was not to be stared at, any more than was the sun. Perhaps no more than ten eyes were watching closely as he passed.

The men around Mike now began to move; the march was underway. Five or six thousand strong, its ranks overflowed on both sides the broad roadway leading to the town. Rain spattered from the low racing rack of cloud, as it had off and on during the day, and was ignored by all.

To Mike, the march toward the fateful square seemed very swift. The column entered the town through a simple, wide-open gate, from which a street led between walls of stone and hardened clay to the broad central plaza. Now he could see the small fort on its elevated ground just at the west side of the town. His mouth was dry again, the mountain water long since drained away. He knew Pizarro had four arquebuses atop the fort, and eight or nine primitive muskets.

The square spread its paved acres out beneath the rainy sky. Only narrow ways led out of it. The first thousands of the Inca's escort, filing in from the constricted street, moved on to the far sides of the plaza to make room for those who pressed behind.

Mike, marching in folded-arm dignity like those about him, had yet to see a Spaniard, but he knew where they were—for the most part, concealed in three buildings, old Inca barracks, low and enormously long, that occupied one full side of the square. Their wide, trapezoidal doors were closed and silent. Behind them, men on horseback sweated in their armor, weapons ready, animals prayerfully held silent.

Though he had tried to watch for it, Mike missed the entrance into the square of the gray-robed friar Valverde, who accompanied Pizarro's expedition as spokesman of the Church. When Mike first caught sight of the priest, he was already standing before Atahualpa, whose litter had just been lowered to the ground from the shoulders of its sixty or so high-ranking bearers. Valverde was speaking animatedly, while an interpreter, an Indian from some northern coastal tribe who had lived some years with the Spaniards, stood by. Mike, some forty or fifty meters away, could not catch the words, but he knew that Valverde was passing on Pizarro's invitation to the Inca to enter one of the buildings there to dine with "governor" Pizarro amid a roomful of Spaniards. Then, through the interpreter, Atahualpa declined, saying that he would not enter with Pizarro until the Spaniards returned all the goods that they had stolen since entering his empire.

"Remember," said Boss's tinny radio whisper, speaking into Mike's ear, "don't mow them down in the doorways. We've got to let them make a real attack." The Directors had reportedly considered and rejected the idea that simply warning Atahualpa of Spanish perfidy might be enough to save his land for him. Even if a warning could be made certainly convincing, it would not be sufficiently galvanic. Swords must be allowed to bite, the power of Spanish arms must be displayed, the Inca's person must be brought into danger, in order to produce a full mobilization of the Andean world that would be capable of resisting European pressure throughout the sixteenth century and afterward.

Valverde had been rebuffed. Now, his voice rising angrily, he was launching into the "Requirement": a peculiar document imposed on Conquistadors by the authorities in Spain. It amounted to an outline of the Faith, and a testimony to the noble intentions of its proselytizers; and it was required to be read aloud by them to the benighted whom they had come to govern before the Spaniards could begin to shed blood in quelling Indian resistance. Meanwhile Mike was thinking that he *was* going to shoot the charging horsemen in the doorways, pile them up there before they could get out and start the slaughtering, whether Boss wanted it done just that way or not. It was not just a matter of defending the Inca. He—Mike—was out here in this bloody square himself, and his plastic armor was feeling more and more thin and insubstantial with each passing moment.

Now Atahuaipa, questioning, had taken into his hands the holy book Valverde had been waving at him. The Inca, who had never before seen writing, much less a bound volume, could not get it open. The friar reached out and would have helped him. Annoyed, the Inca shoved the robed arm away, and a moment later got the book open by himself. There fluttered before him pages of incomprehensible markings. It may have seemed to him a joke, a trick, something as rude as the insulting message just stammered out by the interpreter, whose unintelligible meaning seemed to be that the Child of the Sun should at once hand over lordship of all his lands to some distant white-skinned ruler that he had never seen or heard of. The Inca threw the Bible to the ground.

The interpreter hastily picked up the volume and handed it to the friar. Valverde took it and turned away. Harshly shouting something which Mike could not quite make out, he strode toward the building in which Pizarro and his cavalry were hiding.

Looking toward its roof, Mike now saw the expected white scarf wave, a signal toward the fort. He shifted his grip upon his ceremonial mace, and with a nervous thumb turned off the safety catch. Without in the least understanding it, he heard some final admonition from Boss come through his concealed radio.

Matchlocks needed time to work, time for priming to ignite and pass fire on to the chambers. The scattered volley from the fort erupted a full two or three seconds after the waving of the scarf. The missiles blasted from the primitive guns were not vastly more dangerous than a volley of rocks from Inca slings; but for men who had not heard or seen the like before, the thunder-weapons were terrible in their psychological shock.

Around Mike, the ruling class of the Four Quarters of the World were turning, gaping at the low sky in search of lightning bolts, and calling upon their gods. Jostled in the press, he sidestepped, raising his mace, trying to get a clear field of fire toward the trapezoidal doors . . .

"Santiago and at them!" The war cry boomed forth in Spanish near at hand, was echoed from the fort, and from the square again. The big wooden doors burst open onto the square. In converging columns from three doorways, the horsemen thundered forth, driving hard for Atahualpa's grounded litter.

Mike aimed his mace and squeezed the hidden trigger, knowing but not caring that he was firing too soon. He swept the rough column of oncoming cavalry from front to rear with invisible force.

There was no immediate effect.

"Hold your fire, hold your fire," Boss kept repeating, with insane calm, in Mike's left ear. At the same time, Mike saw the first weapons thrust and cut, heard the screams of the day's first slain and wounded.

Still no Spaniard had fallen. He was squeezing the trigger, wasn't he? And the safety had been taken off. But nothing worked. He might as well be snapping photographs. The mounted men came on, oblivious.

To Indians who had never seen or imagined such a charge before, who indeed had never before seen a horse, the cavalry onslaught must have brought terror as of monsters from an alien world. But yet the need to defend the Inca was still overriding. As fast as the men of Atahualpa's escort could be knocked down by horses, run through by lances, hacked out of the way by swords, others threw themselves into the Spaniards' path. The great litter had been heaved aloft again by loyal arms, its bearers trying to retreat through a great press of men.

Blades flashed, steel and crimson. War-horses screamed like anguished men and reared, struck with their hooves at feathered men who ran beneath their bellies and tried to push them back. In every frame of vision, Indians were going down. Thousands would die today inside this town. Blood spattered on fine plumage and vicuna wool. The voices of fear and rage and triumph rose up deafeningly.

"Fire!" The order from Boss was piercing plain when it did come. Oh, fire, you bastards, Mike pleaded with his comrades. I'm going to have to sit this one out, guys, don't know what's wrong with this damned hunk of junk . . . For perhaps the seventh or eight time, his fingers checked over as best they could the mechanism of the stun-maser built into his bronze mace. He could check it blindfolded, after all the time they'd spent in practice. In practice everything had always worked. And it all checked out now. Each time he pressed the trigger, the unit responded with a faint vibration, the designed signal that the beam was operating. Any complex nervous system, a man's or horse's, say, caught by that beam within a hundred meters' range, should be disorganized for seconds or even minutes. Repeated jolts could kill, or so they'd taught him. All the Castilians and their horses should now be staggering and weakened, or sprawled convulsing on the pavement. Then the Indians should rally, no doubt to slaughter the Spaniards before they could recover. Then Tawantinsuyu would be saved, warned, inoculated and immunized against European power and perfidy. The empire of the Incas, within this branch of history, should continue to exist, and its existence should change the world.

Mike tried again. What else could he do? He sighted this time at an unmounted killer, a graybeard on foot who might well be Pizarro the poor horseman, preferring to trust to his own two legs in the melee. The man's eyes flashed blue beneath a morion helmet; his sword was leveled toward the Inca's swaying litter; his whiskered cheeks were stretched to roar a command or a war cry. Mike hosed the man—or tried to hose him—with radiation that should have dropped him in his tracks. He steadied his aim and held the trigger down. The man gave his head a fierce shake, as if something had stung or distracted him in the midst of battle. But then he moved forward again, striking vigorously left and right.

Where was Pizarro's Mask? Not on his face. But still . . .

"Boss, my weapon's jammed somehow . . ." That was Gunner's voice.

"—not getting any output from this—" That sounded like Sparks.

"Negative here, too. Malfunction . . . " Might have been Samson.

"Get closer!" Boss was ordering them all. "Everyone, keep firing! Move on in . . . "

The Inca's litter was still borne high on scores of sturdy arms and shoulders. So far his attackers had not been able to get within a lance-length of it. They were kept back not by battle but by slaughter—human flesh forcing itself forward by the ton, clogging the Toledo-steel blades of the meat grinder. In the background somewhere, the muskets and the cannon kept up a slow erratic barking. Meanwhile, in the confused press of bodies, the men who carried Atahualpa could not maneuver to carry him away. Whenever they began to find the space to move, some horsemen managed to come at them from a new direction.

Whether under some hypnotic compulsion to follow Boss's order, or infected by the fanaticism of those around him, Mike found himself trying to get closer to the great litter. A few yards off he could see Gunner, also pushing his way forward. Mike aimed and fired, aimed and fired. Totally ineffective, as before, but what else was there to do?

A Spaniard spurred his horse, the animal's half-ton of driving weight forcing its way close to the litter, while its rider thrust and cut at the bearers to bring the Emperor down alive. Mike saw one of the blue-clad noblemen lose an arm; the man leaned his red shoulder-stump under the pole, continuing to bear a portion of the load.

All around the roaring struggle went on, endless, mad, hypnotic. Horses tripped on the piling bodies of unarmed men. Men and horses slid and fell in puddling blood.

Pizarro—that graybeard climbing over bodies had to be him—and where, where, was his Mask? Hidden somewhere in his baggage, if only someone could—Pizarro roared curses at his own men, some of whom seemed to have given up the attempt to capture the Inca and to be threatening to kill him if they could hurl themselves close enough. On his swaying litter, the Inca himself sat as impassive as a mummy; there was nothing he could do unless his men could first get him away.

Still, incredibly, the Spaniards could not quite manage to get close enough to kill or capture him. No sooner had one of his litter-bearers been cut out of the way than two more climbed upon the bodies of their fellows, happy to die for their great lord. And wounded bearers still upheld the poles, until their strength had bled too low to let them stand.

Jammed in by struggling bodies, Mike could do no more than any of the men immediately about him. The narrow gates of the square were all clogged with humanity—masses of Indian men striving to get out, perhaps to arm themselves—while others tried to push in to reach the Emperor's side.

Mike saw, within a few yards of the Emperor's litter, Sparks's head almost severed by a sword cut that struck just above his concealed body armor. A moment later, another Spaniard seemed about to strike at Atahualpa with a dagger. Pizarro was on the spot in time to intervene, shooting an arm forward and taking the blow on his own hand; it was the only wound that he or any of his men were to receive during the day. Around their leader now the horsemen surged forward together, yelling.

At last the gay-plumed litter overbalanced. The remaining bearers, stumbling over corpses, felt the blood-wet poles slide through their helpless hands. The litter toppled, spilling its contents sideways. Dismounted Spaniards, contending with their own horses in a perilous scramble, seized the fallen Inca's arms.

It was as if a switch had closed; a core of gravity dissolved in an explosion that sent shock waves across the square. The thousands of Indian men still alive within its walls were left with only one instinctive purpose: flight. Mike was swept with them, away from the spot where Atahualpa's arms were being bound. He could do nothing but struggle to avoid being trampled in the rush.

Again a cannon or a musket fired. Spanish voices screamed: "Santiago and at them!" Mike knew the killing was far from over. When the crowd about him loosened enough to give him room, he ran, rain whipping into his face from the sky that seemed to have been steadily darkening forever. Before him, one of the long white walls of the square of Cajamarca crashed down, broken outward beneath the impact of a thousand running, climbing bodies. Not far beyond lay open country—and a chance.

Mike ran. There came hooves hammering behind him, now closing right on his heels in a terrible avalanche of sound that brought blind panic. Something smashed with a giant's power at his left shoulder blade. He was lifted and hurled forward into another running man, the two of them rolling together on the pavement as horse and rider thundered gigantically by.

Dazed, unsure of anything but being still alive, Mike rolled to his feet and staggered on, beginning to run again when he found that his legs still worked. The pain that had been beaten into his back persisted, but he had no sense of broken bones or bleeding. Blindly following a horde of moccasined and sandaled feet that flowed around him on both sides, he clambered over pieces of the fallen wall, and kept on going. If only he had his Mask . . . Why hadn't it warned him of this ahead of time, shown him the right way to avoid it?

There was a street to run, among a few more buildings, and then the open countryside ahead, the almost barren plain. Men ran through fields, shouting in cracked voices of the fallen Inca, a shock in their voices as if the sky had broken like a pottery bowl above their heads. A thousand nobles, some of whom might have managed to stop a rout, lay dead, back in the square. Demoralized at one blow, the vast Inca army scattered into leaderless confusion.

Behind Mike there came again the sound of hooves, and he forced his aching, pleading lungs to grab him air to let him run. At last his lungs could do no more, and he must either stop or fall. He turned, aiming and firing as he had been trained, with the mace that somehow still stuck in his hand. He sighted at the dark-bearded face, high atop the horse that from this peasant's angle looked unstoppable as a tank. The red sword lifted, and Mike turned and threw himself down . . . Something sang in the air above him as he rolled away. The rider galloped on without a pause, charging after other game. Mike scrambled to his feet and found that after all he could still run.

At last he had to fall, and fell, and lay there gasping, very near a faint. The thin air . . . of course, the Spaniards had to breathe it, too. But they were not compelled to run, and run, and run . . .

When enough breath and control had come back to let him raise his head, he found himself alone except for one man who sat nearby, his head and shoulders outlined against a dismal, gloomy sunset. The walls of Cajamarca might be half a mile distant across the plain. It was a white-haired man but maybe not an old one who sat there with his elbows on his knees, twiddling his thumbs in an un-Indian-looking way.

Mike grunted something that might have been in Quechua, and got up to a sitting position himself. In the distance, in the dusk, he still could hear screams and war cries.

"My name is Esperanza," the white-haired man said in English, turning to look at Mike. He had a huge nose, almost broken-looking. "I talked to you once on the telephone." It was the same resonant actor's voice. Esperanza was wearing some kind of cape.

"Good God," Mike said without much vehemence, or reverence, either. "I'm not sure what world I'm in."

"Well, it is hard to tell sometimes. But at the moment you're in Tawantinsuyu-16, as the Directors's jargon has it. Sixteenth-century Peru, and if one of those Spaniards stabs you, you'll be dead. Never doubt that for a moment."

Mike felt no doubts at all on that matter. He sat there breathing hard, gripping his mace, developing a fierce anger that the other seemed so sure that he, himself, was in no danger of being stabbed. Esperanza looked too relaxed for that.

Mike said, "You're doing this to me. What're you going to do next? Whadda you want?"

"It's probably useless for you to question me." Esperanza shook his head, and Mike could see his big nose briefly in silhouette. Cyrano as a prizefighter. "Tell me, Gabrieli, what are your plans? Beyond mere survival, I mean. This is an awkward time to talk to you, I know, but I have to get in this visit when I can."

"If you're such a goddamn friendly visitor, give me a hand. Get me out of this."

"I can't. Literally. Can't even tell you anything very useful. If I tried, I'd be gone in a paradox loop before *I* could find out anything from *you*."

"Where's Tom?"

"Finding your brother is still a high-priority matter for you. That's very—"

Esperanza was gone. No fuss or fanciness, just gone. If he had ever been there. If he were not merely some result of a concussion.

"Report in." It was a tinny and tiny, but reassuring, Boss's voice, coming through the left ear-ornament. "Gunner. Rocky. Sparks. Report in, please, and head for rendezvous." The call was repeated, with slight variations and an enormous weariness of tone, as if Boss had been sending it for some time. If so, Mike hadn't heard it until just now.

"This is Rocky," he answered, low-voiced. "I'm . . . " Where was he? Out in the valley somewhere. "I'm on my way to rendezvous. Sparks isn't, though. I saw him get killed, back in the square."

"Rocky." Boss sounded relieved to get an answer. "You're quite sure he's dead?"

"Quite." With a shudder that turned into a shiver of Andean chill, Mike got to his feet. He started walking away from Cajamarca into the moonless, starless night.

Boss asked, "Any sign of Gunner?" Evidently Boss knew the fate of Samson, whatever that might be.

"No."

"Wait . . . I think I may have a bearing on him here." Boss was evidently carrying some special gear to help him keep track of his troops. "Proceed to rendezvous, Rocky. We'll try to meet you there."

"Understand." Radio silence fell. He stumbled along, in gusts of rainy wind. As he got onto higher ground, it required some effort to keep from falling over a rock or into a ravine. He had turned on the homing device in his right ear-ornament, and the beeping tone kept strengthening. Its pattern varied depending on whether the transmitter was to his right or left. He was shivering uncontrollably now with bitter cold.

He still had the bronze mace in his hand. A weighted stick. He stuck it in his belt. Probably not as effective as policeman's billy, but if the cavalry came after him again, he was going to turn around and try to smash their heads in with it. No, he wasn't. He knew damn well the cavalry was not going to come out in these hills after dark. Right now the Spaniards were behind walls in Cajamarca, fearing the Indian counterattack-by-night that was never going to come, taking turns guarding their royal prisoner, snatching sleep in their armor while their horses stood by bridled and ready to go. He was carrying his mace for another reason—to bring it back to the Fort and find out why it hadn't worked.

At last the modulation in his right earplug altered to a pattern that meant he was within a hundred meters of the rendezvous point. And still no one else in sight.

He was getting the ten-meter signal before a figure ahead of him detached itself from deeper darkness, stirring and scraping among the rocks. It looked quite tall and heavy-shouldered.

"Samson?"

"Rocky." The big man pushed away from the rock he had been leaning on, came closer by a few steps, then sat down all in a heap. "Did you see—?" The dazed question trailed off into silence. There seemed no need to try to answer it.

"Hello, up at rendezvous." It was Boss's voice again. "I'm coming uphill from the south—need a bit of assistance."

Going to give help would be no more unpleasant than standing around here shivering. "All right, I'll be down." Somehow Mike got his exhausted body moving. Pain radiated through him from his back. His lungs and his whole chest ached.

"Boss?" This sounded like Lola's voice on radio. "We're coming in fast. I've got the whole valley on radar now. No sign of Tenocha interference. Let me go in with some of this good hardware I've got on board and try to break the Inca free."

"No." Boss's voice was weary and inflexible as a ghost's. "There's no such contingency plan. You must simply stand by, and not use your 23–weapons unless the Tenocha use theirs first. In this case, the side that strikes first is at a disadvantage. And what if you killed Atahualpa? The problems are incalculable, at least by us here in the field. We're pulling out, back to the Fort . . . We're not in shape for anything else."

Mike could hear the last low-spoken words from right in front of him. Climbing down a few more steps, he reached Boss, who proved to have Gunner draped against him; Boss was half-carrying the wounded man along. Gunner was clutching their two weapons.

"Careful, Rocky, don't grab his arm."

"Ah."

Between the two of them, they somehow manhandled Gunner up the hill, getting back to rendezvous just as the muted whistle of rotor blades was coming down. The warmth and air in the cabin of Rusty's flyer somewhat revived them all, except for Gunner, whose arm was nearly severed. Boss had a pressure bandage on him, but Gunner's face was gray with shock under his phony Indian tan. He kept on shivering, and his slow-blinking eyes were empty. The flight back to the Fort took less than half an hour, under a rotor that screamed like police sirens through the night. No one had even cared if the Tenocha were looking in on the operation. Maybe all armies in all wars were inevitably fouled up in their own blunders . . .

It was Mike who carried Gunner in across the flight deck. Doc, with Cori standing by as steadily as an experienced nurse, had a cart ready for the wounded man, and a bottle that they plugged into his arm even before they wheeled him off.

The three men who had managed to come back on their own feet slumped into chairs before their lockers. They had all put on parkas in the aircraft, and still wore them, open, over bloodstained Inca finery. Samson, who had hardly said a word since rendezvous, gazed into space. Boss and Mike stared at each other for a while. It seemed as if perhaps they shared a secret.

Cori came back, very businesslike in her white smock that now was also marked with blood. "Are any of you wounded?" she asked in English. "Doc wants to know."

Mike reached his right hand back to feel his aching shoulder blade. He shook his head, and tried to raise a smile for the girl. It would be something—some kind of achievement, salvage, whatever —if they could get her out of this to some sort of decent life.

Before Boss could give his delayed answer—if he was planning one—Lola appeared in the doorway of the operations room. "We had an alert signal on the panel earlier," she informed Boss. "It went away. But now I've got a signal for friendly aircraft coming in."

Boss nodded, not surprised. Looking gray and shrunken as he slumped there in his parka. "Rocky . . ."

"What?"

Boss grimaced. "Ah, this foot is giving me hell." It was the first time he had mentioned trouble with a foot. "Will you step out and greet them?" It was a request, not an order.

New and bigger rotors were audible by the time he got out onto the flight deck again. A flyer bigger than any he had seen before, shining its own lights down onto the darkened deck, descended from broken clouds. The golden sunburst on its metal flank was more elaborate than those on the craft Mike had seen. He had a momentary impulse to turn and run, as if from before a Spaniard's lance. But he was all run out.

As he crossed the deck toward the landed flyer, he was confronted by two Inca men in modern gray uniforms, who had evidently just dropped from the ship's belly. Between them there suddenly appeared a taller third man, who wore a woven sunburst on his parka's breast, and came forward with his hood thrown back as if this were a sunny day at some spring altitude.

"Where's Boss?" The demand came in understandable Quechua, though with an intonation quite different from the language Mike had learned.

"In there."

"Alive?"

"His foot's hurt."

The tall man started to push past Mike, then paused momentarily. "You're—Rocky." It came out almost *Roca*, as in the name of mighty Inca Roca, Atahualpa's ancestor.

"That's right, sir."

"Call me Tupac. Let's go inside."

Inside, Tupac kept his parka on, though the heat and air pressure had been turned up for the benefit of the wounded. He towered over Boss, ignoring Boss's one tentative effort toward getting up. "What went wrong?"

Boss met his eyes for a moment, then blinked and looked away and made a gesture. "The guns wouldn't work. None of them."

"Stun-masers wouldn't work?" Tupac shifted into English, which came from his mouth strangely accented. "Were they not all tested?"

"On the firing range downstairs." Boss still sounded ghostly. "We followed all the tests you people gave us, and the guns met all the specs. Then out in the field, nothing. I'd get a firing indication, but no effect on target. At least I saw no effect on any man or animal I shot at."

Tupac looked at Mike, who nodded, and said, "I thought I got a small effect one time, but it was minimal. Man just shook his head and went on." He gestured the wielding of a sword.

Tupac looked at Samson, who said, "I might as well have been taking their pictures."

The tall Inca rounded on one of his escort who had come in with him. "Collect whatever of these suspect weapons you can find. We'll take them back to Cuzco." Suddenly he swung back to Boss. "Did any of the people flying cover report Tenocha action?"

"I didn't," said Lola, still looking out from the operations room. "There was nothing detectable." Boss also signed a negative.

Tupac paused for thought, puffing out a long breath. Then he spoke decisively. "Roca. You go out and get into my flyer. Don't waste time packing. I want you to come with me. I'll be along as soon as I get a few more details straightened out in here."

Mike's eye caught Cori's worried one before he reached the door to the flight deck. He found energy enough to wink.

9. Mictlan

Aboard Tupac's flyer they told him little or nothing, beyond repeating that they were taking him to twenty-third-century Cuzco. Inside this craft the furnishings were superior to anything that he had seen in Tawantinsuyu so far. But he spent most of the flight sitting alone in a small alcove of the main cabin that made almost a private cubicle. He had no way of seeing out, and the flight ended with a landing directly into a vast hangar whose doors were shut overhead before Mike got out of the flyer, so he saw nothing of the outside world. From the hangar he was escorted directly into a connected officers' quarters or hotel or whatever, a maze of corridors and doors, where his assigned room turned out to be much like his old quarters back at the Fort—even to the lack of windows. He slept at once, exhaustedly.

The first time he awoke there, he wasn't sure if it was a good day's or a good night's rest he had just enjoyed. The only time frame he felt at all sure of was the century—he believed he was somewhere in the 2200s, because they had told him so, as casually as he might have believed a distance marker on a highway. After what he had been through recently, the idea of a jaunt into the future hardly seemed shocking.

The little he had seen of Tupac on the flight had left Mike with the impression of a man fretting, unable to act effectively at the moment, but still desperately pressed for time. At first this assessment didn't seem to make sense, applied to a man who had time travel at his command. But all indications were that the ability to move from century to century was strictly limited, that the past could be reentered and remolded only in certain places, and with difficulty. Besides evidently severe natural limitations, Mike supposed there might be whole years or decades held impregnably by the enemy. Maybe there were months or days of peril, natural or man-made, that jutted up like dangerous reefs to snag the unwary spacetime voyager. More helpful was another analogy that occurred to him, that of two twentieth-century men in his own branch of the world. One rode a supersonic airliner, eyes fixed in a hungry stare at his quartz-crystal wristwatch; the other walked a dirt road at an easy pace, squinting up at the sun to gauge the passage of the day. Which was most at the mercy of time?

After awakening in Cuzco for the first time, Mike lay in bed beginning to wonder whether yesterday's interview with Esperanza had been as unreal as it now seemed, the product of some delirium. He had of course mentioned it to no one, and reacted with a guilty start to a melodious ringing from an instrument at bedside, much like one of the communicators at the Fort.

He gave English a try. "Hello."

"Tupac here. I want to see you. Someone will come to get you in about ten minutes."

And that was that. Maybe in the days when Boss was touring Cuzco they had had time—there was the seeming paradox again—to show him the sights, provide philosophical interludes to convince him of the rightness of their cause, let him mingle with people great and small. Now things were moving at a quicker tempo.

Laid out on a carved chest at the foot of his bed, Mike found a new uniform—he couldn't remember if it had been there when he tumbled in last night. Naturally it was a perfect fit. Its shade of brownish gray was a little different from that worn at the Fort, and it was still without insignia of any kind. He had turned in his malfunctioning mace to Tupac's aide last night, but the ruins of his Inca garb were still where he had tossed them when undressing, along with his plastic-mail shirt. Mike looked briefly but reverently at the scarring on the links that had protected his left shoulder blade against a trefoil lance head, and went to inspect his back in the bathroom mirror—a discolored lump had arisen, but he wasn't maimed.

Washed, clothed—since the pills had given him an Andean complexion, shaving was practically unnecessary—and feeling well on the road to normalcy, he answered the door just eight minutes later. A girl in brown-gray, wearing meaningless insignia, beckoned him to follow her and led him on a long, entirely indoor walk.

Some of the ways they passed along were wide as city streets, and crowded like rush hour. The people were mostly Indians, in a myriad variations of the familiar uniform, but whites and blacks were present in a small admixture, and he saw side by side two faces that he took to be definitely Asiatic. Nowhere could he catch a glimpse of the outside . . . and nowhere a green door, strange mandala, or studded panel of a kind to fit his visions given by the Mask. He was beginning to doubt that those visions would ever be fulfilled. The damned thing had brought him here and then had blown a transistor or something. It was broken and feeding him repetitious nonsense. Had it, like the stun-masers at Caja-marca, fallen under the influence of Pizarro's Mask? Had the Con-quistador a somehow superior model that could produce coincidental breakdowns even in another Mask? Tupac had been so certain that there was only one . . .

The black-haired girl he followed was attractive, but only in a remote, impersonal, abstract way. He wondered if chemicals would be put in his food here, as at the Fort . . .

He followed her through a silvery, circular doorway that blinked its iris sharply shut behind them. In a vast room, Tupac sat behind a desk on which two trays of food were laid. The fragrance of coffee wafted from large cups, and a spouted pot stood by. On the plates were fat pancakes and sausages that Tupac was already attacking with his fork. The girl gestured Mike forward and then left.

On second glance, the place was not quite a room, but rather an area within some larger enclosure. The ceiling was quite high enough for basketball. From beyond translucent partitions voices drifted, speaking Quechua, sometimes faintly echoing as if they came from really cavernous regions. Maybe it was the hangar where timeflight had ended last night. There came also sounds suggesting tools and machinery.

"Come. Sit down. Eat." Tupac was still practicing his English, which needed work but still might be better than Mike's Quechua. On the wall closest to his desk there towered a bigger version of Boss's map of Tawantinsuyu-16. On this map, what must be Tawantinsuyu-23 extended clear across the continent, marked with a thousand varied symbols, standing for cities or God-knew-what. Brazil still seemed to be nonexistent. On an adjacent wall, a flat picture of a globe of the world spun slowly in a good illusion of three dimensions. Mike took the time to notice that the nations of Europe, at least, looked about the way he remembered them—and there, the good old U.S.A. right where it ought to be.

On Tupac's desktop there were no papers to get mixed up with the food, but rather a flat translucent and segmented screen which occupied most of the horizontal area and upon which passed a steady parade of images. Sharing out the space in orderly fashion were graphs, columns of figures, headlines, color photographs, and charts indecipherable by the savage mercenary from three hundred years in the past. At intervals one thing or another vanished, to be replaced by new displays. As he ate, Tupac scanned his desktop with an expert eye, sometimes reaching out to a series of controls mounted in proximity to his right hand, with which he temporarily altered or froze the flow of information.

Mike sat down. With what had become almost involuntary reflex, he scanned his surroundings for a crimson-slashed mandala, or a green door that stood ajar, et cetera.

"Try the corncakes, Arnie."

Arnie? There was no one else visible in range of conversation, so Mike picked up a fork and cut into one of the fat pancakes on the plate before him. It was very good and made him realize his hunger.

His plate almost cleaned off, Tupac swallowed coffee and put his mug down with a small but unconcealed belch expressive of enjoyment. "Ahh. Well, to business. I have your background record here." In one corner of the desktop, a thousand words or so of small print sat immobile; with it the image of a man's head that revolved in the flat screen as solid-looking as that flat globe upon the wall. Was that supposed to be Mike Gabrieli's face? Looking at it upside down, Mike supposed there was some resemblance, maybe a close one.

Tupac was reading the dossier. "Arnold Francis Dearborn. Born Kansas City, 1948. In trouble for juvenile delinquency, as you people call it, in the sixties. Then infantry service in Vietnam. Somewhat overenthusiastic service, as your own superiors thought. Let's just say that timidity and tenderheartedness were not your problems. Still, you were basically amenable to discipline. Yes, you went on our lists away back, along with thousands of others . . . Then, when your little sister of whom you are so fond acquired leukemia, our computers really zeroed in. By the way, I can now give you a good report on her. The remission continued, as we promised. Two days after you were recruited officially and left for the Keys, she was discharged from Michael Reese Hospital, Chicago. Complete remission, which as usual has the doctors puzzled; so you see, we've kept our part of the bargain."

The desk coughed faintly, and from somewhere spat a photograph into Tupac's hand. Girl with traveling bag in hand, big smile plain on her face, approaching a car whose Illinois license showed plainly and whose door was being held open for her. A smiling older couple was at her side. No one was looking at the camera. Photo taken how and by whom? Our spies are everywhere. So that was how they handled the recruiting. Save a loved one from cancer or the equivalent, and you've hired yourself a loyal worker; it fit in with everything he'd heard.

The only problem was, the man they'd hired for one job was evidently an experienced killer named Arnold Dearborn. He had started for the Keys, for that house in Marathon where the couple owned the cabin cruiser. But the man who had actually come to their door in the middle of the night was a former clerk-typist named Mike Gabrieli.

Tupac was still speaking, words that demanded much more than half an ear. " . . . so, according to this dossier, and a creditable performance in the field so far under difficult conditions, you're now our first choice to take over Boss's job. The pace of operations is going to pick up." Tupac probably did not realize just how that last bland announcement sounded, right after Cajamarca. "If you accept the job, there'll be additional compensation involved. In the form of—what do you call it?—a rain check for future medical treatment. A limited additional number of times you'll be able to call on us, after you get home, for yourself or a family member."

It hadn't occurred to Mike that he was going to be offered a promotion. He'd vaguely thought he was being called in to give some kind of testimony in an investigation of the failure at Cajamarca. The prospect of being promoted didn't elate him, either. It felt like being made captain of the ship when it was on the verge of sinking. What if he turned down the promotion, though? Then they might not send him back to the Fort at all, and what would happen to the Mask he had left there? Whereas, if he went back as commander . . .

"I'll take it," he replied, and then asked, "What's happening to Boss?"

"He is finished there, whatever you decide. I'm not blaming the defeat on him, but we want to make a change. We'll bring him here to Cuzco-23, get him out of your way. Give him some kind of a staff job—I believe that is the proper term—until the issues are decided and you can all go home." Tupac's abrupt smile indicated that there were no problems with tooth decay in Cuzco-23. "Good enough?"

"Good enough." Mike took another bite of the excellent sausage, demonstrating to himself how calm he was. Then, yielding to a sudden impulse that skidded wildly close to self-destruction, he asked, "But suppose I wasn't Arnie Dearborn?"

Tupac blinked, but then his eyes held on to Mike's. "What do you mean? Who else could you be?"

"Well . . . " Surely his subconscious had some retreat prepared, to let him blurt out a thing like that. Yes, here it was. "That trouble with the guns. Suppose that was some kind of sabotage. Someone at the Fort deliberately screwing things up. Maybe someone who's not what he or she seems to be."

Tupac shook his head once. Once was enough. "We know who you all are. Believe me, we very carefully recruited you and checked you out and brought you to the Fort." The way he said it made it almost believable even to Mike. "Have you any reason to suspect anyone at the Fort of—what do you call it? Sabotage?"

"No. Except I don't understand why the guns suddenly didn't work."

"All of their beam generators had been accidentally misset. There was an exactly corresponding mistake made in calibrating the test equipment you used at the Fort, so it showed the guns were putting out the proper power when in fact they weren't." The Inca smiled humorlessly. "The Tenocha test their weapons on live targets and don't have comparable trouble. Of course we are not so incompetent that blunders like this could normally happen. Nor was it sabotage in any ordinary sense. This coincidence of mistakes was an effect of the weapon that Pizarro bears against us, whom he does not even realize that he is fighting."

Mike, hunger suddenly gone, pushed back his tray. "The Mask."

"The Mask." Tupac's arm swept trays, dishes, and leftover food all together into a wide chute that yawned suddenly at one side of his desk and then closed again. The coffeepot had survived. "One of the things your new job will require is that you learn some more about the enemy we're fighting . . . Hmm. Where to begin?"

"Do you know where the Mask comes from?"

"We don't know who made it. It comes from the far future; it first appears in our segment of time among the fourteenth-century Tenocha."

"I understand that. Tupac, you know for some time it's struck me as peculiar that the Aztec-Tenocha and the Conquistadors should be allies."

Tupac poured more coffee into two fresh cups that popped from somewhere. "It shouldn't. The history of warfare is full of strange allies. And Cortes in Mexico and Pizarro here did often ally themselves with one Indian tribe or faction against others. And this war that we are fighting ramifies into so many regions of space and time that—well, from your viewpoint or even mine, it no longer makes much sense to ask who all of our enemies are, or all our allies either. Don't think that the grand headquarters for our side are here in Cuzco-23. In twentieth-century terms, this building we are sitting in is maybe like an army corps headquarters, no more. And the Fort, of course, is only an outpost." Tupac rubbed his head and added, seemingly more to himself than to Mike, "Though it seems to have become a damned important one."

"All right." Mike waited, thinking. So how do we know our side is any better than theirs?

Tupac paused as if he sensed the question and wanted to take his time and set it right. "In the branches of history where our enemies rule, people exist chiefly if not solely for the service of the State. For the State's chief servants, all others must be always ready to offer up their labor and their wealth, their freedom and their blood. I am not speaking of special sacrifices required at moments of great peril for society. Here in Cuzco-23 we ask those sometimes; so does any government. I am speaking of a routine mode of life and thought. Of daily rites that include the cutting out of living hearts, the cannibalism of limbs from living human beings. Both old Aztec-Tenocha habits, and not just in the sixteenth century. They are practiced in the twenty-third, and later. I can show you filmed records of these rites, if you have doubts—?"

"I saw enough blood and guts at Cajamarca."

"That was only war. Well, never mind. You had a better view of that than I can ever have, and obviously it shook you, even after

Vietnam. Personally, I find all scenes of slaughter monotonously alike."

"Sir, is there any more you can tell me about this Mask Pizarro has?"

"Call me Tupac. In a real sense, Pizarro doesn't 'have' the Mask; it has him. Does a man who jumps onto an avalanche possess real power because his mount sweeps villages and forts out of his way?"

"Well." Mike felt a shiver as of Andean cold. "But suppose instead of him, someone else was carrying it—or another Mask like it—around."

Tupac gave a short laugh and studied his big brown hands, spread out on the shifting patterns of his desktop. "I suppose if today's Inca announced he had one, Parliament would immediately insist he give it up. And they would have good reason. It might bring him to any goal he wanted, but it might be devastatingly rough on his friends and associates as well as on his enemies." He shook his head. "I tell you frankly, we will probably never be able to kill Pizarro as long as he heeds his Mask's advice. Assuming he wishes to remain alive."

"That powerful?"

"That powerful. From how far in the future it comes, I do not know."

"Tupac—forgive me if I keep pushing at this point, but if I'm to be the commander out there, I've got to know just what I'm up against. If someone walked in here and offered you another Mask, just like Pizarro's, would you take it? What would you do?"

Tupac's smile was sardonic. "If I were strong, I would accept that Mask, and then try to have it destroyed at once. I say 'try' because it would not be as simple as melting down a mere lump of gold . . . Do you know what a black hole is?"

"Some kind of astronomical thing? An infinite mass . . . ?"

"Not infinite, just very concentrated. Of absolutely crushing gravity. As a power source, orders of magnitude better than nuclear energy. The only black holes now left in nature are those of astronomical mass, because thanks to the blessings of quantum mechanics, the little ones, of which there were a great many when the universe was made, decay in finite time. Our scientists think that the Mask may contain one of those early little black holes as its power source, one brought for that purpose from billions of years in the past.

"Anyway, if someone brought it to me and caught me in a weak moment, I think I might put it on my face and look through the eyes. Then we would see which way the world would bend, for me . . . but no one will bring a Mask. I am sure that there is only one."

Mike opened his mouth and let it close again. He slumped down in his chair.

"Speaking practically now," Tupac went on, "if you or anyone else in the field should get the chance, Pizarro's Mask should be melted down on sight, along with anyone who happens to be holding it, wearing it, or just standing in the way. And from now on you are going to be using some weapons that can melt things."

"I thought we weren't able to use that kind of force in the sixteenth century."

"Our wisest computers assure us that from now on we should try." Tupac got up briskly and went to stand beside his vast map. "On 26 July, 1533, some eight months after his capture, the Inca Atahualpa was—is—will be—executed by Francisco Pizarro, despite his full payment of the ransom demanded by the Spaniards. For you to rescue Atahualpa now would involve too many paradoxes, we think. But, shortly after the execution, Pizarro and his small force begin a three-month march to Cuzco, fighting several battles along the way against unpacified generals of Atahualpa's army. You people at the Fort are going to interfere in some of these battles—this time using weapons that work."

Tupac spoke on, his eloquence making this new scheme sound not too difficult, just exciting enough to maybe produce a pleasant tingle. Mike felt a fading of his sudden new hope that he might now be granted an understanding of just what was going on. Damn Tupac!

Not that Tupac seemed like a robbing, murdering Conquistador. He was no Aztec-Tenocha, either, cutting out a bloody heart or two each day to please his gods, savoring human flesh. Here was celebrated only the more subtle sacrifice to Inti, and only on occasions of special need. But unfortunately for the victim, he was left just as dead. Come, climb this exciting mountain with us, Sonny, enjoy the marvelous view. Now we've reached the top, we'll give you a big mouthful of delicious coca, so you won't notice the cold a bit, and now how about a nice cozy nap? Don't mind us while we pile these few small rocks upon your head. They'll help to keep the wind off . . . and the condors, too.

Mike found himself briefly distracted from his own situation, thinking of Cori, wondering what the future or futures in all their unguessable complications might hold for her.

A minute later, he was getting to his feet. The interview was over, Tupac was shaking his hand to congratulate him on his promotion, and his escort had come to lead him out.

Before they sent Mike back to the Fort, they taught him something about chronophysics. Shortly after leaving Tupac, he was conducted to a lady mathematician, who lectured him in strangely accented English.

Fifteen minutes after they started, she was saying to Mike, "Any time travel would entangle the universe in hopeless paradox were it not that changes introduced by a time traveler can literally split the world, causing a real branching of physical reality. If you go back and try to murder your grandfather before he can sire your parent, you might conceivably succeed. The universe can divide itself to accommodate such an act. A new branch, in which you were never born, comes into being."

"Wait a minute, wait a minute. A whole new universe, stars and galaxies and all, just because I pull one little trigger? Where does the energy come from for such a creation?"

"From the same sources whence came the energy to make the universe that you already know. Does its existence seem incredible?" Formidably patient, his teacher was prepared, as he had already begun to discover, to snow him blind with mathematical support of every word she said. She would write out the proofs electronically on a wall-sized screen if he preferred; it wasn't her fault if he could scarcely begin to understand a symbol of them.

"Okay," he gave in, with a small sigh.

"Okay." Her broad Andean face creased with a smile. "However, though your objection is not theoretically accurate, it does have a certain practical validity. Consider an analogy. When you walk across this room, your motion has a undeniable, though of course not measurable, perturbing effect on all the bodies of the solar system. 'Thou canst not stir a flower without the troubling of a star.' Hey?"

"Um."

"Similarly, a small act—the pulling of a trigger—may produce an actual new physical universe and earth. Practically speaking, the new creation will almost everywhere diverge from the old by only an immeasurably small amount. That is, from the physicist's point of view. Societal effects, of course, are something else again."

"I think . . . I don't know. Maybe I begin to see."

"Of course you do." She began to explain that while the gulfs between the different historical branches of the world might be very narrow, they remained unbridgeable. To get from one to another, you had to go back in time to where the branches diverged, then forward again at a different angle, as it were.

Mike kept reminding himself that a lot of smart people didn't understand relativity, either.

One could sometimes draw power, though, from this branched quality of the world. So the Fort was powered, and so was the enemy's comparable installation, known to be somewhere in Tawantisuyu-16. It was code-named Mictlan, from an Aztec-Tenocha word for hell, and before they sent him back to the Fort they taught him something about Mictlan . . .

He was in Cuzco nine days altogether, if the count he tried to keep was accurate, and he might almost have been in Atlanta for all he found out about the place. He spent almost all his time on cram courses in chronophysics, in the nature of the enemy, and in a few other subjects, and he emerged feeling not much wiser than before.

After nine days or so, they flew him back to the Fort. Tupac came along. This time Mike was able to look out a window shortly after takeoff, and when the timejump came he could appreciate its weird visual effect, sun and bright sky shifting instantaneously their quality of light, as if a quick cut had been made in a movie. Timejumping was never done on the ground, they'd told him; large solid objects in the locus of a rematerializing traveler presented too great a hazard.

On the flight deck at the Fort the surviving garrison were lined up in cold-weather gear to meet him—Doc, Gunner (with two functional arms), Lola, Samson, Rusty. And there was Cori, no longer identifiable among the others at first glance, so tall had she grown. In time, as measured at the Fort, Mike had been gone for several months. At the reunion, no one mentioned Boss; Tupac had remarked casually en route that the former commander was already back in Cuzco, awaiting reassignment.

Tupac kept them all standing on the deck while he gave Mike his official blessing. A short pep talk, snappier than Boss's used to be, a few words that rang clear in the thin air while the great rotors behind and above the speaker never stopped completely. In about one minute, the Inca and his escort were gone.

Mike smiled, uncomfortably, at the twelve intent eyes that watched him, the new commander. "Let's get inside."

One of the first things he did after getting in was to go to the commander's quarters. He opened the doors of the office and adjoining bedroom with a key that Tupac had handed him a little while ago.

Samson asked him, "Want some help bringing stuff over from your old room?"

"No thanks, I'll pick it up myself. There isn't much."

Alone with the Mask, he was encouraged—almost elated—when it promptly showed him something new: a picture of himself putting it, still in his humble traveling bag, on the floor of his new closet. After that it went back to monotonous showings of the red-slashed mandala, the green door, the studded panel.

Cori was Mike's first visitor in his new office. "Welcome home, Roca Yupanqui," she offered from the doorway. After putting the Mask away, he had left the door open, in a sudden mood of something like loneliness. Cori's dark eyes were sparkling, really glad to see him. Home, hey? He realized vaguely that the women must have been helping her fix her hair again.

The Honored Roca smiled back. "Thank you. And how are you?"

"I do well."

"You're certainly learning English."

They talked a little about the other things that both of them were learning: about machinery and customs and the awesome history of the world. Then she took herself away, saying he must be busy.

He just sat there for a while, staring at the door that she had closed behind her. He had mentioned her to Tupac, who had explained there was some complex kind of paradox-danger that forbade moving her to Cuzco-23, at least for the time being. Tupac had also thought, and Mike agreed, that the girl's knowledge would probably prove useful to them in Tawantinsuyu-16.

Problems seemingly more urgent were at hand, and Mike soon brought his gaze back to his new desk-chronometer, a gift from the Directors, as Tupac had put it. It was 27 July, 1533. The Inca Atahualpa was dead, strangled yesterday by his Spanish captors after a sham trial. Having squeezed what wealth he could out of his royal hostage, Pizarro was now free of Atahualpa's embarrassing and potentially dangerous presence. Soon the pliable youth Tupac Huallpa, half-brother of the slain monarch, would be crowned as the first puppet-Inca, reigning at Pizarro's pleasure; and soon after that the conqueror would be on the march to gain the gold and souls of Cuzco.

Gunner flying solo in one heavily armed aircraft, Mike in another, were at a sunny 2,000 meters above the mountain town of Jauja. Let the inhabitants of Tawantinsuyu-16 now see, if they cared to look, great birds thundering in the sky; they were shortly going to see sights even more marvelous than that.

On the land below, Pizarro's hundred and thirty or so effective fighters—a small garrison of the less healthy troops had been left behind—had now progressed more than half the distance from Cajamarca to Cuzco, a march of some weeks along the Inca's royal roads in this region where a road was likely to turn suddenly into a stairway, or abruptly leap an abyss on a swaying fiber bridge. Almost a year had passed in Tawantinsuyu since Mike had first arrived there.

Today Pizarro had run into his first serious military opposition, an army of several thousand under the general Yucra-Huallpa. On a small height overlooking Jauja, Pizarro was just sending his steel-armed and armored horsemen to smash like a mechanized column into the dense ranks of Indian infantry, men armed with woolen slings, and clubs and blades of bronze and wood and copper, and protected with quilted cloth.

The outcome of this first shock of battle was as expected by the observers in the sky. "There they go," Gunner commented shortly on the radio. Like an organism shattered into its component cells, the Inca forces were torn open by the impact, fast disintegrating into a fleeing mob. Later their leaders would rally them, and they would try again. And again after that, with fresh troops brought in by the thousands, conscripts from the land, and veteran profession-als from the far corners of the empire. And yet again after that . . .

but courage and determination were going to avail them nothing, unless they got some help.

"Hold position up here, Gunner. Watch for a Tenocha counterstrike. I'm going down." Handling these craft, fast though they were, was easier than driving a car.

"You're the chief." No one had yet said "You're the boss."

Mike aimed his ship's nose at the Spanish column. He switched his target screen to change ranges automatically and set his thumb ready on the trigger in his steering column. Stun-masers would fire from that trigger, with a rapid automatic cannon cutting in if the trigger were held down for three consecutive seconds. Should cannon fail, the rocket-launchers were cut in. So the Directors thought to circumvent Pizarro's Mask. Mike expected it might not be that easy, but his own Mask had given him no warnings against making this effort.

He went down fast. Horses grew in his screen, and silent yelling fighting faces, and then one gray-bearded face beneath a morion helm, its whiskered cheeks stretched out to shout commands. Pizarro was mounted today. Where would he have hidden *it*? Inside that bundle tied behind his saddle?

Hurtling closer—

The world went blank and empty for a timeless interval, and then refilled itself with sound and light that seemed to take a year receding to levels that were no worse than intolerable. Pain wrenched at his head, the panel before him only a red-hazed blur. He thought it was some internal sense rather than sight or hearing that let him know his flyer was in a dive and that its speed was very high.

"Gunner—what—"

There was no answer. Vision cleared, and Mike saw from the panel indicators that his flyer's defensive missiles had been launched. Something modern had come after him, but so far he was surviving. His machine was pulling itself out of the dive. Far below, the ants in steel armor and those in quilted padding played out their savage battle, too busy to notice the giants' blows being exchanged across their sky.

The flyer gave back control when his hands reached for it. But response was sluggish, and damage lights were showing.

"Gunner, come in. Where are you?" Then at last he saw the other flyer, lying broken on a high rocky slope. There was no sign now of the Tenocha, in the sky or on his panel, but they might strike again with as little warning as before.

As usual, flat space was at a premium. It took Mike a couple of minutes to set his flyer down within climbing distance of Gunner's wreckage. He had to try, though, the cabin of the wrecked flyer looked reasonably intact, and there seemed grounds for hope. Getting out of his own ship, he clambered across a rock face where in some cooler moments the risk of falling would have frozen him. He wrenched at a door, and at last got it open enough to look inside.

Gunner hadn't made it this time.

Teeth bared, Mike turned and started back for his own flyer, pondering his next move as he climbed. Pizarro was protected, as by steel walls . . . but so, apparently, was he, Mike Gabrieli. Together they could probably rule the world.

But after Cajamarca, Mike would as readily have formed a partnership with a cancer virus.

So he was going on playing with Tupac's team. Would the Inca legions of the twenty-third century now be able to move in, with advantage? So far, there was no help in sight; only the Spaniards far below still intent on chasing and slaughtering the fleeing Indians.

Getting airborne, Mike found it at once problematical whether he was going to stay that way. The shuddering of the airframe was more pronounced than before, and the Fort was hundreds of kilometers to the southeast

Again, something struck at him out of the sky. Not an explosion this time, but an invisible wave of power that left him sick and paralyzed, hands sliding from the controls. Before unconsciousness closed down, he had time to think that this must be what the stun-masers were supposed to feel like. His last sight was of a huge aircraft bearing insignia like blood-red lightning bolts.

There were recurrent dreams—or, rather, recurrent awakenings to a state as terrible as the worst dreams could ever be. Perceptions of blood-dripping limbs, intermittent giggling laughter, questions he forgot as soon as he had answered them, all imbued with that utter inner terror that bubbles out in nightmare.

The next clear scene was of himself, propped up in a soft chair. At first he saw his own body as if from outside, from a locus suspended in the air a few feet off. Only gradually did things arrange themselves so he inhabited this slumped figure, garbed in a white gown as if for a hospital or the tortures of the Inquisition.

Looming over the low chair in which he rested was the figure of a brown-uniformed man, who sat on the edge of a long table, below bright lights.

"Arnold. Arnold. Arnold." The man was speaking to him, speaking with monotonous patience, and Mike knew that it had been so for some time. "Arnold, you are awake now." The man's English was peculiar in a different way from Cori's or Tupac's.

"Yes." The only emotion he felt was a kind of pride in having managed to wake up.

"That is fine. That is just fine." Satisfied, the man got off the table and walked around it to take a chair on its far side. He made a tent of his fingers and looked across them. Dark Indian face. On his arms, red daggers crossing.

"How long have you been working for the Incas, Arnold?" The tone was bright; the question sounded as if it might be prompted by nothing stronger than polite curiosity.

I must be in Mictlan, Mike thought, without urgency. "How long?" he echoed aloud, involuntarily. He felt no fear, but only curiosity to see what happened next.

"Yes, Arnold. Ar-nay? Ar-nee, I should say to you. How long."

"I don't know. Who can keep track, with all this funny time-travel business going on?"

"Let me put it this way. How many days of your life have you actually spent at it, do you suppose?"

"Lessee—before Cajamarca, about three months. Since then, I was nine days in Cuzco . . . Cuzco . . . Cuzco . . . " He seemed to be stuck.

"Who did you talk to there, in Cuzco-23?"

"Tupac. Others."

"What others?"

"Professors. Teachers." He just answered, without thinking. He had no choice about answering or not.

"Which of them was an old man—no, let me say a white-haired man, with a big nose?"

"Uh."

"Whose name perhaps began with 'E'?"

"Not there."

"All right, let that go for now. Now I want you to think back, Ar-nee, very carefully. What was the date, in your own calendar, when you were first approached by a recruiter for the Incas? Think, now."

All Mike could do was look back at his questioner hopelessly. Very sad that he wasn't going to be able to answer the question. It had no answer, but that wasn't something he was allowed to say. How awful. Now he felt sadness, and his eyes began to brim with tears.

"Very well, if you can't say, you can't." And the interrogator gave an obscene, incredible little giggle, as in those nightmare intervals before awakening. His red-marked sleeve moved as he adjusted something. "You will have use later for all your tears. He—ee—ha. Now, what name did their recruiter use who first approached you? In Chee-ca-go, wasn't it? Right after your sister, Joanna, contracted leu-kee-mee-a?"

His tears had stopped. Names and names went rattling in his head. A horde of foreign file clerks had tramped into his brain, were rummaging in all the dusty drawers. But Mike Gabrieli had never been approached by an Inca recruiter, and there was no answer to be found. If the man once asked Mike a sensible question, like "What's your name?" Mike would have to answer it. But this Tenocha was bent on questioning Arnold Dearborn, doubting his identity no more than Tupac ever had. Mike could only grunt and shake his head.

"Ar—nee, Ar-nee." Gloomily. "I wish you could tell me who put these blocks into your brain. They present a really formidable barrier. But we, of course, shall persevere, and in good time we shall prevail. Do you doubt that?"

"No." The truth came automatically when it could.

"Have you heard the name 'Tom Gabrieli'?"

"Yes."

"You have met a white-haired man with a big nose."

"Yes."

The interrogator almost got to his feet, settled for leaning forward on the table. "It is possible you still don't think of him as an agent for the Incas. But you have seen him, several times, since your involvement began."

"Yes."

"And his name is?"

"He told me Esperanza."

"Ha!" A hurried sort of triumph. "The Spanish word for 'hope,' of course. How hopelessly, stupidly coy these friends of yours can be. But now you have seen for yourself just how incompetent they are. First at Cajamarca . . . and then they sent two of you out in those little aircraft, into a zone we had so well covered that . . . Tupac knew he was sending you to be killed. Do you realize that now?"

"Uhh. Yes."

"It is only by the wildest chance that you are here alive. And the Inca plan for which you were sacrificed has come to nothing also. Do you understand?"

"Uhh."

"Well, you at least realize the possibility—even the likelihood —that I am telling you the truth."

Mike had to nod. It made his head ache briefly.

"Your whole operation there at what you call the Fort has been a failure, is it necessary to add? Now there are only four people left there alive—for a little while."

Mike managed to count it up. Himself and Gunner subtracted, there should be five. Probably the Tenocha didn't know about Cori.

His questioner's interest lay elsewhere. "How often did Esperanza come to see you at the Fort?"

"Never."

"In Cuzco, then?"

"No."

"What other names did Epseranza use, when you knew him back in the United States?"

And so it went for some time. They knew they had him fixed somehow so that he was incapable of lying to them. But they also knew with the same unquestioning certainty that he was Arnie Dearborn, which made hash of all their results, as it might have made of many fine Inca calculations back in Cuzco-23. It looked as if only the old man with the big nose might be ahead of the game so far—whatever he might be playing for. At least he must be these bastards' enemy. Three cheers for Esperanza. But there was no emotion in the thought.

After a while, Mike began to undergo blackouts in his chair, periods of nothingness that were at first isolated and momentary but grew more frequent and lasted longer. Finally someone came up behind him, and there was a wrench of pain that felt as if they had torn a hole in the top of his skull and pulled his spine up through it.

Lolling in his chair like a dead man, he was rolled out of the interrogation room, while the pain in his head subsided to a mere blinding throb. He raised a hand and found a shaven scalp with a few drops of blood. It would seem that they had pushed something down into his brain.

So the Tenocha and their pawns, the Conquistadors, were the victors in Tawantinsuyu-16, which would soon become Peru in this branch of history as it had in others. So it seemed. But the Tenocha wanted something more, or they would not be questioning him. Nine out of ten of their questions had to do with Esperanza, but they never mentioned the Mask—any Mask.

Ahead of Mike's rolling chair, a door slid open by itself, and hands reached from behind him to grip him by the arms and dump him forward like a load of laundry, into a small cell. His brown-uniformed keeper turned the chair away, and the door slid closed. Mike was alone, as if inside a giant egg; the cell was lighted from no visible source, and lined in smooth curves of what felt like tough plastic. He stood up in his white gown. He wasn't physically weakened, but felt as if he ought to be, and he was somehow abnormally relaxed. Holding his mildly aching and fevered head, he thought that inhabiting this cell was almost like being inside a giant tooth through which some sadistic dentist was about to thrust a drill.

The second interrogation session (the second one he could remember—there might well have been others somewhere along the line) was much like the first, save that this time he was fully conscious when they pushed their hair-thin probes down into the top of his skull. This time two interrogators, a man and a woman, were seated across the table from him, and they raised their heads momentarily in reaction to his scream, then went back to studying some paperwork spread out before them.

As soon as the probe was fully in place, the whole procedure became quite painless and not even frightening. He tended to drift off, though.

". . . get around these inner barriers of yours." The woman was talking to him. She had come around to sit on his side of the table.

"You understand now, Arnie, don't you, that there is no point in trying to fight us? No reason for you to adhere to Tupac and that bunch?"

Her voice was almost kind, and he would have liked to agree with her, but truth was enforced upon him. "No."

She sighed. "Well, we are going to have to overcome your subconscious reluctance to face facts." She motioned to someone behind Mike and spoke a few words in some language he had never before heard. It occurred to Mike that the next time they pulled out the probe, he would probably faint or die. Emotionlessly, he wondered how dying was going to feel?

Into his field of vision some men now wheeled his brother, lying on a kind of cart. Tom was in a white gown, too, a short one, and both his legs and one of his arms had been cut off. All the stumps were swathed in precise bandages. His remaining arm—his left—was strapped down. Their eyes met, and Tom's face, already badly altered, wrinkled horribly, as if there might be something he was trying to do or say. Tom's head had been shaved, too, but some time ago, for now stubble like a new beard had a good start on growing back. The woman put a hand on the cart. "Now this gentleman was another protégé of Señor Esperanza. His name is Tom Gabrieli, and you have heard of him; whether you have met him before or not is immaterial now. You can see how much good his service to the Incas has done him. He has been dwelling in a food locker lately, and when his last limb goes, he goes."

At least those were the words he thought he heard the woman saying calmly. Maybe if he didn't think about them, the sounds could make some other meaning.

. . . the cannibalism of limbs from living human beings . . . not just in the sixteenth century, but in the twenty-third and later. I can show you filmed records . . . That was Tupac's remembered voice. Hey, Tupac, you were right. I must admit it.

" . . . family grieving for this man, at home in the United States. And for his brother, whom we had to put out of the way in Flori-da. On those highways, not hard at all to make an accident. No one takes much notice . . ."

At Marathon in the Keys, the car like the one he, Mike, had been riding in, gone smash through the rail and into the water. They were fishing it out when Mike rode by. Some mix-up by the Tenocha field teams, coincidental of course, and they'd killed Arnie

Dearborn in that car and never guessed it. Now Mike could no longer follow his own thoughts, for he was being questioned again, and his attention was compelled.

"Was Esperanza on hand when you left Flor-i-da?"

He blacked out.

And came to. Tom and the cart were gone, the torturers conferring in their own language.

What had he, Mike, been concentrating on, the first time he wore the Mask? On finding his brother. Amazing, absolutely amazing results, all across the centuries as well as miles. And his second wish had been . . .

When the probe was pulled out this time, he screamed and fainted but he did not die.

Mike came out of his faint again while being wheeled back to his cell. He had the feeling that the foundations of Mictlan might be moving beneath his chair, hell ready to launch itself like a giant spaceship. Tom on the cart. Not Tom. What once had been Tom.

When he saw the brown hand descending on his shoulder, he hallucinated for an instant that it was holding a laser-cleaver like the one in the kitchen back at the Fort and was going to lop off his arm. But it was only gripping his white sleeve, tilting him forward. The featureless door of his featureless cell was sliding open as before, and he was dumped limply inside.

Looking out before the door slid shut again, he saw his escort already turned and wheeling the chair away. On the wall beyond the man were the red daggers of the Tenocha sigil, red daggers like . . .

. . . like those in the endlessly repeated visions shown him by his Mask.

Nursing, with a finger, a droplet of blood from his abused scalp, he sat back on the floor and tried to think. Anything to keep Tom out of his mind. The door had closed now, cutting off his view of the insignia outside, which had been similar to the mandala of the vision, but not identical. Still, the mandala must be somewhere inside Mictlan. In his recently befogged mental state, Mike might have had it before his eyes without really seeing it. Yes, the snakes in it curled so—

His cell door slid open, and he involuntarily cowered back. But the narrow corridor outside was empty.

He had been thinking of the—

The instant his imagination formed the picture correctly, the door slid shut smoothly.

Months ago, the Mask had given him this cell's key. It was a secret key that no jailer need fear to lose, no prisoner could hope to steal. But it had not been out of reach of the Mask's powers.

He stood up. He had almost forgotten that he was riding on the avalanche. He might be carried through hell, but hell's gates could not hold him if he kept his footing. The Mask would take him where he had asked to go. To find his brother, then to put the Mask itself back where it belonged. Those had been his original wishes when he put it on. One accomplished. Two more now added: for his own survival, and for the destruction of Mictlan and all that stood behind it.

Out in the corridor, Mike remembered to think his cell door closed behind him. Without any real surprise, he saw the green door standing ajar to his right, a dozen strides away along the slightly curving passage. He walked there silently and pulled it fully open.

It was a chill storeroom of some kind, with other passages leading off at its far end, and smooth drums and cubical sealed containers piled about, some on tall shelves. At a table half a dozen steps into the room, a working figure had its brown-uniformed back turned to Mike. A Tenocha man, busy wrapping something on the table—some bundle about the size and shape of a man's arm. A surgeon's or a butcher's tools were laid out on the work surface, where a drop or two of fresh blood marred the room's pastels.

The worker had heard someone come in, and he started to turn, calmly and unalarmed. Some paces beyond him, Tom's upturned face showed sightless eyes above the rim of a huge metal bin.

The table made a light sound, skidding back; the uniformed man had pushed against it as Mike's fingers clamped his throat. The Tenocha's eyes bulged; trying to pull away, he staggered back and back, stopped at last by a tall metal rack laden with anonymous plastic drums. The butcher was not big or heavy. Mike hammered his head again and again against the metal rack, but when he released the throat, the man fell only to his hands and knees. A sharp metal implement that had fallen from the table came up into Mike's hand, and with it he struck downward. Struck again. And bent to make the job quite thorough.

He stepped away from reddish streamlets on the floor and went to look into the bin. Tom was naked, his chest ruined. His heart must have been cut out at the end.

Tears were running on Mike's face. Mandala and green door were behind him, studded panel next. But it was nowhere in this room. Outside in the corridor there were loud voices getting nearer, speaking Tenocha.

Mike chose at random among the passages in back, and followed a narrow way amid piled crates and boxes. Air hissed somewhere, bringing first a change of pressure and then a breeze flavored with open snow and mountain rocks. Unhurried but unhesitating, he went on.

He came abruptly onto a loading dock, its glass doors now closed against the glare of sun upon a gray, snow-blasted slope. What land and century? He didn't know or care. Parked right against the outer hull of hell, its open hatch latched to a docking port, a flyer waited, rotors motionless.

The cabin was warm and pressurized when he stumbled into it, still wearing his hospital gown. This was not an Inca flyer, of course, but still the constellations of controls were half-familiar. Among them the expected panel of the vision waited. Mike's hand reached out, and as he brought it down, he hoped the stud would detonate the mountain underneath Mictlan and raise it to crash down upon them all.

10. The Royal Road

Peru, 1533

The stud he slammed down produced not cataclysm but instant engine power and quiet rotor movement overhead. With a series of soft noises, the hatch undocked from Mictlan and folded itself inboard. Mike let himself slump into the pilot's chair. The ship was going straight up, fast, in what was obviously a programmed takeoff sequence. Airborne over the geodesic shape of Mictlan, he could see that it was somewhat bigger than the Fort, and placed in a landscape generally similar to the Fort's setting, mainly upthrust and splintered arctic emptiness. The sun was low in the sky behind a rank of distant clouds.

Only when the craft had borne him a little higher did Mike realize that the enormous mountain upon whose slope hell perched was a volcano. First he saw the thin smoke-plume, reaching into the upper atmosphere, zigzagged at various levels by disagreeing air currents. With another gain in height there came into view the crater itself, a mile or more in width. Now Mictlan was shrunken to a mere wart on the mountain's side. Mike looked down into a different kind of hell, its fissures glowing vaguely even in daylight with their internal fires.

A thousand meters or so above the volcano's rim, the flyer came to a hovering halt. Now he was evidently going to have to take over the controls, or at least feed in some instructions. If the instrument panel before him was arranged at all like that of the Inca craft that he had learned to fly, then maybe *this* would get him a map to show his position.

A screen on the panel sprang into colored life. In its center was the sharp green dot he had expected—that must represent the position of his flyer; and right next to the dot there appeared a round formation that was surely the volcano crater. But the coordinates and even the alphabet of the words marked on the map were alien and unreadable. Well, switching scales on the map should now be possible with *this*.

On the second try, he got it. The largest scale let him see in outline enough of South America to give him a rough idea of where he was. His green dot was up near the equator, hundreds of miles north of the region where he had been captured, and almost at the northern limits of the Inca empire.

Geography lessons absorbed at the Fort came into use. The towering cone below him was almost certainly Cotopaxi, near the city called Quito in the country known in most branches as Ecuador. In 1534 an expedition of Spaniards striking out from Peru into these northern provinces was to be pelted with ash by Cotopaxi, at a distance of a good many miles. But evidently the Tenocha had no fear of an eruption.

With a minor false start or two, Mike established himself in control of the flyer. He aimed it south and stepped on the gas, relaxing a little when he had the ominous egg of Mictlan well out of sight behind him. The top of mighty Cotopaxi would take a longer time to lose, but it was dwindling fast. He saw no other traffic in the air. Was his escape already discovered, his craft being automatically tracked? He couldn't guess. No blasting missiles came, no paralysis struck out of the high air. For all he knew, it might be hours before they realized that they were short a prisoner.

He set his course as straight as he could for the Fort, aiming for the middle of the natural mountainous redoubt in which it lay, a little north of the town of Abancay, and only sixty kilometers or so, as the condor flew, from Cuzco. What Mike could see of the ground below revealed no modern roads, cities, or signs of mechanized cultivation; he found no reason to believe that the Tenocha had timejumped him out of the sixteenth century.

Coming in alone toward the Fort in a strange craft reminded him of his first arrival, on that morning that now seemed so long ago. But today he faced the pressing practical problem of the Fort's automated defenses, which seemed likely to shoot down an incoming Tenocha vehicle before a friendly occupant could convincingly identify himself. Still, trusting to the Mask, and fearing the pursuit that might already be closing in, he dared to press straight on at high speed.

At about thirty kilometers' distance he prudently veered off and began to fly a slowly constricting spiral, meanwhile continuously calling in. Trying to call in, rather—he couldn't be sure that any signals from this Tenocha equipment would really be listened to by anyone on duty in Operations.

"Doc, Samson, anybody—don't shoot! This is Rocky, in the Tenocha aircraft." It was going to be a job, explaining his escape from Mictlan, but give him the chance and he would think of something. If all else failed, he might even tell the truth. "I'm coming in peacefully. This is Rocky, the chief, remember me? Landing instructions, please."

He was answered by an ominous radio silence. He was within ten kilometers of the Fort before he got a good look at it through a telescopic lens. A moment later he had left his spiral course and was driving toward the building, low and fast.

The Fort was a ruin, scorched and battle-blasted. Not only had the domes and antennas been blown clean away, but much of the doughnut-shaped upper story as well. The few remaining windows were all shattered. Explosions had torn through concrete walls that were more than a meter thick; the whole structure was now tilted within its broad, natural rocky cup and looked like a ship about to sink. Four or five flyers had slid together in a jumble on the slanted deck. Some of their rotors were bent up at broken angles.

A break in the deck's slab had left a portion of it nearly hori-zontal, and Mike set his flyer down there. In a locker on board he found a pair of boots, some leggings, and a gray parka that fit well enough to get into. He shut off his flyer's power, released the cabin air pressure, and climbed out into an intense silence, troubled only by a whine of wind around the jagged ruins.

How long ago had the Tenocha struck? The metal of the wrecked and tangled flyers was already showing heavy rust, but that was no reliable sign. Mike had been taught that all modern materials used in Tawantinsuyu-16 were designed to disintegrate rapidly after sustaining heavy damage, so their debris would not trouble future generations with any paradox. Within a decade after the attack, the entire Fort would probably have disappeared.

Freezing wind rushed past him into an open doorway, tilted and irregularly enlarged. He stuck his head inside. "Rusty? Doc?" All light and warmth were gone from the interior. Upon undamaged carpet, snow was piling up in little untracked drifts. "Cori? Samson?"

He had no flashlight, and finding his way amid the slanted ruins was difficult until his eyes began to get used to the gloom. Then he discovered Lola, dead and apparently well on the way to mum-mification by freeze-drying. At least, he thought it was Lola. The body, in the usual pullover and slacks, was badly shot up, and the face had been damaged.

Now he stopped calling people's names, went to his locker, and got into some cold-weather gear that fit him properly. By the time he had finished changing, he was staggering and had to sit down for a few moments' rest. He couldn't take much of this cold and altitude, not today. And now, before he did another thing, he had to find the Mask—

There came a little noise, which spun Mike round to face a figure that leaned against a ruined wall, holding a heavy shoulder weapon leveled at him. A slight figure, inside the bulky garments and the boots.

Mike said in Quechua, "Little one, it's me."

She set the firearm down carefully before she came to him across the tilted floor. Ten seconds later, she was crying like a helpless child. Hugging him, holding him desperately, all the while sobbing on his shoulder.

"They came . . . they came . . . Roca, we could do nothing . . . All the others are dead, all hunted down. Me they didn't know about, and I could hide."

"I know, I know. But it's all right now. It's going to be all right."

He led her into the violent disorder of what had been the commander's quarters, and there found an emergency lantern to turn on. In a choked voice, she told him of how she had been managing to survive since the attack. Field stoves had provided her with some warmth in a hideout she had established on a lower level, and food had been available from emergency stores. For days she had been keeping herself alive with the desperate hope that he or Gunner might come back, or that the Directors might send some kind of rescue party. This mountain was steeper than the one on which she had been given to the Sun, and from here there was no hope of getting down on foot.

His desk chronometer, buried in debris but still working, announced 13 November 1533. Coincidence once again. From the history that had been drilled into him, Mike remembered that on this day Pizarro was disposing of another eminent prisoner, in this case by burning alive—the recalcitrant Inca general Chalcuchima. This man was accused—perhaps correctly—of poisoning the first puppet Inca, who had died recently in the Spaniards' camp at Jauja. And on this day also the next applicant for the vacant post of Emperor was freely presenting himself to the European invaders—this was Manco, a younger brother of Atahualpa. Manco, one of Atahualpa's opponents in the recent civil war, and therefore on its losing side, had just emerged from hiding. Today, like many of his kinsmen, he viewed Pizarro as a timely savior.

In the commander's apartment the closet door stood open. His humble bag, still zipped, ignored by friend and enemy, lay on its side, secure as a bank vault or maybe more secure. The golden weight came out into his hands, and with something like reverence he lifted it to his face. There was a gasp from Cori.

At once, he beheld a scene of himself and Cori throwing blurred objects into backpacks, then climbing into the Tenocha flyer and taking off. All right. Gripping the Mask, he led the way to where the packs should be available, and good things to go into them.

First he selected medical items. Then a little high explosive—you never knew, and Mask or not, he had no intention of being taken alive again. He gnawed through two bars of field rations while packing up some more.

Cori helped him pack. But once, her hands holding his arm, she interrupted his busy movements. "Roca Yupanqui, you came back for me. As you brought me from the other mountain where I was freezing, so from this." There was something like worship in her eyes.

He gave her a brief hug, almost impersonal through the thickness of two parkas. "We'll get down from this one, too. Now help me pack."

He clipped a high-powered stunner on a handgun mount to his belt. Twice before they were ready to go he had to stop and rest, seeing the world bleach gray around him. Cori hovered in concern until he motioned her to keep on working. No, he wasn't going to last long at 18,000 feet. The surge of strength that had seen him through his escape was ebbing, despite the nourishment he had taken. At last, Cori now doing most of the work, the two of them got their packs aboard the flyer, and he fired its engines up.

Before he reached for the controls, he donned the Mask. Right away, to his surprise, it showed him that he should carry his sidearm on the left, ready for a cross-draw. Then, as he had expected, it projected for him an airborne image of the Tenocha flyer, which he need only follow.

The course set by the Mask led at first straight down the mountainside, at a level almost as low as Boss's flight when he had flown to pluck Cori from the shrine. Then, off across some relatively flat barrens to the south. The flight took only a few minutes. In a small, steep-sided canyon, innocent of any sign of man, the imaged flyer ahead of Mike set itself down upon a tiny mesa. He followed, and cut power. Here the Tenocha craft would be invisible to anyone approaching on foot until they had climbed almost within arm's length of it.

Here the altimeter indicated a mere 10,000 feet above sea level, almost a balmy altitude. His own Mask-projected image and Cori's were already climbing down from the mesa, and he guided her quickly after them. Daylight was already failing, the sun well behind the tall peaks to the west, and the sky clouding over.

When they had made their way down the first steep upper slopes of the mesa, the Mask bombarded his eyes with a burst of colored noise and then abruptly made its own eyes opaque. Mike stopped to take it off and put it into his pack. Seeing the wide-eyed look on Cori's face, he managed a smile and wink for her. "Secret," he said. She nodded solemnly.

Beneath his parka's hood, his shaven scalp was hot and tender. Even at 10,000 feet, down from 18,000, he didn't feel too good. The sons of bitches with their probes had naturally done some damage, and he wondered if now he was getting an infection. He stopped walking again, this time to choose an antibiotic pill and pop it down.

Where he was going he did not know, but he supposed that a goal would eventually become obvious. The wrinkled land in its descent changed gradually from barren rocks to hardly more fruitful soil. Soon after he took off the Mask, terraced fields came into view a little below the level where they walked, fields girdling mountain after mountain, into the distance. And now, abruptly, there appeared a switchback loop of Inca road, a pebble's roll ahead. Half a kilometer away, Mike could see some villagers moving about, near their huts of stone or mud and thatch. He guessed they might have spread potatoes in the sun to dry and were now getting them into a shed, in expectation of rain.

When they had reached the road Cori stood still beside it, looking first one way then the other. "I know this place." She pointed to her left. "That way the road goes to Cuzco. Back the other way, to Abancay, then Vilcashuaman, then on to the provinces of the north."

He consulted the Mask again; it gave him only faint traceries of light. Probably common sense was all he needed here. "We must go to Cuzco," Mike said thoughtfully, packing the golden weight away again. Pizarro would not be many miles ahead in the direction of the capital; the Spaniards must have passed over this very road only a few days ago, with Manco their new puppet and his entourage of Indian supporters. For a long time now, Cuzco would be the stage for the central scenes of the Conquest.

While getting clear of the Fort he hadn't really thought of where he and Cori were going, but now it was obviously time to take stock. There wasn't going to be another Fort for them to live in, or another flyer in which to travel. Wherever the Mask was leading them, they must live now as Andeans. He looked at his and Cori's modern clothing, which would have to go, and at the packs they carried. He seemed to recall that the Mask had advised packing, but he had probably overdone it.

Cori had walked out onto the road and was looking east along its descending curves, toward Cuzco. She said: "There is a *tambo* near, where we will be able to spend the night."

The road was mainly downhill, but to Mike it felt as difficult as a climb, and he could sense his fever rising. Night had fallen, full and sudden, before they reached the *tambo*; so far, a moonless night, with stars a prolonged white explosion from one sawtooth horizon to another. The air was like fresh ice, and despite cold-weather gear Mike shivered violently.

The *tambo*, a combination inn and storehouse, was a low stone building that looked deserted when they reached it. In normal times, supply clerks would probably have been on duty, dispensing needed goods under a system of careful control, and innkeepers, operating a kind of motel for the upper classes. Common Indians under the Inca's rule did not journey, except to some nearby village to trade on market day or festival, or when herding animals or marching in the army. Tonight the wooden doors to the store-rooms, all ranged around an interior court, were standing open and unwatched. One or two of them had been chopped from their hinges.

"I will serve the Honored Roca," Cori murmured in her own language, and bent down in the disused corral to scratch up some dried llama dung in preparation for a fire. Mike mumbled some-thing feverish and went to rummage through the storerooms. Other liberators had recently been there before him. The great wooden bins were pulled open; some had all their contents strewn about. He got out a small flashlight; there were several bits of technology it would really hurt to give up when he went Indian.

The Spaniards in their monomaniacal search for treasure had scattered many things but taken few. There were still tons of Inca clothing, sandals, unwoven fibers, and stacks of pottery. Great gra-nary jars still brimmed with maize and ground cornmeal. Huge baskets waited, filled with dried fish and *charqui*. Every storable necessity of life was hoarded in the *tambos* by a paternalistic gov-ernment against a time of need for any of its people.

So far even civil war and invasion had not broken down the sturdy mechanism of the moneyless economy; but in three or four years matters would be different. The stored goods would be wasted wantonly, or used up without provision for replacement. The people would be dying en masse of disease, and of starvation previously almost unknown. Those who survived would be broken free of the rocklike mold of their old lives, but reenslaved as Spanish chattels under a new dictatorship as harsh as the old and far less concerned with their material welfare.

Mike buried parka, trousers, and boots inside an ancient dung heap. With his teeth chattering, for the time being he retained a T-shirt of his thermal underwear. He quickly put on an Inca loincloth, a fine sleeveless tunic, and a woolen cloak, choosing his new garments from the smaller bins evidently reserved for the nobility. There were no gold ornaments in stock to put into his pierced ears, but ornaments were not vital. Pulling a cap of llama wool over his shaved and punctured scalp, he rejoined Cori at the smoky fire that she had undoubtedly started by means of some quick modern technology. She seemed far from deft tonight at juggling stewpots and hot stones and food; at home, before the Fort, there had undoubtedly been servants to do these tasks for her. Suddenly he realized that the chance of Cori's seeing her family again was no longer astronomically small. He wondered how the thought of it affected her.

"You had better change your clothes, too," he told her, speaking Quechua. "I will watch the fire."

She came back shortly in dress and mantle of red and white, with a kerchief folded over her head, and soft, beaded moccasins on her feet. After eating they moved the fire, or some of its brands, inside one of the hostel rooms. In the little white-walled chamber, a ceiling hole let some of the smoke out, and a hide curtain at the doorway held in some of the heat. Creature comforts were not the strong point of the Inca culture. What was? In his present fevered state he couldn't think of anything. Let the damned Spaniards have it all. No, that was the fever talking. After Cajamarca, he would let them have nothing. And after Mictlan . . . He had not yet disposed of the packs, and he gave himself another dose of medicine.

It was true, though, in Tawantinsuyu people had to be practically of royal blood to merit as much as a low stool in the way of solid furniture. And the Inca himself often had no better illumination at night than one of these damned flaring dung-fires. Of course he didn't have to try to read by it, having never heard of reading, and for watching a dancer or grabbing at a concubine, it should be light enough . . .

Mike fell asleep before he realized that sleep was near. In the middle of the night he awoke, fevered, shivering like an old man and enjoying as an old man would the warmth of the young girl's body rolled against his own under the woolen blankets. Straw matting held them above the earth floor, and tiny life moved in the straw. Maybe the same cooties that had here feasted on royal Inca blood during some imperial progress of the past. If the Inca spat or took off a garment or picked his nose, the object separated from his person remained sacred. Therefore why not these lice? Anyway, Mike could feel no bites. At the Fort they might have given him some immunity to vermin, sacred or profane.

Lying against him, Cori kept twitching in her sleep. Bugs or bad dreams? He meant to open a pack and take more medicine, but before he could do so, he slept again.

In the morning Mike felt a little better, but still swallowed another dose. Cori went out to see if they were still alone in the *tambo*, and he fitted the Mask onto his aching head. It gave him nothing but visual noise, and he stowed it away again, this time in his Inca belt-pouch, which it nearly filled.

While Cori worked to make dried corn and dried fish palatable for breakfast, Mike winnowed through the backpacks. What could not be carried in their pouches or under their clothing somewhere must be discarded. The handgun he retained, after the Mask's earlier warning on how it must be carried. He abandoned the high explosive, breaking gelatinous capsules and scattering the contents as harmless powder. Cori stuffed her own belt-pouch and an extra one with the Fort's emergency rations and medicines; when he suggested they might not need it all, she looked at him as if he were mad. He also found room in his pouch and hers for a tiny set of two-way radios, capable of recording incoming messages electronically or as printouts.

Continuing toward Cuzco, they struck out on an empty road. Near midmorning they passed a deserted-looking village, its guinea pigs still rooting about in the house yards. About midday they reached what Cori said was the town of Curahuasi. There Mike sat on a stone at roadside, letting his fever appear somewhat greater than it now was, while Cori, with her much greater facility in language and custom did some talking. The townsmen gestured their respect for her aristocratic accent and bearing, and expressed their willingness to serve as litter-bearers for her and her father—or it might be she was presenting him as an uncle, the word in this context was the same—but there were no litters to be had.

In these troublous days, no one apparently thought it very strange that two of the nobility should be stranded without vehicles or attendants. Mike gave the local men to believe, when he finally spoke to them, that he and his daughter/niece had suffered robbery and assault at the hands of passing Spaniards. No doubt his lack of golden earplugs made this convincing. The tale won him no great sympathy, however. This close to Cuzco, the faction of nobility at odds with Manco, and therefore presently subject to Spanish attack, was looked upon somewhat as imperialist Yankee carpetbaggers had been in the vanquished South. Against this northern faction the Spaniards were proving—so far—to be very valuable allies. The village leader of Curahuasi, inviting the travelers into his mud hut for a noontime snack, spoke of how he had yesterday himself seen Manco greeting the Bearded Ones and forming an alliance with them.

Emboldened perhaps by Mike's bedraggled looks, the headman went on to verge on insolence, remarking that the days of the great Huayna Capac (who would have tolerated no such nonsense as a civil war) were coming back. The Quitan armies—he meant the northern, anti-Manco armies, who a few months ago under Atahualpa had believed themselves the virtual rulers of the world—were going to be driven out of this part of the empire. Their general Quisquis, while retreating a few days ago toward Cuzco—which, as the headman correctly foresaw, he was not going to be able to hold—had destroyed the long suspension bridge that carried the highway over the Apurimac, but this very day the people of the riverside villages had started to rebuild it.

Yankees and rebels? No, the Incas' internal politics was more complex than that. More like the Wars of the Roses, with great houses and branches of nobility contending for the crown, in tangles of family relationships and loyalties and intrigues too intricate for any outsider to really comprehend. Not wishing to seem too passive in his guise of ailing noble, Mike looked a little sternly at the headman, who cut short his almost insubordinate news commentary. Mike signed to Cori that they should not tarry here for long, and after a brief meal, they were soon out on the road again.

Apurimac translated as "Great Speaker," and the voice was audible well before they came in sight of the river's gorge, into which the retreating Quitans had dropped the remnants of the highway bridge. The echoing roar was impressive, even though the rains had not yet come in earnest, and the river was still drought-shrunken in its canyon. Score one more incredible stroke of good luck for Pizarro's version of the Mask. At any other season of the year, the cutting of this bridge would have stopped the Spaniards cold—at least until Manco could have conscripted labor to rebuild it for them. As it was, horses and men had been able to ford the river in the gorge and were as close as ever on Quisquis's heels.

Other traffic had been backed up, however. Trains of llamas looked with forlorn dignity for forage along the barren roadside, while their drivers crooned to them and fed them now and then from their own cargoes. And near where the road was broken at the gorge, the hillsides were a swarm of human activity—the populations of several villages, who served as *chaca camayoc*, the keepers of the bridge, were hard at work. Normally the bridge had to be replaced every two or three years, as its fibers decayed, and this was a routine job.

As the first clouds of the afternoon formed above, numbers of children beat piles of grass with sticks, turning stiff blades to supple strings of fiber. Women, sitting down and gossiping a mile a minute as they worked, handspun these strings into twine, and the twine into slender yellow rope. Men, chanting as the women talked, twisted what looked like miles of rope into thick and progressively thicker cables, ending with a product nearly a foot in diameter and long enough to span the gorge—Mike guessed something more than a hundred feet.

Meanwhile, young men on opposite banks of the river far below appeared to be playing at a game. They tossed out into the river lightly weighted strings woven of straw, and tried to tangle the strings from the two banks together in midstream. Soon after Mike had let himself down, with a sigh, on a handy boulder that offered a good seat from which to watch proceedings, the tangling was accomplished. A compound line of straw was pulled up, taut and dripping, from the Great Speaker's sullen-mumbling throat. Against that endless voice a higher, more fragile yell of success went up from a hundred or so human tongues.

"Now they can pull a rope across." The English words came from close at Mike's side, in tones as resonant as the Apurimac's.

Mike turned his head and glared at Esperanza, who stood there dressed as a llama-driver. His white hair and a newly seamed face made him appear to be on the brink of retirement to the Inca equivalent of Social Security in some peaceful village. His bare brown legs were hairless and gnarled as weathered wood beneath his simple tunic's folds. Cori, Mike saw, had gone a little distance off to join a small gathering of momentarily idle women. Maybe she was trying to get some information. Probably she'd said to him where she was going, and with the roaring of the river and the pressure of his own thoughts, he hadn't heard.

Mike continued to give Esperanza a long stare. The other, his white hair sticking out from under his woolen cap, imperturbably watched the stringing of the ropes.

"You bastard," Mike said at last. "If I thought you had anything to do with what happened to Tom . . . "

"I tried to help. As I told you on the telephone, I warned him, but he wouldn't listen; don't blame me for any of his troubles. And now the Mask is yours."

"One of them is."

Esperanza ignored the comment. "You want to hand it over to me, Gabrieli? It's meant a rough time for your brother and for you. I can probably get you home safe if you hand it over now. If you hang onto it and stick around, there're going to be more rough times ahead." The head turned, aiming the big nose at Mike.

Looking Esperanza in the eye, Mike shook his head very slowly.

The other smiled a little. "Good. I was just checking. Don't really want the thing."

"You just want to know what I'm going to do with it. That's what you usually ask when we have these séances."

Esperanza nodded; it was almost a bow. Down below, the young men had got a real rope of straw across the river and were pulling a thicker rope over with it. Next, Mike supposed, they would string one of the big cables.

He turned back to the man beside him. "I'll tell you what I'm going to do with it. I'm going to stick it to the Tenocha as much as I possibly can. That includes you especially, if you're on their team after all—if all that in the interrogation was somehow just for show

"All *what* in the interrogation?"

"Well, they made it sound like you're really on their shit list, you know? I think they overdid it. Nine-tenths of the questions they asked me were regarding you."

Esperanza didn't pretend to be ignorant of what Mike was talking about. "That's of interest. Thank you." The words seemed genuine.

Now one end of the first huge cable was being made fast to a massive stone bollard wedged in place against the living rock of the gorge. Nearby, coca leaves smoldered on a ritual fire, propitiating spirits. The tang of the smoke when it blew toward Mike was really something else.

"You know," said Esperanza, "after this bridge has been rewoven a few more times, it will be named for San Luis, the good King of France. Then, after the *chaca camayoc* have learned to neglect repairs, and it falls down with people on it, someone will write a book about the accident."

Mike shook his head. "Now you are speaking of Peru," he said, in his best Quechua yet. "This is Tawantinsuyu, here."

"And you are beginning to boast like an Indian as well as look like one. This Indianization gives me hope for whatever plan you may be trying to effect. Did you tell them anything of me, when they interrogated?"

"I would've told them all I could, which wasn't much, if they'd had sense enough to ask the right questions. You knew I was getting into that, I suppose, you bastard."

"Want to tell me what your plans are, Mike? Or do you prefer the name of Roca, now? How can I persuade you, how can I influence you to tell me? More depends on your decisions than you can realize."

Mike still couldn't trust this character. "Tell me first something that *you're* going to do. Or even what you've already done. Did you make the Masks?"

Esperanza gave a weary, discouraged headshake. "My time is up," he said, and turned and stumped away. Mike started to call after him, but did not. He watched Esperanza's figure blend with those of three or four other llama-herders along the road. Then there were still only three or four of them, and he could no longer be picked out. Cori came back toward Mike. She took no notice of an old man passing, going the other way.

Her report was cheerful. "Roca, the women are sure that soon the bridge will be complete, and we can go on. They also say the road is clear to Cuzco from here on."

"Come sit here with me. Watch them work."

Soon four big cables were across, two side by side to form the basis of a floor, two more cables higher for the handrails. Men ventured out on the new bridge, weaving thin ropes thickly to make a floor and barrier networks on the sides, dense enough to keep the smallest child safely enclosed. The last step was a layer of twigs, woven in among the floor ropes so that feet—human or llama—could not poke through.

The sun was almost down before the work was done. The llama-drivers had been contending for some time to be the first to get their caravans across.

"It should be our right to go before them," Cori complained.

"Let us wait, if waiting in silence will make us less noticeable."

The wait was brief, but night had come before they crossed the swaying bridge above the roar. Downhill to the middle and then climb; it trembled like a nervous animal beneath them.

He asked her, "Is there another *tambo* near?"

"I don't remember. We can follow the llama-drivers, and there will be some shelter." After a little while, she added, "Back at the town I told them that the Spaniards had shaved your head and tortured you, trying to find more gold. I also told them that we lived near Cuzco, that they might not think you of the Quitan faction. But the truth is I do not know where you are from."

The thin air was chilling rapidly, but he didn't feel the cold nearly as much as he had last night. "My home is very distant, Cori."

"I know that. And your wife must be sad that you are gone from it."

He took a dozen steps or so in silent thought before he answered. "In my land, many things are different. There it is common for a man to be a bachelor after he is twenty years old. And so I have no wife."

"Oh." It was a soft monosyllable, which told him little.

"Cori, I don't know exactly where your home is, either."

She hesitated. "My family that gave me to the Sun are dead to me now, and I to them. I have thought much about it, and it must be so. Inti, the Sun, did not want my life, and so he passed me on to you, the Fort people, *pokara-runa*. You are the chief of the Fort people now, and so my life is yours, *apu*."

Apu. Lord. Probably not half a dozen men in the empire would commonly be so addressed. Awed, he groped for words, but could not find them.

"I hear llamas ahead, Roca Yupanqui. I think there is a *tambo* near."

In the *tambo*, Cori went to borrow fire from the llama-drivers who camped in an outer courtyard, as an excuse to talk to them. Coming back to the small room she and Mike had taken, she relayed their gossip, none of it new, about politics and road conditions. "All my uncles are quite old," she added, as if in afterthought. "So tonight I did not say you were my uncle."

"But what?"

"My husband." Looking away, voice very low.

Mike was a long way from smiling. Suddenly he felt like a young teen-ager himself, both in mind and body. It had been many days now since he was dosed with anaphrodisiacs, and maybe there was some rebound effect. Cori was about fourteen, not at all young for an Inca girl to become a bride; and chastity before marriage was not considered a matter of importance among her people.

A long time seemed to pass. He cared—he cared a hell of a lot—what happened to her. Then he whispered, almost choking, "Come here." And with enormous tenderness he pulled her in between the blankets in the dark . . .

In the morning he woke looking at her face, and marveling.

11. The Square of Joy

For some reason this morning, Mike felt almost afraid to don the Mask, but when he put it on it showed him nothing but noise. Dressing and packing were the work of a minute, and after Cori and he had eaten, they were quickly on the road. All this while Cori was cheerful, talking more than he had ever known her to do. But after they had been walking an hour or so, she grew silent, and he sensed that something was bothering her. It took some persistent questioning to get an informative answer.

"I . . . I now miss some of my family."

"Well, if any of your relatives are in Cuzco, we may see them there." He looked at her thoughtfully. "They may not recognize you, you know." He was wondering what they would make of her returning from the Sun.

Cori was silent, walking. He took her hand. At last she said, "It is my parents that I miss. Even though—they did what they did, they are not cruel. They meant me to be happy with Inti. But we will not meet them in Cuzco, for they live in the Collasoyo. In Cuzco there is only the house of one of my uncles. He is an important man, and often traveling on military affairs."

"Will this uncle know that you were given to the Sun? What is his name?"

"I do not know what he will know. Quizo Yupanqui is his name . . . Roca, what is wrong?"

He had stopped in his tracks for a moment, staring at her. Now he walked on. "Only that I have heard his name." In the standard histories of the earliest years of the Conquest, it could not be found. But in 1536 . . . Patience. That was three years from now.

Some forty miles of road lay between them and Cuzco, and to walk it took them two more days. Small *tambos* along the way all gave evidence of having been ransacked by the invaders, but retained supplies in plenty and offered shelter during the cold nights. On the way, Mike and Cori made the swaying passage of four more suspension bridges; the fleeing Quitans had not bothered to cut these, which crossed no barriers as formidable as the Great Speaker's gorge. At neither bridges nor *tambos* were there authorities to take note of and perhaps question travelers; war had swept all such guardians aside, blinding the eyes of the Inca to vagrancy and laziness throughout his realm. Not that either was widespread as yet. Peasants tending llamas or working in the fields were often to be seen. Sometimes these folk looked up at the travelers and sometimes not. Let those who walked the roads in terror or triumph come and go; the land remained and held their lives rooted fast.

From time to time Mike and Cori met, or were overtaken by, other parties of displaced persons on the road. Men and women with bewildered faces, come in search of tools or food or clothing that had not arrived at their home villages on schedule. Others, whole families, leaving destroyed homes and ruined fields, wandering they knew not where. Once Mike on impulse dosed a sick baby from his small medical kit, the mother pleased that an evident sorcerer should show an interest. He didn't wait to see what effect his efforts had.

The place was called the *urcoscalla*, where with a last dramatic twist the *Capac Nan*, the Royal Road, showed to the traveler Cuzco, the Navel of the World, fitted into its valley at 11,000 feet above the sea. At home Mike had heard Cuzco called the oldest continuously inhabited city of the western hemisphere. And he knew that during his visit to Cuzco-23 he had passed, almost without being able to see it, through one of the great metropolises of another branch of history.

At the *urcoscalla* Cori stopped to offer fervent prayer, plucking her own eyelashes and blowing them, together with little feathers from the trim on her fine cape, toward the local *waka*, a grimly weather-beaten shrine of natural rock that seemed to stand beside the road as a sentry. Mike made a motion or two in the same direction and turned to watch the town.

Cuzco of Tawantinsuyu-16, he estimated, might hold a hundred thousand people if the populations of its satellite towns were counted in. In general, he knew, the upper class lived in the city itself, amid its palaces, storehouses, and shrines, while servants and other workers dwelt in the adjoining suburbs. Across the valley ran rows and rows of houses of mud or stone, painted red or yellow or white beneath their roofs, the new thatch yellow, the old straw weathered gray.

Two small rivers crossed the valley and the city, to join near the far side of both. And upon its hill to the northwest brooded the Fortress of the Speckled Hawk, Sacsahuaman. Within the gargantuan masonry of its walls the city's entire population might have found shelter. Far on the opposite side of town, close to the confluence of the streams, the Temple of the Sun reared white walls high above the narrow streets and crowded roofs. The living sun winked pure gold from the frieze on that high cornice, now in its last days of glory before systematic despoliation by the Spaniards stripped it bare. Pizarro was already within the city, of course, but still too intent on consolidating his position to divert any of his men's energies to serious looting.

"It is more than a year since I have stood here, Roca Yupanqui." Cori had turned from her thanksgiving prayers and was enjoying the prospect with him. With the coming into view of the city before them she had brightened, like some fresh reflection of the sun, or like a flower turned to its light. "Then I was but a child. Have you seen this before?"

"No. It is a marvelous sight."

They descended into Cuzco's valley, to find themselves quickly surrounded by llama corrals and suburban hovels. On the right the stench of a tannery drifted from a side road, and on the left appeared extensive barracks, long, low buildings like those that had concealed the attackers at Cajamarca. Meanwhile traffic on the road around them had of course increased, with business as usual the order of the day despite political upheaval.

Servants in plain garb hurried by, not being lazy, not wasting time—the penalty could be death for repeated offenses of that kind. Eminent visitors from outlying provinces, in distinctive head-gear and multicolored finery, were borne past in their litters and hammocks. Masons clanked bronze tools on stone, with movements incredibly quick and adroit, and hoisted dressed ashlars in great slings of the ubiquitous grass-fiber rope. Messengers with *quipus* in hand were sometimes forced by the density of traffic to walk rather than trot. Sweepers were busy, darting onto the road and off; the pavement was remarkably clean, considering the numbers of people and animals that passed.

Now the city proper enfolded the Royal Road within its anonymous walls, behind which lay the low, sprawling town houses of the ruling class. The dozen palaces of the past emperors were ahead, Mike saw now. Halfway between the fortress Sacsahuaman and the Temple of the Sun, they bordered the central square of the city, massive structures rising to twenty-five or thirty feet, looming above the surrounding ranch-style houses of the lesser nobility.

The highway ended abruptly, debouching into that vast, sand-surfaced central plaza. "*Waykapata,*" Mike muttered, distracted in a certain awe. He doubted that anything in Cuzco-23 could have produced a comparable feeling in him.

Cori had stopped by his side. "Yes, the Square of Joy. I remember when I was a child, coming here for the great festivals. The workers put all work away for a few days, and the nobility all their planning and their quarreling. All were happy, drinking and singing, for a few days . . . " She turned aside and with a prayerful gesture blew kisses toward another shrine, erected precisely where the highway entered the square. At the four corners of the Square of Joy terminated the four great Royal Roads. Tribute and hostages came in along them from the Four Quarters of the World, and conquering armies looking for more tribute and hostages, devoutly spreading the worship of the Sun, went out—so it had been for more than a hundred years of Inca rule in Cuzco.

Until this year, when invasion as from another planet had turned the whole world upside down.

Overlooked by the stone palaces of a dozen former Incas, the enormous acreage of the Square of Joy was bisected by the paved-over channel of the Huatanay, icy supplier of clean mountain water to the city, and efficient remover of its sewage. Now a small horde of young men were sitting along the masonry that held the river, and in the nearby sand, chatting and laughing among themselves. Many had woolen slings wound round their heads, and clubs and shields lay all about. Mike supposed they were some part of the army of four thousand that Manco now was raising, at Pizarro's request, to help harry the Quitans under Quisquis completely out of this central portion of the empire.

From one of the distant sides of the Square there came a sound so familiar that Mike was starting unconsciously to ignore it. But he caught the sharp turn of Cori's head and beheld her wondering stare, and looked around himself. Horses, of course, picketed before the palace of the legendary Pachacuti, that Pizarro had taken for his own. The sun glinted on morion helmets there, and a rank of campaign tents was visible through a gateway in the outer palace wall. No doubt a sizable proportion of Pizarro's small cavalry force was always armed and ready, day or night, for instant action.

The house of Cori's uncle was a short walk beyond the Square of Joy, through narrow streets shadowed by constricting walls, in the direction of the Temple. Like those of the other nobility in this sector, the house proved to be a two-story structure with a peaked, thatched roof. Like the wall around its grounds, it was made of finely fitted stones laid in regular courses. A gray, stooped doorkeeper, his staff of authority in hand, stood vigilantly at the main gateway open to the street. The sight of two well-dressed folk approaching moved him a little aside, enough to allow them to step inside to state their business. The interior walls of the courtyard were plastered in red and yellow; three empty litters waited under an awning at one side. A few guinea pigs trotted about. Great pottery vessels, which Mike guessed were full of grain or other foodstuffs, stood in another section of the yard. There, between a stone grinding mill and a clay outdoor oven, a doorway led into what was doubtless a kitchen, wherein two women could be heard arguing.

"We have come to see Quizo Yupanqui," Mike announced to the gatekeeper. Cori had been coaching him somewhat on etiquette and grammar. "His niece is now my wife."

The old man took a limping step sideways, his eyes widening. Mike thought: What hideous mistake have I committed? Only a half-second later did he realize that the man's surprise had nothing to do with him.

Wrapped in a blood-spotted cloak, a young warrior lounged against the gatepost; he had evidently entered almost on Mike's and Cori's heels. No, not lounged—he was leaning against the wood from weakness. His eyes, looking back at Mike, were those of an animal nearly cornered, who must decide instantly which way to run. His gasping breath was that of a runner at the top of a long climb.

Weakness made the warrior's decision for him. He started to fall, and Mike stepped forward instinctively to catch and hold him up. The gatekeeper was just reaching to lend a hand when two more figures appeared in the open entrance. Steel flashed about their heads and bodies, and long steel in their hands.

"There he is, Gonzalo!" one Castilian voice roared out. "Almost found another den here, looks like."

"By the saints, we'll get a good tail-hold and pluck him out." Gonzalo, the larger of the two, with black and bushy sideburns, took a confident step forward.

Mike reached across his body for the stunner, stuck in his belt precisely where the Mask had told him it should be carried, and the weapon came out smoothly into his hand. It was nearly leveled at Gonzalo's navel, when the arm of the exhausted warrior, thrashing in some last desperate attempt to do his own fighting, knocked Mike's wrist a light blow at what seemed to be the precisely disastrous angle. The little stunner flew from his fingers and skidded neatly across the paving of the yard toward Cori.

The gatekeeper had fallen down, whether through accident or design; and, whether through age or prudence, he stayed there. The blood-stained warrior was in no better shape, though he had drawn a bronze dagger from his belt and waved it feebly. Mike let him slide down to the ground, and snatched up the doorkeeper's staff. It was of stout wood, and had a lot more length than any dagger, but it was not Toledo steel, nor was he D'Artagnan. No choice, however. Big Gonzalo with his bushy sideburns had already started across the yard after Mike. The other Spaniard had turned partly away, his alert eyes probing the doors and windows of the house for any sign of more resistance. Inside the kitchen door a flurry, as of retreating feet.

Mike backed slowly away, holding the big wooden stick as he thought a man might be supposed to hold a quarterstaff. Robin Hood . . . how had Errol Flynn . . . The sword leveling toward his midsection looked enormous, and very real. The armored figure brought back Cajamarca, brought back the urge to scream and run. Mike fought it down. Now the sword feinted a quick thrust, stopped, and then—

It fell down ringing on the flagstones of the yard. From the corner of his eye, Mike saw Cori aiming, unorthodoxly, the silent gun clenched in her two small fists down at her midsection.

The Spaniard whose sword had fallen from his suddenly deadened fingers looked in utter bewilderment at Mike for just a moment. Then Mike's crude but heartfelt swing of the staff caught him alongside the head, tipping up his helm. It was a clean knockout.

The second intruder had been hit by the stunner, too, and his legs were tangling themselves so he could hardly stand. But he still held his sword and was therefore still very dangerous. Mike switched his hold on the club to the more familiar grip used on a baseball bat, and tried a little fancy footwork, dancing in and out. The sword took off the end of the staff in the first brisk passage, but the swordsman overbalanced with his efforts and fell down.

"Santiago!" he roared out in an impressively loud voice as he toppled. Mike clouted his sword arm, gave him the butt of the staff as close to the solar plexus as he could aim, then laid a finisher right on the bearded jaw.

The winner stepped back, breathing hard. Then he spun round. Dashing into the courtyard from one of the doorways of the house came an enthusiastic-looking warrior, his short-cut hair still raven black although his face was deeply lined. Short and sinewy, he brandished a *makana*, the standard Inca sword-shaped club of wood. This man halted, seemingly in mid-bound, to goggle at the scene before him. Armed retainers, pouring right after him into the courtyard, froze there in the same surprise.

At this moment there came a hammering on the street gate, which its keeper, just recently back on his feet, had had the wit to close and bar. "Santiago!" a Castilian voice bawled from the street. "Fight on, we are coming!"

Mike turned, swallowed, tried out his Fort-learned Spanish. "*Por Dios*, I am only struggling with a wench. I thank you for the offered help, but in this fight I hope to win without it."

Brief silence outside, and then guffaws. Mike looked at Cori, who had also taken some Spanish lessons at the Fort; she understood what he wanted, and managed a sound between a laugh and a whimper. More laughter echoed from outside, and heavy footsteps crunched away.

Throwing down the shortened staff, Mike turned to the old warrior, who by now was leaning on his *makana*. "Honored Quizo, I thought that these two men in metal meant harm to some of your household. As your nephew by marriage, and your guest, I thought it would be well to act without waiting for your permission."

A silence began to stretch. Leaning on their implements of war, Quizo and his men stared almost blankly back at Mike, alternating the direction of their gazes toward the two men he had felled. Aspects of the comical had come into sight when the man the Spaniards had been pursuing broke the spell by stirring feebly and letting out a groan. Cori, who had long since put the gun quietly away, bent down at his side at once, then looked up quickly. "Uncle. Let me direct your servants and see to it that this one's wounds are cared for. He bleeds."

Quizo emitted a single, expressive, Hollywood-Indian grunt. His servants hurried to tend their fallen countryman. Shortly Cori rose to her feet and began some formal introductions.

"Husband of my niece," Quizo said when these were finished, "it would seem that these two *suncasapa* are your prisoners." Vast respect was in his voice. More than likely, Mike thought, Quizo had already seen on the field of battle what Spaniards' swords could do.

He thought over his response carefully before he spoke. "If that is so, uncle of my wife, then I think I will release them, that they may tell the other Bearded Ones to be careful how they offend the men of Cuzco."

Quizo's eyes narrowed, then brightened a little. "And will you throw them into the gutter?"

"With your agreement, Honored Uncle, I will first take them somewhere far from your house." He didn't want to bring the Spaniards down on Quizo's house in force; the scrambling of short-term memory was a common effect of the stunbeam, and if he gave Gonzalo and his friend a little further treatment with it before they were dumped, the chances were small that they could ever remember in which house or street they had been clobbered, or by whom.

Quizo doubtless understood that the idea was to avoid massive Spanish retaliation. He signed agreement. Mike promptly bent to pick up the Spaniards' fallen swords, and offered a present of one of them. "Take this, Uncle." Quizo grunted again, and accepted the keen blade reverently.

In the end the job of disposing of the fallen was left to some of Quizo's retainers. The two Conquistadors, relieved of their weapons, departed the house inside two curtained litters. Meanwhile the wounded Indian, still no more than semiconscious, was put to bed, his bleeding stanched, and a physician summoned.

Cori was taken off by one of Quizo's senior wives who claimed to remember her from a small girl, and who, in some natural confusion, evidently believed it was one of Cori's sisters who had been sacrificed to Inti something more than a year ago. Disappearing into the friendly woman's clutches, Cori cast back a glance that Mike hoped was meant to be reassuring.

The general took Mike into another room, and offered a fine little silver box filled with coca, of which Mike accepted a small pinch. It was another custom of the nobility that everyone had tried at the Fort.

Sitting, Quizo dealt coca sparingly to himself. Mike, sitting on a mat opposite, could see from his new vantage point that this house was not far short of being a palace. Within an inner atrium garden, a listless Amazon monkey crouched on a sunbathed branch, not requiring the restraint of the fine silver chain and collar that bound it to its tree. It languished here, far above its wet, low-altitude jungle, ignoring the rare birds chirping and cackling round it in their cages of delicate silver wire. Mike could quite appreciate the monkey's feelings; after that one brisk bit of sparring, he had been more than ready to sit down. How did the Spaniards do it? The more he learned about them, the more their toughness demanded his respect.

As if sharing this thought at the same moment, Quizo commented: "The army of Quisquis slung ten thousand stones and javelins against the *suncasapa*, and swung at them with ten thousand maces, *makana*, daggers, clubs. The enemy numbered only a few score, and yet Quisquis, who is a valiant warrior, was driven from the field."

And so, thought Mike, you naturally want to know how in hell I ever clouted two of them down with something like an old hoe handle. Knowing that modesty would not be expected or understood, he began some moderate brag about how this was not the first time that enemies had fallen before him; that he had been known to deal with more than two opponents at one time, et cetera, et cetera. Which recitation of course really explained nothing. Quizo was undoubtedly going to put his victory down to some kind of sorcery, no matter what he said. All right. Something close to sorcery had been required—let it go at that. The odds were enormous that neither the gatekeeper nor the fallen Inca had noticed Cori's action with the handgun, nor could they have connected her silent gesturing with the Spaniards' fall.

Waiting for Quizo's deliberate reply, Mike found himself still unable to keep from marveling at the almost unbelievable toughness of those few score Spaniards who had routed thousands of strong armed men. Think what you might of their morals, you had to give them that.

Cori's little jolts with the stunner, though only grazing, partial hits, would likely have sent ordinary men of US-20 on their way to the emergency room of the nearest hospital. And yet Gonzalo and his friend had continued to think of nothing but fighting, and one of them had come close to getting at Mike with a sword.

The Conquistadors were burned by day in the Andean sun, frostbitten by night, malnourished by any good dietary standard, often half starved for oxygen. They battled sometimes for days on end, usually greatly outnumbered by their enemies, who were tough men fighting fanatically to save their hearths and families and gods. Isolated beyond hope of help in this alien world, they depended only upon God, the saints, and their own comrades.

These last stood by them in combat to the point of death, treated their open wounds with crude stitching and the application of hot oil or melted fat, and might sometimes try to swindle them out of a fair share of the spoils. In the face of all this, the more successful Spaniards not only survived, not only conquered, but maintained multiple mistresses, sired bastards by the score, and ruled estates, cities, and a nation, with energy enough left over for bloody hair-trigger quarrels among themselves. Francisco Pizarro himself led the field in most of these events, and he had been in his mid-fifties when the adventure started.

Quizo put his silver snuffbox of coca aside, on the shelf of a perfect trapezoidal niche built right into the masonry of the wall. Mike had thought such elegant construction reserved for the Inca's own buildings. Of course Quizo, or one of his ancestors, might have been given this house by an emperor. In a moneyless society, such rewards were common.

Fine weavings hung on Quizo's walls, and others equally good were jumbled carelessly amid the straw mats of the floor. A ceramic brazier held real wood ashes from last night's fire. Between great chests carved from some Amazonian hardwood Quizo sat chewing on his quid of coca; now and then, great golden earplugs swinging, he turned and spat into a small Mochica bowl. Bring the furnishings of your living room to US-20, Quizo, and I'll guarantee a fortune for both of us . . .

In the world as redecorated by coca, time seemed to drift. Maybe altitude, mental strain, release from danger, and recent physical exertion also had something to do with this disconnected mental state, which was dangerous now when he should have all his wits about him. Quizo offered more of the drug, but Mike declined, thinking he could now do so without being impolite. He was not really hungry when women came to serve food to him and the general, but he began to eat and developed an appetite as he did so. Ordinarily, Mike supposed, the ladies would have joined them for dinner. But today he was being especially honored.

Roast guinea pig, squash, beans, and sweet potatoes. Shy maids served the dishes silently and flashed away. For dessert, popcorn—Mike couldn't remember if it was grown near Cuzco or had to be brought from some far corner of the empire.

Quizo belched, rubbed his stomach. "Has the Honored Roca traveled far with his bride?"

"It has not been a long march, Honored Quizo, but a hard one. Today's encounter with the *suncasapa* was not my first." Let his wounded, shaven scalp and missing earplugs speak for themselves.

Quizo peered at him, scowled as if at his own forgetfulness, then clapped his hands to summon servants. Quickly several matched pairs of golden ear-ornaments were brought in, all of which the general pressed upon his guest. No more than fair compensation, Mike supposed, for a Toledo sword. He chose a pair for wearing, and at once a comely concubine approached to help him put them on. Half-stoned as he was, all he could think of when her fingers touched his skin was Cori. So it looked like this thing he had started with his little teenager was something serious. Good God, it certainly seemed to be, for her. Be careful of her, man, don't ever leave her on another mountain. He tried to imagine himself and Cori coming home to Atlanta, the tall old house, the black yardman next door looking up from trimming the hedges. Good God. As far away as Mars.

When the chosen earplugs had been installed, and servants waved away, Quizo spoke to him again. "The man the Bearded Ones were chasing is a distant relative of mine. He is also from the north, and perhaps you know him. His name is Chuqui Huaman. Swift Hawk was in the army of Quisquis, and fell wounded in the fighting on the heights above this city. He was sheltered in another house in Cuzco, but some of those who would have Manco as Inca lived there, and betrayed him. And so he fled the *suncasapa* through the streets."

Mike had not actually said that he himself was from the north; but let Quizo assume it if he chose. "No, I had not met Swift Hawk before. But I knew him for a valiant man when, wounded, he turned on the two sword-carriers and tried to fight them with a small knife. I was glad that I could give him help. Will he live or die?"

"My women tell me that he has stopped bleeding and is sleeping now. Tomorrow he may come and eat with us."

The sun was gone now from the atrium, and a servant came, to take the monkey in, maybe to where it could find some warmth beside a fire.

Quizo made it plain that his house was Roca's, however long the victor over the two Spaniards cared to stay there with his bride.

A few days passed in welcome rest. As Mike had expected, no repercussions developed from the brawl. He could picture the two Castilians coming to themselves, slowly and painfully, in an alien gutter. Its burbling stream, fresh from the Huatanay, might at least be cleaner than most European water supplies of the time, but he had arranged to have some chicha poured about them when they were dumped. When they rejoined their comrades, stinky with stale booze and weaponless, half-dead with blows and the aftereffects of an invisible radiation about which they could know nothing, unable to tell where they had been or what had happened, Pizarro would probably order them a dozen lashes each, as a reminder to keep out of trouble in the future, and lose no more steel weapons. Of necessity, the Governor ruled his men with a taut and sometimes ferocious discipline.

Mike's host did not go abroad wearing his sword. But Quizo brought it out to show, in the evenings when other men, all *pakoyoc* loaded about the ears with yellow metal, dropped in to dine, to drink, to sniff a little dope, above all to talk. Mike very soon confirmed what had already begun to seem distinctly probable: Quizo's house was a potential center of rebellion, against both the Spaniards and Manco's collaborationist faction of the native aristocracy. Once Quizo had described to his other guests the incident of the two Conquistadors, and had shown them the gatekeeper's old staff, whittled like a wooden butt for sword practice—Mike looking at it now experienced a certain queasy sensation in his gut—once Quizo had done this the other men all spoke freely in front of Mike, and much of their speech showed their disaffection. These grumbling magnates represented only a minority. Most of their peers in Cuzco were, at the moment, solidly behind Manco, whose time of official coronation was fast approaching.

Anyway, Quizo's cronies did not expect immediate renewal of civil war in Cuzco, or fear midnight arrests, though such things might come. The present situation among the Incas was, Mike thought, more like a vast and deadly family quarrel than anything else. Almost any two of the *pakoyoc*, if they looked back a few generations, could discover some blood relationship. The ruling class or tribe of Tawantinsuyu, whom he thought of as Incas though that name strictly belonged only to the ruler, formed in effect a single family of several thousand members. Each successive ruler might have scores of wives, and several times that many children, though not all considered legitimate. His chief wife was most likely his own full sister, and almost every one of the nobility shared to some extent in the blood royal.

"Roca Yupanqui has not said of which lineage he comes," one distinguished guest remarked one evening, glancing down the room in Mike's direction. Like so many distinguished beggars, these lords of Cuzco were all sitting on the floor, fingering chunks of meat out of little stewpots and drinking gravy.

Mike had given this expected question some advance thought. It was a point on which the Mask had been no help. In fact he had noticed that the Mask never seemed to care what its wearer said, but only what he did.

Now he paused for a sip of chicha. "When my head was injured by the enemy," he began, "much of my life before that time was taken from my memory. But to replace old things, new things were given. A vision, in which I struck down men in shining armor, and in which it was given to me to speak and understand their language. And more things were given, also, of which I may not yet speak. That I must serve the Inca faithfully was told me in the vision; and it was told me also that the details of my lineage and family no longer mattered, for the world of Tawantinsuyu is to be born anew."

The men looked closely at Mike and were impressed. The evening was rather quiet after that, until the time came for the visitors to take their leave.

It was now the middle of December, 1533. A couple of days after his remarks about his visions, another, smaller gathering took place in Quizo's house. This time besides Mike there was but a single guest, to whom Quizo himself deferred. Willak Umu, Servant of the Sun and high priest of Inti's Temple, who dwelt in its Golden Enclosure, *Coricancha*. The night before, Mike's Mask had shown him the visage of an unknown Indian man, stern and ascetic, who seemed to be beckoning him forward through a great golden doorway—and this man, Mike saw as he joined Quizo in welcoming their distinguished visitor, was Willak Umu.

When the social preliminaries had been disposed of, and the time for serious discussion was at hand, the high priest announced: "The Bearded Ones are insane with their craving for gold. And He-who-is-to-be-Inca indulges them in it. I fear that once his coronation is over, the most sacred treasures will not be spared."

"Quisquis may yet defeat Manco and the Spaniards," Quizo asserted doggedly. "They have not yet returned from pursuing him."

"Quisquis and his army have fought them time and again," the high priest pointed out. "At best they manage to break off battle before great numbers of our men are killed. At worst they are badly beaten. I do not think this time will be different."

Quizo was gloomily silent.

"I have decided," Willak Umu went on, "that there is some gold that must be saved. Already many gold plates have been pried from the walls of the Temple, to help make up Atahualpa's ransom. All will be taken in the end, down to the last speck, for the *suncasapa* are madmen in this regard."

There was a pause, the other men both waiting in silence for the high priest to continue. Mike suspected he knew what was coming, and the suspicion made a prickling down his neck.

"The great *punchao*," the high priest breathed. "The Sun at Dawn. At least we must save that, at any cost."

Quizo at once made a solemn sign of agreement. "I know a good place to hide the Sun," he offered quickly, as if he had already been making plans along that line. "How and when might it best be removed from the Temple?"

Mike had a thought on that subject, and when no one else seemed anxious to offer a plan, he put his into words. "Perhaps it could best be done on the day when Manco accepts the *maskapaycha* from the hand of the white man called Pizarro. All of the Bearded Ones, and all of the men of Tawantinsuyu who are now their allies, will be present at the ceremony."

"On that day I must be in the Square of Joy myself," said Willak Umu. "The Inca will require it."

"I also," Quizo put in.

"But not I," said Mike. "The Inca will not remember me, nor note my absence. And those of my lineage think that I am dead."

By the time the great day of coronation came, Mike had lost count of the exact date, but he thought it might be Christmas. Early in the morning Willak Umu sent to Quizo's house a half a dozen anonymously garbed men. Mike thought them probably some of the Temple's more fanatically trustworthy priests. They showed him to a litter emblazoned with the sun-signs of the Temple, hoisted him to their shoulders, and trotted off in its direction. Using the smaller streets, they moved against the flow of the crowds glimpsed on the main thoroughfares, who were headed from every outlying portion of the city and its suburbs toward the Square of Joy.

The outer Temple walls showed raw holes, where the mounting bolts for its gold-sheathing plates had been torn out some months ago in the futile garnering of Atahualpa's ransom. A small gate opened quickly when a bearer tapped. Mike was carried in and set down in a narrow space between the outer wall and the rear of one of the Temple buildings, while the low, trapezoidal gate was quickly barred again.

Another, larger doorway stood open to the interior of a building, a single vast and nearly empty chamber. Here too the stone walls were raw where gold plate had but recently been stripped away. Mike's escort walked ahead, he followed. Without warning, Coricancha burst upon his eyes.

The Enclosure of Gold was a courtyard within the Temple precincts, forming their heart, wide enough to be a park, completely open to the Sun. In the first shock of seeing it, all that was within it seemed to be brightly aflame with yellow light. Here for generations had labored the great artists and metalworkers of an empire. Into Coricancha now for a hundred years had come the Inca, to offer to Inti, upon the greatest occasions, the blood of snow-white llamas.

Twenty golden llamas, life-size, now made a motionless caravan across the court of Coricancha. Six large buildings fronted inward on the court, all but their rear roofs invisible from the streets outside. On all the rooftops facing toward the court, thatch of straw drawn from pure gold caught at the Sun and hurled it glinting downward. Below, the herders of the llamas, also full-sized, were golden too, down to their slings and staves, each figure of them a Midas dream of wealth.

In the center of this square of miracles, a massive golden fountain gushed with living water, not the molten yellow metal that the eye now half expected. Pure liquid gold would seem no more than what was required to nourish the long straight rows of maize, all silver, gold, electrum, no two plants quite alike, all life-sized and perfectly wrought down to the tiniest kernel. Gaping as he walked between the rows, Mike stumbled on a clod of earth . . . too hard for earth. He looked down. Pure gold, the size of his two fists, the outline of a golden weed hand-modeled on one side.

There came to him the thought of Tom, whose lifelong wish had been to get within reach of wealth like this, and who for a single golden Mask had thrown his life away. But even Tom in his worst fit of avarice would have seen more here than the mere weight of metal. Unlike the Spaniards, who like so many dragons would have as their first thought the idea of melting this down to make the handling easier, then sitting on it, hiding it away out of the reach of other thieves . . .

His chain of thought went glimmering. He was standing in front of what he had come here to see. Above the singing fountain in the center of Coricancha, fixed to a wall above an altar that was worth an emperor's ransom in itself, was that which could obliterate even the thought of golden life-sized llamas . . . *punchao*.

The word might mean simply daylight, or the appearance of the sun. Here it meant the face of Inti, shown as he came in majesty in the Andean dawn to wipe away the dark, the cold, to blind the stars and deny with his own immortality the fact of death. Round as the great sky-disc that now sent down its flame to share, and surrounded by long, radiant streaks all of pure gold, it was everywhere sparked and patterned with what must be sapphires, emeralds, diamonds. A Biscayan braggart, Manico Sierra de Leguizamo, was to claim that he had had this *punchao* in his possession one night in Cajamarca, and in a night of dissipation had gambled it away before the real sun could rise—his boast created a Spanish proverb, but few of his contemporaries believed him. Pizarro would never have suffered *this* to fall into any common soldier's hands. But no historian, in Mike's branch of history or Tupac's, would be able to say with any certainty where this *punchao* had really gone.

Coricancha numbed the mind of the newcomer, but to the priests who made up Mike's working crew it was their workaday world. Already one of them had brought out bronze and wooden tools from somewhere, and others were standing audaciously upon the altar, getting ready to detach the *punchao* from its mountings. Before laying tools to metal, however, they were pausing, looking at Mike. He must have been represented to them as a sorcerer of great power, whose orders were to be strictly followed in this enterprise. "To work," he told them, as decisively as he was able, and leaned back with folded arms against a llama worth no more (he guessed) than the New York State budget for a year.

The sun of noon was burning down, solstitially almost straight overhead. Soft bells—golden, no doubt—tinkled somewhere inside the Temple complex, and a procession of holy women filed into view, bearing gifts of food and drink to place before the Sun. Naturally, Mike thought, no one had remembered to tell the *mamacona* to keep out of the way today.

White-robed, demure, and graceful, the Chosen Women of the God passed one by one before the altar, the priests hopping awkwardly out of their way. There was one woman taller than the rest, with hair that looked almost blond where it escaped her veil. She couldn't be a native here, of course; some hostage or captive, then, from . . .

Where in the western hemisphere could she have come from?

Not only the hair. She looked like—

Mike took three steps, stood where she must almost run into him as she filed with the other gift-bearers back toward the women's cloister.

"Sal. Sally Zimmerman."

Her face was no more tanned than it had been at Key West, but it was vastly less prettified and harder and more real. It looked at him blankly for a moment, an Inca *mamacona*'s face startled by an exclamation in a foreign language; and then Sally Zimmerman inside it breached the surface, as if ascending from a long, breath-holding dive.

She didn't know him right away; he must have been changed far more than she. "Who?" she croaked in somehow rusty-sounding English. "What did you say?"

"I said your name, Sal. It's me—Mike. Mike Gabrieli." Maidens were piling up in confusion behind Sal where she had stalled, while the front half of the procession went on away from her with measured dignity.

"Mike. Oh, God help me. I thought that you were dead."

He took her by one loose sleeve and pulled her gently from the line, indicating with a nod to the women behind her that they should move along. "And I had some doubts about you." He was hissing at her almost angrily. "How did you get out of that house? Aunt . . . Aunt Whatsername's house?" At the moment he couldn't recall his own relatives properly. Of what lineage were they? "And what happened to the town?"

"Esperanza came for me. You know, the white-haired man—"

"I know."

From the distant Square of Joy, ten thousand voices roared; Manco Inca had perhaps just received the royal fringe from the invader's hand.

"Anyway, Esperanza got me out while those men were hunting you. He said Key West would be back to normal in a few hours, and nobody there would realize that anything weird had happened."

Some more priests were coming out of another building now, halfway across Coricancha; it was a busy day in the Temple, for what he had thought would be a secret mission.

Sally went on: "Esperanza said I had to come here for a time, for reasons of paradoxes and whatnot. I don't understand, but I've been going along." Her voice, growing anxiety and all, was becoming almost as he remembered it. "What else can we do?"

"I know the feeling."

Sal held his hand now, as if he might vanish otherwise. She said, "Tom wound up in this world, too."

"I know. I've . . . seen him."

"Have you?" Sal nodded past Mike's shoulder. "Here he comes now."

He started to turn, then tried to say something, then did turn. The priests who had just emerged from a building had separated. One of them was now coming toward Mike at a trot. The sun on a thousand fortunes of pure gold was transmuted into a strange kind of fire that burned out sense and reason from the brain. The metal maize stalks seemed to topple, the molten figures of llamas melted, wavering toward pure light.

"Mike! You ugly sonovabitch, you're still alive!" And even as he heard the words in the familiar voice, he knew that he was fainting.

12. Old Peak

As he sat in his and Cori's room in Quizo's house, the Mask was showing him another room inside another house of polygonal stone, wherein there stood another Masked figure, looking back at him. It was no mirror image; the other man's clothing was European-16, and a wisp of gray beard escaped incongruously from under the enigmatic smile of his Mask.

These last few days, Mike's Mask had brought him nothing but noise, and these apparently pointless visions of Pizarro. The Governor, too, was always Masked when Mike saw him, always alone and indoors. No doubt he was somewhere in the Casana, the palace of the mighty Inca Pachacuti, that Pizarro had commandeered for himself as the most magnificent on the Square. No doubt Pizarro also saw Mike; at least Mike was hoping and assuming that this apparent interference of the Masks was mutual, and that the Spaniard was as stymied by it as himself. Also Pizarro, thank heaven, probably had no means of guessing from which house or even which city his enigmatically Masked opponent was gazing back at him.

Mike heard a small noise and took his Mask off, trusting it to continue to block Pizarro's vision. He saw that Quizo had pushed the door curtain aside and come into the bedroom. The air was gray and chill with early dawn. Cori, who tended to be a slow morning starter except in conditions of emergency, stirred sleepily, bundled in a woolen blanket.

By now Quizo had seen the Mask several times and accepted it almost as Cori did, as nothing very surprising for a sorcerer to possess.

When he was sure that Mike was through with the Mask for the time being, Quizo said to him, "You and Cori, get up now. It is time to go."

This was a surprise. "Go where?"

Quizo only smiled, perhaps pleased that he could still surprise the visionary, and took himself away.

"Damn." It irritated Mike when people cutely refused to answer. But the general's directions were not given lightly, and he stirred Cori with a foot, found her already half awake. They both began to dress quickly. Not knowing what sort of journey Quizo had in mind, they packed their few valuable possessions about their persons.

Bowls of oatmeal-like *quinoa* were waiting for them in a common room on the ground floor, and out in a courtyard three litters stood with bearers ready. As he began on his hot cereal, Mike saw Quizo himself appear out there, obviously ready to board the first vehicle in line; Mike took Cori by the arm, and out they went.

He wished he could send a word to Tom, over in the Temple, before setting out on whatever expedition Quizo had planned. But someone would let Tom know. Mike got into the second litter in line, and looked back to see Cori step into the third. With a slight start, he now recognized that third one as the Temple litter with the false bottom, in which the *punchao*, disassembled, had been carried from the Temple here to Quizo's house. Eight sturdy-looking bearers grunted now as they heaved the vehicle to their shoulders. Obviously they were burdened with much more than Cori's slender weight.

Mike thought of Cori's curvy little bottom bouncing an inch above the lordly staring eye of Inti. Well, if the priests saw no sacrilege implied, he was not the one to suggest it to them. Actually, the more he thought about it, the less likely it seemed that Inti would object.

The house gate opened just before the litter train and closed again immediately it was through. The bearers moved at a quick pace, almost trotting. Avoiding the Square of Joy, where Spaniards were ever-present, and the eyes of the *yanacona*, most active collaborators, were the busiest, they traversed side streets to intercept the Royal Road that led out of the city to the west, the same road that Mike and Cori had entered Cuzco by.

As they departed the city, Mike closed the side curtains on his litter and tried on the Mask again, hoping to learn what this sudden journey might portend. Nothing but noise in his eyes, a color TV gone mad. Damn. Well, Pizarro was no doubt doing some damning of his own just now.

Mike put the Mask away but left the curtains drawn. He felt a sudden guilt at being carried about like an invalid on the backs of other men; never mind that the other men thought nothing of it and would have been surprised to know his feelings. Guilt had not assailed him on his ride to Coricancha and back the other day; he supposed his mind had been too busy then.

Damn again. It nagged him that he had not been able to talk to his brother today before leaving Cuzco.

Recovering from his faint in Coricancha a few days earlier, Mike had soon made sure that it was really Tom who stood before him. Only—and this doubt seemed to occur to both of them simultaneously—there was no immediately obvious way of making sure that they were Tom and Mike from the same branch of history.

"Tom, I tell you, goddamn it, I saw you lying there dead. All hacked up. Arms gone, legs gone, chest cut open." Mike recited it in an under-breath monotone, as if confessing some terrible fault. He drew a deep breath. "I got out of Mictlan with the Mask, no other way I could have made it. Of course if it wasn't for the Mask . . ."

"We'd neither of us be into this. Yeah." Tom nodded. "Yeah, that Mictlan sure sounds like hell. But I was never there."

They stood there talking English in their city-Georgia accents, and the folks at home would have thought them both made up for the minstrel show, if minstrel shows were still being given any-where. Tom looked dark and Indian, too, though he hadn't been changed as much as Mike. All around them the absurd golden wealth of Tawantinsuyu shimmered, as from a sun gone mad.

Tom said, "Look, that must have been—well, me, from another branch."

"I guess." Mike shook his head and wondered if he should try to laugh.

"Look, Mike, I don't *know* of anything bad that happened to you in my branch, I just assumed . . . Look, I left you that Mask in that red paint can, just like you found it. Then I went up to Miami Beach, like a real numbskull, didn't know what I was getting into. The Tenocha showed up, and I had a second or two to think, my God, what have I done to Mike, getting him involved? 'Course I didn't know then who in hell the Tenocha were, but I could see they were some bad onions. Just starting to give me a real rough time, when here comes the cavalry. Like John Wayne with all the trumpets blowing, let me tell you."

"Let me guess. Esperanza."

"That's him. How'd you know? Anyway, he got me out of that fight and dragged me off here, in what I first thought was only a helicopter. Here I discover he's already brought Sal. The priests here seem to think he's a ship captain, you know, one of those balsa-raft deals the Incas have. I guess they never get farther than a little bit up and down the coast. Believe me, I didn't know *what* was going on at first. You think you were confused, inside that Fort you told me about? I didn't have the advantages you did—of any orientation classes, or being given a regular course in the lan-guage.

"Anyway, I figured first that he was somehow peddling me and Sal as freaks, to Willak Umu, who I know now is the high priest of this establishment. At least I figured it was better than being murdered, which I was on the point of back home."

"I'll have to go along with that."

"Except now I'm realizing there must be more to it. He didn't bring Sal and me here just to help us out, the way he tells it. You know what I think?"

"What?"

Tom swept his arm about them. It took Mike a moment to understand. "Oh. The gold."

"Of course!" Tom glared at him for being stupid. "Sonovabitch! *Nobody's* going to let someone else carry off all this loot and melt it down, if he can prevent it. Esperanza wants it, just like the Spaniards do, but some of these paradox problems that he talks about prevent his just carting it away. We're here to play some part in helping him."

"Yeah." Mike nodded, then shook his head. "But we're all having a few greater problems than getting gold, in case you haven't noticed."

"Like what?"

Mike sighed. "Like people getting raped and murdered right and left."

"Oh, yeah, this war that Esperanza keeps mentioning, but he can't or won't explain it. War and politics go on. Hey, buddy, they've really changed you around. Look at your ears. With me it's basically just some dirt and sunburn. Hey, listen, have you got a razor? It's a hell of a job trying to keep shaved. Bronze butter-knives and old broken seashells, they use. Hey, you get yourself a little *coya* yet? One nice thing about bein' a priest here is there's none of this celibate nonsense. Poor Sal—I guess things are different for the girls."

"I guess. Listen, junior, if Esperanza wants you to be a priest and Sal a nun for a while, you just better stick with it. That's my advice."

Before Cuzco was many kilometers behind, the litter-bearers turned north, leaving the Cincasoyo Road that Mike and Cori had traveled earlier. Now they were on a branching road, equally well paved but not quite as broad. At the first *tambo* stop, near midday, where the bearers were replaced by waiting relief teams, Mike asked again: "Where are we going, Honored Quizo?"

Quizo's eyes almost twinkled. "Where the *suncasapa* will not come." Mike decided he was not going to repeat the question.

Shortly they were under way once more, Cori indicating with a helpless little shrug that this was a new part of the world to her also. Still going north, they made a long climb through a valley where lakes were visible on either side of the road. Then they passed a town. Mike leaned from his litter to ask a bearer, "Where are we now?"

"Chinchero."

If he had ever heard the name, it now meant nothing to him.

Making frequent rest stops, and now moving at a deliberate walk, the bearers by dusk came out on the bank of a large river that Mike, consulting hazy mental maps, tentatively identified as the Wilcanota. Gradually during the day he had shed most of his feeling of disgust at being carried, and by night had even stopped trying to lift his own litter by gripping at the side poles during difficult ascents.

That night they stayed at a large *tambo* near where the road began to run northwest along the river. Quizo camped in one small room and Mike and Cori in another, while their taciturn bearers tried to get along with some more convivial llama-drivers out in a common barracks. Talking privately with Mike, Cori confirmed that she had not seen this road before, and had no idea where they were going. They estimated that they had come twelve or fifteen miles during the day.

In the morning, Quizo roused bearers and passengers early, and they were on the road before the mists were gone. In a few hours they met a group of men trotting toward them; these turned out to be a relief crew of bearers arriving for a prearranged rendezvous. After all had shared a morning meal, the newcomers bore the litters on northwest, while those relieved hiked back toward Cuzco.

During the rest of the day the scenery grew ever more savage and spectacular, the climbs and descents steeper. The road branched again, left the Wilcanota behind and far below, shrank drastically in width, in places to a mere three feet, and burrowed twice in constricting rock-carved tunnels through jutting mountain shoulders. And once the wingtip feathers of a condor, soaring over an abyss, came so close to Mike's litter that he could have reached out to touch them, except that reaching out would have involved the risk of looking down. He gripped the side poles of his litter and tried to think of something else.

Out of nowhere, seemingly, appeared a military checkpoint, sheltered behind a low stone wall on a place of vantage where it seemed a half-dozen men should be able to throw back an army. A young officer wearing checkered tunic and bronze *canipu*, with feathered magic trailing from the rim of his dress shield, dropped to the road and halted the bearers with an upraised arm. Quizo stuck his head out through his curtains and spoke, and the officer bowed aside.

Past the checkpoint the road went down, to a nearby *tambo*, where the travelers spent the night. Mike and Cori were both lost, though he estimated they might be no more than thirty miles from Cuzco.

Sometime near mid-afternoon of the third day's travel, Quizo suddenly and unexpectedly called a halt. There seemed no human habitation near, and today they had seen no other traffic on the road. The only arable land in sight was forested, not planted.

Upon alighting, Quizo at once sent the bearers back whence they had come, taking his empty litter and Mike's with them. Cori's remained; she stood patiently beside it. Scarcely had the two empty litters vanished around a bend in the road, then down the mountainside above the travelers came six men in what Mike took to be a variation on priestly garb. These sturdy newcomers greeted Quizo with deference. Then they took up Cori's litter, without her, but still laden with its hidden burden of the Sun.

Leaving the road behind, Quizo led the way up the trackless hillside. In a fold of the land, one more small village waited—a couple of huts, rather, looking misplaced here in the wild. Then on up, into raw wilderness. Mike and Quizo several times had to give a hand in heaving the litter upward. If it were an honor for the nobility to bear the Inca, it could hardly be less of one to help Inti himself to a hiding place in time of peril.

There was timber ahead, and a hard climb brought them into it, Mike gasping, and the others showing some signs of strain. Shortly they emerged from the belt of trees. They had gone up and down so much since leaving Cuzco that Mike felt as uncertain about altitude as about location, but the timber indicated they were not at any extreme height.

Around them forbidding rocks grew steep, and steeper still. Quizo marched on like some patriarchal mountain goat. The muscles in his lean calves looked like the granite that they spurned behind. The rainy-season clouds had been gathering close above their heads when they started upward from the last huts, and now the climbers were going in among the clouds. The world closed down to small inclined planes of damp and slippery rock. White radiance brightened slowly and fitfully ahead as they climbed on.

There were flashes of blue and gold ahead, from the sun's lashing of the clouds' tops. Now brief glimpses of purged sky and hard-edged rock appeared in that clean light.

Mike came out atop a ridge, into a radiant world, where he found Quizo already standing with his arms outspread. The lowering sun, behind them as they reached the ridgetop, made Brocken specters of their shadows falling on the cloud-bank at their feet—seemingly gigantic images of themselves, shadowing vast clouds and whole mountains dimly glimpsed beyond. Round Mike's own shadow's head he saw the glory—meteorologists' jargon for a rainbow halo. He heard a suppressed little cry from Cori standing at his left, and saw Quizo at his right pull hairs from his eyebrows and blow them like kisses to the Sun. Quizo and Cori, Mike knew, must each have seen themselves, and no one else, honored by the glory, and must each have taken it as a great sign. Meanwhile the litter-bearers, perhaps in some humble wisdom born of greater experience on these heights, disregarded the meteorological phenomena and stuck with their job.

From the ridge on which they stood, the mountain went on even higher, and around it went the narrowest path yet. Mike thought at first that the litter was not going to make it, but those who carried it knew better. They shifted grips and bore it on without a pause.

At a point that Mike took to be about halfway round the mountain, the path broadened enough to give them all a place to rest. Here was posted a single sentry, who, unsurprised at their appearance, saluted Quizo casually with his javelin.

There was something that had begun to trouble Mike as he looked about him at these mountains, something less obvious than altitude or fear of falling. The great peaks, wooded and rocky jumbled together as far as the eye could see, with glimpses of

jungle lapping at their bases, and the voice of a great river somewhere far below—it was all oddly like a scene remembered. Déjà
vu taunted his mind and danced away. What name might this
river bear?

His earlier resolve against asking questions was momentarily
forgotten. Almost without thinking he tapped the nearest bearer
on the shoulder. "Where are we going?"

"*Wayna Picchu*," the cheerful answer came, the man meanwhile
pointing straight ahead.

New Peak? The panting refugee from the lowlands cautiously
edged a few inches forward. He saw a smooth mountain, standing
up to its waist in clouds. Something very familiar . . . but certainly
not part of the scenery around the Fort.

Mike edged on, past the resting men, where there was barely
room. The mountain that he stood on, he now saw, was connected
to New Peak by a high saddle of land, and on that saddle an Inca
city rode amid a herd of clouds. Below the crowding of its thatched
roofs and walls of polygonal stones, vertiginous terraces of varied
crops made stair steps down the mountain for a hundred meters
or so, before its sides steepened too much for even Andeans to
carve their farmland from it.

It hit him. Small wonder that this place looked familiar. He
had seen it in a hundred photographs, before he ever heard of
Tawantinsuyu. If that was New Peak over there, this mountain
that he clung to here would be, of course, Old Peak. In Quechua—

"Machu Picchu," said the bearer, and smiled a little to see how
much the warrior-sorcerer was impressed.

That was all in early January, when the terraces of Machu Picchu
were thick with crops, its cisterns brimming from the chill rains
that came each afternoon. It was not until May that Mike climbed
the same trail again, returning from his first journey out, he and
Quizo and Chuqui Huaman and a few others hiking up to the
secret city in the clouds. In May, 1534, the dry season had arrived,
water was being husbanded, the land resting. It was the month for
Inca armies to march forth to war. Quisquis was still in the field,
somewhere. But around Cuzco and Machu Picchu, all the land
was held in a troubled and unsettled peace.

Mike was impatient on the last leg of his journey back, urging
the others on. He was suddenly fearful that something bad had

happened to Cori during the weeks he had been gone on business of politics and the hunt. It was not a particularly rational fear—the Spaniards, in every branch of history that Mike knew about, had failed to discover Machu Picchu at all. In Mike's home branch, the very name—though not that of the homonymic mountain—had been forgotten, and the ruins of the lost city were rediscovered only in 1911, by an explorer from the United States.

In Machu Picchu the great Inca Huayna Capac, father of Atahualpa, Huascar, and Manco Inca, had rested sometimes from his long work of conquest. Here scores of cloistered holy women had worshiped at the shrines he had established. In 1534 there were still priests and Chosen Women here to serve those shrines, and there were artisans and physicians in residence. Mike thought of the latter and drew some comfort; when he had left Machu Picchu in April with Quizo, to attend the Inca at the Royal Hunt, Cori had suspected she was pregnant.

As he came round the ledge on New Peak, Mike saw that the terraces had not yet dried out; tropical vegetation still sprawled over the granite bones protruding here from ancient compound fractures of the earth. Now Quizo's elevated quarters came into view; somewhat less luxurious than those of his house in town, but usually well staffed with servitors and concubines. The general's windows loomed from a crag on the eastern side of the mountain, overlooking a mere sketch of a path below, which seemed to lead nowhere at all. At the end of that path the *punchao* had been hidden, in a crevice among gigantic shards of granite, almost impossible to reach by climbing. The face of the Sun had been swathed in heavy wrappings so no glint of it could shine forth, but otherwise left open to the sky.

And now his friends said good-bye with a few ribald jokes and let him hurry on ahead. Now he was on the final stairway leading up to the apartment that he and Cori shared, like garret-dwellers in the old-time Paris of any of a dozen known branches . . .

Cori must have been watching from a window, for here she came, barefoot and with her hair blowing wild. His heart jumped to see her safe, and he guessed she was not pregnant after all, for here she came running like an Olympic athlete down the stairs to greet him with an almost savage embrace.

"I missed you."

"I, too, oh so much."

He held her at arm's length, looked around. There was no one. In English he said, "You know something I've just realized, while we've been separated? You're my wife."

Cori started some kind of answer, giggled, started another, then half collapsed, contending with a mixture of emotions. "The women . . . ," she got out finally, "the women here have been asking me . . . when and where we were married . . . and I have had to put them off."

"That first night in the *tambo* together; give them that date. And tell them anything you like about where. Tell them in Coricancha if you want to. Willak Umu himself will say that is so, if I request it."

Later, with Inca nightlife going on in the city round them, dancers' bells and flutes and pipes announcing a mild celebration of the return of the men who had walked out into a changing world and come back safely, Mike leaned on a high windowsill, feeling like a peer of the Moon, and looked out across Machu Picchu in the night. Mike drew in a chestful of the air. He no longer minded the cold of the high mountains, though at great elevations his breathing still troubled him and he knew there could be bad long-term effects from the altitude. But this was not the night for worrying. Below him was spread a world of sugarloaf mountains, enchanted waterfalls in moonlight, the endless rumble of the Urubamba far below—fantastic land and plants and clouds and sky.

Now he was telling Cori of his journey. "So Quisquis was driven clear back into the north, and the Inca returned to Jauja, to rest from the campaign and entertain his Spanish guests. Therefore the hunt . . . Quizo and I met Swift Hawk there—remember him?"

"Of course. Has Chuqui Huaman recovered from his wounds?"

"Oh, yes. In fact he was just back from Teocajas, where another great battle was fought not long ago. That place is—how shall we measure it?—about a hundred miles south of Quito. One of Pizarro's chief men, Sebastian de Benalcazar, was leading about two hundred *suncasapa*, chasing rumors of gold in that direction. They shattered an army of some tens of thousands, under Ruminavi, old Stony Eyes. From what I hear about Ruminavi, he must be a man a lot like Quizo.

"Anyway, when Quizo heard about this fighting, ending in another bloody defeat, he bit his tongue—I mean he really bit it, I think deliberately in grief and anger, so I could see the blood running from his mouth. Then Quizo spoke of joining Quisquis in the field, but Willak Umu and I persuaded him he should stay loyal to the Inca and wait for the time when Manco's mind can be changed about the Spaniards.

"Then of course we had the great hunt. I suppose you know what they are like, if you haven't seen one. Ten thousand beaters make a circle, whoop it up with lots of noise, drive all the game into closer and closer confinement. When the animals are almost on top of each other, all in a panic, the *pakoyoc* grab up their favorite weapons and jump in, killing or trying to kill whatever they like, from puma and bear to ground squirrel."

"And did you enjoy the hunt, brave husband?"

"I . . . yes, I guess I did. It was exciting. The Spaniards I believe really thought it was pretty tame stuff. Mostly they watched, though they were polite about it and took part to some extent. It was in Pizarro's honor, after all, that Manco ordered the hunt to be held."

"Then did you meet the *sapa* Inca?"

"Yeah." Alone together, he and Cori still mixed English into their speech. "I got to crawl up before his throne, barefoot, with this little pack they put on your back as a symbol of subservience. Manco said something like 'How are you?' and I answered 'Fine, Your Majesty,' or words to that effect. I was a little worried that he might ask what province I was supposed to be from, or how my job was coming along, but Willak Umu and Quizo were there to back me up in case of awkward questions. Hell, there must be hundreds of the nobility around that Manco can't recognize on sight, or know what branch of the tribe they're from, or what their job is supposed to be. He talks more to the Spaniards than to us." The "us" came out quite naturally, and only afterward did he have a peculiar feeling about it.

Cori sat curled up, leaning against the wall, a woolen blanket round her legs. "Tell me more about the Inca. What does he look like?"

"Oh. Handsome, I guess. In his very early twenties, looks even younger. He seems flattered by having a man like Pizarro bowing to him, listening closely, asking his opinions on everything. Pizarro's quite a diplomat, along with his other talents . . . wait, though. As I kept telling Quizo and the other—wait."

"Mike." She hesitated. "You know the things that are to come. Is it not so?"

"Not quite. I have a—call it a special knowledge of what *ought* to happen, sometimes." He had carried the Mask with him to Jauja, but had not used it there, fearing that Pizarro in one of their Mask-to-Mask confrontations would see from the background that his mysterious opponent was nearby. He wondered if Pizarro had given up trying to use his Mask also; watching the man at Jauja, Mike had been unable to get any hint of his plans.

"Anyway, Cori, one thing I'm anxious to tell you, something I'm excited about. At the battle of Teocajas, Chuqui Huaman captured a Spanish horse, alive, and he's still got it. He brought back one of those mummified horse-hooves, too, that Willak Umu and the other priests all crave. But the live animal is what interests me, and it's near here now, grazing in one of those meadows down by the river. Under a strong guard, of course."

"What do you want of Swift Hawk's horse? Not just a chance to ride on it, I don't suppose."

"No. I've played with the idea of getting other horses, breeding them, equipping cavalry of our own. But that would take too many years—years we don't have. Still, the horse is in my plans—at least indirectly."

Cori got up and came to join him at the window, kissed him, then moodily paced away. "Roca, how many *suncasapa* are there in Tawantinsuyu now?"

"There must be about a thousand." He grimaced. "The newcomers are no doubt the greediest of the bunch, kicking themselves for not having got here in the first wave, when they imagine they would have been able to plunge in right away, up to their armpits in loose gold. Some of 'em wouldn't have enjoyed that first march over the mountains with Pizarro, though, or the sight of Atahualpa's army outside Cajamarca. Nor will they enjoy what's coming in a year or two."

"What is coming?" Cori had an entrancing way of liking to listen to him, even when it seemed she must know what he was going to say.

He moved away from the window. "We must fight the *suncasapa*. Drive them out. That was really my job at the Fort, and it still is. And it is the job of all the Inca people, too."

"But if the Fort has fallen, and our armies could not kill the Bearded Ones when they were but a hundred and sixty . . ." Cori clenched small fists. "How shall we kill them when they are a thousand? And when half the empire's subject tribes are anxious to make cause with them?"

"Their own cruelty will cost them allies. It's more than cruelty. Through sheer indifference they will starve whole peoples and tribes. Make life impossible for whole nations, something no Inca ever did as supreme ruler. As for how to fight the Spaniards—it can be done. I feel sure that we can find ways. But the time is not yet ripe. The Inca himself must lead his people back to war."

Next day Mike met in conference with Chuqui Huaman, Quizo Yupanqui, Willak Umu, and others. The theme was the war yet to come, the rebellion which must rid Tawantinsuyu of its conquerors. After some flowery rhetoric had been disposed of, tactics, strategy, and weapons were all on the agenda.

Mike had some thoughts he had been developing on all of these. Take weaponry, for example. He had to face the fact that he was no Connecticut Yankee master of all trades, able to teach the metalworkers of Tawantinsuyu how to improve their bronze until it might compete, edge against edge, with Spanish steel. No, whatever improvements he could achieve in the way of hardware would have to be put into effect by native craftsmen using the skills and materials already at hand; and the improved weapons would have to be usable by infantry, preferably with only a minimum of special training.

What were the world's master war technologists of the sixteenth century, the Europeans, doing on their home battlefields to offset the inherent advantage of cavalry? Not using firearms, or anyway not yet using firearms with any convincing success. Gunpowder was on the verge of transforming warfare, but only on the verge. If Pizarro had relied on the best arquebuses and cannon available as his chief weapons, he would not likely have survived his first battle in Tawantinsuyu. Anyway, the technological difficulties in the way of his, Mike's, trying to arm the Indians with machine guns or even muskets were of course insurmountable.

Then there were the famed English yeomen, who with their longbows at Agincourt a little over a hundred years ago had mowed down the charging armored flower of French chivalry. But Mike suspected he wouldn't be able to make a good longbow if he tried, and was certain that he wouldn't be able to use it properly; he had read somewhere that years of practice had been required. The Inca armies already included companies of archers, tribesmen from the Antisuyo, where trees grew plentifully and choice wood for bows or anything else was readily available. But the men who could use those bows did not thrive here in the high country where the key battles must be fought; and Mike doubted also that their weapons were as powerful as the English yew was said to be, capable of driving a slender wooden shaft right through a metal breastplate at close range.

And, now that he thought about it, the defensive armor of the Conquistadors was no doubt better than that of the French more than a century earlier. With a sigh, Mike gave up all thought of archery.

Try again. In this fourth decade of the sixteenth century, just who were the best infantry in Europe, and why? Once he had put the problem in that form to himself, a sunburst like Inti's face seemed to explode above his mental landscape. Of course!

To the leaders who had assembled grimly today to hear him, Mike said, "In the part of the world from which the *suncasapa* come, there is one land with many high, steep mountains, even such as stand here in the center of Tawantinsuyu. Few men of that mountainous land own horses. They go to war on foot, as do the Incas. Yet never is their country successfully invaded by the surrounding tribes of men in armor. And the fighting men of that land are even in great demand as soldiers elsewhere."

Not one voice was raised to ask him how he knew all this. It was accepted as a sorcerer's vision; whether it was accepted as true was another question.

Swift Hawk tasted his tobacco, a delicacy esteemed and used as snuff among the aristocracy. In a voice that held both real interest and polite doubt, he asked, "And can these men who fight on foot beat equal numbers mounted on horses?" He viewed his captured horse—and rightly—as a great prize.

Mike took thought. "Yes, they sometimes can. They cannot out-run the men who ride. But they can stand against them."

Quizo asked, "In open fields?"

Memory presented the untimely suspicion that Agincourt's field had been a bog. But that was irrelevant to the capabilities of the

Swiss. "It is so. If the Honored Quizo will place at my disposal a blademaker and a good carpenter who has worked on weapons, I will soon have something to show him."

"It will be done."

The talk moved on to strategy and tactics. Reading history with a few hundred years' hindsight had enabled Mike to come up with some thoughts on those subjects, too. But he kept quiet for the time being, not wishing to be cast as the upstart who knew all things better than his elders. First, to get the weapons working.

The longest piece of wood readily available within the walls of Machu Picchu was a spare roof beam, about three meters from end to end. Mike conferred with Quizo, and the two of them searched various buildings for longer timbers that might conveniently be taken out and used. Nothing more satisfactory was located, and messengers were dispatched to the forested Antisuyo, their knotted *quipus* jiggling as they ran.

Meanwhile Mike set the artisans in metal and wood to work upon the nine-foot roofing beam, supervising them closely at every step. The result, which he could show to Quizo and the others two days later, was quite close to his memory of what an eight-foot halberd ought to look like. The tough shaft had been trimmed of excess weight, and a long bronze head bound on with metal straps and riveted securely. On one of its sides the head was an ax-shaped blade, and on the opposite side a pick-point curved into a hook. In the middle, it rose as a short spearhead, in a straight continuation of the shaft.

The bronze points and edge were not going to penetrate steel armor. But they could certainly damage any exposed limbs of the rider or his horse, while the man who wielded the halberd stayed out of range at least of the horseman's sword, though not his lance. Therefore the new weapon was already an improvement over the *makana*, or the bronze-studded mace. But the hook, of course, was the real key to the halberd's effectiveness. It could catch on armor that it could not pierce, or dig into exposed flesh or clothing, and give the man on foot a fighting chance to pull a rider from his horse.

Maybe nine times out of ten, thought Mike, the halberdier on foot would lose against the mounted knight; when evenly matched, maybe nineteen times out of twenty. Still, even those odds when translated into casualty statistics would mean a great improvement over the Incas' record thus far against the Spaniards. And the combats to come would not often be simply even. Numbers remained one of the chief Inca advantages.

Quizo and the others looked thoughtfully at what the workmen had wrought, but they had little comment yet to make. A real test was going to have to be arranged; how else could a man know anything about a weapon?

It took a few days for the timbers to be brought from a hundred miles or so away, and a mile or two less altitude. Borne most of the way on human backs, they came as ordered, twenty feet long and perfect. Another Inca strong point, probably more valuable than mere numerical superiority, was a genius for logistics, for getting men and material to where they were needed at the proper time, and with a surprising degree of secrecy when it was called for. Again Mike and his mechanics went to work, this time with Quizo and other anxious warriors frequently hovering near.

The trial was held some thousands of feet below the high saddle of Machu Picchu, in a broad meadow beside the Urubamba. Here for some days now, Swift Hawk's captured horse had fattened with its grazing. Two peasant worker-soldiers came along, draftees sent into war as needed and then replanted in the soil. Mike had put in several hours' practice with them, putting them through a drill he had devised as he went along. The pikes were about five meters, or some sixteen feet, in length. Their business ends, normally to be long, bronze spearpoints, had been left blunt for this trial and were padded with quilted cotton armor bound on tightly. At Mike's suggestion, Chuqui Huaman's horse had also been well quilted, as if for a bullfight.

Swift Hawk leaped onto the animal's bare back with a skill and confidence that showed he, too, had been practicing, probably for more than a few hours. He waved aside the blunt imitation of a Spanish lance that Mike had had prepared, and instead grabbed from an aide what he proclaimed to be his own favorite weapon, a wood-bladed *makana*, much like the one Quizo had been prepared to wield in his courtyard in Cuzco.

Mike and his two pikemen took their places at one end of the meadow; Swift Hawk urged his animal to the other end, then turned it round. The trial was to be one against three, if they counted only the number of human contestants; if instead they went by weight and strength, the odds swung sharply to the other side. No one was trying to kill today, but Mike fully expected that this was going to be a damn sight rougher than any football game that he had ever seen.

Once again, with mouth dry and hands sweating, he knew the feeling of the little man on foot awaiting the centaur-monster's onrush. But this time, with the stout wooden shaft of the halberd in his hands, and flanked by pikemen who—he hoped—were not going to turn and run, the feeling remained endurable.

Chuqui Huaman kicked his animal in the ribs, urging it forward.

"Ground your weapons," Mike growled in Quechua to his troops, and saw to his relief that they remembered what the command meant. As he had taught them, hoping he was teaching correctly what seemed the only sensible tactic to repel a charge, they squatted to dig the butts of their weapons deep into the turf, meanwhile holding their points at the height of the horse's chest. They swiveled their pikeshafts steadily to keep them aimed at their charging opponent.

Swift Hawk came on, letting out wild yells. Mike raised his halberd, looking for the chance to use it, remembering coldly that the Mask had shown him nothing one way or another about this game, and hoping that he would neither be trampled to death nor make an utter ass of himself.

At the last moment the nerve of one of the pikemen failed, or else he lost a good grip upon his weapon. The long shaft was knocked twisting from his hands by a blow from the *makana*; but Swift Hawk, confronted by those leveled shafts, had also turned at the last moment, or else his horse had simply shied away from impact. Now the horse skidded sideways, its flank being punished by the other pike, whose owner wrestled gamely to hold control of it. The triangle of forces overcame brute weight and strength; the animal cried out and reared, nearly throwing its self-taught, unsaddled rider.

Now, thought Mike, moving to step in. But he was too unpracticed and too slow. Tugging on the horse's mane, Swift Hawk wheeled his mount and raced away. At the other end of the meadow he turned again. The man whooped out another war cry, and man and horse, both savagely tough, came back for another charge. Swift Hawk's face was contorted, as if for real war, and he had his own deadly weapon upraised to strike. He couldn't be intending to kill. Could he? The cotton helmet on Mike's head felt suddenly as thin as tissue paper.

This time Chuqui Huaman veered his animal completely around the pikes, then curved back toward Mike. But the momentum of the charge was broken, and the horse ready now to shy away. Mike managed to parry the *makana* when it swung at him. He made an effort to snag the rider with his bronze hook, but missed wildly. He was reminded—not that he needed reminding—that in this business of using hand weapons he was an utter beginner playing with professionals. By this time Swift Hawk was halfway down the meadow, turning his horse. And now here he came again.

The rider faked right, faked left, then tried to go between the pikes. Whether through cleverness or luck, one of the novice pikemen raised his point at the last moment. The horseman took the padded impact full in the chest and went off neatly over his horse's rump. The riderless horse shied off; Mike stepped forward, a little late but going through the motions, and brought his halberd down. He meant to pull the punch, but the weapon was too top-heavy to be perfectly controlled. Swift Hawk, trying impulsively to jump up, got enough of a knock on the head to stretch him flat and motionless.

In a moment Quizo, Willak Umu, and the other warriors were swarming about the combatants, gabbling as excitedly as boys in a playground. Swift Hawk's head was prodded and pronounced unbroken, and his knockout dismissed as nothing more than a good joke. Quizo and the pikemen, all differences in rank and dignity forgotten for the moment, got into a spirited argument as to how the weapons must be gripped. Meanwhile the high priest was declaring that he wanted to try the halberd himself.

As predicted, Swift Hawk began to come around in a few moments. Shortly he was on his feet, frowning when he heard a laugh or two, and claiming loudly that his horse had tripped beneath him. In a few minutes the game was on again, this time with the Honored Quizo swinging the halberd, at some peril to his pikemen. Mike took a turn with one of the long weapons, wanting to get the feel of how it must be held.

Again, on the first try, Swift Hawk got around the pikes—although had there been an entire rank of pikemen for him to try to outflank, it would obviously have been a different story. His weapon and Quizo's clashed, clashed again—and then, as the horse ran past the man on foot, the halberd's hook snared Chuqui Huaman neatly by the tunic. A moment later he was once more stretched out on the grass.

The workout went on a little longer, but nothing happened to seriously change the results of the test thus far. The horseman was unable to simply run over his adversaries or drive them from their chosen positions. On the other hand, Chuqui Huaman lacked Spanish arms and armor, and he had had no chance to develop methods of attack. Climbing their slow way home toward Machu Picchu, the Incas were still doubtful. Quizo was obviously intrigued and pleased by pikes and halberds, but Willak Umu noted that there was more than the tactical effectiveness of the new weapons to be considered.

Said the high priest: "It will take many tall trees to thus equip an army."

"Trees can be cut and carried," Quizo answered doggedly.

Willak Umu sighed. "And even if the weapons were all at hand to be distributed, the Inca would not hear of it. He still embraces the *suncasapa* as his friends."

"We must wait until the right time comes," said Mike. "But we must be ready when it does."

The high priest was returning at once to Cuzco, and the bearers waiting to carry his chair away were lounging, squatting, beside the place where the trail started. Except for one who waited standing, a little apart from the others. An old man for a bearer. Also his nose looked rather large. Mike walked closer.

"You," he said in English.

"You can get a lot of meaning into a monosyllable, Mike. I see you're doing well."

"A raft captain last year and a porter now; you are really managing all this, aren't you? Including me."

"Because I drop in for a word of conversation now and then, you think I'm running the show? If you only knew the effort these simple visits cost me. If I were really managing all this, as you put it, I'd force you to tell me what I want to know instead of asking for information like a beggar."

"You always want to know something. I'm always supposed to give answers, but I never get any."

"Mike, if I try to tell you anything, put an idea into your head that's not already there, chances are I'll have to leave abruptly. It's the way paradoxes work. Now, I can tell you *that*, because it seems you already know it. But no more than the Incas of Tupac's time can I drop information into this past, for it is my past, too."

"Sure, you just come to get information. What do you want to know this time?"

"As always, your intentions as Mask-wearer. And I believe I have already discovered them, thanks to being able to watch the demonstration today."

Mike looked around. Everyone else was busy chatting; no one seemed to be paying any attention to his conversation with a porter. He looked back. "You arranged for the Mask to fall into my hands, didn't you?"

Esperanza shrugged. "I'll try to answer that. If I should vanish suddenly in midsentence—well. What I did was to drop the Mask into your branch of history. It then—selected—you. Much as a computer—which the Mask is, among other things—comes up with a particular number in answer to a particular problem.

"Pizarro's Mask and yours are of course in a sense the same, though our enemies have selected him much as I have chosen you. In a year or two, when you and he come into direct opposition, only one of you will be able to—"

And that was it. Willak Umu's crew was starting back for Cuzco a man short, but Mike was willing to bet that no one would ever notice it.

13. Manco

Cuzco, Peru, 1535–36

"It's the lady *coya* that we want, Señor Inca. All this silver is fine, but she's the one we're after!"

Gonzalo Pizarro was speaking, one of Francisco's much younger brothers, surrounded by half a dozen of his compatriots, all heavily armed. Not the Gonzalo whom Mike had knocked out, but resembling that one. And he was speaking now to Manco Inca, all of them standing in the Square of Joy in front of Manco's just-completed house. "Palace" would have seemed too grand a word for this edifice; it was dwarfed by Pachacuti's old palace next to it, the Casana that had been taken over by the Governor.

Manco looked noticeably older than he had at the Royal Hunt a year and a half ago, the last time Mike had seen him. Manco in the gateway of his new house also looked half paralyzed, like a man who did not know which way to turn. Not, after three years of occupation, so much incredulous that this foreign gangster should be demanding his—the Inca's—principal and most beautiful wife. But incredulous that such an offense could have become not only conceivable but something to be expected. So Mike put it to himself.

It was December again, and the afternoon summer rains were threatening. Cori and the baby were doing well, but she wasn't ready for any arduous trips yet, and Mike had left her in Machu Picchu while he made this first journey into Cuzco for more than a year. He had not needed the sputtering Mask to tell him that the time was ripe for eventful change in the capital; his studies of history had told him that. All the histories spoke of this scene that was now before him.

Quizo had come into the city with Mike, the two of them intending to go straight to the Temple and talk with Willak Umu, but before they had crossed the Square they had been distracted by the confrontation going on in front of Manco's house. Mike and Quizo stopped at a few meters' distance from the scene, watching and listening. Here they had also found the man they were looking for. Willak Umu stood at Manco's side, scowling toward Gonzalo Pizarro and his crew of bullyboys.

At the Spaniards' feet in the sand of the Square were bags and boxes spilling silver. There were *canipu*, necklaces with gems, ornaments for limbs and hair, small boxes, combs, and mirrors. No gold was visible in this offering; probably Manco had none left to give, or at least none that he was going to sacrifice in an effort to retain a wife.

"I can find no more gold, Señor Gonzalo." In the last couple of years, Manco had learned passable Spanish. "These presents are yours; my wives are mine. Now bother me no more."

Francisco would never have bothered him in this way. He preferred to keep the Conquest on friendly terms as long as possible. Nor would Hernando de Soto or many of the other leaders. But Francisco was far off on the coast, overseeing the construction of Ciudad de los Reyes, the city that would one day be called Lima, and as his *corregidors* in Cuzco he had named his brothers Gonzalo and Juan.

So now Gonzalo only grinned. "Ah, Señor Inca, I really can't stand it anymore, this waiting. We know the *coya*'s in your house—now bring her out. I have heard marvelous things about her beauty, and I want to get a good look."

Juan Pizarro, a younger and handsomer version of Gonzalo, had become aware of Mike and Quizo standing nearby. He turned halfway toward them, one eyebrow faintly questioning, one hand moving with slow assurance toward his sword hilt. Manco now turned to the newcomers also; he stepped forward out of his gateway and with a gesture of his head indicated that they should go through it into his house. Meanwhile the high priest stood unmoving, confronting the Spaniards with a fixed glare.

Inside the gate, Mike paused at the door of the house itself, turning back and trying to see what was going on out in the Square. He had the stun-maser in his belt, but he wanted to let the day's events run out their normal course, of great importance for the future.

"What's up?" The words were English. Tom, his priestly garments hung on him carelessly, had come out of the house to stand with Mike. Meanwhile Quizo had gone on inside, perhaps finding the Inca's degradation too much to watch.

"Trouble," Mike whispered. "But according to plan." Then he looked more closely at his brother. "Last I heard, you were still living at the Temple."

"Dominicans ran all of us priests out, and Manco is putting some of us up here." Tom found it funny enough to grin about. "Spaniards are getting ready to build a church over there, I think. Thought I might try out my altar-boy Latin on 'em, but I decided not."

"Good thinking," said Mike dryly. Then he pulled his brother back into the house, for here came Manco stalking in through the gate, Willak Umu a step and a half behind him.

Mike and Tom, with Quizo and various members of the household, all bowed aside from the doorway as the Inca swept in. Only one faced him—a lovely woman who must be Cura Ocllo, his sister, wife, and queen. As she came out of an inner room, Manco seemed to have a little trouble looking her straight in the eye. Instead he swept a sharp glance round him at the others. "Where is Inguill?" he demanded.

Cura Ocllo took a step forward, and as if there were no one else around, addressed her husband familiarly. "What do you want with her?"

This time he did not drop his eyes, but blustered. He barked at his queen to be quiet and snatched the royal shawl from her head. "I tell you, send me the woman you have named Inguill. It must be her or you, and *they* do not know your face. What other comely women have I left? In all Cuzco there is hardly one that they have not already raped."

Bowing her bare head, a hand to her face, the *coya* retreated into the room from which she had emerged. The witnesses were standing with bowed heads, hearing and seeing no evil, and Mike made haste to drop his own eyes when Manco again swept an angry glance around. But Mike looked up a moment later, in time to see Sally Zimmerman coming out of the *coya*'s quarters.

Her relief was evident when she saw him and his brother. "Tom? Mike?" Manco had turned away. "What is this? I don't understand what they want me to do."

Tom said, in English, "Nothing you haven't done before, the way it looks."

Manco had been gathering queenly garments from fluttering servant girls, and now he turned on Sal and thrust them at her. "You will go to the men outside, and you will say to them that you are the *coya*."

"You'd better do it," Mike advised when Sally turned her puzzled face to him.

Tom took her arm and spoke in English. "It's some of the Spaniards. Look, Sal, your going with them could mean a hell of a big chance."

Sal said nothing, but kept on looking fearfully at Tom, while the maidservants started to gown her as the queen.

"What I mean, try to find out where the gold is stashed." This whispered in English.

Meanwhile, Willak Umu could no longer hold his peace. Giving Manco a look that verged on the rebellious, he stalked outside. Mike slid over to resume his former station at the door, where by looking out through the open gate he could observe a large part of the Square. He could not hear exactly what the high priest was saying out there to the Conquistadors, but Gonzalo Pizarro's answer came back loud and clear.

"Who said you could talk that way to the King's *corregidor*? Don't you know what kind of men we Spaniards are? By the King's life, if you don't shut up, I'll play such games with you and your friends that you will never forget them. I'll cut you up alive!" The words were no figure of speech; they were uttered by a man with his hand on the meat cutter at his side.

Willak Umu did not condescend to retort, apparently, but neither did his erect figure retreat a centimeter. Tension in the Square remained drawn, like a steel cable near the breaking point, until the women had finished their hasty work on Sally and had thrust her out the door.

Her face was partly covered now, but her eyes flashed, bluer than any Indian's should be, and her figure was tall and voluptuous under the shawl.

There was a moment of silence, and then a joyous shout went up from the Spaniards. "Señor Inca!" Gonzalo bellowed, "let me have her right away! I can't stand waiting any longer."

Manco had come out just behind Sal, shoving her impersonally forward. "Yes, congratulations. I give her to you. Do what you like."

Gonzalo had never thought of doing otherwise. He grabbed Sal by an arm and pulled her close, then used both hands to grapple. He put aside her shawl and kissed her full on the mouth, employing vast energy if no finesse. Manco, and even Willak Umu, whose brow had been ready to hurl lightning, were suddenly laughing in sheer amazement. That a man should act so in public, with a woman whose face he had not even seen before!

Sally took it quite differently, cried out, and fought herself halfway free. "What is this?" she burst out, mixing Quechua and English. "I will run away rather than face such people!"

"You will go with them!" Manco roared. Her eyes passed quickly over other faces, from which she might once have expected help. Then she ceased to struggle. Gonzalo loaded her with his share of the silver to carry, bags and boxes, before he and his party left the Square of Joy.

It was tough on Sally, but then there were other people in this war who had things even tougher. And Mike hadn't dared to try to change that scene. The woman Inguill, sent off with the rapists in place of the queen, was in the history books already. That Inguill could be Sally . . . He reminded himself there was more to time travel and branching history than he was prepared to try to understand.

Quizo had gone off somewhere on his own, too bitter, perhaps, to speak to anyone. Mike, Tom, and Willak Umu walked now toward the Temple through the changed streets of the city. Mike had expected the city to be changed, but still the reality was shocking. Random rubbish was strewn about, and animal droppings splotched the pavement. Here and there Spaniards' graffiti marked the superb masonry of the walls.

But the worst changes of course were in the people. Inca beggars had begun to lounge in front of the Casana and elsewhere, asking for food when a Spaniard or *pakoyoc* passed. Idlers not quite beggars sat at gates and sills along the streets. The children passing were often dull-eyed and fat with the starchy obesity of the ill-fed.

Mike found the golden straw all vanished from the roofs of Coricancha. Nothing had replaced it; many of the roof beams had fallen in. Gone, of course, were the golden llamas, with their herders, the rows of maize, the altar—the treasure all gone, like stuff that dreams are made of.

At the edge of a pile of rubble where a wall had recently been knocked down, a young priest of Christ, in a brown habit, stood arguing with a minor priest of the Sun.

"When your high priest returns," the Dominican was saying, in slow and careful Spanish, "tell him that I was here, wishing to talk to him. He will remember me, Cristobal de Molina, from Almagro's expedition to the south last winter. We often walked together, he and I, and talked . . . "

Molina's eyes followed the shifting attention of the man that he was talking to. "Ah," he said then. "Willak Umu." His pronunciation was bad, but he was trying; Quechua didn't fit easily on a Spanish tongue. He picked his way across the rubble to stand before the taller Inca. "My friend—I do think of you as my friend. I am relieved to see that you came back in good health from the south."

Willak Umu looked at him, as if from atop a mountain peak, or riding on a cloud.

"I have just been speaking to Bishop Valverde about you, Willak Umu," the priest went on. "It is his hope and mine that you will come to know the One True God."

"His name is gold?" the Indian asked.

The priest flushed, looked down, tried to look back, then burst out at last in heartfelt emotion. "High priest, I am sorry!" he cried.

"I know what you must think, for few of the Indians that Almagro took south as porters and bearers are still alive, and fewer still of those whom we met along the way. After you—departed, escaped, what you will—I saw things that I do not want to remember, but I cannot forget. Spaniards having their horses' newborn colts born in litters by Indian women, who themselves were weak with starvation. Cruelties without cause . . ."

Willak Umu was looking at him. Through him, rather.

"I am sorry!" Molina cried again. "But you—you must not judge the Church of Christ by the wrong that men do, who claim it as their own."

In his agitation he would have paced about, but the broken stones about him made him stumble. Then, as if changing the subject, the Christian priest began to explain that the Church of Santo Domingo was soon to be built on this site of Coricancha. Already some Indians who seemed to have nothing else to do had been set to work removing the old buildings . . .

Mike had turned away, and was the first to see—without surprise—Manco come pacing toward them, unattended in the street. Mike reached out to touch Willak Umu on the arm.

The rubble of the Temple about his feet, Manco faced them all, and again, something about him had been changed. "Gonzalo Pizarro has taken my wife, after all."

The deception had not worked—at least not for more than a matter of minutes. Sally had got away from the Spaniards, but not before a couple of them had abused her. But they had the real *coya* now, had carried her off almost under Manco's nose.

At a meeting held in his house that day as the shadows of the western hills lengthened over the city, Manco declared: "I have decided. I am no longer Inca, if I am willing to remain in this city now, swallowing the insults I have suffered. Time and again these men have offered me outrages. One night I was forced to flee this house, when looters and vandals came into my very bedroom . . ."

It was all going right on schedule, thought Mike, with a mixture of anxiety and grim fatalism. Tonight the Inca was going to sneak out of the city. And tomorrow . . .

Mike had made sure not to be chosen as part of the escaping monarch's retinue, by announcing ahead of time that he was compelled to work some special sorcery that very night. He would rejoin the *sapa Inca* later, wherever Manco might be; so he pledged in fealty, and was sent on his way.

Others at the meeting were not so loyal. Manco's litter had not got far beyond the city limits when the sounds of mounted pursuit echoed along the narrow streets and out onto the Royal Road. Mike listened from inside Quizo's house. He put a calming hand on the old general's arm. The time was not yet; these scenes still had to be allowed to play. Manco was petulant, Manco was hurt, Manco was angry—but not yet enough.

Presently a drawn-out scream came through the night. The Spaniards had caught one of the Inca's party, caught him and twisted a rope around his genitals, trying to force him to tell which way the Inca had gone. But they learned nothing and had to press the chase in several directions. This, with mounted speed, they could do successfully. Manco was overtaken, mouthing weak excuses for his sudden departure from Cuzco, while all the others of his entourage fled. Manco was bound and dragged back to his capital like a taken thief. Gonzalo Pizarro chained him up, tossed the keys to some of his less-civilized underlings, and went back to bed. For a few days following, other problems and activities claimed most of the *corregidor*'s attention, and Manco was left helpless in the charge of Francisco de Solares, Alonso de Mesa, Alonso de Toro, Pedro Pizarro (an adolescent cousin of the Governor), and Gregorio Setiel. They stole what silver remained in Manco's house and amused themselves by raping his remaining wives before his eyes. For sport one night they burned his eyelashes with a lighted candle, and on a wager tried to push the candle up his nose without extinguishing the flame. Another night, three-quarters drunk, some of them urinated on the Inca.

Mike did not see Manco again until January, on the day that Juan Pizarro ordered his release. This was after the Inca had been chained to a wall for the better part of two weeks. Rumors of his maltreatment had reached the ears of Juan, who had forebodings that in the court of the Emperor Charles it would not be thought fitting that any monarch, even the veriest heathen puppet, be so abused. Charles had been royally displeased by the execution of Atahualpa a few years ago. No king liked to see another king badly treated at the hands of a mere viceroy or governor; there was something about *lese majesty* that kings found offensive.

Meanwhile, Francisco Pizarro had still not returned, and was not expected soon. Juan was very brave and handsome, and smarter than Gonzalo, certainly, but still he was not among the most perceptive and intelligent of men.

"Señor Inca," he stated, having just seen the chains unlocked and cast aside, "if all the things that you allege are true, it is very, very—*annoying* that you have been so treated. This I understand, and you have my sympathy. On the other hand, this is a province governed under the Emperor Charles, and you must conform to the wishes of the Governor sent by His Majesty, and to the orders of that Governor's *corregidors* when he himself is absent. Your duties require that you remain in Cuzco."

"I see now that I must." Manco's voice was ordinary. He had not rubbed his wrists when the chains fell off.

"Good. I hear that you have been studying your letters, and have read in Christian books. Have you learned much, Señor Inca?"

"*Sí.* I have learned much."

A bone-chilling drizzle was falling when they walked outside, Manco, Willak Umu, Mike.

Manco, looking ten years older than when he had tried to flee the city, pulled his cloak about him. "We will wait for the end of the rains," he said simply, almost absently, looking around the Square. Then he drew a deep breath.

He was quiet, too, at the start of the meeting convened that night inside his Cuzco house. But in the middle of the first tentative discussion of future policy, he rose and stalked from the room. He came back gripping in one hand the wooden foot-plow that he had been forced to use, for want of the old sacred golden implement, in breaking ground at the festival of Inti Raymi almost a year ago. He gripped the foot-plow in one hand, as if it were a straw, though he was not large of frame; and the foot-plow and his whole frame were shaking.

Most of the men assembled cowered down and raised their cloaks to hide their eyes when they beheld their Inca coming back. Manco raised the foot-plow at arm's length and swung it down amidst them, smashing furniture and pottery.

"*Haylli!*" He roared out in a voice suddenly terrible; even Mike, cowering with the others, closed his eyes under his raised cloak.

"*Haylli!*" The farmer's word for plowing, spading, subjugation of the land. And also his war cry, yelled out when smashing skulls and bones in battle.

Pretending to be going to conduct some religious ceremonies and to gather more hidden gold—which latter suggestion worked on his captors' monomania to rob them of their senses—Manco Inca left Cuzco with Willak Umu, free as a bird, on 18 April 1536. It was Wednesday of Holy Week. The end of the rainy season was almost at hand.

14. The Last Giving

Peru/Tawantinsuyu, 1536

The ten thousand thatched roofs of Cuzco were on fire, and the smoke of their burning rolled up in a great pall across the glaring face of Inti. Would that Quisquis, slain by his own rebellious captains in the north, had lived to see this day—and also Ruminavi, executed at last by the invaders when they had taken Quito.

Now, out on the northern hillsides above the capital, the massed legions of Quizo Yupanqui, Tiso, other generals of every faction, had diverted most of the rivers' water, making swampy ground to hamper the city's horsemen if they should sally out, and also cutting down on the water available in the city for fighting fire.

Thus far none of the Spaniards in Cuzco had tried either to sally out or to fight the holocaust of flame. There were fewer than two hundred of them, busily fortifying themselves in a few buildings around the Square. The rebellion had struck them with stunning surprise. Before the Conquistadors were even sure that the departed Manco planned to strike at them, Inca logistic genius had invested Cuzco with an army of a hundred thousand men, mainly peasants freed for the season from the land.

Francisco Pizarro, not to learn for a few more days the full story of what was happening in the interior, was at Ciudad de los Reyes, the city that was to be Lima, with a few hundred more of his compatriots; and an equal number of Spaniards were scattered about on more or less isolated estates, *encomiendas*; many of these were dying today, in simultaneously timed isolated ambushes and skirmishes.

Manco's men had succeeded in occupying Sacsahuaman before the Spaniards in Cuzco were alerted, and now along one of its vast terraces the Inca rode upon a captured horse, bellowing war cries at an unending column of his troops who marched toward the city itself. Trotting to keep near his emperor's side, Willak Umu also shouted.

Riding a general's litter amid a phalanx of two hundred pikemen, Mike answered them with a salute, bowing his head and stretching out his arms. He then felt reflexively at his side, making sure the Mask was in his belt-pouch, though it had been totally useless now for months.

It was near mid-morning of a clear day, except for smoke, as Mike led the troops that he had armed and trained into the first attack on Cuzco. Again he felt at his belt, this time making sure that his unit of the two-way radios was where he could get at it handily. Cori had the other unit with her at Machu Picchu, where she still nursed their firstborn son; if it hadn't been for the baby, he would have had a devil of a time trying to keep her out of the combat zone, where thousands of other women had come to share the risks of battle with their men.

As the encircling army launched its first general attack, inside Cuzco were those who had been too inert, too apathetic, or too terrified of Manco to flee; the last category included a few thousand active allies and collaborators of the Spaniards, most from tribes with old, unhealed enmities against the Inca.

The roofs of the city's houses nearest to the Fortress of the Speckled Hawk had been set afire early this morning by red-hot stones hurled from slings that smoked and burned in half after a toss or two. The straw of the roofs was dry and the wind favorable, and fire had leaped into the city from house to house, almost as fast as a man might walk.

Through twisting streets, between scorched walls whose roof timbers had already burned away, Mike's specially trained hundreds pressed into the city, with thousands of the Inca host advancing on their right and left. The smell of burning choked; the streets were almost impassable in places with hot debris from the buildings. Three ranks in front marched in close order, pikes ready; the bronze spearpoints of the second rank bristled three feet behind those of the first, and those of the third rank were an equal distance behind. Let the Spaniards charge if they dare, and hurl themselves upon this porcupine.

So Mike bragged in his own mind, until the horsemen did appear, a score of them at an intersection some fifty meters ahead. Then he turned his head, calling to his reserves to close up ranks behind him.

Ahead, the cavalry turned off on the side street and vanished in a roaring column. Maybe they had seen the pikes and were going back to headquarters to report this innovative weaponry. But here, as his men advanced, was the side street now coming onto his flank. He shouted to move some of his men into a defensive guard there.

Barely had three short ranks maneuvered into position than from around the curve of the street the horsemen came. The toothed hedge of pike-points frustrated their charge, and Mike heard cries of Castilian outrage. The Spaniards were too professional to obligingly impale themselves or their mounts. Jockeying their horses near the pikes, they used their swords to lop off some of the bronze heads.

But now a swarm of the Inca's forces came howling, leaping, dancing on the bare walls that lined the streets, where for once they stood higher than their mounted adversaries. A hail of slung stones struck the Spaniards at close range, denting helms, bruising horses, thudding into padded armor and ricocheting harmlessly from steel. The men on the walls flung javelins, and when the cavalry came in reach, swung down at them with halberd, mace, and *makana*.

The leader of the cavalry—was it Juan Pizarro? Mike could not be sure—cried out orders, and his men's horses wheeled in orderly retreat. Mike also had to shout, to keep his own ranks from dissolving in a disorganized pursuit. He took all the time he needed to get his men re-formed in perfect order; only then did he order the advance cautiously resumed.

When at last he could climb a broken wall and look out upon the Square of Joy, he beheld it swept by such a rain of slung stones that he did not dare order his men out into the open to try the cavalry again. From positions among the denuded, blackened remnants of buildings on this side of the Square, thousands of slingers were sending a continuous spray of missiles across at the Casana, whose roof had somehow miraculously escaped burning. Those wide, trapezoidal doorways over there, behind which the enemy must have gone to earth, were beginning to fill up, as if the hurled stones were drifting snow. No man standing in those doorways could have survived for a second.

Fierce as the barrage was, it conferred no great military advantage when it could not be followed up with a charge across the Square. Mike spent some time sending messages to his neighboring commanders, trying to coordinate a plan of action. But communications were poor, and the native discipline too loose. As the slingers ran out of ammunition or decided that they had performed heroically enough for one day, they simply retired, usually as stragglers.

Meanwhile, incoming messages to Mike's command post consisted mainly of rumors that the cavalry was outside the city, ravaging Indians in the open and threatening to retake Sacsahuaman. Not knowing what to believe, but playing it safe, Mike marched his troops back through the city, looking for action. When he finally returned to it, the fortress was quite secure. Still on his horse and in a fever of excitement, Manco rode up and demanded a full report from the front lines.

Again in mid-afternoon Mike marched his pikemen out, toward rumored heavy fighting in the area of Quizo's house. Buildings were still burning there, and Andean bodies littered the streets for a couple of blocks, but all was quiet. Coming back wearily to Sacsahuaman near sunset, he found Tom waiting for him.

"How'd it go out there?" his brother asked, coming up to his litter before it was set down. "You look about half dead."

"I am. And we didn't accomplish much." With darkness, the day's fighting would be over—unless the Spaniards came out on some desperate midnight sally. They might try that, but not tonight. They must be utterly exhausted and would need the time to tend their wounds, try to strengthen their defenses, and grab some rest. If Manco and Willak Umu could only be persuaded to launch a night attack of their own . . . but that did not seem likely; the Moon was not in the right phase. Mike was going to try again to argue the point; he had requested an audience with Manco.

"Talk to you, Mike."

"Come along. I've got to sit down somewhere, get some rest." He had been carried back and forth all day in a litter, but yet his throat and lungs and even his arms and legs felt worn, as if he had been fighting for hours with every muscle. Casual horror scenes from the day kept belching up into his memory; he had yet to see a dead Spaniard, though a few reportedly had been killed. Their bodies were evidently torn to pieces at once, or dragged quickly to the rear so the embalmers could quickly begin the process of making their skins into ritual drums. But the day's dead Indians would not march quietly out of his awareness. One little, two little . . .

In a quiet upper room of the fortress, Mike let himself sink down to rest. "What is it?"

"You know what, Mike? This ain't your war, now, is it, really?"

"It ain't your gold, either. How's Sal?"

Tom sat back, looking almost hurt. "All right the last I saw of her. She's camping here, too—there's a lot of DPs here from the upper classes. Look, what's with you—all this volunteering for the front lines? What're you gonna get out of it?"

"Try and take Sal out of here. If events run true to historical form, the Spaniards are going to be doing some bad things to the women that they capture as the siege goes on."

"Take her where? Anyway, I guess they already did a few bad things to Sal. She gives bad reports of Gonzalo Pizarro's friends."

"All right." Mike sighed. "I'll talk to someone, get you two shipped out to Machu Picchu. When I say 'bad things,' I mean like cutting their hands off. It's called terrorism, and sometimes it works."

"Oh." Tom was squelched for the time being.

. . . guiltily Mike caught himself up from slumber. He must have dozed off, trying to talk to Tom.

It was a day since he had looked into the Mask, and now he pulled it from the pouch at his side. It showed him Pizarro, looking back at him from inside whitewashed walls. This time the Conquistador held a small flask in his hands, and as soon as visual contact was made he sprayed and sprinkled what it held in Mike's direction.

Holy water, no doubt. Mike made an insulting Inca gesture back at the Governor, followed by one that he had seen some Spaniards use. Pizarro must be getting really worried; he must have learned by now of Manco's getaway, if not of the general revolt. He would not take that first piece of intelligence as lightly as his brothers had at first.

Now Mike put the Mask away, got his small radio out, checked for recorded messages and found none. He had to call three or four times before Cori answered, but she was still safe in Machu Picchu and in good health, as was the baby. She had been changing a diaper.

"Little mother, have you decided yet what we should call him?"

"Father Roca, as I keep telling you, it is too early for a real name. Right now he is only a *wawa*."

He and Cori had talked for a little while, when he looked up to see Chuqui Huaman standing near, waiting politely for the sorcerer's attention; the Inca was now willing to give Roca the audience he had asked for. Mike hastily signed off and followed Swift Hawk.

He found Manco now in an exalted state, almost as if the triumph were already won. Evidently Manco had just finished confession, for Mike caught a glimpse of the high priest dropping into a sewer a small bag with woven symbols on it that might well contain the royal sins.

This time there was no crawling before Manco with a symbolic burden; this was an army headquarters in the field, and anyway Mike had the feeling that a lot of protocol had been left in the Casana's prison cell. He shook off his tiredness as best he could, and delivered his arguments on tactics and strategy, which were mainly these:

The scattered skirmishes around the country could be allowed to take care of themselves, provided decisive battles could be won at two places. First, here at Cuzco, the Inca's sacred heartland. Second, on the coast at Ciudad de los Reyes, where Pizarro now had his back against the sea but still retained a solid beachhead and could eventually receive strong reinforcement.

Mike pleaded that the battle at Cuzco, against a surrounded and vastly outnumbered garrison, could surely be won even without new weapons, if attacks were pressed day and night without a pause. Willak Umu must dispense for the duration with all religious ceremonies and taboos regarding the phases of the Moon. Also, Manco should commit no more than ten thousand of his troops to the attack at one time, recalling them after an hour or so and sending in ten thousand fresh. Another ten thousand should be kept in resting reserve, ready for emergency, and ten thousand more set working on such construction projects related to the siege as might seem useful. The remaining thousands should rest and eat and sleep; in a few hours, their time to fight or work would come.

The Spaniards' discipline and equipment might make them, man for man, a vastly superior military machine; but not even supermen could fight around the clock and around the calendar without rest.

It had already begun to grow on Mike, however, and the conviction was strengthened in him even as he spoke, that the key to victory was really not here, but at the coast. Pizarro and his Mask were there for one thing; and if the Spaniards' beachhead were wiped out, none of their forces trapped in the interior could reasonably hope for victory.

When Mike asked to be allowed to lead his pikemen to the coast, the Child of the Sun gave permission. He would march with Quizo Yupanqui, who had been put in command of the army attacking there.

Mike's litter rode behind Quizo's through the mountain country that defended Cuzco from the sea. In a narrow defile on the upper pampas, amid landscape that made that around Machu Picchu seem merely hilly, Quizo's picked legions caught Gonzalo de Tapia's force of seventy cavalry in the neck of a difficult pass. Tapia had been sent inland by Francisco Pizarro to try to relieve Cuzco. Tons of rock were toppled onto his men, confined on a narrow road where they could neither defend themselves nor flee. They were wiped out except for a pair of wounded prisoners.

Quizo mourned that all the horses had been killed. The two prisoners, their hands impartially bound, through one of them seemed to have a broken arm, the flesh of their shoulders threaded with ropes to lead them by, were sent stumbling along on the way back to Cuzco, a gift to Manco Inca from his most successful general. Seventy *suncasapa* wiped out at a blow!

That night Mike lay awake, wrapped in wool beneath Andean stars, seeing the faces of the two tortured Europeans. If he had seen Inca cruelty before that of Cajamarca or Mictlan, which side would he now be on? With a little effort he could argue himself free of the troubling question—or ninety percent free, anyway.

The next morning, a *chusqui* came gasping over the mountains from the east to report that the Spaniards in Cuzco had succeeded in making a foray out of the city, getting far enough to massacre a thousand Inca troops in the plain behind Sacsahuaman. The pikes had stood against them fairly well, but still the enemy had been able to outmaneuver the plodding infantry and strike where conventionally armed troops could be thrown into a rout.

"And has the fortress fallen to them?" Mike asked.

"No." The messenger was surprised by the question.

Mike relaxed a little. The siege of Cuzco was progressing somewhat better than it would have if he had not laid violent hands upon its history.

A day or two later, and miles closer to the coast, Quizo fought another victorious battle, this time in the high country near Parcos, his forces wiping out another thirty mounted men. This time the pikes played a part, blocking the Spaniards' egress from a tight spot, but the day could have been won without them, such a powerful ally was geography when it could be used to best advantage. The acceleration of gravity on boulders weighing tons provided a weapon that even tanks could not have resisted. But Mike and his special corps of pike and halberd played a larger role in the next fight, near Jauja. There Quizo took a score or two of Spaniards by surprise in their encampment and, after a struggle of several hours, exterminated them to the last man.

The marching and fighting through the mountains took weeks. Quizo was very careful and methodical. All passes must be blocked and held, while reinforcements and supplies were fed into Quizo's army, and he maneuvered it toward the city by the sea.

It was the month of Purification and Sacrifice—Mike had to stop and think to recall that it was also August. He radioed Cori to leave the baby with a nursemaid and go to the town of Abancay.

She quickly agreed, and added: "Mike, there is good news. Tom and his wife are here."

"His wife? A tall woman with fair hair?"

"Has he more than one wife? I thought one wife only was the custom in your land. Yes, that is she. He calls her Sal."

"Okay, I was expecting they'd show up." Thinking, Mike bared his teeth. Of course he didn't want Tom getting slaughtered at Cuzco, but it also might be touchy to have him poking around at Machu Picchu, where the *punchao* was hidden. "Tell him to come with you to Abancay, and the woman, too. If they argue, put them on the radio to talk with me."

"I will do it."

From the radio he shifted to the Mask, in which he caught Pizarro. The Governor was also wearing his golden smile, as he always was when the two of them made their tenuous contacts in this way. Mike's opponent sat on the doorsill of a house in tropic sunshine, lush low-altitude flowers growing profusely around him. And there was such grim weariness in the lean figure's pose under that face of serene and ageless metal that Mike was reminded of Marceau on stage, miming the maskmaker who cannot tear off the smiling false face from his own . . . In the background Mike saw a girl he thought must be the teenaged Ines, as the Spaniards had christened her. She was Pizarro's favorite concubine, playing now with their two tiny children.

A great and sudden shout went up in Quizo's camp. Mike stripped off his own Mask, put it away, and stuck his head out of the tiny tent he had acquired for purposes of sorcery. Around him was the vast bivouac of the Inca army, filling a broad draw between two rows of gentle hills. When he climbed the line of hills to the west, he could see in the distance the city that would one day be Lima—or instead, depending on how the fighting went, would soon revert to being part of a coastal desert. The new buildings shimmered with the heat and distance, and just beyond them lay the incredible sea, to whom all centuries were almost one. From Quizo's encampment the land generally sloped and smoothed toward that sea and city, in the last mile or so becoming practically level. On that flat solid ground, ideal for cavalry, Pizarro was going to have to be finally beaten. If history flowed on in its unaltered course, Quizo's army would be shattered in the attempt, the back of the rebellion broken.

Around Mike now, men and women leaped and whooped and danced in jubilation. Before he could reach Quizo's swarming tent, he had the news from a dozen voices: Cuzco had fallen after three months of bloody, deadly struggle. Mike let out an Indian whoop and leaped himself, then paused for a moment of more private satisfaction. The chains of history had been broken!

When Quizo had a chance, he greeted Mike and reported the details. Juan Pizarro had died in battle. Gonzalo had been captured, had lived a day with feet and hands cut off, and then his skin had been stretched and made into a drum, the mouth left open so that when the belly was beaten puffs of sound would come from between those glossy-bearded cheeks. It would be a prize exhibit in the Inca archives of conquered enemies. Only a few Spanish prisoners remained alive. Their fate was still uncertain.

Quizo's face turned grim, as he reported a second item of news that had come with the same runner. The Inca sent orders that Ciudad de los Reyes be attacked and destroyed at all costs. Francisco Pizarro was to be taken alive if possible.

There was a third important piece of information, told by the messenger on his own initiative. He and the men before him who had sped the news through the mountains had seen and heard Illyapa the Thunderer preparing to enter combat. It was not yet the season of rain, and the sky remained cloudless, yet they had seen lightning flash from horizon to horizon among the peaks, and had heard the reverberations of its sound.

On hearing this, Mike hurried back to his own tent, where he found that his radio had just produced a printout: THIS TIME THEY WERE THE ONES WHO HAD TO STICK THEIR NECKS OUT, AND WE WERE READY. KEEP UP THE GOOD WORK. TUPAC.

But Tupac's legions could not come down to help on the plain before Ciudad de los Reyes. Because of omens witnessed, Quizo had decided that he and other leaders must march and fight on foot this day. The general exposed himself in the front rank for the attack on the city, his chief lieutenants marching at his side except for Mike, who insisted on staying within his square of pikemen. Mike also wished for the better view of the field that a litter would have given him, but that he could not have. When the hills had been left behind the marching host, and cries from ahead announced the coming of the Spanish cavalry, Mike put on his Mask and wore it openly.

Pizarro must have seen the gold face flash from afar and certainly understood its importance, for he diverted the full weight of his cavalry in Mike's direction, bypassing the exact Inca center where Quizo walked. And this time the Governor himself was mounted, leading the charge with leveled lance.

Mike gripped his halberd in two hands and shouted orders at his men. Around them rose the whining of ten thousand slings, with war chants, whoops, and yodels. The thundering of hooves built up to drown out all other sounds.

Through a sleet of stones the cavalry hurtled against the massed pikemen and halberdiers. The Inca line bent backward in the center, but it did not break. Mike saw Quizo and the other marching generals vanish behind a cloud of dust. But there was no sudden rout, no slaughter of the Indians as the historians had recorded for this day. The mass of men on foot resisted the disciplined, concentrated pressure of horse and steel, and then surged back in counterattack.

Through whorls of violence and dust Mike could see the Spaniards, having to fight like madmen now to try to extricate themselves. Many were surrounded by masses of foot soldiers who could not be simply brushed aside. He had a good view of one horse, hooked by a dozen halberds, pulled screaming off its feet, its rider vanishing beneath a mass of Indians.

The neat ranks of pikemen had dissolved now, but not before achieving their purpose. Most of the Spaniards were entangled, either as individuals or small groups, within the great mass of their enemies. There was savage fighting on every hand, men being dragged from their horses screaming, horses screaming, too. As at Cajamarca, the bang of musket and arquebus sounded, but almost unheeded now. And horses once more lost their footing on piles of Indian dead.

From somewhere a horse came to knock him down. Senses reeling for the moment, Mike had one clear thought: I knew I'd never get through this alive. He had lost his halberd and groped for his stun-maser. The Mask was still on his face, and its eyes were clear, though it projected no useful images.

He had been knocked down among Indian dead men, still warm of course, one still twitching, another quiet, gray-haired, too old for this nonsense . . .

. . . gray-haired, and with a big nose, and an awful lance-wound that had gone right through his throat . . .

For some endless time, Mike stayed there on hands and knees, staring down at Esperanza. Maybe this death was no more real than Tom's had been. Maybe . . .

Something warned him to get up. Here came Pizarro on his mount, cutting and thrusting right and left, his bare face contorted into a theatrical mask of murderous fury, driving straight toward the Indian man on foot who wore the Mask of gold.

Feeling numb, Mike brought the stun-maser up. But before he squeezed the trigger, Pizarro had gone down, pulled from his horse by a bronze hook.

He used the maser, though, stunning three Indians in order to be himself the first to reach the fallen Governor's saddlebags. Even as he rummaged in them, he kept looking right and left for the effort the other Spaniards must make to rescue their fallen leader. There was none, no last charge to glory. Mike realized then that the battle was over.

No time, though, to savor victory. Now in his hands he held Pizarro's Mask, unmistakable though wrapped in layers of padding. Mike tore the wrappers away and at once raised the thing, strung with a silver cord, to his own face.

While it attuned itself to him, presenting first opacity, then noise, then spotty visions, he could hear Pizarro somewhere nearby, still alive, profaning, praying, snarling at the brown hands that held him down, perhaps hoping to be killed quickly. Then Mike, following firm new visions, ignored the Governor and headed for the city as fast as he could trot. His legs drove hard, his lungs drank in the rich, thick air.

Some buildings in the city were already burning; some of the victors already claiming loot, bickering above the noise of scattered fights still going on. In the streets, some of the Indian women who had attached themselves to the Conquistadors were behaving hysterically. Mike yelled at them to follow him.

He strode boldly into the *casa* that had been the Governor's, moved furniture, raised boards, and shouted into a secret cellar for Ines, telling her to bring her children out, to follow him and they would not be harmed.

Carrying one baby part of the way himself, he saw her and other dependents to the harbor, where in the name of Quizo he barked out orders that one of the Spanish ships captured in moorings be preserved, her crew held safe on shore. Aboard her he placed the women and children he had managed to rescue, and then, with the Mask's help, he picked out men to post as guards. This accomplished, with Pizarro's Mask still on his face and his own at his belt, he hiked back to confer with Quizo.

As he strode amid howling looters, smoke, and flame, Mike checked his radio and found a new printout: ROCA, WHERE

ARE YOU? REPORT IN. STAND BY FOR FURTHER ORDERS. TUPAC.

"A few things to get done first," he said aloud in English, without turning on the transmitter. The device was vibrating faintly in his hand, though; another communication coming.

REPORT IMMEDIATELY ON PIZARRO'S STATUS. STAND CLEAR OF THE MASK. WE ARE GOING TO DESTROY IT BY REMOTE CONTROL.

Mike bared his teeth, this time in what was really a smile. Of course Tupac's destroying the thing at a distance was easily conceivable. But Tupac's taking the trouble to warn a now-useless mercenary first was a little harder to believe. And this power of destruction must have been magically acquired just today, or it would have been used long ago. Evidently Tupac had a good idea of where Mike was, knew that Ciudad de los Reyes had just been taken, and therefore that the Mask-wearer Pizarro had somehow been brought down to defeat.

There was Quizo, not far ahead, blowing kiss after kiss of thanksgiving toward the sun at zenith. Waiting to approach the general, Mike raised his radio to his lips. No need to choose a channel; Tupac would be listening to them all.

"Roca reporting. Francisco Pizarro is now Quizo Yupanqui's prisoner; I hope and expect that he'll be brought before Manco essentially undamaged."

While delivering this message, Mike received more instructions from the Mask he wore. He thought a moment or two, then switched to the radio channel on which Cori should be standing by

"Cori, we've won here. I'm all right, but it's not all over yet. There's something you and I put on a shelf once, that second time I helped you get down from a mountain. Get that thing for me now—it's going to be needed. I hope to see you soon."

His wife acknowledged briskly and signed off. The wording of his instructions might have been obscure enough to put any listening enemies off a little. But mainly he was relying on the Mask that had ordered her mission to help her through with it.

Turning his back on the burning city that would never become Lima, and on the victory celebration of Quizo's thousands, Mike started to walk back to the deserted hills. Going alone up one of their barren slopes, he could feel the radio vibrating faintly, and smiled a little. Sorry, Tupac. Now I do things my way.

But why not talk back to him now? Mike pulled out the communicator, took one look at the last printout and almost dropped it. MIKE, THIS IS ESPERANZA.

He switched quickly to audio, and heard:

" . . . recording before the battle for Ciudad de los Reyes, but it's only going to be sent to you afterward, if I don't get back here and turn off the transmitter." It was the unmistakable resonant voice, speaking English.

"Now for once I'm not asking you anything, Mike, and can tell one or two things at least. Because if you ever hear this, the chances are overwhelming that I will be dead, and out of reach of any paradox.

"I'm going into the fighting today, carrying one of your pikes—there are good scientific reasons why I can now do this much, but can do nothing more than this, to help the cause. So this much I must do, because the cause is so important.

"Keep up the good fight, Mike. Human civilization, way down the line, depends on it. Of course that's true most of the time, for all of us, though we may not think of it till we start doubling back in time. There are more pivotal moments in each branch of history than you'd guess.

"Anyway, good luck to you, and your wife and child, and to your brother and Sal. Get them all home if you can. People of my time will be standing by to help, if you can win in Tawantinsuyu-16."

Distracted by Esperanza's words, Mike jumped when he saw the red sigil on the descending flyer's side. Then he remembered. Cori set it down on a small rise and ran to embrace him as he came running toward her. Behind her, Tom, awkwardly carrying a bronze-tipped mace, and Sally, a dagger at her waist.

The first greetings over, Tom stepped back, staring at his brother's still-covered face. "You're wearing it all the time now?"

"For a little while longer."

At this indication, Cori got back into the pilot's seat. "Where are we going, my husband?"

"Fly north." The imaged flyer projected for him by the Mask was tearing a hole in the air in that direction. "I may take over the controls later."

For several minutes Mike closely watched the next series of pictures presented by the Mask. Then he took it off.

"What's the matter?" asked Sal, getting the first good look at his face.

He gave them all a brief smile. "If all goes well, we'll soon be on our way home—all of us." He tried to show Cori some reassurance. "The *wawa*, too."

"What're you doing now?" This was Tom. "M'God, you got two of 'em now."

Mike had pulled some cord from a locker and was now binding the two Masks tightly together, back-to-back, making a Janus-head, as one of them had shown him how to do it. "Just getting ready."

"For what?" Sal's voice was taut.

"The end of the war." If he started trying to explain now, Tom would argue and maybe even fight. Mike still had the pistol, but he wanted to avoid that route.

"Bear about five degrees east, Cori." Of course he no longer had an image in the sky for guidance, but he was looking over her shoulder at the panel, and he knew their destination.

"Five east it is."

THIS IS TUPAC. REPORT IN. EMERGENCY. It was coming in on the flyer's communicator as well as the little belt-worn ones.

"Oh, all right. What the hell." He answered while looking forward past Cori's shoulder, to where the wild, deserted-looking mountain country around Cotopaxi was illuminated with irregular flashes, bright as Inti's face, sudden as Illyapa's thunderclaps. "Rocky here, Tupac. Looks like you're having a little action now around Cotopaxi. What was the name of that place you once told me about? Mictlan?" From the corner of his eye, Mike saw Tom's startled face turn in his direction. The Mask had shown Mike what was happening in the north. As Manco had assailed Cuzco in the south, there, too, an Inca host surrounded entrenched enemies.

THIS IS TUPAC INCA, ORDERING YOU TO REPORT IN FULL. HAVE YOU PIZARRO'S MASK?

Tupac didn't say *the* Mask, this time. Maybe at headquarters they were catching on at last.

"Yessir, I do. And my own Mask as well. Relax. You've been trusting me with one for four years now, though you didn't know it. I'm not a politician. You can trust me a little longer."

WHAT ARE YOUR PLANS?

"Now you sound like someone else I used to know. I'm not discussing secrets on the radio." Probably it would make no difference at this stage if he did, but let them stew a little longer.

Without warning, advanced weaponry from Cuzco-23 began swatting at the flyer. A couple of near-misses were deafening. Sal cowered, Tom grabbed at Mike's arm, mouthing "What the hell is this?" His voice inaudible beneath the noise. Looking back, Mike saw two fast Inca flyers that had risen in pursuit, colliding with each other now, by accident, of course, one disintegrating in a brief flash after their wings had brushed.

As the noise diminished, he could hear Tupac raging on open channels, chewing out the commanders amid whose cragged emplacements the flyer passed unharmed. It was passing through the siege-ring around Cotopaxi, and Tupac wanted to get his forces out of the way of the double Mask-bearer, the augmented avalanche.

Even as the Inca barrage fell silent, the Tenochas opened up, their fury obscuring the cone of Cotopaxi, still distant but now swelling rapidly. They were not impressed with the red insignia, but their efforts were futile, too. Aztec missiles blew up in the wrong places, or went wildly off course. Death-beams aimed from different angles blended fortuitously, heterodyning each other into a cone of harmlessness through which the flyer bore its passengers unharmed. Inside Mictlan, equipment must be failing, men toppling with unforeseen heart attacks, a thousand years of luck converging into a minute.

Now Cotopaxi loomed gigantic, through fumes and blasts of weaponry—and there was Mictlan, its geodesic shape monstrously enlarged by what must be layers of defensive forces or material. On orders, Cori drove straight toward it, Mike watching, reading to himself the range, and waiting—

"Turn right!" he cried out suddenly.

She swerved, in hair-trigger reaction, just as the space ahead along their previous flight path was filled by a chain of awesome explosions.

"Around the mountain, Cori—right around it."

She obeyed, rock-skimming at great speed. Now most of the heat and roar of battle had been left behind. They flew in something like the eye of the storm.

"Now fly up over the rim. Circle inside the crater." As she followed his orders, Mike dropped to his knees, pulling at the bottom hatch to open it. Clutched in his right hand were the two Masks bound together.

He had an eye out and was ready when Tom came jumping at him, yelling "No!" Mike dropped the Masks and yanked the pistol out and jammed its muzzle under his brother's chin. It would be very rough at contact range, but still it wouldn't kill, and Tom must have known that he would use it.

Mike said, "Listen, stupid, I'm doing this my way. The Masks have to go." And when Tom tried to talk, to move, he jammed the pistol in harder. "Listen, *I* know where the *punchao* is! Understand me? Know what I'm saying? The *punchao*!"

That did the trick, and Tom slid out of the way, eyeing Mike respectfully, rubbing a little at his throat. He let Sal pull him to a seat.

Without a pause for second thoughts, Mike dragged the hatch open, caught a scorching breath from bubbling magma that flew past at some unguessable short distance below. He dropped the Masks together into it, letting the stun-maser fall out, too, so he could slam the hatch again a fraction of a second quicker.

"Cori, straight on north! Pour on the coal. Let's get us out of here!" He scrambled to get himself strapped into a seat.

They were out of the crater in the blink of an eye, the bulk of Cotopaxi already dwindling behind them, the sounds and sights of battle fading.

Then it came. A glare that made the world a photographic negative, a wave of shock that flung their flyer like a scrap of film.

Cori fought for control and got it back. Then she was limply ready to move over for Mike. He circled slowly back toward the south. The weapons flashes from both sides were stilled. He could not see anything of the volcano at first; a sullen, humpbacked cloud dwelt there, with chunks of debris still falling through it and around it, their speed reheating some of them to incandescence on the long drop back to earth.

Mike circled, looking, listening. Inca voices, that had been stunned, were coming back now on the radio. When he flew back near where Mictlan had been, half of Cotopaxi's slope was gone. Thick lava flowed over it toward the distant sea.

Mike was standing in the open air, on a vast landing deck, with the solid and fantastic shapes of Cuzco-23 spread out before him and below.

"But now," Tom beside him was protesting to the Inca Tupac, "there's no Mask to go on a ship for Spain and be lost in the Gulf. It won't be there for anyone in the twentieth century to find. Hell, I suppose there's not even any treasure-hunting company."

"And you might suppose correctly," said Tupac with a kind of enforced patience, "that even Florida is now known by another name. But your branch has not been so affected. The same home world that you left is now open to you—as much as any home can ever be the same, for any returning traveler. And your way to it lies open." Tupac spoke the last sentence as if he found it something to be marveled at.

He turned to Mike. "We will provide you with some help there, of course. Some may be needed, I imagine, as you are returning to your family with a sixteen-year-old Indian bride and a child."

"Thanks." Mike smiled at Cori, who was smiling back. She had already faced wonders greater than those of US-20, or at least their equal. "We'll manage, as long as you don't just drop us out of the blue on Peachtree Street."

"Oh, of course not. I understand arrangements are made to offer you a choice of cover stories, and you will have time to decide; your trip home will take a day or two, subjective time." He shook his head, as if again he marveled. "You have some powerful friends."

"I guess I do."

The Inca came a step closer. "In Cuzco-16 we are still faced with some difficult problems of reconstruction. So I would like to ask before you go: have you any final advice for Manco?"

"A little. Yes, I guess quite a bit. First, that he send ambassadors to the Emperor Charles—go over the heads of all the Conquistadors to try to keep them off his neck. Being converted to Christianity might give Manco some political advantage, but I doubt there's much chance of that. As a gesture of goodwill, he might send Pizarro home alive, after a few lashes for infringing against the laws of the Inca kingdom."

"Whom did you suggest he might send as ambassadors?"

"He has a lot of smart Indians around. And as interpreter, maybe one of the sympathetic priests, like Molina—I hear he survived. And of course Charles would love to get some presents of gold, if there's any left to scrape together."

Tom's head turned to look across Tupac at Mike.

Mike went on: "Manco should establish relations with other European powers as well. Trade for their technology, but allow no settlers. Massacre on sight any Europeans bearing arms. Make firearms. Raise horses . . . establish a written language."

"All right, all right." Tupac made gestures. "All good advice. You might have written the plan, as we would like to see it. I believe your ride is coming."

Esperanza's friends. Cori sucked in her breath and clutched the baby. Sal squinted upward, as if at a holy vision, and moved away from Tom, who had just come to stand beside her. In the cloudless sky a ship from a thousand years in Tupac's future had materialized and was descending, slowly and with no visible support, glowing like a mild, beneficent sun.

. . . the sun. And I know, Mike thought silently, where lies the great *punchao*. In a crevice on the eastern flank of Machu Picchu, where the rays of the first light can sometimes find it, and light its golden fire, now that the wrappings must have rotted and fallen off. When I get home, no eyes will have seen that fire for four hundred years and more. To hide it there was Willak Umu's idea, not mine, and so it should be there in my branch, too. But it will stay there till the mountains fall, for all of me.

Cori moved a little closer, brushing his arm, and he looked down. It didn't pay to reach too fast for gold.

The Fate Line

by

Walter Jon Williams

The Valley of the Kings lay stony and barren beneath a blazing sun. The mortuary temples where the old kings had once been worshiped were abandoned, and the village of Set Maat at the opening of the valley held only a few dozen souls. Small looted tombs, those of officials and servants who had wanted to be buried near their kings, gaped in the valley walls, and the valley floor was scarred by piles of rubble left by thieves.

No one had built a tomb here in nearly a thousand years.

Shaded by his woven sun hat, Perseus advanced on muleback down the ancient valley road, followed by his work gang of Lycians and a supercilious Armenian scribe. He had been assured that Lycians were expert at carving tombs—their own leaders were laid to rest in magnificent cliffside tombs carved to look like Greek temples. And the Armenian, for his part, was the only member of the expedition to know how to speak and read Egyptian.

But Perseus was not here to build a tomb—he was here to rob one, or if possible more than one. It was a task he found both distasteful and frustrating, not the least because it might get him killed.

Perseus had the misfortune to be a royal bastard. His mother had been a dancing girl who had died in childbirth, and his father

195

had been the king, Ptolemy Philopater, or possibly Philopater's own father Ptolemy Euergetes—the Palace retainers who remembered that time had never been certain. Perseus had never been acknowledged by his father, whoever he was, so he had been raised in the Palace at Alexandria amid an anonymous swarm of children, the offspring of dancing girls, servants, courtesans, and minor officials. The Palace was an odd, magnificent nursery, a place of marble columns, shaded porticoes, tinkling fountains, and the Temple of the Muses . . . and also a place of rumor, scandal, intrigue, and deadly violence. Perseus was amazed that he had actually survived to adulthood.

Perseus' presumed father, Philopater, had died seven years earlier, leaving the kingdom to his five-year-old son, Ptolemy Epiphanes, whose nickname meant "the God on Earth," and whose coronation heralded a series of massacres. First the late king's court favorites had ordered the execution of the new king's own mother. Then a rebellious general had captured the pharaoh and butchered the court favorites. An insurgency broke out in the Delta. Crops failed. King Philip of Macedon declared war on Egypt along with Antiochus, the king of Syria, who invaded Egyptian possessions in Palestine with an army of fifty thousand professional soldiers and a hundred fifty elephants. Most of Upper Egypt had broken off under a Nubian pharaoh named Hyrgonaphor.

The godlike qualities promised by Epiphanes' nickname were not yet made manifest. He was barely twelve, and already his kingdom was falling apart under his feet.

To preserve his reign and his own existence, Epiphanes needed to hire soldiers, and soldiers cost money. The treasury was bankrupt, and the peasants—those who weren't in rebellion—had already been taxed beyond their capacity to pay. Temples had been forced into making voluntary contributions. Tariffs had been raised at all the ports.

Courtiers, of course, would not be taxed on their enormous wealth. If the administration ever dared such a thing, the officials who gave the orders would be assassinated and the young king would have a whole new series of advisors forced on him at sword's point.

This being the case, there weren't a lot of options left. Tomb robbing was among them.

And so the king's half-forgotten half-brother, Perseus, was sent with a gang of Lycians into the Valley of the Kings in the faint hope of finding a royal burial that hadn't already been robbed. He traveled with Lycians because no one dared employ native Egyptians. If the locals found out he was here on an expedition to loot the tombs of their great kings, their outrage would probably extend to rebellion—*another* rebellion, on top of those already in place. When he'd passed through Thebes, and later Set Maat, he'd let it be known that he was on a mission to survey and preserve the remains of the pharaohs.

What he hoped to preserve was his own skin. If his mission failed—altogether likely—he could be executed for his failure. If he succeeded, he might become too prominent an alternative to the current king, and he'd be executed anyway.

He was having a hard time envisioning a happy outcome for his mission.

Perseus led the expedition to a cliff on the western side of the valley and ordered the group to make camp. At least the site would be shady in the afternoon.

Then he sat in the shade on a stone, sipped some of the sour wine the expedition had brought with them, and contemplated his task.

The expedition had not been equipped with a map. The first thing he needed to do was make a survey. And for that, he would need the skills of the scribe, a man who seemed to have no name other than Armenios—"the Armenian."

But that would be a job for the morrow. For tonight, he would drink his wine, eat his dinner, and contemplate the odds of his own survival.

The survey began well. Some of the larger tombs seemed to have been looted only partially, which left open the possibility that further excavation might produce results. Armenios the scribe recorded the names inscribed on the looted tombs, and they proved to belong to kings of the eighteenth, nineteenth, and twentieth dynasties, the period when the Egyptian Empire was at its height. Ahmenhotep, Rameses, Thutmose? Perseus had never heard of any of them.

Examining the plundered tombs only depressed Perseus. He wondered if the tomb of Alexander the Great, where the great conqueror reposed in a pair of golden coffins, would one day lie as wrecked and lost to memory as the sepulchers of these forgotten rulers.

It was one of the Lycians who found the untouched tomb. While taking his midday meal, he had found himself staring at the rubble at the base of a rockfall. And there, above the rubble, he'd seen something that looked like a door—but only with the light shining at a certain angle.

On viewing the door, Perseus concluded that only someone like the Lycian, with personal experience of knowing where on a rock wall it was possible for a tomb to be carved, would have had a chance to see the portal.

The door originally had been concealed by a pile of rubble, but the rubble had eroded to the point where the lintel and upper part of the door were now faintly visible. The Lycians set to work with shovels and picks and soon cleared away the entire door.

The door had been sealed with clay, but the seal had been so damaged by the Lycians that Armenios was unable to read the characters inscribed on it. Perseus gestured for Armenios to step back.

"Break down the door," he said.

The Lycians set to work with a will. The masonry sealing the door was smashed and cleared away. A short entrance hall was revealed. Perseus called for torches.

His worries of his own future had vanished. His mind filled with visions of treasure, wealth beyond his greatest dreams.

Heart pounding, Perseus advanced down the corridor, and the sight took his breath away. The room was filled with furniture: beautiful chairs of ebony, tables with carved ivory legs, caskets of carved alabaster, faience vases, chests of marble. There were life-sized wooden statues of soldiers, effigies of Egyptian gods, and a disassembled chariot.

"Get this junk out of here!" Perseus ordered.

King Ptolemy already had all the nice furniture he would ever need.

The Lycians picked up the furniture and hurled it out onto the broken stone of the valley, revealing in the process another sealed door.

The walls were covered with Egyptian writing, eyes and hands, horizons and falcons. Armenios pointed to ovals that held more Egyptian characters.

"It's a royal tomb," he said. "Only the kings are allowed to have their name inscribed within a cartouche."

Armenios' eyes glittered in the torchlight. Even he had caught the fever of gold.

"The pharaoh's name was Ahmose," he said.

"Was he famous or something?" Perseus asked.

The Armenian's lips quirked. "I have no idea," he said. "But this tomb is small compared to some of the others. Either this is a minor king, or this tomb is very, very old."

The inner door was smashed down in a matter of minutes. Beyond was another hallway, this one occupied by wooden oars scattered on the ground. Perseus kicked his way through these and thrust his torch into the interior.

The entire room was occupied by a vast wooden chest far too large to fit through the corridor, beautifully carved and cunningly made of slats that had been fitted together on the spot. There were doors in the chest, fixed with metal pins and sealed with clay. Perseus was too impatient to work out the method of unlocking the doors: he took one of the picks and smashed the doors to bits. He was rewarded with his first glimpse of gold.

"Tear the chest apart!" The chest was cleared away, and Perseus stood amid the wreckage, his eyes devouring the solid gold coffin now revealed. It was so huge that it must have been carried down the corridor with only a finger-breadth of clearance on either side.

Perseus tried to imagine how many soldiers that coffin would buy for Ptolemy.

The effigy on top showed a youngish man with regular features wearing the false beard of an Egyptian king. It took eight men to wrestle the gold lid off the coffin and reveal what lay beneath.

Inside the outer coffin was an inner coffin wrapped in a linen shroud, plus four canopic jars of carved alabaster that held the pharaoh's viscera. Perseus had the jars tossed in the corner—King Ptolemy already had more jars than he could count—then tore open the linen shroud, revealing another gold coffin.

Inside the second gold coffin was an inner coffin made of silver, inside of which was the mummy of Pharaoh Ahmose. He was wrapped in many layers of bandages, but the details of mummification were not what attracted Perseus' attention—rather his eyes were dazzled by the cloisonné gold collar, the gold amulets, the gold-hilted bronze sword . . . and the gold mask that covered the pharaoh's head, its eyes glittering in the torchlight. The sight took Perseus' breath away.

But he hadn't entirely lost his head.

"Armenios," he said.

"Yes?"

"I need you to make an inventory of every object in the tomb made of precious metal. Never mind the rest. Then you'll have to carry the inventory back to the king to get more men and supplies, because we'll never wrestle these coffins out of here with the men we've got."

"Very good, sir."

Perseus turned to the Lycians. "The rest of you get more lanterns and torches. We need as much light as possible."

Armenios' pen scratched as he made note of every precious object visible. It was he who noted that there seemed to be more gold ornaments partially concealed by the bandages. It was also he who noticed the discrepancy in the pharaoh's golden mask.

"This isn't the same face that was on the coffins."

Perseus looked in surprise at the pharaoh's mask. Armenios was right: whereas all three coffins showed the effigy of a young man with regular features, the mask showed a longer, leaner face with a broad, frowning forehead set in an expression of fierce concentration. It was still Egyptian work, and the mask still bore a pharaoh's false beard, but it was clearly a different face.

"Perhaps one of them isn't a pharaoh, but a god," Perseus said.

"Deceased pharaohs are always portrayed as a god," Armenios said. "Osiris, usually, and sometimes Re."

Perseus looked at the mask again. The eyes glimmered, almost as if the pharaoh had opened his lids.

"Maybe he's not deceased in this one."

What material had been used to represent the eyes? he wondered. Mica? Glass? Whatever the material was, it was disturbingly lifelike.

"Maybe another man was buried in the king's coffin," he said. "A court favorite, perhaps, or a general. And the king's body is hidden somewhere else."

"Perhaps," Armenios said. "But this body has so much gold on it, it's hard to conceive it could be other than a king."

In the end, Perseus decided, it didn't much matter. The identity of the corpse was irrelevant: the gold and silver were what was important.

At nightfall he ordered everyone out of the tomb and guards placed on the doors. He laid his own pallet in the first chamber, and he set a lantern burning nearby, so that he'd know if anyone tried to enter.

Outside, he heard the Lycians and Armenios celebrating with wine and Egyptian beer. He lay in the semidarkness, watching the hieroglyphs on the walls dance in the flickering light of the lamp, and considered his own future. Discovery of the tomb would raise his profile to an uncomfortable height. Previously it had been possible for the courtiers to ignore an unacknowledged royal bastard, but now they would have to acknowledge his existence. And that meant that he would become a rival of Ptolemy whether he wanted to or not. Which meant that he would die.

To avoid these morbid thoughts, he decided instead to consider the dead man in the next room. Ahmose, hidden in the next chamber for over a thousand years, coffins nesting within one another, alone in the dark . . .

He thought about how the eyes of the mask had glittered. Mica? he wondered. Mother-of-pearl?

Without quite making a conscious decision, he rolled off his pallet, took up the lantern, and walked into the inner chamber. The coffin gleamed in the wavering light. He raised the lamp high and looked down into the inner coffin. The eyes of the mask glowed out of the heart of the coffin, like daylight seen through chinks in a curtain.

He reached for the mask, hesitated, reached again. It came off the body with a kind of sigh. A face had been painted onto the bandages beneath the mask, the even features of the young man depicted on the coffin.

Perseus stepped away from the coffin and held the lantern high in one hand to get a better look at the mask. The fierce face gazed back, eyes glittering. Perseus turned the mask around and blinked in surprise. Seen from the rear, the eyes glittered from beds of a soft gray material. He balanced the lantern on the edge of the coffin, then probed the material with his free hand. It was soft to the touch, and was clearly meant to cushion the brows against the metal of the mask.

The mask was intended to be worn in life, therefore. A corpse wouldn't need the interior padding.

Light shimmered and shifted in the mask's eyes. Again Perseus wondered what they were made of.

If he put on the mask, he thought, he would at least know what it was like to be a king before his half-brother killed him.

He took a breath and pressed the mask to his face.

In the next hour he learned many things, not the least of which was the fact that he, personally, needed to carry the news of his discovery to Alexandria.

The Captain sent Demetrios uptime to report to the Colonel, and when he stepped out of the flyer he found himself at the nameless academy where he'd trained—functional buildings that sat on carved mountain terraces set in the Andes at four thousand meters, the better to get recruits accustomed to Andean altitude. The spectacular views had never quite made up for the thin air that had Demetrios gasping for breath during the exercises.

He was eight hundred years uptime from where he started. His crazy aunt Eudoxia, who was a palm reader, had always said that the breaks in his lifeline indicated that he'd travel far in his life. She probably hadn't had this in mind.

The Colonel was a youthful-looking Quechuan with prematurely gray hair, who sat behind a clutter-free desk of polished onyx. His first question was a surprising one.

"How well do you speak Greek?"

"I was born on Cyprus," Demetrios said. "We emigrated to Australia when I was twelve, but we still speak Greek at home."

The Colonel's eyes narrowed. "Do you speak classical Greek at all?"

"You mean like Sophocles and them?" Demetrios asked. "No, not at all—and you don't *speak* that lingo, it's a dead language, all you do is read it."

The Colonel gave him an appraising look. "Well," he said, "you're going to learn to speak it. Reading will be optional."

Demetrios was thankful. He hadn't ever been one for reading.

"Am I going to ancient Greece?" he asked. He was under the impression that the Quechuans were focused on their enemies, the Tenocha, and had nothing to do with the Old World.

"Well," the Colonel said, looking a little weary. "Perhaps it's better to say that the ancient Greeks have come to us."

"There are many worlds, of course," the Colonel said later, after Demetrios had been introduced to the four soldiers he would command. "We have quiet little listening stations in many of them, alert to any interference by the Tenocha. It was in one of these worlds—we call it Cuzco-81–when we first detected an anomaly in Mexico, in the Christian year 1304."

Constantine, the unit's communications tech, raised a hand.

"Wasn't that before the empire of the Tenocha even began?"

"Correct," the Colonel said. "In all our timelines where the Tenocha exist, their capital of Tenochtitlan was founded in 1325. But instead we find that Mexico was invaded before the Tenocha even founded their state."

"Invaded?" The word slipped from Demetrios' lips without his meaning to let it go.

"By the Conquistadors?" Constantine said.

The Colonel looked at Demetrios.

"No," he said, "by the Greeks. By the Greco-Egyptian empire of the Ptolemies."

In all the histories the Colonel knew, he explained, Egypt had been conquered by Alexander the Great and subsequently ruled by Alexander's general Ptolemy and his descendants. The Egyptian Empire waxed and waned as Alexander's various successors battled among themselves, but began a steep decline under Ptolemy V Epiphanes, who inherited the kingdom as a child, lived much of his reign as a puppet of powerful courtiers, and despite his best efforts lost Egypt's overseas possessions to his rapacious neighbor, Antiochus the Great.

But in the world of Cuzco-81, Ptolemy V had employed a brilliant staff officer, Perseus, who helped Ptolemy's general Megas to defeat Antiochus decisively in an unconventional night attack. When Megas died on campaign, Perseus assumed command and defeated Antiochus again, capturing him along with his treasury and his entire family. Perseus annexed Syria to Egypt and left the rest of Antiochus' realm in the hands of a Seleucid relative who preferred half a kingdom to no kingdom at all.

Perseus then returned to Egypt with an army flushed with victory and loot and overthrew the boy king. Claiming to be a Ptolemy himself, he took the throne as Ptolemy VI Eponoios, the Uniter. He killed corrupt courtiers, married Antiochus' daughter Laodike, ended rebellions in Egypt, conquered Libya and Asia Minor, and defeated a Roman army sent by a republic alarmed at his sudden rise.

His descendants, beginning with his son Ptolemy VII Hipponax, had equal success. As a descendent of Antiochus, Hipponax reclaimed what remained of his grandfather's kingdom, then added Parthia to his realm. Subsequent Ptolemies absorbed Macedon and Greece, Carthage, Numidia, and Mauretania. They alternately beat Roman armies in the field or used the immense wealth of Egypt to buy off Roman politicians. Rome was reduced to the boundaries of Italy and became a client state and a provider of mercenaries for Ptolemaic armies.

In the early fourteenth century, 1500 years after the general Perseus had overthrown his boy king, a Ptolemy still ruled in Alexandria, monarch of an empire centered on the Mediterranean. The dynasty had an astonishingly long life, longer than any in any history. "Even the bad Ptolemies were amazingly lucky," the Colonel said. The empire reached from the Tagus to the Indus, with colonies and trading stations that girdled Africa and dotted the coast of India and Southeast Asia. The kingdoms of northern Europe fawned on Egypt and did their best to imitate it.

Ptolemy reigned over an enlightened world, where Greek philosophy and science had enjoyed an uninterrupted reign over an empire wealthy and at peace. The Ptolemies had supported practical technologies: navigation, scientific agriculture, mechanics, architecture, ship building. Primitive steam engines now pumped water from mines, shifted water from the Nile to irrigation canals, and provided auxiliary power to ships.

Egypt had traded with the New World for some time, but now Ptolemy turned his attention to conquest. Armies carried in powerful ocean-going ships had subjugated the major islands of the Caribbean. In 1296 Ptolemy invaded Mexico in person with an army that swept all before it. Having secured his conquests, he built a fleet on the Pacific coast of Mexico and was now exploring up and down both coasts of the Americas, making contact with the locals. It was only then, in 1304, that the Egyptians had come to the attention of the Quechuan observation post hidden high in the Andes.

"We were looking for electronic signals that might indicate an incursion by the Tenocha," the Colonel said. "We weren't looking for wooden ships carrying armies of Egyptians. Not in that era."

"So the Gippos knocked out the Tenocha before they even got started," Demetrios said. "What about your lot?"

"In 1304 the Sapa Inka rules only the small area around Cuzco," said the Colonel. "None of the rival Andean states are any larger. Ptolemy could knock them down like dominoes."

"And with our help?" Demetrios asked.

The Colonel looked grim. "We *tried* to help. We sent back a number of agents to approach Ptolemy, and when they failed to get close to him, we tried sending in teams to take him out. Every mission was a disaster—there were technical problems, weapons systems failed at crucial moments, transport crashed . . . even simply gathering *information* was difficult. Just retrieving the history book that provided basic information about the Ptolemies cost three lives. There were a lot of good men lost."

Demetrios looked at the other four members of his team, all of whom were drawn from the twentieth century, and spoke twentieth-century Greek.

"We're the next sacrifice?" he asked.

"No." The Colonel was firm. "Absolutely not. We're not going to repeat that mistake. We're going to intervene at an earlier date, well before Egypt moves on the New World." He stood, made a subtle gesture with one hand, and a holographic timeline appeared in the air. He pointed at a date.

"You're going to 196 B.C. Just after the general Perseus returned from defeating Antiochus and installed himself as Pharaoh. You're going to change this alternate timeline before it even gets started."

The flyer dropped the team amid the papyrus ocean of the Nile Delta, a day's march from the city of Tanis. From Tanis, Demetrios and his companions could travel by canal and the Nile's own branchings to the capital, Alexandria.

In three months' special training, using the Quechuans' techniques for implanting knowledge in the human mind, the team had all become fluent in the Greek of the third century B.C. They still spoke with accents—ironically enough accents that belonged to the remote descendants of the people with whom they intended to converse—but they had adopted a cover story that would account for any eccentricities in their speech. They would present themselves as traders from remote Bactria—a distant Asian kingdom that Alexander had conquered generations ago, but with which Egypt had fallen out of contact.

It was a measure of the importance of their mission that the team had been provided with every conceivable piece of equipment. High-technology weapons concealed in ordinary objects such as walking sticks, boots, and gloves. Hidden navigation aids. Communicators disguised as earrings or pendants. Edged weapons, belonging to the period, of a higher quality than any smith of the period could hope to achieve. Chain armor made of unbreakable plastic rings that resembled iron. Mules to carry their goods. Gold and silver in modest quantities.

But it was what the mules carried that would establish them as merchants of note: five hundred pounds of pepper. In the third century B.C., pepper was produced only on the Malabar coast of India, and in Europe it was so valuable that unscrupulous merchants sometimes cut it with hunks of far less valuable silver.

The team would sell their pepper in Alexandria, buy or rent a home with the profits, and insinuate or bribe their way into the court. The usurper pharaoh Ptolemy Eponoios would be dispatched by modern weapons—to anyone outside the team, the death would look like a stroke or heart attack—and then Demetrios and his comrades would exfiltrate back to the Delta and send out a call for a pickup.

The flyer roared back into the sky, the wash from its rotors flattening the papyrus and sending silver spiderwebs over the surface of the Nile. Demetrios looked up as the vehicle disappeared into the night sky, and then the normal night sounds returned, the frogs and birds and the sough of wind through the reeds.

The team waited the hour till dawn and then set out on a path in the direction of Tanis. The papyrus grew twelve or fifteen feet high on all sides, and the trail offered very little visibility. They met few people that day—a few peasants who had farms or fishing camps, fishermen in small reed boats, and slaves harvesting papyrus. The team found a woman baking bread and bought a pair of loaves. The narrow track they followed turned into a road, two ruts sunk into the muddy soil.

The party camped on a kind of island, a football field–sized area a little higher, and drier, than the surrounding marsh. It was home to three palm trees and a mud-brick house slowly crumbling in the sun.

The mules were unloaded and currycombed. Tents of waxed linen were raised. Other people had camped here in the past, and there was enough animal dung to make a fire. A clay pot was hung over the fire, and onions, beans, and salt pork were stewed together. All the food, though perfectly ordinary for the period, had come from thousands of years in the future.

A crescent moon rose in the east. Demetrios wandered off the island to answer a call of nature, then he continued walking to clear his lungs of dung-fire smoke. He was in the vast sea of reeds again, the moist ground soft beneath his boots, the feather-duster tops of the plants rising far above his head. Papyrus rustled around him and waved in front of the sickle moon.

"Ho, man." Demetrios almost leaped out of his skin at the resonant baritone that seemed to come out of nowhere. He gazed wildly at the man who stood politely at his elbow.

Ho anthropos. His words had been Greek, a standard greeting.

"Sorry if I startled you," the man said.

Demetrios looked at the stranger carefully in the light of the rising moon. The man had snowy hair and a large nose. His voice was as sonorous as an actor's, and his face bore an expression of tolerant amusement. He wore a simple wool tunic with a blue border.

"I didn't hear you walk up," Demetrios said.

"I didn't walk up," the man said. "*You* walked up. I was here all along."

"Just standing here," Demetrios said, "in the marsh, for no reason."

He began to suspect the man was a part of a bandit gang that haunted this part of the road, waiting to ambush travelers. Yet the stranger seemed to carry no weapons.

"I didn't say I had no reason for being here," said the white-haired man. "I had a perfectly good reason. I was waiting for you—or for someone like you."

Demetrios felt his neck hairs prickle.

"Someone like me," he repeated. He realized he was unarmed except for a belt knife.

"A stranger from another place," the man said. "From—one might say—another world."

Demetrios struggled to mask the sudden blast of fear that chilled his spine. His hand drifted toward the hilt of his knife as he held the man's eyes with his own.

"And why did you wish to meet someone like me?" he asked.

"To warn him," the stranger said. "I wanted to say that the mission is doomed to fail. Ptolemy is too well protected."

Before the man finished speaking, Demetrios drew the knife in one smooth movement and had the point pricking the stranger's throat. Demetrios patted the man down, looking for weapons.

"I'm not your enemy," the man said with perfect calm. "In fact, I'm trying to keep you alive."

Demetrios found no weapons. He took the man by the arm and faced him in the direction of the island.

"Who are you?" he hissed. He didn't want to make noise in case the man had friends nearby.

"My name is Elpidos," the stranger said. Demetrios began marching him in the direction of the island. He offered no resistance.

"How do you know about me?" Demetrios demanded.

Elpidos gave a sigh. "The answer to that question," he said, "is rather complex."

A shout came from the island. Demetrios recognized the voice of Helen, one of his team. There was a clattering and more shouts.

Demetrios felt Elpidos slump. "I'm too late," the stranger said.

Cries and screams rose above the papyrus swamp. Demetrios dug the point of the knife into the stranger's throat. "What's going on?" he said.

"Ptolemy's soldiers are killing your friends," Elpidos said.

Demetrios gave a growl of rage, shoved Elpidos away, and began a sprint back to the island.

"Don't go!" Elpidos called after him. "You're too late!"

Indeed he was. The sounds of combat had faded by the time he returned to the island, and Demetrios slowed and approached cautiously, trying to remain silent as he slogged through the boggy ground. He slithered between the tall stalks of papyrus and saw a troop of light cavalry, twenty at least, moving over the island with their lances at the ready. He saw only two of his team, and they were clearly dead, lying where the long spears had flung them. The other two were not visible, but Demetrios was sure that if they were still on the island, they shared the fate of their comrades.

Demetrios knew he would be spotted if he ran for any of the team's weapons, so he remained where he was. And in any case he didn't understand how the team had been wiped out. Admittedly they were taken by surprise, apparently by an enemy that knew exactly where to find them, but their hidden weapons were within easy reach, and any one of them could have disposed of these attackers without trouble—in fact they could have burned the papyrus to its roots for five hundred meters in all directions.

What had happened?

Ptolemy is too well protected.

The memory of Elpidos' words was so powerful that Demetrios looked over his shoulder to see if the white-haired man had materialized behind him. He saw only papyrus. He clenched his teeth and turned again to the site of the disaster.

The soldiers dismounted and searched the island. They looted the bodies, collected any obvious weapons, and collected the mules. The stew pot was kicked over. Looters found the sacks of pepper, which resulted in whoops of delight. The murder of Demetrios' team had made the soldiers rich.

The troopers remained on the site for half an hour or so, then mounted and trotted off into the night, leading the mules loaded with booty. The dead were left to rot.

Demetrios entered the site of the massacre, limping on legs cramped from crouching in the reeds. His examination of the site led to more questions than answers. Two of the team had died holding energy weapons that should have annihilated any attacker. Helen had apparently thrown her stunner away, then tried to run and been speared in the back. Constantine had attempted to fight with a short sword but had been overwhelmed. The attack had been unexpected, and none had been wearing armor.

The cavalrymen hadn't recognized the energy weapons—they were disguised as walking sticks or horsewhips—and had left them where they'd fallen. The edged weapons they had taken with them, along with the team's armor.

The first thing Demetrios did was check one of the plasma weapons. It hummed to life as it always had in training, and holographic gauges and aiming aids appeared before Demetrios' eyes. He didn't dare fire it with the cavalry so near.

Demetrios could do very little for his friends. He lacked the tools to bury them, and there wasn't enough dry wood for cremation. He dragged the bodies into the old mud-brick hut, then covered them with one of the tents.

He didn't worry about the bodies beyond that. He'd lost comrades in the past, and he had learned not to waste time in mourning.

He preferred revenge, if he could get it.

The best thing he could do now would be to flee back uptime and report the catastrophe that had overtaken his mission after less than twenty-four hours. Then, if he was lucky, he'd get another crack at Ptolemy.

Except that, apparently, he would be unable to signal for pickup. There were certain times, arranged in advance, when he would be able to call for exfiltration, and a rescue team would arrive to carry him off. But he had to be able to make the signal, and he could find none of the communicators. One had been disguised as a piece of jewelry that Helen had worn, and it had been looted; the other was a polished bronze mirror, and he couldn't find that, either.

He decided to wait till dawn and search the island thoroughly. If he couldn't signal for a pickup, he would be stuck in Ptolemaic Egypt for the rest of his life.

He spent the rest of the night in misery, drowsing with his back to the mud-brick wall of the hut, the plasma weapon cradled in his arms. The crescent moon crawled slowly overhead. He felt completely alone, engulfed in darkness, lost in a violent, barbarian age.

He would have liked company, even if that company was Elpidos.

Morning brought luck. Searching the island, he found one of the sacks of pepper had been sliced or kicked open in the fight, and had spilled much of its cargo. The team had been carrying long pepper, more valuable than the more common black pepper, each pod looking like a tiny, blackened ear of maize. Carefully Demetrios picked up each pod from where it lay in the grass, and then wrapped his treasure in a piece of tent fabric.

He scoured the campsite and found packages of food that should keep him going for several days. His own cloak and blanket had not been looted.

But he couldn't find either of the signaling units. He seemed to be well and truly marooned in the second century B.C.

Demetrios considered his options while he packed the few belongings he would be taking with him. Continuing on to Tanis was clearly out of the picture, and he was unable to call for rescue. He would have to head in the opposite direction and look for a way out of the Delta.

With the pepper as his grubstake, and his knowledge of technology and future events, he should be able to make a life for himself somewhere outside of Egypt. He could marry, have children, maybe go down in history as the inventor of the windmill or the telescope or the hula hoop.

Or, he thought, he could continue the mission alone. If he killed Ptolemy, or even just succeeded in creating enough chaos, he might attract the attention of the Colonel and the Quechuans. Then they might be able to find him and pull him out.

This last plan seemed by far the most attractive. And it offered the only chance of escape.

He swung his belongings onto his back, picked up a plasma weapon in one hand and the sack of pepper in the other, and marched away into the dawn.

Demetrios had never been particularly impressed by his employers. They had the benefit of technology beyond his comprehension, but they still hired people like him to do their fighting for them. He couldn't fully respect people who refused to butcher their own meat.

Still, the Quechua had saved his life, and he supposed he owed them a debt of gratitude. In the Western Desert, his unit of Australian infantry had been surrounded and cut off south of Gazala by Rommel's Germans. Demetrios had managed to escape the encirclement at night but found himself alone in the desert without food and water. He was on the verge of collapse when the Quechua found him.

The Quechuans' war seemed a good deal safer than fighting the Desert Fox, and after some years guarding stone-age Peru from the cannibals of the future, he would be returned to the twentieth century with a new identity and a pocket full of cash. The offer had seemed generous at the time, but then he'd never expected to have to face swarms of mercenary cavalry in the swamps of Egypt.

Still, he reflected, he was better provisioned now than when he'd wandered off into the Never Never with an empty canteen.

He made his way through the papyrus marsh for half a day, and then stole a reed boat that a fisherman had drawn up on the bank. Raising the sail, he almost capsized twice before getting the hang of the craft. Through canals, a lagoon, and the Nile's own wandering byways, he managed in a night and a day to get from the Tanitic to the Mendesian branch of the river, and once there to the ancient city of Mendes. There he sold some of the pepper, and with the silver bought deck passage on a merchant ship bound for Alexandria.

That night, beneath the light of the crescent moon, the boat made its way westward, its sail filled by the land breeze coming off the Delta. The air was scented with the odor of the Nile: rotting sedge, fertile muck, and silt carried all the way from Ethiopia. Demetrios drowsed on the foredeck, his blanket stretched out on the planks, the bag of pepper his pillow.

"Do you speak English?" came a voice.

"Yeah," Demetrios replied automatically, and then fear jerked him awake and he sat up, reaching for his knife. He looked in fear and surprise at the white-haired man who squatted amiably on the deck.

"If we speak in English," Elpidos said, "the others won't be able to understand us."

"You weren't on the boat earlier," Demetrios said. The ship wasn't any longer than twenty meters: he'd seen everyone aboard during the course of the day.

"No. I wasn't."

"And you're here now."

The older man spread his hands.

"Self-evidently," he said.

Demetrios narrowed his eyes. "Why?"

"Because I still have your best interests at heart."

Demetrios gave a snort of derision. Elpidos looked at him mildly.

"I came to warn you two nights ago that you were in danger."

Demetrios was surprised by the anger that burned in his voice. "My mates were killed anyway, while you were ear-bashing me in the swamp."

"If you'd been present, you wouldn't have been able to affect the outcome." Elpidos peered down his big nose at Demetrios. "Let me guess," he said. "Your friends were well supplied with weapons, but the weapons didn't work."

"Yes."

"There were power failures. Or the weapons were calibrated incorrectly. Or the safety mechanisms were stuck."

Demetrios looked at Elpidos in wonder. "They all checked out when I tested them."

"The king is protected." The older man's mild eyes turned hard. *"The king is protected against all who wish him harm."*

"Protected by what?" Demetrios asked. "Some kind of technology?"

"By the laws of chance," Elpidos said. "You might just call it . . . luck."

Even the bad Ptolemies were amazingly lucky, the Colonel had said. But how could luck be inherited?

Technical problems, the Colonel had said, *weapons systems failed at crucial moments, transports crashed . . . even simply gathering* information *was difficult*

Realization struck Demetrios with the force of a slap to his ear.

"Your name is Elpidos," he said. The white-haired man nodded. "Elpidos," Demetrios continued, "is the masculine variation of *elpida*, which is Greek for 'hope.' And—" he pointed at the old man.— "and the Spanish for hope is Esperanza."

The man bowed. "At your service."

"They told us about you," Demetrios said. "They said they weren't sure what side you were on." Suspicion bubbled up in him. "They also said you'd been killed."

"I was uploaded from backup," Elpidos said. And, seeing Demetrios' blank stare at the unfamiliar terminology, "Let's just say that where I come from, death can be a temporary phenomenon."

"Huh," Demetrios said. "It's like the universe can't do without you."

The snowy-haired man's superior expression only seemed to deepen.

Another idea struck Demetrios, and he felt his nerves sizzle as if he'd been struck by lightning.

"You died," he said, "in the War of the Masks."

Elpidos only gazed at him. Demetrios felt moisture on his cheek as spray flew from the bow.

"I'm an officer," Demetrios said, "so I got a briefing on the Mask, and how to recognize if an invader is using one. And among the problems that an enemy Mask would create is that our side becomes incredibly *unlucky*."

Elpidos said nothing. Starlight glittered faintly in his eyes.

"But the Mask and its double were destroyed," Demetrios said.

"And I was killed," said Elpidos.

Demetrios frowned. "There are duplicates of *you*," he said. "Are you telling me that there are more copies of the Mask floating around?"

"I'm not telling you anything," Elpidos said. "You understand that I have to be careful in speaking with you—if I say anything wrong, I could create a paradox and be pulled rather violently out of this continuum."

Demetrios grinned. "But I'm allowed to speculate, right?"

"I can't stop you from thinking."

"Fair dinkum," Demetrios said. "So if Ptolemy has a Mask, it would show him the future, yeah? It would show him anything that might threaten him—like my team. And it would show him right where we'd be well in advance of our arrival, so that he could send his soldiers to deal with us."

Again Elpidos said nothing.

Demetrios' words slowed to match the pace of his thoughts.

"And if Ptolemy's wearing the Mask right now," he said, "he can see me on this boat, coming to Alexandria. And he'll have people in the harbor, waiting for me."

"There is a small boat being towed astern," Elpidos said. This was true: the ship's boat had been shifted both to make room for deck cargo and to keep its planks from drying and shrinking in the heat and becoming useless.

"Perhaps," Elpidos said, "you and the boat could disappear some time before dawn."

Demetrios rubbed his chin and thought about it.

"There doesn't seem to be a snowball's chance in fighting Ptolemy," he said. "Not as long as he's got the Mask."

"He is protected against all who mean him harm," said Elpidos. "A category that includes your friends in the future. You'd do better to leave Egypt and find a life for yourself somewhere else."

Demetrios gave Elpidos a careful look.

"Why are you so interested in my welfare?"

"There's already been enough bloodshed," Elpidos said. "Peru and Egypt have no reason to go to war."

"Egypt's on the verge of invading Peru. The Mask must have told Ptolemy to invade the Americas before Peru could become a rival."

"That's only happening in Cuzco-81. Not in the timelines where you or your superiors come from."

"My superiors see it differently."

Elpidos looked stern. "This war will only benefit the Tenocha."

Apparently that statement was too much for the time-space continuum, because the white-haired man abruptly vanished, leaving a startled Demetrios staring at empty air.

The light of the Pharos, Alexandria's magnificent lighthouse, had been visible for hours before Demetrios wandered aft, past the sleepy helmsman, and then slipped over the side and clambered down the rope that led to the ship's boat. He had the plasma weapon stuck in his belt and held the bag of pepper in his teeth. Once in the boat, he cast the boat free, raised its sail, and set off toward the Egyptian shore.

He had to admit that he was beaten. The king was protected against anyone who wished him ill, and so Demetrios had no hope of harming Ptolemy. He knew better than to pursue a hopeless cause. The usurping king could live a long, happy, successful life as far as Demetrios was concerned.

Long life to Ptolemy, he repeated to himself, as the waves thumped against the boat's hull. *Long life to Ptolemy. Long life to Ptolemy.* Maybe the Mask would hear his thoughts.

But however much he had given up on his mission, Demetrios had not entirely surrendered the idea of revenge.

Morning found the ship a mere white speck on the horizon. Demetrios continued to sail along the coast until one of Alexandria's suburbs came into sight. He left the boat on the beautiful sand beach and walked toward the city, leaning on the cane that held his plasma weapon.

He had been well briefed on Alexandria. The great metropolis, he knew, was the largest city in the world. It held more Jews than any city in Palestine, and more Greeks than any city in Greece. The city's monuments were famous even in Demetrios' own time: when he was a child in Cyprus he'd been taught about the Pharos lighthouse, the Library with its half-million volumes, the Museum that had been host to the greatest collection of scientists the ancient world had known, and the great tomb where Alexander the Great lay in a pair of solid gold coffins.

Outside the city, however, Demetrios soon found himself wandering through a vast cemetery. The Alexandrines buried their dead outside the city walls, to the east of the city, and so Demetrios walked past hundreds of tombs, some bright with marble, some old and crumbling. Some of the tombs had been broken into, and poor people lived in them. Atop or alongside the tombs, statues of gods stood alongside portrait-statues of the deceased, the young modest seated women with their hair coiled about their heads, the young naked men called *kouretes*, the older married couples sharing a couch and holding hands. The impressive Alabaster Tomb and the Tomb of Stratonike loomed above the other monuments, and Demetrios was able to use them to orient himself.

Demetrios found himself thinking of his team lying beneath the waxed linen tent in the old mud hut north of Tanis, and sadness warred with anger in his mind.

The city walls loomed ahead, and the fortifications of the Canopic Gate. People were moving in and out freely, but still Demetrios felt tension tautening his shoulders as he entered the city. Warned by his Mask, Ptolemy might have had killers waiting at the gate.

But Demetrios wasn't killed. Instead he walked through the gate into the Jewish Quarter. The Jews were crammed into tall tenements that shadowed the road, and they spilled out into the streets. The gutturals of Aramaic rose in the air. Many were dressed in Oriental fashion, the men in robes and turbans, the women in long veils that reached to their ankles; and others were dressed in the simpler Greek style. Everyone had kohl-rimmed eyes. Preachers of one Jewish sect or another harangued the crowd from street corners. The smells from the cooking stalls made Demetrios' mouth water. With some of his change, Demetrios bought sliced lamb wrapped in flat bread, along with a cup of heavily-resined wine that seemed mostly vinegar. At least it served to quench his thirst.

He kept his bag of pepper in his hand, not trusting the crowd well enough to set it down.

He headed deeper into the city and came to a bridge over a canal. A procession was moving along on the canal, a series of barges filled with soldiers in glittering armor. Citizens crowded the bridge and the banks of the canal, cheering and waving. Demetrios asked one of the citizens what was going on.

"The king's leading the army out," he was told. "Hyrgonophor's marching on Thebes, and the king's going to meet him."

Hyrgonaphor, who had featured in the Colonel's briefing, was the rebel pharaoh who led the native rebellion in Upper Egypt.

Just as Demetrios turned his attention back to the canal, he saw the royal barge appear. It was low, to fit under the city's bridges, and its strakes were vermilion. The blades of the oars had been gilded. A falcon carved on the bow, and another on the stern, overshadowed the man who stood there wearing the diadem of kingship. He wore a brilliant white tunic and the purple cloak of royalty, and he stood beneath the falcon acknowledging the cheers of the crowd.

Other than the gilding and finery that surrounded him, Ptolemy Eponoios seemed perfectly unremarkable.

"Well," said Demetrios' interlocutor, "with all the soldiers gone, maybe the prices will return to normal."

Oddly, Demetrios was not tempted to use his plasma weapon to kill the king. He knew it would be a waste of time—someone would stop him, or the weapon would malfunction, or explode, or it would turn out that his target wasn't the king at all, but a double cleverly substituting for the real thing.

Or a meteor might fall on his head.

His respect for the Mask was complete.

Demetrios asked directions to the spice market. It was farther west, past the round Temple of the Muses, near the port from which the spices were shipped to the rest of the Mediterranean.

On his way to the market he gawked at the Museum and the Tomb of Alexander. Once there he offered his pepper for sale. He'd decided that carrying cash would be easier and safer than carrying an awkward sack. He spoke to several spice merchants, had the pepper weighed, and accepted the most generous offer. By the end of the day he had an apartment near the Palace, a new suit of clothes, and had deposited most of his money in the strong-box of a local moneylender who acted much like a modern banker. He wouldn't pay interest on deposits, but he'd keep them safe.

Demetrios spent the next few days getting oriented in the vast city. He saw the temples, the monuments, the harbors filled with hundreds of masts. He viewed the markets, the shops, the mansions of the rich, the tenements of the poor. He was looking for a way of earning his living. His profits from the pepper might last a couple of years if he was careful, but if he was stranded here, he'd need an income.

He could go into the spice business, he supposed. He'd learned enough about it as part of his cover. But becoming a spice merchant would require travel, and he didn't want to leave Alexandria for any length of time.

In his meanderings he noticed that it wasn't only the Jews who had prophets. A host of seers infested the town, dressed in faded, torn tunics, their hair and beard wild and untamed, their eyes gazing pale and eerie beneath heavy brows, looking mad as hoopoe birds. Fortune-tellers set up their tables near the temples, and astrologers offered consultations from small shops. Witches plied a less wholesome trade in curses and spells.

Most of the fortune-tellers seemed far from starvation. Alexandria, with its Museum and Library devoted to science and philosophy, sat atop a deep foundation of sorcery and superstition.

Perhaps, Demetrios thought, he could go into the prophecy business. After all, he already knew the future.

As he pondered this possibility, he realized that nowhere had he seen palm readers. If chiromancy was being practiced anywhere in the world, it wasn't in Egypt.

Nor had he seen tarot cards, which his daffy aunt Eudoxia had assured him were Egyptian in origin. The Egyptians, it turned out, lacked cardboard and couldn't make cards if they wanted to.

Eudoxia had been a practicing palmist and a card reader, as well as an astrologer and a believer in numerology. As a boy, Demetrios had paid no attention to the astrology or numerology, but he vaguely remembered the times she'd looked at his palms and explained the lines and the mounts.

And it didn't matter what he remembered, really. If he took up palm reading, he could make it up as he went along.

After all, there was no one here to contradict him.

It took several days to nerve himself to the point of doing it, during which time he hired a sign-painter to make a sign for him, and wondered if this were the first of millennia worth of signs to feature a garish hand divided up into segments by lines and bright colors.

It required even more courage to begin decorating his eyes with kohl. He did not come from a time when males wore makeup.

Demetrios decided to practice his art at the great temple to the sea god, known simply as "the Poseidon," which was near the Theater and in the same district as the Palace and the barracks for the city's garrison. The priests required a daily rent, paid in advance, before they let Demetrios set up his table, sign, and stools on their grounds. After parting with the money, Demetrios thought that being a mountebank must be profitable indeed if he was to be able to afford the priests' extortions.

His first customer was a small, heavily pregnant woman who wanted to know if her husband would be returning from the king's war against Hyrgonaphor.

"Chiromancy isn't prophecy," Demetrios said. "It mostly tells you about yourself. But"—he pointed to an ear—"sometimes a god whispers a prophecy to me, and I will tell you what I know. Your husband is in little danger. The rebels will be crushed in a very swift campaign, with small losses to our side."

Demetrios had no qualms in making this prediction. Ptolemy had a Mask. Hyrgonaphor didn't. Ptolemy would therefore win with great efficiency and little loss.

In any case, the woman believed him. "That's what my husband told me!" she said, as if that confirmed everything. She also believed Demetrios when he said that her palms showed that her pregnancy would be oppressive, but would have a happy outcome; that her money worries were constant but not desperate; that she needed to eat more red meat for the health of the child; that she should refrain from wine or beer until the delivery; and also that it was best to drink water only after it had been boiled. Her appearance told Demetrios all he needed to know: she was in good health but seemed a little anemic; her clothes and jewelry were modest but clean and neat; and the medical advice was clear enough to anyone from the twentieth century.

Her utter faith in his advice gave him confidence. Demetrios spent the day making commonplace observations and giving commonplace advice. He told obese men to go on a diet and get more exercise; he told soldiers that attention to their kit and their duties would earn promotion; he told a housewife that her love line strongly suggested that this was not the appropriate time to get involved with a married neighbor.

He told everyone he met that the king would defeat the rebel pharaoh in a brief campaign. People took him seriously. Everything he said was given force and significance by his mantle of occult power.

At the end of the day, Demetrios had to bite his lip to keep from laughing when one of the Poseidon's priests came to have his palm read.

For six days Demetrios continued dispensing his advice, never forgotting to mention the glorious victory that soon would enhance Ptolemy's reputation. The novelty of chiromancy helped to bring a constant stream of customers to his table. On the sixth day he looked up to see a supercilious man staring down at him, with a royal guardsman on each side. The man's hair was beautifully cut, with little spit-curls on his forehead. His jewelry featured gold and emeralds, he wore soft green leather shoes with elevated heels, and he scented the nearby air with the fragrance of *chypre*. It was no strain to assume the man was a courtier or royal functionary.

"Can I help you?" Demetrios asked.

The man sneered just a little.

"Is it true that you have been making prophecies about the king?" he asked.

"I have been telling people that the king will crush his enemies," Demetrios said.

"Are you aware," the courtier said, "that it is illegal to make prophecies about the king, or to cast his horoscope?"

Demetrios raised his eyebrows. "Even to speak of his victories?"

The visitor looked stern.

"He who prophesies victory today may prophesy defeat tomorrow," he said.

"In that case," Demetrios said, "I shall avoid mentioning the king at all."

The man scowled. "See that you do," he said. He frowned. "Your accent is unfamiliar," he said. "Where are you from?' "

"Bactria."

"The back of the north wind." The man sneered. "No wonder."

"Allow me to demonstrate my Bactrian art of chiromancy," Demetrios offered. "If you'll sit, I'll give you a reading free of charge—and I promise not to mention the king."

A wave of *chypre* preceded the courtier as he sat on the stool Demetrios had ready for customers.

"I am Demetrios son of Agamemnon," Demetrios said. "May I know your name?"

"Armenios." The courtier spoke the name as if it would be familiar. It meant "the Armenian," and Demetrios wondered what right a half-barbaric Armenian had to sneer at Bactrians.

Already, he realized, he was thinking like an Alexandrian.

"Are you right-handed?" he asked. Armenios was, and Demetrios asked for his left hand. The hand was soft and well manicured. The right hand was also visible on the table, and Demetrios saw the marks of ink on the fingers. He also saw a large signet on the right thumb, which indicated that Armenios probably held a royal office and needed to sign documents.

"The proximity of your lifeline to the mount of Saturn shows that even though you have responsibilities, you have an easy life," Demetrios said. "But the whorls show that you should be careful to take sufficient exercise."

Demetrios reflected on life in the Palace, and how the courtiers would fawn on the king while conspiring for favor, office, and rewards. The life of a courtier was filled with anxiety—particularly now, since the new king had began his reign by executing many of the former king's advisors, then confiscating the wealth they'd earned from embezzling state funds and from the sale of offices.

"The deepness and clarity of your lifeline indicates that you avoid being manipulated by others," Demetrios said. "But the breaks in the line show that others are constantly trying to undermine you. And the crosses in your head line show that you have many momentous decisions ahead of you."

Armenios seemed uneasy at this revelation.

"Go on," he said.

"The curve in your heart line shows that you have deep, strong emotions, but that you try to hide these from other people. You feel as if other people don't know you."

This was something Demetrios told all his clients, and since it was true of everybody, they all believed him and gave him credit for enormous powers of perception.

Demetrios continued the reading, comparing the left hand with the right. He emphasized the uncertainty and paranoia of the life at court and the violence that lurked under the surface.

"The lifeline on your right hand approaches the mount of Zeus-Ammon," Demetrios said, "the king of the gods. This means that your best chance for thwarting those who wish you harm is to remain close to—" He fell silent.

Armenios lifted one eyebrow. "Who?" he said.

"We have agreed not to mention that person," said Demetrios.

Armenios gave a thoughtful frown. Demetrios reckoned he had just given good advice: the greater a friend Armenios made of a Mask-wearer, the greater his chance of survival.

Armenios rose.

"Thank you, Bactrian," he said.

Demetrios rose. "Come at any time," he said.

His business prospered. He read the palms of courtiers, of important merchants, of priests, of officers in the army. Armenios never came to his table at the Poseidon, because he didn't want to be seen consulting a fortune-teller, but he invited Demetrios to his home. He learned that the Armenian had started as a scribe, but that the new king had promoted him, and he was uneasy over his sudden elevation.

Dismayed at how his physical conditioning was deteriorating, Demetrios started attending a gymnasium near the Palace, and there he worked out with prominent members of the community, then shared a cup of wine and a rubdown. He began to know quite a number of important people socially. He moved to a larger apartment and began to entertain.

He was more discreet about telling others of the king's impending triumph, but he did whisper into an ear here or there.

He missed tobacco, whisky, potatoes, chocolate, and even bully beef. Sometimes the cravings were so strong that he stopped whatever he was doing and simply tasted the memories of his old life.

One day he was sitting at his table at the Poseidon when he heard a deep, resonant voice behind him.

"What do you think you're doing?"

"Have a seat, Elpidos." Demetrios made a graceful invitation with a hand. The snowy-haired man sat opposite him and frowned.

"I advised you to leave Egypt," he said in English.

"Are you right-handed?" Demetrios said.

"Yes."

"Then give me your left."

"Why are you here?" Elpidos demanded.

Demetrios shrugged. "I've got to be somewhere, yeah?" he said. "I've got to earn a living. Alexandria is the richest city in the world—and the only advantage I have over any of the locals is that I know the future. So I've set up as a seer."

"That's very dangerous," Elpidos said. "You're too close to the king. One word from him and your throat is cut in the street."

"He—well, the Mask—has no reason to cut my throat. I've abandoned my mission, I have no intension of harming him in any way."

The other man's big nose was pointed at Demetrios like a sword. "You're up to something."

"From your heart line," Demetrios said, "I see that you have deep feelings, but you conceal them from others. You feel as if others don't know you."

Elpidos scowled. "You're not very good at cold readings," he said.

Demetrios hadn't heard the term "cold reading," but the meaning was plain enough. He grinned. "I'm doing well here. I seem to be good *enough*."

Elpidos said nothing for a moment, apparently thinking hard.

"I can't tell you anything directly," he said.

"But I can speculate, the way I did before."

Elpidos' dark eyes stared intently at Demetrios. "Speculate, then, on the origins of the Mask."

Demetrios decided he was willing to play along.

"No one knows for sure, but folks think it was created by the Tenocha of the far future, and given to their ancestors in other timelines."

"Speculate," said Elpidos, "what might be the case if that were untrue."

Surprise slowed Demetrios' thoughts. "Well," he said slowly, "if the Mask is here in ancient Egypt, it might be a lot older than the Aztecs."

"Speculate," Elpidos demanded, "who might have created the Mask if it was *meant* to be in Egypt."

Demetrios was finding himself a little flustered beneath Elpidos' demands.

"Well," he said, "*Egyptians*, I suppose. Egyptians from the future, and probably from another timeline."

"Speculate on their object."

Demetrios blinked. "Object? There's an object besides the Mask?"

Elpidos sighed. "What were they trying to achieve with the Mask?"

"Create an alternate timeline much like their own."

"And what—given what you see around you—might that future Egypt be like?"

Demetrios grinned and pointed at Elpidos. "This is that Socratic method, yeah? That I heard about in one of those Museum lectures?"

Elpidos nodded wearily. "Yes," he said. "I suppose it is."

"And your future Egypt? Starting from"—Demetrios looked around the city, seeing the crowds, the great Poseidon, the tall buildings on all sides—"here?" He thought about it. "Well, it would have science, wouldn't it? You start with the Museum and the Library and go on to being able to create things like the Mask. And you'd have philosophy. And really great architecture."

Elpidos nodded. "That is very much the country where I was born."

"So you're not Quechuan? Or Tenocha?"

Elpidos gave a weary smile. "Since you've come to the most important details without my telling you anything directly, I think we can dispense with the circumlocutions."

Demetrios laughed. "Whatever those are, mate."

"The Mask," the older man said, "was created for the pharaoh Ahmose, who lived at a time when Egypt was in crisis. The Hyksos invaders occupied Lower Egypt; the Nubians threatened from the south. But Ahmose couldn't put a foot wrong—he drove off the Nubians, then crushed the Hyksos so thoroughly that they vanished from history. He founded the New Kingdom and began the Egyptian Empire. And then . . . " Elpidos shrugged. "The Mask—originally it was a pair of goggles—was set into a mask of the Egyptian war god Menthu. But Ahmose's descendants did something incredibly foolish. *They buried the Mask with him.*"

Demetrios could only laugh.

"Leave it to the Gippos!" he said.

"It happened in one timeline after another," Elpidos said. "And so it was *our* turn to do something foolish. We gave up on Egypt, and gave the Mask to the wrong person."

Demetrios' laughter died in his throat. He stared.

"The Tenocha?"

"We knew there were drawbacks," Elpidos said. "We knew their religion was violent. But we thought that once they developed advanced civilization, the Tenocha would leave all that behind."

Demetrios snorted in amazement. "You didn't reckon that their ruling class would establish a totalitarian state and invent a thousand recipes for dining on human flesh."

"Well." Elpidos spread his hands. "Who would?"

"Anyone," said Demetrios, "who had fought the Nazis in the Western Desert. For a start."

There was a moment of silence. "Now," Elpidos said. "Here in Cuzco-81, Perseus dug up Ahmose's Mask, and he's on his way to founding an enlightened state." He looked at Demetrios. "Why stop him?"

"I'm *not* stopping him," Demetrios said. "I told you that."

"Some timelines are dominated by the Quechuans, who have an enlightened, scientific state, with a king and a parliament. Some are dominated by Egypt, who are likewise. What difference does it make to you?"

Demetrios gave him a puzzled look. "Well, mate, what difference does it mean to *you*?"

"You're a Greek. I'm a Greco-Egyptian. You should be on our side."

"What *side*?" Demetrios looked at him. "Why am I getting the feeling that there's a whole mess of conflict somewhere in time that you're not telling me about?"

Elpidos seemed exasperated. "There's a lot of things I *can't* tell you about!"

"Use the Socratic method, cobber. That seems to be working well for you."

Elpidos' hands tightened into fists. "I advise you to leave Alexandria."

Demetrios glared. "If you want me out of here, you can bloody well take me home! Back to the twentieth century, with a sack of money for my time and trouble."

Elpidos was outraged. "I can't!" he said. "If I did that, I'd—"

And then the snowy-haired man vanished. Apparently he'd said too much, or was about to.

Demetrios glanced around. Though the area around the Poseidon was crowded, no one seemed to have noticed the shouting, vanishing stranger.

Even when Elpidos was present, he thought, he seemed not entirely to be here.

In the autumn the king returned victorious. He had scattered Hyrgonaphor's armies in a lightning campaign, and the rebel pharaoh died on the battlefield. So complete was the victory that Ptolemy's control now extended to the Third Cataract. The ferocious war taxes that had so oppressed the kingdom were repealed, and celebrations ensued.

The realm was at peace for the first time since the death of Ptolemy Philopator, six years ago.

On the way home, Ptolemy had visited Thebes, where his old enemy Antiochus was held under house arrest along with his family, and married Antiochus' daughter Laodike.

The combined victory and marriage was celebrated with a parade, public banquets, and a festival of theater, poetry, chariot races, and games. Amid the fuss, it was hardly noticed that a half-dozen officials vanished, charged with conspiracy against Ptolemy, their property confiscated by the state.

Amid the public display there were also private parties and receptions, given by, or in honor of, returning veterans. It was at such an event that Demetrios met the king.

The occasion was a banquet thrown by an obscenely wealthy Syrian merchant named Heiro. Seven dining couches, each for three men, were set in a U shape, with tables set along the U's inner curve. There were no women guests, but rather flute-girls and gymnasts, entertainers whose occupation extended to casual prostitution.

It was a boys' night out, and one of the boys was Ptolemy.

Demetrios was surprised by the lack of pomp that surrounded a Macedonian king, at least in a private gathering. No one bowed, no one threw himself on his face, and no one called the king "your majesty." Ptolemy was addressed by his name, or politely as *kyrios*—which meant "lord" or "gentleman"—or *archon*, which meant simply the person in charge.

Ptolemy came with some friends; but if there were guards, he left them outside. He dressed simply, with a border of royal purple on his tunic, and his royal diadem was a simple strip of linen tied around his forehead, soon covered by the reveler's vine leaf crown that Heiro gave to all his guests.

Demetrios supposed that Ptolemy had every reason for being casual. The Mask would have informed him of any threat to his person, which would have been removed long before Ptolemy left the Palace.

As before, Demetrios thought that Ptolemy—once removed from the glamour of office—seemed a very ordinary person. He wasn't tall; his nose was beaklike; his chin was weak. Demetrios thought that he and the king were of an age, about thirty.

As soon as Ptolemy entered and the servants had finished washing his feet, he took a tour of the room and addressed each of the guests. He looked intently into their faces as he did so, and when his turn came, Demetrios found himself trying not to flinch from Ptolemy's eyes. He wondered if the Mask had shown Ptolemy his face, and if he'd doomed himself simply by being in the room.

"Congratulations on your marriage, *archon*," he said. "I understand the bride is beautiful."

Ptolemy's mouth gave a cynical quirk. "Beautiful or not," he said, "the marriage was necessary."

"I hope that fate, ah, coincided with your inclinations." Demetrios was pleased that he'd managed that on the spur of the moment. He was not very good at the sort of flowery, elaborate language that prevailed around the court.

Ptolemy gave him that searching look again. "You're the Bactrian soothsayer, aren't you?"

"I am."

A hint of grim weariness crossed the king's face. "I doubt I'll need your advice," he said. "I get plenty of advice as it is."

"I would never try to advise the king," Demetrios said. "I'm too foreign and too ignorant of Alexandria to be of any use. Besides, I am a chiromancer—and chiromancy tells us about the subject, not about the future." He held out his right hand. "If I may see your palm, *kyrios*?"

Ptolemy hesitated for a moment, then offered his left hand. Demetrios looked down at the palm and knew at once that he was in luck.

"You have a fate line," he observed. "Not everyone does." He traced the line with a finger. "It's deep and distinct—this means that fate controls you, *kyrios*. You may be king, but you are not free."

Through his contact with the hand he felt Ptolemy stiffen. Over Ptolemy's shoulder, Demetrios saw the eyes of his host, Heiro, widen in horror.

"Ptolemy," Heiro said, "perhaps you'd like to meet more of my guests. Philhippos, here, has just returned from Rome . . ."

"Of course," Demetrios continued, "the pharaoh is of special interest to the gods. Perhaps a god commands you—and for the good of your realm, you obey."

He had rehearsed this speech for months, and had the pleasure of seeing it strike home. At first Ptolemy's face hardened, but then the hardness vanished, replaced by the searching look Demetrios had seen before.

"You're not an ordinary seer." Ptolemy spoke dryly. He freed his hand from Demetrios' grip.

"I'm very ordinary," Demetrios said. "Common as dust."

Ptolemy only offered a cynical smile, and then moved on to greet Philhippos, and ask the news from Rome.

The summons from the Palace came three days later, with three uniformed guardsmen appearing by Demetrios' table at the Poseidon. Demetrios marched along between them, uncertain whether or not he was under arrest. The guardsmen didn't know either.

Demetrios sat in an anteroom while a troop of soldiers, veterans of this last campaign, marched in and received awards. The courtier Armenios drifted through the room and gave a start of alarm as he recognized Demetrios. He ghosted away in a cloud of *chypre*, pretending not to know him.

After half an hour Demetrios was then ushered into a room with dainty Ionic columns, a polished marble floor, and Ptolemy's chair, which was rather too modest to call a throne. He was dressed more formally today, with a purple cloak and a metal diadem, almost a crown, with spiky golden sun's rays, an asp, and a pair of golden ram's horns meant to identify the king with Zeus-Ammon.

Ptolemy rose, shrugging off the cloak and leaving it on the chair.

"Demetrios the Seer," he said. "Come with me."

He led Demetrios to a terrace overlooking the Royal Harbor, with its sheds for the Egyptian warships, its views of the Poseidon and the temple of Artemis, and just across the water the Pharos, the enormous lighthouse with its trail of dark smoke that marked the harbor by day. Demetrios was stunned for a moment by the view.

"Lovely, isn't it?" Ptolemy's tone indicated he was preoccupied by something other than the view.

"Your city is beautiful, *archon*."

"And at peace." Ptolemy frowned. The sun glittered from the spikes on his diadem. "At peace for the first time in years."

"Is the peace under threat?" Demetrios asked. "If that's so, there's very little I can do to help you. I'm not a politician or a military man."

"Antiochus wasn't our only enemy," Ptolemy said. "While he was fighting with us over Coele Syria, Philip of Macedon took our Aegean islands as well as Lycia and Caria in Asia Minor. But since then, Philip's got into a war with the Romans." He stroked his receding chin. "I'm advised to strike at Philip now, when he's distracted by the war in Greece, and regain our possessions."

"The advice is logical enough," Demetrios said.

"But yet," said Ptolemy, "Egypt is at peace. We are a rich country. As things stand now, Egypt and our Syrian possessions are protected by secure frontiers. Greece and Asia minor are in continual flux—if we take Lycia and Caria back, we're in a constant military dance with Macedon, with Bithynia, with Galatia, Pontus, Pergamon, with the Achaeans and Aetolians and Spartans . . . and with Rome. Their intrigues are never-ending—I could find myself in a war started by any of them."

"It's a wise man," said Demetrios, "who knows the meaning of the word, 'enough.' "

Ptolemy looked at him from under a cocked eyebrow.

"And yet," he said, "it's not just Asia Minor that's in flux—it's the whole world. The Romans have just crushed Carthage and taken their possessions in Spain. Now Rome has armies in Greece fighting Philip. I've disposed of Antiochus myself. It could be argued that I should grab what I can out of the chaos and establish as secure a position as I can, before some other power—Rome, say, or Pontus—takes everything, and then marches on *me*."

Demetrios looked closely at Ptolemy. "*Has* someone argued that position, *kyrios*?"

"I am receiving advice to that effect, yes." Ptolemy's face was carefully neutral.

"From a trustworthy source?"

"Oh, yes."

Demetrios felt his heart beat faster. "A trustworthy advisor," he said, "is beyond price to a ruler."

Ptolemy said nothing. Demetrios considered his next words carefully.

"Is it a god, *kyrios?*"

Ptolemy's eyes flickered.

"Though you make no such claim yourself," Demetrios said, "the Egyptians say that the Pharaoh is the god Harpocrates. So it wouldn't surprise me if gods spoke to you."

Still Ptolemy said nothing. Demetrios stepped closer, spoke in a tone of intimacy.

"A god spoke to Diodotus, the founder of my own country. The god spoke through a kind of mask." Ptolemy gave a start. "A mask of Hermes," Demetrios said, "like you see in the theater when a god steps onto the stage. Diodotus followed the advice of the mask, and he defeated his enemies and created a great kingdom."

There was a passionate intensity in Ptolemy's eyes, but calculation as well.

"I am a tolerably well-educated man," he said. "I was brought up in the palace, and have heard the ambassadors of many nations speak. When I was growing up I listened to many historians and many philosophers lecture in the Museum, and I never heard this story about Diodotus."

Demetrios smiled. "In every family there are secrets that are never shared with outsiders." He nodded his head at the king. "I am a descendant of Diodotus, though now in exile like the rest of the family. Though you are a king and I a fortune-teller, *kyrios*, we share one thing in common: we both have the name of bastard."

Ptolemy's face was hard. "Where is this mask now?"

"Diodotus ordered it melted down on his death. But his heirs were unable to destroy it, so they buried it with the king."

Grim lines settled around Ptolemy's mouth. "Why did he want it destroyed?"

"He felt it had usurped his freedom. Though its advice led to his success, Diodotus felt he had become a pawn of the god. And the mask demanded certain acts which he found repugnant."

"Like kill a child," Ptolemy said, half to himself. "A child that had done no harm to me, or to anyone." He straightened, looked out over the Royal Harbor. "Yet it can be justified." He made a sweeping gesture, taking in the Palace, the temples, the warships, and the smoking Pharos. "No thirteen-year-old boy could have held *this*. I have brought a victorious peace that the boy could never have achieved." He raised his brows, turned to Demetrios. "Yet now my . . . my Oracle . . . wishes me to start another war. To jeopardize the peace I've built. To take those ships out of their sheds, pack them with men, and send them to Lycia."

"Your Oracle has brought you success so far," Demetrios said. "I won't advise you to disregard it."

He wasn't about to give the Mask a chance to kill him.

Ptolemy spoke on stubbornly. He had begun a confession, and now he would finish it. "I would be happier," he said, "if the Oracle explained its reasoning. But no—instead it's *go here, do this, issue this order*. It even ordered me to marry a spoiled fifteen-year-old princess, which was not my inclination, and still isn't." Ptolemy suddenly looked very weary. He paused, and then continued.

"When I was in Thebes the Oracle instructed me to send soldiers to a house on the northern edge of town and kill everyone there. I don't know why—I don't know what crime these people committed or if they had committed a crime at all." He frowned. "They did have some rather remarkable chain mail armor. So perhaps they were assassins, though they didn't otherwise seem very well armed."

With a shock Demetrios realized that this was another of Cuzco's attempts on Ptolemy, one that had apparently met with the same fate as his own.

The Quechuans hadn't worked out yet that Ptolemy had a Mask. Demetrios wondered how many lives would be lost before the Colonel or his superiors realized what they were up against.

Not that the Quechuans would *care*, Demetrios thought bitterly. They didn't do their own fighting, and more mercenaries were easily procured.

They weren't willing to face the Mask themselves, he realized. That's why they used soldiers for hire.

Ptolemy continued without observing that Demetrios' had become distracted. "And when I returned to Alexandria," he said, "the Oracle told me to have certain people arrested and executed. It didn't tell me why. They may have been conspirators, they may have been thieves—or perhaps the Oracle simply used them to create an example."

"It seems to me," Demetrios said, "that even though the god doesn't explain himself, he's more trustworthy than any mortal."

Ptolemy looked skeptical. "Perhaps," he said.

"If the god is advising you to invade Asia Minor, he has good reason for it. Though the war may be evil—the same way killing a child is evil—yet it may prevent a greater evil."

Ptolemy raised an eyebrow. "A greater evil than a general war in Greece and Asia Minor?" he said. "*That* is evil indeed." He raised his hands to his head and took off the diadem. He held it before him, the spikes and ram's horns glittering.

"Do you know," he said, "I never believed in the gods. The philosophers at the Museum say they don't exist, and I followed their teachings. But now I know the gods exist, and that they are *terrible*—far worse than any man." He lifted the diadem again, and placed it on his brow. He turned to Demetrios.

"I am a king and a god's slave," he said. "It is my fate, and I seem unable to avoid it."

"Asia Minor?"

"I will invade." He made a gesture with one hand, as if throwing something away. "The god wishes it."

"And your son?" Demetrios asked. "Will you wish him to endure this slavery?"

Ptolemy seemed to consider the matter.

"I would wish my son to be free," he said. "And if the realm is secure by then, perhaps he will be."

"The king is wise," Demetrios said. He held out a hand. "Will you let me read your palm? After all, it's the only thing I'm good at."

Smiling, Ptolemy gave his left hand.

Looking down, Demetrios looked at the deeply creased fate line, and gave his reading.

It was impossible to fight the Mask, he knew. And he wasn't going to try.

Nor was he going to advise the king to disregard the Mask's advice. That might mark him as an enemy of the Mask, and then the Mask would tell Ptolemy to slash his throat.

He had based his advice on the understanding that the Mask advised its owner of the best course of action to take . . . *for that owner.* It would tell Ptolemy what was good for Ptolemy—not for Ptolemy's son, or wife, or horse. Only for Ptolemy. It wouldn't give Ptolemy's son Hipponax any instructions unless Hipponax actually possessed it, and then it would shift its allegiance to the son.

Therefore, Demetrios had reasoned, as long as he advised Ptolemy to follow the Mask's advice, he—Demetrios—would be safe. And if Ptolemy himself decided to keep the Mask a secret, and not to pass it on to his son, then the Mask would not object, because the Mask's duty was to benefit Ptolemy personally, not other members of the family.

If the Mask were buried here with Ptolemy Eponoios, then it wouldn't be around to advise a far-future Ptolemy, 1500 years hence, to invade Peru.

Demetrios figured he owed his employers that, at least. They had saved him from the Libyan desert in 1942—and if they'd subsequently abandoned him in ancient Egypt, it hadn't precisely been their fault.

The only drawback to his plan, Demetrios thought, was that he'd have to wait a long time to find out whether or not it worked. If he remembered his briefings correctly, Ptolemy Eponoios wasn't scheduled to die for another twenty-eight years, when he would finally be overtaken by some illness—cancer, heart disease—that the Mask had no way of preventing.

Twenty-eight years, Demetrios thought. That was an awfully long time to wait for a plan to come to fruition.

But then, he thought, he had enlisted in a war of many centuries. And at least if his scheme failed, it wouldn't affect him personally. He would continue to live in the greatest city on earth, enjoying the patronage of its elite.

And in the meantime he could continue to advise the king, and read his palm, and urge him to ensure that his son remained free.

And perhaps he would invent a few things that would make life here more comfortable. Windmills, pumps, the printing press.

And maybe he could find tea. He would really like a good cup of tea.

After all, he would be here for a very long time.

Afterward to "The Fate Line"

I first met Fred Saberhagen sometime in the mid-1970s, shortly after the Saberhagens moved to New Mexico. He had a sinister smile that made me just a little anxious, and I found myself uneasy in his company. It was only later that I realized he was wearing vampire fangs—very subtle vampire fangs that had been created for him by an orthodontist, and which weren't at all obvious at first glance.

That episode served as a very good introduction both to Fred and to Fred's style of humor.

I've joked elsewhere that there were at least three Freds somehow shoehorned into his skull. There was the logical, rather optimistic Fred who wrote the Berserker books and *The Empire of the East* and its sequels. There was the sardonic, world-weary cynic who wrote the books about Dracula. And there was the Fred From Another Planet who wrote such strange and wonderful one-offs as *Love Conquers All*, *Century of Progress*, and *The Veils of Azlaroc*, the latter of which is certainly in the running for the title of Weirdest Science Fiction Novel of All Time.

Fortunately I got to know all three Freds over the years. Plus of course the guy who wore the vampire fangs.

While I'd read and enjoyed Fred's work over the decades, I'd never fully appreciated his skill as a craftsman until I attempted "The Fate Line." *Mask of the Sun* is a novel involving time travel, parallel worlds, and a gadget that confers something like omniscience on the user. Any single one of these elements would try

235

the skill of most writers—time travel and parallel worlds are subjects that dazzle the creator with far too much possibility, and omniscience is a device that completely does away with suspense (if the hero's got it, he wins; if he doesn't, he loses). Yet Fred juggled *all* of these elements to produce a complex, intriguing, entirely original and perfectly suspenseful novel.

I confess to being completely intimidated by the thought of mastering all these components. It was only the thought of deep time that saved me—I realized that if you were fighting a war over all of history, the war wasn't necessarily won or lost in one encounter. And furthermore a war needn't be fought with weapons—what my protagonist could do against an invincible antagonist was plant an *idea*, and then wait the necessary decades to see if it bore fruit.

Wax, Clay, Gold
by
Daniel Abraham

"The Mask now in his hands had no high cheekbones, nor mouth or chin, nor was it gold. It was not much more than a large pair of goggles. A century would pass before the Mixtec slaves encased it in a gold model of a smiling face."—The Mask of the Sun

We four were soldiers in a war not merely without end but without boundaries: time travel, precognition, multiple universes. None of us wore the faces we were born with. Our homes might not have been in the same reality. A semi-infinite Aztec empire had spread out across a still-semi-infinite-but-smaller-subset-of-possible universes and guided by a golden mask that was, for all practical applications, the voice of the Prophet that wanted to show us our still-beating hearts as we died. So what was our big problem?

Killing time between missions.

Base camp this time meant a high-tensile Habitrail sunk under a bed of the Amazon. All the good hidden Andean peaks in this version of reality had been mapped and mined, and when you can't aim high, you shoot low. The murky, muddy bottom of the River Sea was about as low as we were going. The five of us sat in the commissary module with nothing to do but reread a paperback copy of *Heart of Darkness* and trade dirty jokes.

" . . . and he said, 'I didn't know your dad was a *pharmacist!*' "

We weren't getting through a lot of Joseph Conrad.

"Okay," our team leader said with a sigh. "So this couple is celebrating their first anniversary, right? And . . . "

She was from San Francisco circa 1867. Turned out the 1860s were a lousy time to have your kid develop metastatic brain cancer, and she'd jumped at the chance to sign up as long as her kid was on the medical plan. Now she had the nut-brown skin and prominent nose of a Mayan matriarch. The special-ops expert was prettier than her, and God alone knew what he'd looked like before he got recruited and remade. His heavy brow and hooked nose left him looking as much a native as any of us, and I'd started life as a Korean girl who weighed ninety pounds soaking wet. The first time I'd seen our special-ops expert, I thought he hated us just from the way he held his mouth in a permanent half-smile, half-scoff. Weeks underwater with him had softened my impression. I kind of liked him.

" . . . 'I thought you wanted a golf club!' "

"Okay!" the demolitions expert said, pain in his voice. "Enough. No more jokes."

"The *Nellie*, a cruising yawl, swung to her anchor without a flutter of the sails, and was at rest?" I suggested.

"Not that," he said.

"Most frustrating mission you ever went on," our team leader said and pointed at me. "You start."

I thought about it for a few seconds while the river murmured against our stationary submarine.

"I was part of a scheme to hijack the mask by dressing up as Quetzalcoatl and getting to the First Speaker before Cortés. Only, the mask saw it coming. The only grain between the drop and Tenochtitlan gave the horses colic. Instead of being hailed as gods, we spent the window trying to get a bunch of Austrian Warmbloods to fart. Cortés rode right past us."

"Ouch," the demolitions guy said. "I was on one to insert an operative into Pizzaro's famous thirteen. Only . . . "

"Only, the mask saw it coming," I said.

"Yeah," he said. "Total waste of time."

"What about you?" I asked the special-ops guy, only kind of flirting with the way I said it. "How did the mask screw you over?"

The special-ops guy was quiet for a long moment. The team lead and I exchanged a glance. This was interesting.

"My worst?" he said. "It wasn't the mask that blew the mission . . ."

Tochtli's cell in the slave pits reached long enough for him to stretch out at night without his head touching the far wall, if he kept his feet against the door. In the morning, Mauhizoh woke him with a shout and led him through the streets with the other slaves to the workshop. Mauhizoh always claimed to be an overseer because the others were the children of war prisoners and enemies of the Aztec while his own father had been Aztec and high-born at that. Tochtli didn't think the *pipiltin* treated Mauhizoh with greater respect than any of the other slaves, but he could tell it made the big man happy to think they did, so he never mentioned it.

At the workshop, they ate a paste of ground corn with bits of grease, drank a cup of something nameless and alcoholic, and went to work serving their masters. Some of the slaves brought the clay, purifying it and working it until it took on the right thickness and consistency. Others stoked the fires in the furnaces hot enough to turn silver, gold, tin and bronze soft enough to pour. Pretty young girls from the village brought bricks of wax still smelling of honey to trade with Mauhizoh for beads and scraps of wire.

Tochtli sat on his stool, knife in hand, making metal sculpture from clay molds, clay molds from wax models, and wax models from wax and blade and his own whimsy.

On the morning that the trouble started, the workshop was baking hot. Tochtli had just poured a crucible of molten silver into a mold, filling the gate channels until he saw the dark, dancing metal lurking at the bottom of the gate holes. Then lifting it by the spinning rope, he made two slow turns, bringing the mold up to speed. The mold was singing in a wide circle of air above his head when Mauhizoh came in with a man Tochtli had never seen before.

"Be careful," Tochtli said calmly.

The new man ducked his head and backed away, reflexively avoiding a blow to the head that was really nowhere near striking him. Mauhizoh put a hand on the new man's shoulder to stop him. In answer to the new man's questioning look, the overseer nodded to the melting oven: blistering live coals with a pot of molten silver still nestled above the hard-fired bricks.

"That," Mauhizoh said, "will burn your skin down to bone long before our little rabbit knocks your brain loose."

"Good to know," the new man said.

"The spinning pushes the metal into all the finer work," Tochtli said. "Pushes out the air bubbles."

"If you say so," the new man said, eyeing the spinning mold nervously. Tochtli slowed his burden, letting the mold come down. The silver was lower in the gate holes now. Tochtli grinned.

"See?" he said, pointing.

The new man nodded. He had a heavy brow and high, lordly cheekbones. His mouth fell naturally into something half-smile, half-scoff. It occurred to Tochtli how good that face would look in silver or bronze.

"We have a new slave for the pens," Mauhizoh said. "Say hello to Cuixtli."

"Hello to Cuixtli," Tochtli said, but no one laughed.

Later, when the sun was sliding down the western arc of the sky and the silver had taken the time to cool, Toctli split off the clay mold and considered the casting. The pendant came out well: a vast monkey leaped, carrying a huge pack over its back. Tochtli ran his fingers over the monkey's belly, the texture of fur made metal. It had translated from wax to silver just the way he'd expected, but next time he might make the cuts just a little finer. He'd make sure the clay didn't get too much grit in it. When there was sand in the clay . . .

"You can stop playing with your monkey," Mauhizoh said coming into the room. "It's not your monkey anymore."

Tochtli sighed and put it down.

"It isn't," he agreed.

Mauhizoh rapped his knuckles on the casting.

"Solid," he said. "It's good work."

"It's not being solid that makes it good," Tochtli said. "But, yes. It's solid, and it's good."

"Cuixtli is a good worker. Smart. Hardly had to tell him what to do before he was keeping up with the others," said Mauhizoh.

"That's nice," Tochtli said, picking up a broom and starting at the far corner of the workshop. He didn't like to leave clay chips on the floor, and the mold always threw off more than he expected.

"I need a favor," Mauhizoh said.

"You always need a favor," Tochtli agreed.

"I'll get you a second blanket," Mauhizoh said.

"You always promise that, and you never do it."

"Of course not. If I actually gave you one, what could I offer next time?"

Tochtli stopped sweeping and leaned on the broom, working through the logic of that. The overseer squatted against the wall, his back against the plaster. His face took on an almost comic look of sorrow.

"You should see her," Mauhizoh said. "Etalpalli, her name is. She brings wax every week. Sometimes it's not even hers, but she carries it for other women. She does it to taunt me."

"What do you want?" Tochtli asked as he went back to sweeping.

"Something small, but pretty. A frog, maybe? She'd like a frog."

"I can do a frog."

"But gold. For this one, gold."

"Gold is nice."

"But I don't *have* any gold," Mauhizoh wailed, putting his hands over his face in despair. Then, a moment later, he peeked through his fingers. "You wouldn't happen to have any spare? Lying around, maybe? It wouldn't need to be much."

"No," Tochtli said. "Overseer won't allow it."

"Fine, hold that against me."

"Not holding it against you. I'm only pointing out—"

"But next time, you could hold back a little? Just a little."

"Enough for a frog, you mean."

"A small frog."

"I can do what I can do." He tapped the overseer's knees, and Mauhizhoh shifted to the side to let him sweep.

"A medium-sized frog would be even better."

"If I can do it."

"You're a genius, little rabbit. You can do anything."

When he was finished with the clay shards, Tochtli considered the ashes in the melting oven. He didn't know why he liked cleaning clay, but hated cleaning ashes. The coals were barely warm. Still, he chose to leave them for the next day, on the assumption that his overseer would be willing to forgive the transgression.

The nights weren't cold, but they weren't comfortable, and Tochtli was pleased when Mauhizoh's shout came in the morning.

He liked his pen well enough, but his workshop was better. As they passed through the city streets, he found the new man making a point to walk beside him.

"They tell me you're the caster," Cuixtli said. "The one who makes all the masks."

"That's me," Tochtli agreed.

"Must be hard, doing all that. Pouring so much of yourself into making things for the people who are oppressing you."

Tochtli frowned, trying to understand how Cuixtli thought he would get enough silver and gold to work if the Aztec didn't bring it to him.

"Not really," Tochtli responded.

"But to have freedom," Cuixtli said, and then, looking down the path toward the workshop, "Never mind. We'll talk more later."

A crowd of men stood at the doorway to the workshop. They wore bronze helmets and brightly dyed garments. The swords at their sides were the bronze blades of the Aztec and the wood-and-obsidian *macuahuitl* that symbolized the Mayan elites that each man had slaughtered. At the head of the group of slaves, Mauhizoh went pale, motioning his underlings to stop work.

Tochtli watched the overseer go forward and bend almost double, twisting at the waist like a dog hoping to be petted. The soldiers barked orders and pushed him back. He retreated. His skin shone pale and clammy. He was trembling.

"Tochtli," he said. "There's . . . someone here. You should come."

Tochtli walked forward with Mauhizoh, and the soldiers took them, walking two before and two behind, to the little workshop. Within, standing by his little stool and looking disdainfully at the furnace with its uncleaned ashes, was the Aztec known as First Speaker. Mauhizoh made a small gagging sound and fell to his knees, pressing his forehead to the ground. Tochtli looked at the guards, knelt down, and tried to match the overseer's posture.

"You know who I am, then," the First Speaker said.

"We are honored at your presence, great lord," Mauhizoh said, his voice trembling.

"Stand. Both of you."

Tochtli stood, rubbing at the spot on his forehead where he'd pressed it to the stone floor. First Speaker looked at them both, contempt radiating from him like heat from a fire. His broad, noble lip curled. Without speaking, he lifted a beautiful beadwork bag from the worktable and drew from it a featureless grey curve of an object. Tochtli frowned at the thing. It was made from no metal he'd ever seen. It glowed like oyster shell.

First Speaker held the object as if to converse with it. His expression was more nearly that of a man considering an equal than it had been when he spoke to the slaves. His eyes seemed to say *Really? These two?* The object made no reply. With a sigh, the First Speaker put the thing on Tochtli's stool.

"You are to cast a mask of gold with this concealed within it. Only in the eyes of the golden mask is this to touch the air. Do you understand?"

Oh, Tochtli thought. *It's a mask.*

"Yes, First Speaker," Mauhizoh said, reverently.

"If you try to wear it, either now or after it is cast, you will be killed in that moment. Do you understand?"

"Yes, great lord," Mauhizoh said.

The First Speaker snarled. For a moment he seemed about to scoop the shell back up, but then he stalked out of the workroom, leaving two of his guards behind him. Silence reigned. The soldiers crossed their arms, blades of the conqueror and conquered clacking at their sides.

"Well," Tochtli said.

"Yes," Mauhizoh said, color slowly coming back to his cheeks.

"We'll need some wax, then."

Tochtli had never had a block of wax as pure as the one Mauhizoh brought him. Tochtli scraped most of the ashes from the melting oven and lit a small fire. He only needed to soften wax, not gold. The temperature of the workshop hardly rose over the warmth of a summer day, but the guards still grew restless. Maybe it was their bronze caps. Once the wax had softened to a clear liquid, Tochtli fixed a bit of woven hair to the shell mask with a bit of gum and lowered it in. The level of wax in the form rose more than he'd expected, as if the mask was physically larger than it appeared. For the better part of the morning, he sat by the cooling wax, making sure the shell within it didn't twist or shift out of position.

By afternoon, the wax was solid enough to take out of its forms and set on his workbench. Then he asked the guards to send for

Cuixtli. The slave's high, lordly brow and subtly cruel mouth would do well in gold. As Tochtli made the first few general, shaping cuts, he found contentment growing in him.

The new man arrived looking grim and determined, which went well with his features. Tochtli considered the man as an object, then started working in earnest.

"A mask, is it?" Cuixtli asked.

"Yes."

"All in gold."

"All in gold."

The soldiers yawned, ignoring the slaves with the powerful indifference of rank. Tochtli smoothed the wax chin, cutting away where the neck would have been, then narrowed his eyes, imagining where within the wax the shell sat. It was a very good thing that the First Speaker had wanted the shell to show through at the eyes. The wax model would encase the inner mask except for those four spots, two for the outer face, two within. The clay matrix would hold it there when the wax melted away during the first firing, and then again during the pour. He'd need to be sure that the eyeholes were large enough to keep the shell stable when the gold poured down around it. Tochtli considered the wax, and the man sitting before him.

"Won't you have to try it on?" Cuixtli asked. "See how it fits?"

"No," Tochtli said.

Cuixtli glanced at the drowsing guards and spoke softly.

"But to make something of such beauty and never even wear it? How can you stand that?"

"It's just a mask," Tochtli said. "And I don't really like wearing jewelry. Could you open your eyes like you were surprised?"

The new slave did a good job of it. It didn't look particularly noble, but it would give more space on the shell for the clay to hold. With half a dozen fast, practiced cuts, the wax fell away. The face within it appeared. Cuixtli, but not. The eyebrows high and surprised, the noble lips pursed and pulled a little apart in a tiny, shocked "o". The eyes wide to accommodate the clay matrix. Carefully, he bored through with the knife until he scraped the shell. It was just where he'd expected it to be.

"Um," Cuixtli said. "Huh."

"You don't like it?"

"It's . . . not how I imagined it," Cuixtli said.

"I knew it," the demolitions expert said. "I knew I'd seen you before. You're it. You're the freaking mask!"

"I'm in a causal loop with it," the special-ops guy said. "The idea was I could get close by being the guy it was based on. They made me look like it so that it could be made to look like me. Snake eating its tail."

"Have I mentioned what a pain in the ass time travel is?" I said, raising my hand. "Total ass pain. Anyone want lunch?"

"If you're cooking, I'll eat," the special-ops guy said. "Anyway, we knew it was a vulnerable point. It's the first time the Aztec let the thing out of their sight in a hundred years. It's in the hands of a Mixtec slave. The idea was to get this guy to put it on, see what he had, and run off with it. If we could get the mask away from the Aztec, we could generate a window of opportunity. Do something that the mask hadn't already told the enemy how to avoid."

I walked to the commissary supply boxes, picked out a couple of meal packs and set off the heating element. The tinfoil packages popped like distant gunfire and started warming in my hands.

"Only the bastard wouldn't put it on, eh?" the team leader said. "And paradox boundaries make it so that you can't stuff the thing on his face or tell him what he's got or you drop out of continuity and he thinks you just disappeared, so . . ."

"No, no, no. He put it on," the special-ops guy said. "It took me a while, but I talked him into it. But the thing was, it was the wrong mask, you know? I mean, you've all seen pictures of it, right? Looks like you just asked whether it farted? Well, the one this guy made was totally different. Sort of Montezuma meets Edvard Munch. I didn't know if I'd set off another pod of parallel universes or what."

"Have I mentioned what a pain in the ass parallel realities are?" I asked, handing him a meal. I sat and peeled the foil off my own. The air suddenly smelled of lasagna and buttered peas. Something —a log or a stone—bumped against the outer wall of the base with a clang, slid along, pulled by the river's flow. "Total ass pain."

"Whose idea was it to make the mask a mask, anyway?" the demolitions guy said. "I mean, what was that all about?"

"I read about that," I said around a mouthful of acidy tomato sauce and rubbery pasta. "The hypothesis is that if it hadn't gotten cast in gold, it would have been stolen about five years later by this girl the First Speaker was boffing."

"So the mask saw that coming and hid itself in with all the other gold crap," the team leader said.

"Have I mentioned what a pain in the ass precognition is?" I said. "Total—"

"It's not like that," the special-ops guy said. "This isn't the One Ring we're talking about. The mask doesn't intend anything. It's not alive; it doesn't have an agenda of its own. It just tells you what you ought to do."

"According to who, though?" the team leader said. "According to it."

"But it doesn't mess with you, even when you'd think it had some stake," the special-ops guy said. He hadn't taken a bite yet. "It doesn't tell you what it *wants* you to do. It tells you what it thinks you *should* do, even when the two are totally different."

"So, okay. What happened next?" I asked.

Cuixtli stayed on for most of the next day as well, though the major work was done. It was strange having all those people in his workroom. The guards, Cuixtli, Mauhizoh popping in and out constantly, and more and more as the mask took form. The face in the wax grew to seem as much a personality as any of the people made from flesh.

The wax form was finished, apart from some fine detail work, but that still left fixing lengths of wax to make holes for the pouring gates and venting holes in the clay mold. Tochtli didn't want to impinge on the front of the mask, where his smoothing would leave a different finish than the cast work. Better to have all that in the back where he could use a roughing stick to rub it smooth and no one would see. Tochtli held up the waxwork carefully, letting himself see where the gold would come in, how it would fill the empty space that the wax took up now. Where would air be trapped, and how much of it? Gently he pressed two thumbnail Xs into the back of the mask where the gates needed to go, and two more for the vents. He'd built short loops in the wax where a leather thong could be attached if anyone wanted to wear the finished thing. He wondered now if he'd made them too big.

"It's beautiful," Cuixtli said. "Really amazing work."

"It's not done yet," Tochtli said with a shrug, but secretly, he also thought it was beautiful. Doing good work left a pleasant warmth in his belly, like the aftereffect of alcohol drunk on a cold night.

"Hope it fits. Comfortably, I mean," Cuixtli said. "Wouldn't want it to rub on the First Speaker's nose or something."

"It will be fine," Tochtli said, though the truth was, Cuixtli's anxiety fed his own. If the pour went well, it would be a very nice piece in the end. He didn't want it to be marred by something as petty and avoidable as a poorly-shaped inner surface. And it would be so easy to check. Press it down onto the bridge of his nose for a few seconds, then take it back off. He could even keep his eyes closed. Surely the Gods and the First Speaker wouldn't object to that.

But constraints were constraints.

As the sun began to fall in the west, the reddened light invaded the pale wax. Tochtli thought it looked like the mask was blushing, like there was blood under those angled cheeks. The guards yawned, and Cuixtli sat forward on the stool, hands clasped between his knees as if he was waiting for something to happen. The right thing, of course, would have been to apply the matrix, let the first layer of clay harden overnight, then put the rest of the mold around it in the morning. But once the matrix went on, there was no chance to adjust the final shape of the mask. It would close the strange shell-eyes. The opportunity would be gone.

Bits of wax had built up under his nails throughout the day, and they ached now as they pushed the nail apart from the quick. He dug the residue out with the point of his carving knife and considered.

"All right," Tochtli said to the surprised-looking wax as much as anyone. "Clay in the morning, then. First thing."

During dinner, Mauhizoh came to his cell. It had been three days since the First Speaker came, but the big overseer looked years older. His skin seemed to hang off the angles of his face and his shoulders were hunched like an old woman's.

"How's it going?" he asked.

"Well, I think," Tochtli said, leaning against the rough adobe wall. His plate of beans and corn sat in the corner, making the air smell earthy and sweet. "But with the guards there, I don't know that I'll be able to keep enough gold back for your frog."

"My what? What? You were going to . . . ? No, rabbit. Don't skimp on the gold. This is the First Speaker! He hand-delivers people's hearts to the gods. Don't try to *steal* from him."

"I thought you'd want me to. For the girl."

"It will be very, very hard for me to woo Etalpalli if I don't have a heart," Mauhizoh said. "Honestly, little rabbit, if you weren't living where someone could take care of you, you'd walk into a gorge because you saw something pretty on the other side."

"I suppose I might," Tochtli said, ruefully. Then, a moment later, "It's going to be a good work."

"That's all I wanted to know."

"Do you think the First Speaker would mind if it didn't fit well?"

The overseer ran a hand over his deep-furrowed brow.

"He kills people who displease him. If you can make the thing perfect, make it perfect."

The words settled into Tochtli's mind with a satisfying click. If it was risking death one way as much as another, that made it simple.

"Thank you," he said. He slept perfectly that night in spite of the chill.

In the morning, walking to the workshop, Cuixtli was at his side as usual.

"I need a favor," he said. "Could you come to the workroom? I need you to distract the guards. Just for a moment while I try the mask on."

He knew that he was asking the man to wager with his own death, so Cuixtli's expression of relief confused him. But then, people often surprised him.

"I'll be there as soon as I can," he said.

Two hours later, Tochtli was mixing the clay matrix, waiting for it to reach just the right point between smooth and stiff, when Cuixtli came in the room with a pitcher of water. They spoke for a moment, then as Cuixtli turned, he stumbled and poured the water across one guard's chest. The guard shouted and pushed Cuixtli back and his partner started laughing. Cuixtli met Tochtli's gaze and nodded toward the mask. Tochtli remembered what this was supposed to be for, hunched over, and pressed the honey-sweet wax to his face.

For a moment, he was blind, the pale gray of the shell filling his sight. The wax was too thick at the brow and pressed in at the chin. It would be the work of a moment to open that space and—

Images flooded him. Like a whisper in the darkness, the pictures fluttered fast and insistent and vivid as the brightest dream. Information, instruction, plan all compressed into the space of a single breath, like it had been waiting to show him. He plucked off the mask. The wet soldier was in the process of kicking Cuixtli's rear as the slave scuttled out the door. The dry soldier was still laughing. No one had noticed.

With a trembling hand, Tochtli drew his carving blade and cut his adjustments into the back face of the mask, replaying as he did so everything he'd seen. Everything the gods had just told him.

"Well," he said to himself and the astonished mask. And again, "*Well*."

The clay matrix went on smoothly. Tochtli rubbed the gray mixture into the places where the lines were finest to keep all the detail work and texturing as near to perfect as he could, just in case. He took particular care in applying clay to the eyeholes, which would suspend the curve of shell in the mask-shaped bubble once the wax had drained out. By the time the coating was entirely applied, he had stopped trembling, and a slow, contented smile had found a new home on his lips. While the matrix set, he took out a block of fresh wax, sat on his stool, and began carving.

The process bored the Aztec guards. Keeping watch over a metalworking slave seemed beneath their dignity. They spoke with each other as if Tochtli wasn't there, and Tochtli ignored them as well. Under his fingers, the wax chipped away, and a tiny, delicate fish appeared. Tochtli blew away the fine chips of wax, considered the shape, and began working in scales with strokes of the blade barely more than caressing the little thing's side. Outside, dogs complained to one another and a woman's voice rose in an angry tirade toward a disobedient child.

At midday, Mauhizoh came with spiced chicken and beans for the soldiers, just beans for Tochtli.

"What's the matter?" the overseer asked.

Tochtli shrugged his question.

"You aren't doing anything. What's wrong?"

"Nothing. The matrix is setting. I'll need the rough clay for the mold soon, though. Can you have it sent in?"

Mauhizoh nodded and shot a covert glance at the soldiers wolfing down their food.

"The new one wants to come in. Talk to you."

"I don't think the soldiers like him," Tochtli said. "He spilled water on the short one."

"I'll bring the clay myself, then. He can find you on the way back to the pens. He says . . . "

Mauhizoh leaned close, murmuring so as not to whisper.

"He says you put on the mask."

"Only to check the fit," Tochtli said. "It's better now."

"You're a madman," Mauhizoh said. "If they find out—"

"Then maybe we shouldn't talk about it?"

Mauhioh opened his mouth, closed it, and nodded. Tochtli handed him the little wooden plank, bean drippings still wet on it. The overseer took it, then paused, staring down at the worktable.

"That's nice," he said, nodding to the tiny fish. "What's it for?"

"Just something I was thinking about," Tochtli said, grinning mysteriously.

"What? Is there a joke?"

"No joke."

"Then what?"

"Little joke," Tochtli said. "It only looks like a fish. It's really a frog."

The overseer left, muttering about madness and badly behaved slaves, but Tochtli could tell by the way he held his head that he was less anxious. The First Speaker's mask was safely in its matrix. With the rough clay around it to support the mold, they could cook the wax out of it in the morning and have the pouring done after lunch. Another day to break the mold, take off the lengths of metal from the gates and vents, polish the thing, and the First Speaker would have what he wanted and leave the workshop. If the Gods were kind, he would never have reason to come back again.

It was almost a shame it wasn't going to happen that way.

The next morning, Tochtli was awake before Mauhizoh came for him. He combed his hair with his fingers, humming to himself with a deep contentment while the other slaves groaned and yawned in their cells. They went to the workshop together. A cool wind had come up in the night, and high clouds scudded across the infinite blue sky. Tochtli thought about what you would need to do to capture the shape of the clouds in wax without making them too solid and ugly.

Cuixtli tried to walk beside him, but Mauhizoh had practically glued himself to Tochtli's side, nagging at him for reassurance that everything was as it should be, that the day wouldn't go poorly.

"I think it will end well," Tochtli said.

In the workroom, the mold sat like a brick. While the soldiers watched, Tochtli tapped the clay, listening to how it resonated. When he was sure that it had dried enough, he set a small fire in the melting oven, put the mold in a high-lipped bronze pan with a catching bowl just below the gate holes, and set them together in the fire. Tochtli watched as, hidden in its earthy cocoon, his careful waxwork unmade itself. It was only a few minutes before the water-clear wax began dripping out of the gate holes.

When the flow stopped, Tochtli waited, then took the pan from the oven. The clay mold had stained slightly where the burning wax had come out. Using a pair of wide tongs, he lifted the mold and set it on the worktable, then, careful not to burn himself, took the bronze catching bowl to the window to cool.

"You'll need to go," he said to the soldiers. "I have to get ready for the pouring."

The taller guard scowled and the shorter laughed in amazement, as if a dog had suddenly learned to speak.

"We have been days without leaving the mask alone," the taller one said. "Why would we go now?"

"Take it, then," Tochtli said. "I don't need it until the gold's melted. I only want the room prepared."

The soldiers looked at each other. It was, if nothing else, a chance to get out of the workroom. Carefully, Tochtli transferred the mold to a tray that hadn't been in the fire. The soldiers took it outside together, and he closed the door behind them. Quickly, he went to the window and dipped his calloused fingers into the spent wax. Heat had turned it black. Cupping his hands, he scurried to the space beside the door where the stones were roughest and let the wax fall in wide, spreading drops.

Using the tongs, he pushed the still-hot ashes in the oven to the side and used his carving knife to pry two of the bricks beneath the ashes apart. The crack between them was hardly thicker than a kernel of corn. He placed his stool beside the door, went to the center of the room, considered it, went back and moved a few inches to the right. Then finally, knife in hand, he took the thick rope he used for spinning the air out of the mold. He didn't cut, only measured off half an arm's length, scraped the cord until it frayed, and curled it up again where it belonged.

He walked the room. Everything was precisely as the vision had shown him. Except one thing. Carefully, he plucked up the wax-work fish. It wouldn't do to have it in the room when he melted the gold. Poor thing wouldn't hold its shape. He wondered if Cuix-tli would keep it for him.

"I wish you could have just stolen the thing," the team leader said, brushing back her hair.

"If there'd been even a chance that I could get away with that—"

"The mask would have seen it coming and stopped you," the team leader said. "I know, I know. But it would have been nice."

The demolitions guy who'd been quiet for a while shook his head.

"I don't think I buy that no-intentionality stuff," he said. "I mean, look, all those visions and plans have to have some kind of opinion behind them, right? Some reason that not getting stolen is better than letting you pick it up. It has to be able to decide what *it* wants."

"You're anthropomorphizing it," I said and took my last bite of pasta. "Just because it has a design doesn't mean that it's thinking for itself. A computer program isn't alive. It's just a list of instructions people coded in. It can behave in complex ways, it can respond to its environment, but all the things you'd call judgments are there because the programmers put them there."

"Even if the programmers weren't aware that they're doing it?" the demolitions guy asked.

"Maybe especially then," I said. "If you look at consequence as the same as intention—"

"Would you all please stop talking about computers?" the team lead snapped. I kept forgetting that she was from the nineteenth century and hadn't ever really wrapped her head around an electronic difference engine. In her world, everything we did might as well be magic.

"My point," the special-ops guy said, "was just that it's not self-interested. If it was built to show only the things that make the Aztec win all the wars, they wouldn't need to protect it. No matter who got it, it would push them toward the same end. What's the difference between telling Montezuma how to win the fight and telling Cortés how to lose it?"

"But it showed Cortés how to win," I said.

"Exactly. It shows you what you should do for yourself. Not for the Aztec, not for the Inca, not for the Pinkerton Corporation. For you. Makes me wish we *all* had one."

The tone in his voice was almost sorrowful. The team lead heard it too, her head tilting a little the way it did when she was trying to solve a puzzle. I felt a weird protective tug. I had the same sense she did that we were on some kind of dangerous ground here. Whatever had happened back there, it meant something more to the special ops than another funny story about how the mask had outwitted us all again. Difference was, she wanted to pry it out of him.

"So anyway, the bucktoothed guy finds you and asks you to hold his fish," I said.

"Man walks into a bar," the demolitions guy said, "goes up to a fella standing there and says, 'Excuse me, but could you hold my fish?' "

The special-ops guy laughed.

"Something like that, yeah. Well, it gets on toward lunchtime, right? And . . . "

The First Speaker arrived with only the warning of a sudden influx of slaves and servants. The fire in the melting oven was at its hottest, the gold running in its crucible like melting butter. Tochtli had stripped to a loincloth, and the soldiers were as wet as if they'd just crawled up from the bottom of a river. It was still a few minutes before the pour itself. Only a few. And, of course, when the door swung open and Mauhizoh came in looking like he'd swallowed a stone, Tochtli had been expecting him.

"It's fine," Tochtli said. "No reason to keep him out. Plenty of room."

"Don't light anything on fire," the overseer said. "And don't let anything hot burn him."

"I won't," Tochtli said, shaking the crucible. The gold sweated as badly as the soldiers. The puddle of it shuddered as only molten gold did.

He saw the surprise on the First Speaker's haughty face when the heat struck him. Tochtli bowed low, and the First Speaker motioned him to keep working, so Tochtli ignored him and went back to his tools. The mold sat on the floor, the gate channels up and ready to receive the metal. Mauhizoh haunted the doorway, and through the window, Tochtli caught sight of Cuixtli hanging from the branch of a tree and craning his neck to get a better view in. None of them mattered.

Carefully, he took the crucible and tipped the gold into the gates. Smoke rose up from the holes, but the clay didn't crack. So that was good. He set the crucible back in its place. In the grate, he could see the dark mark of the crack between loosened bricks. A thin, bright trickle of gold slipped out the vent hole, just as it was meant to. Tochtli capped it off. With bare and accustomed hands, he lifted the mold into the ropes and took it to the center of the room, swinging it around in a slow but quickening circle. This was the moment. He took a deep breath and swung the clay and gold in earnest.

To his right, the First Speaker backed away, avoiding a blow that was nowhere near his head, and onto the rough stones behind the door. Another whirl of the mold. Another. The First Speaker turned toward the guard to say something, but his foot slipped on a drop of spent wax, melted by the room's heat. The most powerful man in the Aztec empire slipped, grabbing reflexively at the taller soldier to steady him. The shorter soldier leaped forward, fouling himself in the stool, tripping, and falling to the ground. The ceremonial *macuahuitl*, symbolic of dead Mayan nobles, flew into the air, its obsidian edges as sharp as any blade forged, and caught the spinning rope just where it was weakest.

The rope broke. The mold flew through the air, shattered against the melting oven, and spilled white-hot shell mask, shards of burning clay, and an evil soup of molten gold down into the burning ashes. The *macuahuitl* struck the bricks. Everyone stood in silence. Mauhizoh's face had gone white as the clouds in the high air. The smaller guard began to babble an apology. Tochtli picked up a pair of tongs, went to the oven, and drew out the shell mask. Despite heat and insult, it was in one piece.

"It's fine. It didn't break," Tochtli said, and he saw the relief flood the First Speaker's eyes, just as he'd seen it do before. "I'm going to need another block of wax."

The second time Cuixtli sat for creation of the wax model, Tochtli made the eyes a little smaller, the expression more dour. There wasn't particularly a reason for the change. He just didn't like making the same design twice. And he had the strong suspicion that the shell mask would have shown him differently if it had been too bad an idea. The soldiers sat beside the window, blocking most of his light, but Tochtli didn't complain.

"Thank you, by the way, for watching after my fish," he said.

"You're welcome," Cuixtli said. Ever since the destruction of the first mold, the new slave had been tentative and careful around him. Tochtli couldn't guess why.

"Mauhizoh said you're doing really well," Tochtli said. "He's very impressed by you."

"That's good. I suppose."

"He's the overseer. It's good that he likes you."

"It is. And still, I'm only a slave. I have no freedom."

The words seemed almost forlorn, like a child trying the same argument that failed the time before.

"Would freedom get you more food?" Tochtli asked, his knife shaping the waxwork lips. When Cuixtli didn't answer, he let the question go. Part of the look of this second mask came from the grim expression of the man. Tochtli wished he knew what was bothering him. In truth, he was starting to like Cuixtli a little.

Mauhizoh appeared in the doorway with three earthenware cups. He ignored Tochtli and Cuixtli, taking the chocolate directly to the guards. Even though the First Speaker had been first to interrupt the pouring, the overseer had been doing everything he could to ingratiate himself to the soldiers. Which often meant giving them the alcohol that normally went to the slaves. Tochtli didn't mind.

On his way back out, the overseer stopped at the worktable. He pretended to consider the model still emerging from its block of wax.

"Good morning, Mauhizoh," Tochtli said.

"Yes, certainly. As you say," the overseer said. Then quietly but urgently, "Did you get it?"

Tochtli smiled and pulled a small object from his sleeve. Cuixtli leaned forward to look. A tiny, rough bar of gold, as long as a furnace brick and as wide as the crack between them. Tochtli slipped it away.

"Is it enough?" Mauhizoh asked.

"It is," Tochtli said, and nodded toward the mask. "I'll put the matrix over it while the mold for this one dries."

"You think she'll like it?" the overseer asked, and the anxiety in his face was colored by joy.

"I think so," Tochtli said. "I think women like fish better than frogs."

Mauhizoh grinned, remembered to be somber, and then grinned again. Cuixtli watched the big man leave, bouncing on the balls of his feet like a boy. The new slave's face looked oddly gray.

"Are you feeling well? Tochtli asked.

"Put it on again," Cuixtli said, his voice suddenly urgent. "Just for a second. While they aren't watching, just . . . just look."

Besides his own curiosity, something in the man's voice made it impossible to refuse. Tochtli finished cleaning out the eyes, smoothed the inner face of the mask, waited until the two men at the window were involved in a moment of private conversation that seemed to promise safety. He lifted the mask to his eyes, paused and then quickly brought it down again.

"What was it?" Cuixtli said. "What did you see?"

"Nothing," Tochtli said with a shrug. He narrowed his eyes, considering the wax face before him, then used his blade to raise the left cheekbone.

Yes. That was better.

The special-ops guy went quiet, then heaved one of the deepest sighs I'd ever heard.

"So there you go," he said. "I did what I was supposed to do. Slave put the mask on. He knew what it was and what it did. And . . . "

He flicked his fingers, all five together, like he was letting something go.

"That's just weird," the demolitions expert said.

"I think about him a lot," the special-ops guy said. "About what he *meant*, you know? It wasn't like the mask didn't have anything to say to him. It did what it always does. It showed him what he ought to do. Only . . . You know how I got into this gig? My dad had a stroke. Bad one. I was finishing my doctorate in cultural anthropology. I didn't even have enough money to get him the best that 2040 could offer. And then this white-haired guy with a big nose shows up and offers me a chance to fix him if I just sign on."

"We've all got stories like that," the team leader said, leaning forward on her knees.

"We do," the special-ops guy said. "But we made those choices when we were scared about someone we cared about being really sick. When we didn't really understand all of the implications. And then here's this slave. Guy gets locked up to sleep every night. He gets the mask, you'd think it would tell him how to get out, but it doesn't. It tells him to stay home. Just makes me wonder what it would have told me."

I blinked and looked down at my hands. I hadn't thought about my sister in years, but I could see her as clearly now as the day I'd signed on.

"The bad guys always win," the special-ops guy said. "They've got the mask. They know how to stop everything we try. Don't even have to know what they're blocking. And it's all spilled out across how many different timelines? Millions? Billions? How do you win that kind of war?"

"We have to try," I said, but my words seemed weak. Around us, the river hushed against the walls, water running to the sea that would never be back.

"I don't know what the hell we're doing here," the special-ops guy said, shaking his head. "I truly don't."

The four of us sat in silence. The smell of our food going cold filled the air. The special-ops guy had hardly taken a bite. Ghosts flickered in the corners of the room: visions of lives we all might have lived, losses we might have weathered. The demolitions expert cleared his throat.

"So," he said. "Medieval Japan, right? The emperor is looking for the greatest warrior, so he puts out the call, and the three samurai who show up, one's Japanese, one's Chinese, and one's a Jew . . ."

The new overseer arrived with the first rains of the season. Tochtli sat in his cell, waiting for breakfast. The other slaves were muttering and laughing and singing to each other or themselves. He just waited. The new overseer's face was pinched and nervous. He stood outside Tochtli's door.

"You're the caster," the overseer said. "The one the First Speaker spoke well of."

"That's true," Tochtli said.

"Did you know that Mauhizoh was going to run away?"

"I didn't know," Tochtli said. "But I thought he might. There was a girl he liked."

"And you didn't do anything about it?"

"I couldn't tell my overseer," Tochtli said with a smile. Something like amusement touched the corners of the narrow eyes.

"You're too clever for your own good," he said. "But as I'm in charge now, is there anything else I should know?"

Tochtli nodded and tried not to grin with pleasure and anticipation.

"He was going to bring me a second blanket," he said, and the overseer considered this, coughed once, and nodded just as Tochtli had seen him do before.

Afterward to "Wax, Clay, Gold"

On Fred . . .

Fred Saberhagen was my first real writing teacher. Back in high school, I was in a program that matched students who thought they might be interested in certain kinds of careers with professionals who actually had those careers. I'd read a lot of Saberhagen books without knowing he lived nearby. I knew the *Berserkers* and the *Books of Swords*. I read *An Old Friend of the Family* before I read *Dracula*. I wanted to write books of my own, and I was lucky. Fred was kind enough to show me a few of the ropes. Every Saturday, I went up to his house with a manuscript in hand. He'd go over it with me, show me where I was going wrong. I was just starting. Most of what I did was wrong. But he kept working at me, and I kept working at it, and around a decade later, I started making professional sales. Without Fred, I wouldn't have.

The Conquistador's Hat

by

John Maddox Roberts

Mexico, 1521 A.D.

They called him Cervantes the Mad. Of course he wasn't really mad. He was simply outspoken and not a respecter of persons. After all, had he not warned the governor, Diego Velázquez, that the rogue Cortés would take control of the trade-and-exploration expedition and enrich himself thereby? And had this prophecy not been fulfilled to the letter? True, he had delivered it while turning handsprings, grimacing and making rude noises, but that was just his way of stressing the importance and irrefutable truth of his message.

"A prophet is not without honor, save in his own country," Cervantes muttered to himself. Cortés surely would have done away with him, but Velázquez had many relatives on the expedition, and they protected him. In fact, they entrusted him with gathering evidence they could use against Cortés at His Most Catholic Majesty's court when they should all return to Spain. So far, he had found nothing of value. Cortés's own actions should have condemned him many times over, but the incredible wealth of Mexico pouring into the royal coffers bought much leniency.

But assuredly there must be evidence, Cervantes was certain of it. Today he expected an opportunity to search for something tangible, something that would secure a noose around that neck instead of a golden chain. The town was all but deserted, for Cortés and all the soldiers still sound of body were marching to the relief of some allied towns menaced by the still-resisting Mexicans. Malinali, whom Cortés had named Doña Marina, had gone with them to interpret between the Spanish and their Tlascalan allies. Today the house commandeered by Cortés for himself and Malinali stood empty. No guard stood at the door. What need had the great captain for a guard, when the very terror of his name was greater protection than a regiment of soldiers?

Cervantes was not afraid. He feared nothing and would balk at nothing to revenge himself upon the haughty captain, who treated him as he would a mountebank, not as a brave soldier deserving of honor. Nonetheless, he scanned the streets surrounding the house before venturing inside. He had avoided the march by feigning a return of the sweating sickness and taking to the house that had been set aside as an infirmary. There were no questions, nearly every soldier and cleric had contracted the disease and suffered its recurrence. The overworked Indians detailed as nurses had paid no attention when he rose from his bed and left. The friar who was usually in charge had gone on the march to render aid to the wounded and hear the confessions of the dying, should there be action.

The square before the house was deserted in the heat of the day. It was for this reason he had picked this hour. Satisfied that he was unseen, he passed through the door, which was no more than an embroidered hanging. The Indians did not use hinged wooden doors like Europeans. The first room was furnished only with crude chairs and tables made by Indian craftsmen under Spanish supervision. They were as innocent of civilized furniture as they were of doors. This was the room where the captain held meetings with his subordinates during inclement weather. Cervantes passed through this room and into the next.

This was more like it—the bedroom Cortés shared with his concubine, Malinali. The broad, rope-based bed was piled with luxurious cushions and rich fabrics, gifts of the dead king Montezuma. On one wall was a broad, thin disk of polished silver such as the Indian nobles used in lieu of a looking glass. From pegs on another wall hung the captain's finest clothes, both Spanish and Indian. There also hung his broad, plumed hat of purple velvet. He had ridden out arrayed for war, dressed in armor and helmet and had left these fine things behind.

His mission was to find incriminating evidence, but Cervantes had a sudden impulse to see what he would look like wearing the captain's fine hat. He doffed his own filthy cap and stood before the silver mirror, trying the hat at varying angles until he found the most flattering. The light was at the wrong angle, so he lifted the mirror from its pegs and shifted it until the light displayed him at his most dashing. There was a vast feather cloak that had once belonged to Montezuma himself, and he had to try that as well, so he draped it over his shoulders and admired the breathtaking vision of himself. The cloak was sewn with what had to be millions of feathers plucked from hummingbirds, each individually sewn to the cloth so that the colors faded and blended with one another so beautifully that they dazzled the eyes. A whole village of Indians surely must have labored for years to produce this cloak.

So lost in admiration for himself did Cervantes become that more than an hour passed in trying on all of Cortés's finest things before he came to himself and saw that the sun was falling lower in the west and soon the square would be peopled and he might be seen leaving the house. Hastily, he put all the clothes back where they had been, last of all the fine, plumed hat with which he was loath to part. He was rummaging through the leather-covered Spanish chest and finding nothing of interest when he remembered the great silver mirror. He carried it back to its place and was about to hang it on its pegs when he noticed that a stone of the wall that the mirror had covered was somehow different from the others. The fine Indian stonework required no mortar, and this single stone stood a tiny bit proud of the others.

Instantly Cervantes remembered the great treasure storeroom they had found in the palace of Montezuma, walled up so cleverly that it would have been safe from discovery by anyone save Spaniards, who could smell gold through stone. This had to be the hiding place Cortés had made for his greatest treasures, which meant for his greatest crimes. Cervantes drew his dagger and, very delicately, pried at a corner of the stone, careful not to scar its fine polish. Slowly, it moved outward until his fingertips could get firm purchase on the rougher sides and pulled it away from the wall.

It was only two or three fingers thick, its back coarse with chisel marks where it had been split away from the original cube of stone. Cervantes knew this had to be the work of one of the workmen Cortés had drafted from the burned fleet, for the Indians had no such chisels. He set the slab on the floor and peered within and saw the glitter of gold beneath a covering of silk.

He withdrew the casually wrapped bundle from the hiding place and looked for more but saw nothing. Puzzled, he unwrapped the thing and found himself holding a fine golden mask of Indian work. His expert hands assessed the weight at more than a hundred pesos of pure gold. It was a splendid thing, but these past two years he and all the Spaniards had seen golden treasures beyond the imagining of any European and this thing was but a paltry consideration in comparison with the great golden sun and other massive golden objects they had melted down or, in a few cases, sent back to Spain intact for their value as barbaric curiosities.

Nonetheless, Cortés had kept it for himself, and that meant he was withholding the royal fifth, the portion of all booty seized that belonged to His Most Catholic Majesty and Holy Roman Emperor, Charles the Fifth. To retain gold even to the value of a single peso that belonged to the Emperor was a crime of *lèse-majesté* and punishable by death. This was the evidence he needed. He would put the mask back and inform the Velázquez party of its existence and location. They would perform a search and find it, and that would put the royal noose around the neck of Captain Hernán Cortés. And it would be the doing of Cervantes, whom ignorant men called the Mad.

But the mask was clearly meant to be worn, and there stood the silver mirror. He had to try it on. He fitted the straps around his head. He knew that they were of human skin, but that did not bother him. These Indians were damnably impoverished in the matter of domestic beasts, so there was little leather to be had. The Spaniards had taken to using tanned Indian skin, which the natives themselves used abundantly in their devil-worshipping regalia.

The view through the eyeholes of the mask was somehow strange and distorted. He blinked a few times, trying to clear his vision. Then he saw himself in the mirror, but there was someone behind him. He whirled, and there in the doorway stood Cortés himself, still in his armor and with a thunderous expression on his face. Cervantes snatched the mask from his head and beheld an empty doorway. Cortés was not there. What devil's work was this? Slowly, he slid the mask back in place. There was Cortés, and now he saw more. In some strange, distorted fashion he saw himself approaching the captain, bowing and cringing, holding out the mask to him. What was this? Cervantes never cringed to any man, even when being flogged. He saw Cortés take the mask with a gauntleted hand, then the captain drew a dagger and thrust with it. The mask went opaque, as if curtains had been pulled over its eyes.

Cervantes took off the mask again. He had seen a vision. He was familiar with visions and had them often, but this one was different. This vision had clearly come from Satan himself, for the mask was the work of heathen devil-worshippers and it did the bidding of their master. Further, he had the distinct feeling that this thing *wanted* him to do what he had seen himself doing in his vision. Well, Juan de Cervantes of Madrid knew full well that when Satan wanted a man to do something, he should do the exact opposite. This was especially true when it was clear that he was expected to abase himself to the criminal Cortés and then probably get stabbed for his troubles.

The clattering of horses' hooves outside shook him from his reverie. Cortés was back already! Something must have made him call off the march. Quickly, Cervantes stuffed the mask down the front of his doublet. Devil's work or not, a hundred pesos of pure gold was a hundred pesos. He restored the cloven stone to its place, rehung the mirror, and then had a new thought. With one last, malicious gesture he was out the window and behind the house, sprinting for all he was worth for the dense tree line a few score paces distant. Then he was lost among the trees.

Moments later, Cortés entered his house, half supporting the ailing Malinali. She had come down with some malady, possibly caused by the foul air of a swamp they had passed. He did not wish to confer with the Tlascalans without the services of his loyal interpreter, so he put off the march for another day. The allied towns could hold out for a few days longer without his help.

Thus preoccupied, it was not until evening that he noticed that the broad, plumed hat of which he was so proud was not hanging from its accustomed peg. In its place was a filthy cap he recognized as belonging to that wretched clown, Cervantes the Mad. He sought for Cervantes earnestly, but the fool was never found.

Germania, The National Socialist Republic of Europe 2032 A.D.

From his office atop the Museum, Chief Administrator Hans Muller contemplated the view of the capitol laid out before him. He could see the imposing triumphal arch, so vast that four or five of the similar one in Paris could have fitted beneath it with plenty of room for wheeled traffic to pass through. Beyond it, down the Avenue of Victory, was the Great Hall of the People, capped by a dome so immense that, when a million people were assembled within it during the great celebrations, their exhalations would condense, forming clouds overhead to rain upon the multitude.

It was all quite tedious. The Founders had been hypnotized by the Fuhrer's enthusiasm for architectural gigantism, and all sense of proportion had been discarded in the intoxication that followed the total victory over all resistance within Europe, western Asia and North Africa. Thus their heirs were saddled with these architectural monstrosities and the almost inhuman maintenance they required. At the outset it had been determined that the marshy ground beneath the old capitol called Berlin was unsuitable for monuments so massive and weighty, but in the first flush of victory it had seemed that nothing was beyond the capabilities of the German people. The ground beneath the future Germania had been excavated and filled with a pallet of concrete to a depth of fifty meters, and the titanic monuments built atop this. In expenditure of material, labor, and life it had dwarfed the building of the Great Wall of China by an order of magnitude. Granted, the life sacrificed had been subhuman for the most part, but still . . .

As he had so many times before when surveying this panorama, Muller sighed at the waste. What marvels might have been accomplished with all that treasure had it been put to some use beyond the glorification of People and Party.

Now, the Museum beneath his feet, that was different. It had been built for a purpose—a glorious purpose. It was not the empty posturing of a generation of men who had started from nothing and made themselves masters of the only part of the world that counted for anything. A genuine visionary, the Founder Hermann

Goering, had built this magnificent institution in his imagination as his invincible armadas of the air had pounded London and Moscow to rubble. When his revolutionary superbombers had crossed the ocean to devastate New York and Boston and Rio de Janeiro into submission, he had envisioned this marvel. While the other Party officials built vainglorious monuments to themselves, he had created the ultimate embodiment of the genius of a whole race, the Museum of Aryan Culture.

Muller stood atop forty stories of art, half a kilometer on each side, containing every great work of art created by his people—the contents once held by the Louvre, the Prado, the Hermitage, the Metropolitan Museum, the Uffizi, the British Museum, the less-famous but nonetheless important collections of Oslo, Edinburgh, Naples, and a hundred, a thousand, unremembered and unimportant collections, public and private, all of them residing now beneath his feet. There were vast laboratories devoted to conservation, research facilities, whole publishing houses, everything needed to preserve the heritage of western civilization. There were even floors devoted to the "artistic" works of the lesser races of Asia and the Americas, even of Africa.

There was only a single exception, a single collection that had escaped the acquisitive voracity of Hermann Goering, and remained independent to this day. It still rankled, and it was much on Muller's mind just now.

"Herr Muller." It was Gruber speaking over the hailer. "The emissary from the Vatican has left the Adlon and will be here in five minutes." Gruber was always very precise about these things. He was sometimes wrong, but always precise. He would never say anything as sloppy as "a few minutes."

Muller went to his private elevator and descended to the atrium. He hoped this emissary would be more reasonable than the last several had been, but he doubted it. The man was staying at the Adlon instead of one of the more modern, world-class hotels that abounded in Germania. It stood to reason that a man who spent his days in a sixteenth-century palace would feel more at home in the grand old lodging that had stood when this city had still been Berlin and was rich with the charm of the Old Regime. It also suggested that he would be a stubborn traditionalist, determined to keep the treasures of the Vatican in Rome instead of here, where all the masterpieces of the race belonged.

But then, Muller thought with satisfaction as he exited the elevator, this time he had been authorized by the government to employ
extraordinary coercion. He crossed the vast atrium's pavement of
fabulous green marble, glorying as always in the presence of the
greatest art the world had ever known. This was the Great Hall of
Sculpture and in its center stood Michelangelo's crowning achievement, the *Florentine Apollo*. The hall was thronged with tourists
and uniformed schoolchildren under strict supervision. High up
on one wall a huge portrait of the Founder Hermann Goering
benignly oversaw his creation. He was depicted as a young man
in his First European War uniform, the *Pour le Mérite* gleaming
blue at his throat. Facing him on the wall opposite was an equally
large portrait of the Führer, aloof, his eyes fixed upon destiny. He
had been a great patron of artists, Muller reflected, but his passion
had been architecture. The city without was his monument. He
had even designed the Museum personally, to assure its harmony
with the rest. But everything inside had been Goering's doing.

He passed through the great doorway, thirty meters high and twice
that in width, walking out onto the terrace that topped the grand
stairway. From here the view was not as spectacular as that from his
office, more than a hundred meters overhead, but it was fine enough.
From here he could see the Great Hall of the People framed by the
Triumphal Arch, quite possibly the most-photographed composition
in the world. The sky was alive with aircraft, the lower elevations
with lumbering transport helicopters and the swifter police and
surveillance craft. High above them streaked jet liners and Luft-
waffe warplanes, always vigilant lest the Chinese grow ambitious
once more. The Avenue of Victory, twenty lanes in width, the
north- and south-bound lanes separated by a broad barrier of magnificent linden trees, was crowded with a miscellaneous traffic of
trolleys, omnibuses, and autos.

When the Daimler limousine pulled up at the base of the steps,
Muller checked his watch. Exactly five minutes. Gruber had been
correct this time. The chauffeur opened a passenger door and the
man who emerged startled Muller slightly. He was accustomed to
the plump, soft-looking bishops and cardinals usually sent by the
Vatican. This one was a tall, quite dark, hawk-featured man who
looked more like a soldier than a churchman. He wore a long black
surplice with red buttons and a red sash, and atop his craggy head
the red skullcap sat ludicrously. He ascended the stairway with

easy, springy steps and was not winded when he reached the top. This must be one of those mountain-climbing, skiing, polo-playing prelates one heard about sometimes.

Muller held out his hand. "Monsignori Aldo Capelli? Welcome to the Museum of Aryan Culture. I am Chief Administrator Muller, at your service." The hand that enveloped his was no more than firm, but it felt powerful enough to crush bricks.

"And I bring you the Holy Father's warmest regards," Capelli said. His German was excellent, but he had an accent Muller couldn't place. It certainly did not sound Italian.

"Please, come inside. I know you would like a look around before we talk business. I can't give you a full tour, that would take weeks, but I can show you some of the highlights."

"I would like that, yes."

"Is this your first visit to Germania?" Muller inquired politely.

"It is. I had seen only pictures. The reality is quite—otherwise."

"I understand. It is always overwhelming to a newcomer." They passed inside.

"A magnificence purchased at a certain human cost, I understand."

It seemed an odd statement. "The Founders were hard men of a hard generation. It fell to them to save European civilization from unparalleled danger. This task could not be accomplished with gentleness. They had known much sacrifice and suffering, and they felt no compunction in . . . employing the enemy survivors to restore Germany, and then all of Europe after the devastation of the War for the West. They accomplished all this, took on such a task, so that we, their posterity, might enjoy the blessings of peace and Aryan civilization." It was of course straight out of the Party handbook memorized by every European schoolchild, but it seemed as good a way as any to explain to foreigners how the modern world had been created. Whatever he was, this churchman did not seem to be a European. But now the man was studying the *Apollo* with an odd intensity.

"A neat bit of sculpture work, that," he said dryly.

"I should hope so," Muller said. "This is held by many, including myself, to be the highest achievement by any Aryan artist."

"I meant the way he's been de-circumcised. That couldn't have been easy. And you can't even tell that the sling was ever there. And turning the stone into a golden apple was clever. It wouldn't have done to have a statue of a Jew as the centerpiece of the museum, would it?"

"The only way Michelangelo could get away with creating the first Classical nude in more than a thousand years was to cast him as a mythical Hebrew hero," Muller said. "The Church authorities, you know. The Inquisition and all that. Our Founders were not the first hard, cruel men to govern."

"Touché," Capelli said, nodding.

"So, our people restored him to the artist's original vision. It is quite clear from his writings that a Greek god was his intent." Muller saw an opening. "You can see, Monsignori, how cooperative the people of Florence have been. Not only is their Apollo so prominently displayed, but the paintings of Botticelli have a wing to themselves. We have long hoped for similar cooperation from His Holiness."

"The people of Florence lacked, shall we say, the resources to keep their heritage intact. The Vatican is by comparison rich in resources and international support and prestige."

Time to back away and try another tack. "Pardon me, Monsignori, but I cannot quite place your accent."

"Ah, that puzzles people frequently. My family is Italian in origin, but we have lived in Venezuela for generations."

"That explains it." It explained a number of other things as well, such as the churchman's coloration and facial features. A touch of native blood there, no doubt of it. Not that Muller was a fanatic in racial matters, of course, far from it. Some of the more daring geneticists held that a very small admixture of genes from the lesser peoples actually conferred benefits on the Race. Hybrid vigor, they called it. This certainly seemed to be a formidable and intelligent man, even if he was not pure Aryan.

"Administrator," Capelli said, "might I ask a small favor?"

"Please do so."

"I know that all the great works of European art outside of the Vatican reside here and in time I hope to see them all, but today I would like very much to see your unique collection of Mesoamerican art."

"Indeed?" Muller said, taken somewhat aback. All the glories of Western art in a single building and this man wished to see the work of savages? But there was his heritage to consider. "Of course, it shall be my pleasure. Do come with me."

They crossed the atrium and passed between the Venus de Milo and the Winged Victory of Samothrace to an elevator. Inside, Muller instructed the uniformed attendant to take them to the twenty-seventh floor. "Monsignori, most of the envoys sent here by the Vatican are from the diplomatic corps. If you will permit me, you do not seem to be of that profession."

The churchman smiled, revealing large, very white and some-how fierce-looking teeth. "No, I am a scientist."

"Truly? And what might be your field of study?"

"Theoretical physics. Not a field much encouraged in your institutions, I fear. Associated too much with certain, shall we say, 'eccentric' philosophers of the previous century."

"So it is. Nonetheless, quite a respectable and legitimate field for research, I am sure." The attendant announced their arrival at the requested floor and they exited to a broad hallway. It was all but deserted, and the trolley that whispered up to them on broad rubber wheels carried no other passengers. This floor was devoted to the arts and crafts of savage races and was not much frequented.

"The von Hutten collection," Muller said.

"As you command, Herr Administrator," the driver said formally.

"An interesting man, Philipp von Hutten," Capelli said. "Sent out to the New World by the Welser family of Augsburg as little more than a clerk, and within a few years he was one of the wealthiest men in the world, discoverer of unimaginable mineral wealth at a time when the Spaniards were wringing Mexico and Peru dry of their last traces of gold."

"Certainly an interesting character," Muller agreed. "The Spaniards earned the greatest fame in the history books, but there were German adventurers out there as well. Von Hutten was made governor of Venezuela, as I recall. Is that the reason for your interest?"

"Partly. His descendants returned to Germany and became very influential, did they not?"

"Decidedly so. Quietly, they became close advisors first to the kings of Prussia, then the kaisers, and later, it is said, to the Party and to the Führer himself, though they never appeared with him in public. Like the great banking houses, the von Huttens preferred to remain in the background. To this day, it is unclear what sort of guidance they gave their sovereigns, but it must have been valuable to have kept them in favor over so many generations."

"Perhaps they could see the future," Capelli said, smiling faintly.

"If so, that would be a valuable talent to have. Is that part of your theoretical physics?" This was idle talk, Muller knew, but it served to pass the time until he could put the thumbscrews to this affable but difficult man. With his great and worldly diplomatic corps, why had the Pope sent this odd scientist as his representative?

"It could be. Some of us think that time itself is not as inflexible as most people believe." The trolley drove them past gallery after gallery. Outside each stood some monument to identify what was displayed within: a towering Tlingit totem pole, a Maori ancestor figure, an arch formed by the tusks of an African elephant, even a huge stone head from Easter Island. "Some of us entertain the theory that separate threads of history may split off when events or decisions other than the ones we know from our own history occur, and these alternate time streams run parallel to ours. Suppose one of those fellows there"—he pointed to a rank of terracotta warriors from the tomb of Shih Huang-Ti—"decided that he really didn't like his emperor and killed him and took his place and as a result now, many centuries later, China is the center of a worldwide empire. Only this empire lies in a universe parallel with ours."

This conversation had taken a very strange turn. "One can see," Muller said, "why the Founders deemed this sort of science decadent and unhealthy. Forgive me, Monsignori, but these speculations seem to me to be little more than a form of insanity. Aryan science is grounded firmly in reality, in those things that can be observed with the senses or with instruments—tested, measured, and their properties assessed."

"Those are adequate for the study of most phenomena," Capelli agreed affably, "but not for everything." The trolley stopped before an entrance guarded by a pair of giant warrior figures from Tula. "For instance," he said as they dismounted, "at this very moment, there could exist an alternate universe right next to ours in which, oh, let us say, the Allies were victorious in the Great War for the West. It might be a world where the United States of America wielded supreme power and where what was then called the Third Reich went down in ruin."

"The 'allies'?" Muller said. "I am unfamiliar with the term. Do you mean the Jewish hegemony? The Bolsheviks and the American syndicate led by Rosenfeld and the British Churchill gang? The Founders saved the world from those brutes, for which we may all be grateful. They certainly would not have been sympathetic toward your Church, so you might say that the Vatican and the papacy owe their existence to the valor and determination of the Führer and his comrades."

"So one might," Capelli agreed as they went into the small but exquisite gallery. There were stone idols and intricately worked vessels and altars that had once held human hearts. Along one wall, behind glass there hung a row of glorious feather capes, their colors faded but still stunning in their complexity and the masterfulness of their workmanship. With them hung shields likewise bedizened with feathers and fantastically painted, and there were warrior uniforms so strange they might have been the work of an alien species.

"The ancient Mesoamericans were certainly craftsmen of high skill, and their color sense was well developed," Muller said, looking down at a glass case displaying a row of sacrificial daggers with obsidian blades and handles that were sculptures in themselves, inlaid with turquoise, jet, mother of pearl and coral, figures that might have been dragons or human or some unearthly combination of the two. "But their imagination was primitive, dominated by terror and superstition. They did not have the breadth of soul one must have to create true art. Their creations divert, but they do not elevate the mind. Their music never rose above the level of the flute and the tom-tom, and as for literature, drama—they had none at all. There was much to marvel at, but theirs was a dead-end culture, and its passing did not impoverish world culture as a whole. It is a stretch even to call it a civilization, despite their admittedly impressive architecture and strict civic control."

"Some of them had highly developed mathematics," Capelli mused, studying a calendar.

"Even that was a sort of idiot-savant accomplishment, developed without reference or application to any other science. They could calculate precise dates thousands of years in the future, but never invented the wheel. They built great cities of stone, but never had the arch or anything more sophisticated than post-and-lintel construction."

Capelli studied a case of small trinkets made mostly of copper but of exquisite workmanship. "Not much gold here," he noted.

"No, by the time von Hutten established himself, there was little left that had not been transferred to Europe. Even these costumes and sculptures were mostly acquired by the family as they expanded their operations into Yucatan and Mexico proper. They had already been discarded as the natives were reduced to peonage by Spain."

"Yet, I believe there was one piece?"

"Ah, you refer to the mask?" Muller said. "You've done your research. It was kept a secret by the descendants of the family until quite recently. They used it in some sort of pseudo-Masonic family ritual for many generations." He shrugged. "I suppose their long sojourn among the primitives infected them with a taste for native mumbo-jumbo. It's here in the back."

He led Capelli to an alcove at the rear of the gallery. Clearly, it had been constructed recently, and there still lingered a scent of fresh paint. In the alcove stood a pedestal of mahogany and atop it a stand beneath a dome of thin, crystal-clear glass. The stand held the mask. It was of massive gold, a stylized human face, smiling faintly.

The churchman let out a sigh. "Aztec."

"Yes, a rare piece that escaped the Spaniards. According to a letter written by Philipp's son, the family founder obtained it from a very obscure conquistador who claimed to have been a member of the first Cortés expedition some years before. Apparently he had spent much of the intervening time making his way to Venezuela, hiding out in the jungle from some imagined fear. Eventually penury and desperation sent him to Philipp, and he offered it for sale. According to the letter, he was quite daft and seemed afraid of the thing. I suspect that he was much like the salty old sailors who hang about bars in the tropics with treasure maps for bargain prices."

"Yet obscure madmen have been known to change history," Capelli mused. "Sometimes with catastrophic consequences."

Muller decided that he had spent enough time humoring this man, who was not acting at all like a diplomat on a very sensitive mission. "Monsignori, you are aware that next year we celebrate the centennial of the founding of the Republic?"

"Ah, yes, the centennial. Your Führer has invited the Holy—"

"Your pardon, Monsignori," Muller said, hanging tightly to his composure, "there was only one Führer. The title was retired with his passing, never to be used by a lesser man. The Republic's head of government is the Chancellor."

"Oh, yes. I keep forgetting." He did not take his gaze from the mask.

"In any case," Muller went on stubbornly, "the government of the Republic desires very much that certain art objects from the Vatican collection be loaned to the Museum for exhibition during the centennial celebration which will occupy the entire year. I assure you that more people will be able to enjoy them in that time than ever see them in the Vatican during the course of a century."

"Is that so?" Capelli said, his attention still on the golden face before him. "I do hope you don't want the Sistine ceiling. It would be awfully difficult to transport."

"Of course not!" Muller fumed. "Just certain of the paintings and sculptures. Michelangelo's *Pieta*, the Belvedere Apollo, the Laocoön, Bernini's—"

"Tell me, Administrator, has the Museum ever returned any work once 'loaned'?"

"Do you question the honor of the Republic, and of this institution?" Clearly, it was time to remove the gloves. "Monsignori, I have been given certain negotiating powers by my government. For many decades now, we have respected the property of your Church within the Republic. We have not interfered with your clergy or your rituals, though of course proselytizing has been discouraged. However, if you persist in resisting our entirely reasonable requests for cooperation in the matter of the Vatican collection, we will be forced to reconsider our stance regarding the Roman Church."

"I don't see any alarm system on this case."

"What? What are you saying? Of course there is no alarm system! Do you think this is a jewelry shop? This is the Museum of Aryan Culture! No one would dare to disturb our collections! The punishment for anything of the sort is death, and not a pleasant death at that."

"So I don't suppose there's any real security here either, is there? Just a few ex-policemen to chuck out the occasional disorderly drunk?"

"Monsignori, it is clear that you are unwell, if not genuinely insane. Shall I summon a physician? If not, I must demand that you return to Rome and rest assured I shall also demand an explanation of why you were sent here on so serious an—"

From beneath his sash Capelli took a tubular object of what appeared to be copper and glass, not much larger than a writing pen. He pointed it toward Muller and pressed something with his thumb. There was no sound or visible display, but Muller found himself quite unable to speak or to move. Oddly, he did not fall, but stood rooted where he was. Capelli replaced the thing, then took the glass dome in his hands and raised it. It came up freely, and he set it carefully on the floor. Then he picked up the mask with an expression of wondering triumph.

"Muller, if you only knew how long we've searched for this thing. Decades of just trying to figure out what went wrong here." From within his surplice he took out a small, folding satchel. With great care, he placed the mask within it. It fit perfectly. Slung from the churchman's shoulder, it looked like an ordinary dispatch case.

Now from a pocket somewhere he removed another, much smaller metallic tube. This he held beneath Muller's nostrils, and there was a sound as of a minute spray. In a moment he felt a slight tingling in his extremities.

"In a few minutes you'll be able to walk again, though it will be an hour or two before you can talk." He looked wistfully around the gallery. "I wish I could take all of this with me. None of it exists anymore where I come from. But the mask is all that counts, really. Now, come along."

Capelli took him by the elbow, and Muller found that he could walk as long as someone was urging him to. By the time they exited the gallery, his steps were no longer stiff and he was walking almost naturally. At Capelli's gesture a trolley stopped and they climbed aboard. The man from the Vatican was silent until they were in the elevator again.

"That conquistador. We think we know who he was now, a buffoon named Cervantes. It took years of research to connect him with von Hutten, who should have been beheaded a few years after he arrived in Venezuela, having accomplished nothing."

They left the elevator and crossed the great sculpture hall, and in a few moments they were out on the terrace. Capelli scanned the spectacle of Germania and shook his head. "Some bad things were supposed to happen in this timeline, but nothing as bad as this."

From somewhere overhead a helicopter detached itself from the orderly air traffic and descended toward the terrace. It did not look quite like any helicopter Muller had ever seen, and its rotors were so quiet they were almost silent. As it settled onto the terrace, gaped at by scores of tourists, Capelli turned to him. "Right about now Aldo Capelli is waking up in his room at the Adlon. Tell him what you like when he gets here. You aren't going to have your centennial celebration. That copter will take me to a place where this mask will go back where it belongs."

None of this made any sense, not his paralysis, not this madman's ravings. Timeline? What was that? The Vatican emissary, or whatever he was, walked over to the helicopter, and Muller noted with astonishment that the pilot was a woman. He had never seen a woman helicopter pilot before. Somehow that was as insane as all the rest. Just before boarding, the man who had called himself Capelli took a last look down the Avenue of Victory and looked at the Great Hall of the People framed by the triumphal arch.

"And I'll tell you another thing, Muller. Your Führer was the most tasteless architect who ever lived." Then he got in, and the helicopter lifted away in near-silence.

Once they were out of Germanian airspace, he unstrapped himself and took off the silly, uncomfortable canonical clothing. Then he sat back next to the pilot, comfortable again in singlet and bush trousers and sandals.

"Get what you came for, Major?" she asked.

"Got it. A lot easier than I expected, too. You have anything strong and liquid? I need to wash the taste of this place out of my mouth."

Without taking her eyes from the controls, she rummaged in a flight bag next to her, then handed him a silver flask. "Here. It's peach brandy from back home. Hey, Major, say what you will about these people, but they really know how to handle air traffic."

He took a long swallow and sat back against the seat, his eyes closed. "Yeah, you're right. That's the kind of people they are."

Afterward to "The Conquistador's Hat"

I knew Fred Saberhagen for many years, but never saw as much of him as I'd wished. *Mask of the Sun* was a masterly exploration of the ever-intriguing concept of parallel worlds and timelines and the perils of meddling with history. When asked to contribute to this anthology, something immediately came to mind: we dwell too much on the doings of great and important people. The fact is that idiots, morons, fools, clowns, and losers have probably had just as much influence on history; they are just underappreciated. Herewith, this story of how a total twit can bollix up history to an unimaginable degree.

Eyewear

by

Harry Turtledove

The sun was going down ahead of them. They were . . . somewhere. Estevánico had no idea where. Neither did his master, Andrés Dorantes. Alonso del Castillo of Salamanca also didn't know. And neither did Álvar Núñez Cabeza de Vaca, who led the four wanderers if anyone did.

Three Spaniards and a Moor, lost in some of the widest country God ever made. Three white men and a dark brown one, seeing things no one of their color had ever seen before. Estevánico didn't *suppose* he would rather have been sent underground to grub out ore with a pick—but it was a mighty near-run thing.

Cabeza de Vaca pointed toward the setting sun. He was thin as a nail—all four of the wanderers were famished all the time. The sun had burned him almost as dark as the natives: he wasn't much lighter than Estevánico, in fact. Neither was Del Castillo or Dorantes, come to that. None of the men wore more than ragged scraps of cloth barely covering their privates.

All the same, grim purpose filled Cabeza de Vaca's voice when he said, "The land of the Christians lies in that direction!"

He said the same thing every day at sunset. Estevánico was sick of hearing it—not that Cabeza de Vaca or either of the other two Spaniards cared a copper what he thought. For that matter,

Estevánico was a Christian only because the Portuguese raider who'd captured him said he would kill him on the spot if he didn't convert. In his heart, he remained more than half a Muslim. But he'd got used to the outward forms of Christianity by now. Even he didn't often dwell any more on what lay in his heart.

Cabeza de Vaca pointed again, this time toward some flat ground by the edge of a creek. "We'll camp there," he said. "Alonso, you have the firesafe?"

"I've got it," Del Castillo answered, and held it up: a hollowed-out branch, the opening almost entirely plugged, with tinder smoldering inside. It was one of their most precious possessions, not that they had many to compete with it.

They gathered fuel. They had to gather a lot; dry brush burned hot but fast, and this wasn't a country for trees. Estevánico caught a couple of fat lizards. Cabeza de Vaca knocked over a rabbit with a rock and then bashed in its head. Split four ways, that wouldn't be much, but it was something.

By now, Estevánico liked lizard meat. Hunger made a better sauce than pepper. A million stars blazed down after twilight faded. No city smokes hid them. No cities here, not for Allah—no, God—knew how many leagues.

Del Castillo woke Estevánico to take the midwatch. He was the slave, so of course he was the one who got his sleep broken up. That didn't especially bother him. Had the party consisted of three Moors and one enslaved Spaniard, the white man would have got stuck with the watch in the middle of the night. How else would things work?

Yawning, Del Castillo curled up by the fire. He soon started snoring. Estevánico walked away from the flames to get his night vision back. He could have run off—but what good would that do him? Then he'd be lost and alone instead of lost and in company. Company was better.

Off in the distance, a little wolf began to yip and yowl, and then another and another, till they sounded like a chorus of devils. No matter how they sounded, they were wary of men. They looked like large, sharp-nosed dogs. The Spaniards said they were smaller and yellower than proper wolves. Estevánico had never seen a proper wolf, but he was willing to take their word for it.

He carried an arm-long club with a flaked stone bound to the end by rawhide thongs. No one in these parts would have anything better. He didn't want to fight, but too often life wasn't about what you wanted to do.

Little by little, the hellish chorus died away, only to start up again a few minutes later. Estevánico yawned. "Can't do that," he muttered to himself in the Berber-flavored Arabic that was his birthspeech. The Spaniards wouldn't love him for falling asleep on sentry-go. He wouldn't love one of them who nodded off, either.

They'd kept on good terms with the natives most of the time in their journey through his unknown land. Still and all, it didn't do to take chances. Estevánico didn't *think* the red-brown men would try to sneak up and do unto them as Cabeza de Vaca had done unto the rabbit. He didn't want to find out he was wrong the hard way, though.

He looped around the fire to watch upstream for a while. Then he looped again to go downstream. While he was downstream, he pissed in the creek. He always eased himself downstream from a camp. The Spaniards didn't care one way or the other. Estevánico found that disgusting, but it wasn't as if you could tell your master anything.

He turned to start yet another loop, but he'd taken only a couple of steps when the side of his right foot brushed something lying in the dirt. He almost thought it was a branch and kept walking. But it didn't feel quite like a branch. At any rate, Estevánico didn't think so. And, since this was the most interesting thing that had happened to him since Del Castillo shook him awake, he squatted to find out if he was right.

As soon as his hands closed on it, he knew it was manmade. And its feel made him grunt in low-voiced surprise. The natives in this western land were splendid basket weavers. Many of their tribes had skilled potters. But they knew much less of metal than either the Spaniards or his own folk.

He hefted this . . . thing. It wasn't heavy enough to be gold—nowhere near. There wasn't much of that up here north of New Spain and New Galicia. There wasn't much of *anything* up here, come to that: only endless leagues of ground thinly settled by hunters and gatherers and a few farmers.

Pánfilo de Narváez had thought there would be more. Well, Pánfilo de Narváez, Satan curse him, had thought all kinds of things that turned out not to be so. His expedition from Cuba was nothing but a disaster. The only four left alive from it on the mainland

were Cabeza de Vaca, Dorantes, Del Castillo, and Estevánico himself. How long they would stay alive lay mostly in God's hands.

Estevánico held up what lay in his own hands. By starlight and
firelight he made out what looked like a pair of ungainly spectacles.
He frowned. Some middle-aged Spaniards wore eyeglasses so they
could go on reading after their sight lengthened. Estevánico, who
did not have his letters, thought them a silly affectation. He was
as sure as need be, though, that no natives wore them or knew
how to make them.

Which meant . . . what, exactly? That some other Spaniards had
stumbled through this wilderness? That other foreigners were
loose in these parts? Estevánico couldn't see what else it would
mean. Officials in Cuba and New Spain wouldn't be thrilled at the
news, which was putting it mildly. Estevánico couldn't do anything
about that, either.

He'd never held eyeglasses in his hand before. Awkwardly, he
set them on his nose. What *did* they do for the people who wore
them? For a few heartbeats, he didn't think these did anything at
all. The lenses were even darker than the night. Then, gradually,
by flecks and sparkles, they cleared, and he saw as well as he
had before.

As well? Better. Starlight suddenly seemed bright as the full
moon. He could *see* some of the little yellow wolves that howled
at the sky. A wildcat slunk along, paying the wolves no mind. Up
near the zenith, an owl glided by all ghostly.

He'd never heard spectacle-wearing Spaniards talk about anything like this. He wondered why not, if this was what eyeglasses
did. This wasn't just an aid to sight. This seemed more like magic.

That thought rose again in his mind as his time to go off watch
neared. The eyeglasses showed him someone who looked like him
walking back to the fireside. He followed the moving figure. It
took off the spectacles before kneeling beside Cabeza de Vaca and
shaking him awake. He wouldn't have thought he could hide them
under his rags, but the moving figure did, and he imitated it again.

"*Madre de Dios,*" Cabeza de Vaca said softly as consciousness
came back to him. "Is it that hour already?"

"*Sí, señor,*" Estevánico whispered back. They tried to keep from
waking the other Spaniards. It was probably wasted care; even on
bare ground, all four wanderers slept like the dead every night.

Their leader eyed the stars. Any man with eyes in his head could gauge the hour by their slow whirling. Cabeza de Vaca sighed. "Well, so it is," he said. "Get your sleep while you can. The sun will come all too soon to suit you." He sighed once more, got to his feet, and ambled off in the direction from which Estevánico had come.

Estevánico curled up on his side near the fire like a cat stretching out by the hearth. Next thing he knew, he knew nothing at all.

He looped a bit of string around one earpiece of the strange spectacles and managed to keep them hidden under his loincloth all the next day. It was what the spectacles themselves seemed to want. And they seemed to want to stay in place, too. They didn't inconveniently fall out as he tramped along, for instance. Maybe ascribing volition to them was foolishness. Then again, maybe it wasn't.

Buffalo moved across the plain. They drew off when they caught the wanderers' scent. Some of the natives constantly hunted them, so they were leery of men. Farming was a bad gamble in these parts: rain came sparse and erratic, and even rivers ran dry. Thunderheads piled up high in the sky, flat on top like God's anvils. If you were under one when it chanced to let loose, the storm would pound you flat. If not—which was more likely—you stayed parched. Puddles dried fast under the savage sun; mud soon baked hard as concrete.

Estevánico could hardly wait for night to come again so he could see what other marvels the spectacles might show him. He didn't even grumble when Andrés Dorantes shook him awake. His master gave him an odd look and asked, "Are you all right?"

"Sí, señor," Estevánico replied, so mildly that Dorantes's curiosity found nowhere to light. Muttering, the Spaniard lay down and went to sleep.

Estevánico walked out beyond the red glow the fire threw. He hoped he hadn't hurt the strange spectacles by rolling over on them while he slept. The ones the Spaniards used seemed pretty flimsy; the lenses broke easily, while the wire frames were always getting twisted and bent. But these were unchanged, unharmed, when he fished them out of his loincloth.

He put them on. As he had the night before, he saw more with them than he possibly could have without them. Even the stars seemed a little bigger and brighter and closer than they did to the naked eye.

Rather to his relief, he didn't see himself, or imagine he saw himself, doing anything before he actually did it. That was alarming. The natives here ate mushrooms and drinks made from mushrooms that gave them visions, but he didn't think what he'd seen was one of those. It was too precise, too closely connected to the real world.

"Hello there." The words, delivered in matter-of-fact tones, came from just behind Estevánico's left shoulder.

He jumped and whirled in the air like a startled cat. Whatever the eyeglasses had shown him, they hadn't shown anybody sneaking up on him. And . . . as his feet hit the ground again, he realized that impossible greeting had, impossibly, come in his own language. Maybe a few other slaves on this side of the ocean spoke it, but surely no one within a hundred leagues of him.

No one, that is, except the fellow standing there smiling. Though at least as swarthy as the sun-burnt Spaniards, he was plainly a white himself: no other race produced men with such a formidable nose. And his white hair was wavier and finer than the natives'.

"Who the devil are you? How did you get there without me seeing you?" Estevánico demanded, clutching his club. Since he was talking to a white man, he asked the question in Spanish. But he was ready to knock the bastard's brains out if he didn't like the answer he got.

"Well, you can call me . . . ," the white-haired man said. Estevánico scowled. He seemed to hear the name deep inside his head, not with his ears at all. And he seemed to hear it twice, as *Esperanza* and *Amal*. He knew you could see double if you got a knock in the head. Could you hear double, too? More to the point, could you hear double if you *hadn't* got a knock in the head?

He needed another couple of heartbeats to realize both names meant *hope*, the one in Spanish, the other in Arabic. That could mean anything—or nothing. Estevánico gripped the club tighter yet, ready—eager—to swing it in a deadly arc. "You still didn't say how you snuck up on me like that," he growled.

"It's . . . complicated." Esperanza/Amal looked and sounded faintly embarrassed. "I can't really explain it to you. If I do it just right, maybe I can show you without getting caught in a temporal loop."

Estevánico also heard that phrase in both Spanish and Arabic. The only problem was, it made no sense in either language. "Talk sense, God curse you," he said.

"I told you—I can't talk so that it'll make sense to you. But try this. Now you see me . . . . Now you—" His mouth open for the next word, Esperanza/Amal vanished like a blown-out candle flame. Not even the miraculous spectacles gave the faintest clue of where he'd gone or how he'd gone there.

Andrés Dorantes would have been disappointed that Estevánico didn't cross himself as a good Christian should have. Instead, the Moor made a two-fingered sign against witchcraft that came straight from his native village.

"Now you see me again," Esperanza/Amal said, once more from behind Estevánico. The Moor spun again, not quite in such horrified astonishment as he had the first time. The big-nosed, white-haired man had an engagingly homely grin.

"How did you do that? What kind of *brujo* are you?" Estevánico still didn't make the sign of the cross, now mostly likely because he feared it would do him no good.

Esperanza/Amal sighed. "I'm no he-witch, only a man who knows how to do things you don't, the same way Spaniards know how to do some thing the natives here don't. If you're really curious, I traveled into the future, took a few steps, and came back almost to the moment I'd left. If I'd tried to come back to exactly that moment, I would have created a paradox. If I was lucky, both of me would have disappeared. If I wasn't so lucky . . . Count your blessings, friend, that you don't know *how* complicated life can get."

His words sounded like a madman's. Estevánico would have been happier had he believed Esperanza/Amal was one. Unfortunately, the mysterious stranger had the air of an artisan who knew his own craft as well as anyone could, even if he struggled to explain it to an ignorant outsider.

And he eyed Estevánico the way a smith, say, might eye an iron bar that wasn't red-hot anymore but that would still burn the hide right off your palm if you were fool enough to try to pick it up. "Speaking of paradoxes and complications, I don't suppose I ought to be surprised you found your charming eyewear. Considering what the four of you pull off . . . " He shook his head, annoyed at himself. "I can't say too much, or I generate a different kind of paradox and I really do disappear—disappear so I can't come back for a while, I mean. But then, speaking of paradoxes, unless you found the toy on your nose there, I don't think you could manage what you do at all."

"Wait." Much too much was happening much too fast for Estevánico. "By some kind of magic you . . . went into the future?" Esperanza/Amal nodded. "How far into the future?" Estevánico asked.

"I can't tell you," the white-haired man replied.

Estevánico nodded. That made sense—a lunatic's kind of sense, perhaps, but sense even so. "However far it was, somebody whenever it is still remembers what the Spaniards and I did, uh, do, uh, will do here." He struggled with verb tenses, but he knew what he wanted to say.

Esperanza/Amal paid him the courtesy of not pretending not to understand. "You said that. I didn't. I couldn't. If I tried—*pffft!*" He made a noise like a man spitting a slippery melon seed out between his teeth. Estevánico imagined him squirting out of this time like a spat seed.

"Tell me one thing, since you seem to know about it. Tell me what I can do with this." The Moor touched the spectacles' frame.

"Every now and then, it will . . . suggest things. Maybe you've seen that." Esperanza/Amal waited till Estevánico nodded, then went on, "If you're smart—and it sure looks like you are—you'll follow the suggestions. There aren't many sets of, uh, eyewear like that. For all I know, maybe there's only the one, except in different phases. Or maybe—"

All of a sudden, he wasn't there anymore. Estevánico hoped he was playing another trick, but he didn't pop back out of nowhere this time. If he'd been on the point of saying too much—on the point of saying something useful to Estevánico, in other words—something or Someone took him away before he could.

Too bad, the Moor thought. The next thing he wanted to find out was how to tell his Spanish companions he had the—what did Esperanza/Amal call it?—the eyewear, that was it.

Since he couldn't ask the man with the white hair and the big nose, he asked the eyewear itself. An image formed, one of him holding the curious spectacles and saying . . . Saying what? Saying something. Whatever it was, the eyewear wouldn't or couldn't let him hear. It worked with and through sight, not sound. *Too bad*, Estevánico thought once more.

He hid the eyewear again before waking Alonso del Castillo to take the last watch. But that couldn't go on much longer, and he knew it. After a meager breakfast of muddy water and some leaves the natives chewed, the wanderers set off again. With the morning sun at their backs, their shadows stretched long before them, then slowly shrank.

They followed game tracks and the natives' trails whenever they could. As long as those headed west, they offered an easier way forward than untrodden ground. But when they forked, the men who'd already come so far often hesitated, arguing over which path to take.

They hadn't been walking for more than half an hour when the trail forked for the first time today. Cabeza de Vaca pointed to the more southerly track at the same time as Del Castillo jerked his thumb at the northern one. The two filthy, skinny, nearly naked Spaniards glowered at each other. Cabeza de Vaca might be their leader, but he wasn't their king. Estevánico saw another quarrel brewing.

To try to head it off, he brought out the eyewear and put it on. Cabeza de Vaca, Del Castillo, and Dorantes all stared at him. He chuckled at their expressions, but not for long. The eyewear showed him four scrawny wanderers heading down the southern track: the one Cabeza de Vaca favored. "I think we should go that way, too," Estevánico said.

"*I* think you want to pucker up on Álvar's backside," Alonso del Castillo said pointedly.

"What is that thing, Estevánico?" Dorantes asked. "Where did you find it?"

"Near our fire, night before last," the Moor answered—why not tell the truth? "It's . . . kind of a compass, you might say. If you look through it, it shows you which way you should go." He held out the eyewear, as it had shown him doing.

His master crossed himself. Nothing weak about Andrés Dorantes's Christianity. Indeed, Dorantes often prayed over sick natives, trying to persuade God to drive out their infirmities. He'd succeeded so often, the other Spaniards and even Estevánico tried their hands at it these days. They might not own a faith quite so firm as his, but they'd all had good fortune more than once.

Cabeza de Vaca held out his hand. "Let me see that thing, Estevánico, if you'd be so kind." He phrased things as politely as one *hidalgo* would when asking a favor of another, which made what he said no less an order.

Naturally, Estevánico was reluctant. He put the eyewear back on for a moment. Through its odd lenses, he saw himself handing it to the Spaniard. Esperanza/Amal had told him to do as the thing suggested. By the way the white-haired man spoke, he knew what he was talking about, too. Estevánico thought he would have worked the same thing out on his own in short order. The visions that came through the lenses compelled belief.

And so, suppressing his momentary pang, the Moor handed Cabeza de Vaca the eyewear. "Ask it which way we should go, and you'll see," he said.

"Never thought we'd find eyeglasses here," Cabeza de Vaca remarked as he settled them on the bridge of his own sharp nose. His mouth turned down at the corners. "I don't see anything . . . . Wait. Now I do. By God, you're right. It shows us walking down my path, clear as if we were already doing it."

"Let *me* see, if you please." Alonso del Castillo was courteous, too, but spoke a challenge nonetheless. Cabeza de Vaca frowned again; he didn't want to give up the eyewear, either. But he did. Del Castillo signed himself, which had to mean the vision was also forming for him. He gave a reluctant nod. "Well, you're right. I do see us going that way. Of course, this thing may be a snare of Satan's, made to lure us to ruin."

That also worried Estevánico. But Álvar Núñez Cabeza de Vaca threw back his head and laughed. "If the Devil wants us so badly, *amigo*, he doesn't have to get fancy to take us. He just has to stretch out his hand."

Dorantes nodded. "That seems sensible to me. May I look through the spectacles, too, please, since everyone else already has?"

Del Castillo seemed no happier to give them up than Cabeza de Vaca or Estevánico had. But, as they had, he did. Estevánico's master peered through the eyewear.

"I also see us going down the southern track," Dorantes said. Then he took off the eyewear and handed it back to Estevánico, which amazed the Moor. His master proceeded to unamaze him, continuing, "If the Devil *is* in the spectacles, better the black should wear them than one of us, eh? And if not, he can use them to guide us well enough. We have to stick together till we find a land where Christians live."

That last had already occurred to Estevánico. If Cabeza de Vaca and Del Castillo hadn't thought of it, they needed only a moment to see it was sensible. "*Bueno,*" Cabeza de Vaca said. "Estevánico, you are now our compass."

"At your service, *señor,*" the Moor replied. They all laughed. Alonso del Castillo didn't even grumble when they started down the path he hadn't wanted. The Devil couldn't have arranged that—Estevánico was sure of it. No, it had to be a miracle, come straight from God's hand.

Even with the eyewear, they didn't go far and they didn't go fast. For one thing, they were too famished to march as quickly or as long as men with full bellies might have. For another, they kept falling in with native tribes. Word that they could heal had gone ahead of them. Whenever they met a group of the coppery-skinned folk who dwelt in these parts, the natives hopefully brought out their sick. The wanderers had to do what they could to cure them.

Just finding out what ailed the natives wasn't always easy. Estevánico had had to learn a new language when the Christians captured and enslaved him. His master, an educated man, spoke several of the tongues common among them. But all the Spaniards groused that each little native band had its own language. As far as Estevánico could see, they were right. They—and he—picked up a handful of words and phrases from each one, and tried to bring them out without mangling them too badly.

Again, the Moor wished the eyewear helped with words and sounds. It didn't—which didn't mean it was useless in the healing game. The natives thought it was an impressive piece of sorcerous apparatus (at least as often as not, so did Estevánico and the Spaniards). Despite failing as a translator, it sometimes led Estevánico to herbs or roots—once to a leaf with mold growing on it—that helped his patients and his comrades.

He and the Spaniards got paid three ways. First and most important, the locals refrained from killing them, which they could have done with ease. Second, they fed them as well as they could. The Spaniards—especially Cabeza de Vaca—and Estevánico were all more easily satisfied than they had been before setting out with Pánfilo de Narváez. But they got more to eat from the natives than they did while traveling by themselves.

And the locals rewarded them with women. The Spaniards thought that was sinful, which didn't keep them from sleeping with the women but did make them feel guilty afterward. Estevánico said he felt guilty, too: a Christian was supposed to, after lying down with a woman not his wife. He was still Muslim enough not to feel *very* guilty.

One tribe made eunuchs, whether from its own folk or from captives Estevánico never learned. Some of the whole men of that tribe lived with them instead of with women. They offered them to the wanderers, too. Estevánico refused with the same horror the Spaniards showed. Laying a woman was good sport. Laying a man, even one without his *cojones*, was a filthy abomination.

Dorantes and the other two white men preached the Christian Gospel to the natives as well as they could. That probably wasn't very well. They didn't speak any of the local languages fluently enough for proper preaching. They thought God would approve of the effort any which way. Since neither God nor the eyewear told Estevánico they were wrong, he sensibly kept his mouth shut about that.

He did wonder if Esperanza/Amal would make another appearance. For several months, there was no sign of the white-haired man. Estevánico wanted to believe that the stranger who could walk through time was only a figment of his imagination. None of the Spaniards had seen him, after all—and the Moor hadn't mentioned him to them, either. Try as he would, though, Estevánico couldn't persuade himself of that.

A good thing, too. One night when the wanderers were by themselves, with no guides from one tribe leading them toward the next, the Moor was, as usual, given a watch in the middle of the night that broke up his sleep. He yawned and rubbed his eyes as Cabeza de Vaca lay down and promptly went back to sleep. When he was sure he was awake himself, he put on the eyewear. However much the Spaniards admired what the mysterious spectacles did, they stayed content to let him wear them.

By now, the Moor almost took the eyewear for granted. Almost. Ordinary arquebuses seemed like miracles to the natives. They'd never seen horses till the Spaniards brought them across the sea. How Estevánico wished he and his comrades in misfortune had some! They would have traveled much faster and more easily. When he donned the eyewear, he felt as much in the presence of the awesome and the unknown as the natives did when a gun went off or a horse neighed.

"*Salaam aleikem.*" As before, the words came from behind Estevánico's left shoulder. *Peace be unto you.*

"*Aleikem salaam,*" he answered automatically. *And to you also peace.* This time, recognizing the dry, intelligent voice, he didn't jump into the air. Instead, he turned slowly and carefully, continuing, "I hoped to see you again one day."

Esperanza/Amal smiled at that. "Well, I hoped to see you again one day, too. It took longer than I thought it would, I'm afraid."

"How can anything take long for you?" Estevánico asked. "Don't you just step up into the times to come and then back to where you need to be?"

"It's not that simple. I wish it were." The white-haired man rubbed his formidable nose, a gesture that somehow showed Estevánico how very unsimple it was. Esperanza/Amal went on, "Besides, I've used up big chunks of duration down in Peru, and I can't appear twice in them. I told you before—complications!" He rolled his eyes.

"Down in where? Piro?" Estevánico scratched at a fleabite. He knew he'd mispronounced the name. "Where's that?"

"South of here. South of New Spain, way south. The people there are even richer than the Aztecs were," Esperanza/Amal replied. His mouth twisted in a sour smile. "So of course they draw *conquistadores* the way dead meat draws flies."

Estevánico laughed—softly, so as not to wake the sleeping Spaniards. How Pánfilo de Narváez and the would-be conquerors who'd gone with him would grind their teeth when they found out about that place! If any of them were left alive, they would, anyhow. They'd gone in the wrong direction. The natives up here had nothing worth stealing.

"Do these other natives fight any better than the Aztecs did?" Estevánico inquired. The red-brown men up here couldn't hope to resist Spaniards. Then again, so long as they had nothing worth taking, they didn't need to worry about it.

"They might, if disease weren't hurting them and if they were sure the Spaniards weren't gods," Esperanza/Amal said. Estevánico nodded. Things had gone that way in New Spain, too.

He said, "Thanks for checking up on me, anyway, even if it took you a while."

"*De nada*," the white-haired man answered. "People have always wondered how you and your, ah, friends made it all the way from where you got shipwrecked to where you end up. It's less surprising now that I know you found the eyewear, but even so . . ."

"Where do we end up? What kind of people wonder? Less surprising than what?" Every time Esperanza/Amal opened his mouth, he made a million questions form in Estevánico's mind. The Moor also wanted to tell him Dorantes, Del Castillo, and Cabeza de Vaca were no friends of his, but the little catch in Esperanza/Amal's voice said he already understood that.

He wagged a finger at Estevánico now. "I can't tell you any of that stuff, not without making paradoxes." He paused, considering. "*Maybe* I can tell you—"

He vanished. A puff of breeze stroked Estevánico's face as air rushed in to fill the space where the other man had been. Estevánico waited for Esperanza/Amal to come back, but he didn't, not that night. For all Estevánico knew, he was off drinking wine and shooting dice with his friends. Or he might really have got trapped in one of those paradoxes . . . whatever they were. Estevánico knew he didn't fully understand them. He wondered whether Esperanza/Amal did.

The next day, as the wanderers neared the mountains they'd seen in the west for some time, a native gave them a hollow copper rattle with a face on the side. As best they could, they asked where the fellow had got it. He pointed north and a little west. Words tumbled out of him. The Spaniards and Estevánico could follow maybe one of them in ten.

Thoughtfully, Cabeza de Vaca said, "It *sounds* like he says there are cities in that direction. Lots of people living together, anyhow."

"We've also seen maize meal the past few days," Andrés Dorantes said. "The natives say they get that from the north and west, too."

"Where there's copper, chances are there's silver. Where there's silver, chances are there's gold." Alonso del Castillo might be a perambulating bag of bones in a filthy breechclout, but the *conquistador* inside him lived yet.

Cabeza de Vaca looked down at his own scrawny arm and laughed harshly. "Maybe there is, Alonso, but I don't think we're going to bring it back with us. Four miserable starvelings against a city? Even in these parts, that's long odds."

Del Castillo didn't argue, a telling proof of how weak he was.

A couple of days later, Cabeza de Vaca cut an arrowhead out of a wounded native's chest with a flint knife and used a deer-bone needle to suture the wound he'd made. He took the stitches out the next day, and the wounded warrior did fine. That impressed the man's tribe, which ate mostly prickly-pear fruit and pine nuts. They fed the wanderers as well as they could.

That evening, Estevánico decided to experiment with the eyewear. As his comrades lay snoring not far away, he put on the mysterious spectacles and thought, *I want to go to the place where that copper rattle came from.*

He didn't have to wait long before the eyewear showed him what to do—or, at least, what to start doing. If he walked away from the Spaniards, skirted a couple of sleeping natives—he hadn't even known they were there, but the eyewear did, all right—and headed up a trail that led north, he'd be on his way.

How could the spectacles tell him something like that? How did *they* know? He hadn't the faintest idea. Some sort of fancy witchcraft still seemed more likely to him than anything else.

But, in the end, *how* didn't matter. What mattered was that the eyewear *did* know, and could show him. He'd seen as much often enough to need no further proof. A man who paid attention to the eyewear and acted on what he saw through it couldn't go far wrong; Esperanza/Amal had known what he was talking about there.

Here in this impoverished wilderness, the eyewear kept the wanderers on the right track toward finding a civilized settlement. If someone else in more settled country used a pair of these eyeglasses with the aim of getting rich, Estevánico didn't see how he could go far wrong, either. Idly, the Moor wondered whether the *conquistador* leading the Spanish charge into that rich new southern country did have some eyewear of his own.

Estevánico shrugged. He couldn't do anything about that one way or the other. He could, and did, mutter under his breath about luck and breaks. He'd found his magical eyeglasses in a land full of nothing. If some other fellow had eyewear in a country full of gold . . .

Richer than New Spain, Esperanza/Amal had said. Estevánico hadn't dreamt a land could be richer than New Spain. But the white-haired man with the big nose plainly knew what he was talking about. For that matter, Esperanza/Amal plainly knew more than he *could* talk about.

"Not fair," Estevánico mumbled. He looked toward the north again, toward the place—the city?—from which the copper rattle had come. If the natives there could work copper, they could also work silver and gold. Alonso del Castillo was dead right about that. *And if some of that silver and gold ended up in my hands*, Estevánico thought. Making his mind work like a *conquistador*'s was the easiest thing in the world.

He must have gone on mumbling, because the first thing Esperanza/Amal said was, "Thinking like a *conquistador* may be easy, but it's dangerous, too."

By now, Estevánico wasn't even surprised when the white-haired man popped out of nowhere. "Tell it to Cortés," the Moor retorted.

Esperanza/Amal pointed to the eyewear. "Cortés had the same help you do, and he almost died half a dozen times even so. Maybe more." He held up a forefinger, correcting himself. "Almost the same help, I mean. His set was mounted in a solid-gold mask."

"It would be." Estevánico couldn't even find bitterness. "So, did he trip over it in the dark, too? That wouldn't be so easy, not with a golden mask."

"Montezuma handed it to him," Esperanza/Amal said solemnly.

"Go on! Now tell me one I'll believe!" Up till now, Estevánico had thought the white-haired man a truthteller. But that had to be a lie . . . didn't it?

"He did. By God, he did," Esperanza/Amal said. Estevánico heard the oath in both Spanish and Arabic. "And, if you're thinking of going north to look for gold, you would do well to watch out for more Aztecs." He let out a glad sigh, as if relieved to have said that without getting caught in a paradox and vanishing halfway through his sentence.

"Now I know you're *loco*," Estevánico declared. "The Aztecs live south of here, not north. And Cortés conquered them years ago. I'm not sure of much, but I'm sure of that. Their empire's dead and gone."

The white-haired man sent him a sweet, sad smile. "As a wise man said—er, will say—many years from now, the past isn't dead. Sometimes it isn't even past. And he didn't know the first thing about journeying through time." Esperanza/Amal looked startled. "Or I don't think he did. But when I tell you to look out for Aztecs if you go north, I'm—" He just had time to look startled again, in a different way, before he disappeared.

"You're what?" Estevánico said scornfully. He answered his own question: "You're talking through your farthole, that's what." Esperanza/Amal didn't come back to contradict him, either.

The four wanderers trudged on . . . and on . . . and on. Estevánico began to think they'd keep marching forever without returning to civilization. But they couldn't march all the time. Rain swelled a river and forced them to lie up in a native village for some time. One of the men there wore an amulet of a horseshoe nail and the buckle to a sword belt stitched onto a piece of tanned hide. Alonso del Castillo almost jumped out of his own tanned hide when he saw it. He brought—dragged—the native back to his comrades. The fellow said Spaniards on horseback had come up to the river and killed two natives with lances.

"We're getting there!" Cabeza de Vaca exclaimed. "By the holy Virgin Mother of God, we really are!"

After more long, hungry marches, the leader and Estevánico, who had got ahead of the other two Spaniards, finally met more mounted white men. The eyewear helped guide them on, but Estevánico hid it as soon as he spotted strangers. The soldiers they met didn't know what to make of a couple of shambling, nearly naked skeletons. They hesitated even after Cabeza de Vaca hailed them in Spanish.

At last, though, they took him and Estevánico back to their captain, Diego de Alcaraz. The officer sent three horsemen and fifty natives off with Estevánico to get to Dorantes and Del Castillo. No one offered to let the Moor ride. He had to retrace ten or twelve leagues on foot. Any thought of showing off the eyewear to the Spaniards flickered and blew out. If they wouldn't do anything for him, he was damned if he'd do anything for them.

And so he looked through the eyewear only in secret, when he went off behind a bush to ease himself or at night. The strange spectacles did help bring him to the men he sought. Neither his master nor Del Castillo mentioned the eyewear once he, the new Spaniards, and the natives found them. Both men probably thought they could use the thing to their own advantage—and in law, of course, anything that was Estevánico's belonged to his master.

They came into Culiacán, by the oceanside, in April 1536. They'd needed four years to pass from the Gulf of Mexico to this arm of the Pacific. When Cabeza de Vaca said it was a miracle none of them had died along the way, Estevánico couldn't very well tell him he was wrong.

Three months later, they rode into Mexico City. Everyone there celebrated them for surviving their dreadful journey. Even Estevánico, dark-skinned slave of uncertain Christianity that he was, came in for his share of praise and his share of the fiery spirit the Spaniards had started brewing from the local plant called *agave*. Islam forbade drinking and drunkenness. Christianity didn't. As far as Estevánico was concerned, that was a fine reason to profess Christianity: that and the fact that the Spaniards would kill him an inch at a time if he slid back into his old faith.

He had clothes that covered all of him. He had sandals. He had a leather belt, and a leather wallet in which he could hide the eyewear. He had enough to eat: nothing fancy, not for a slave, but enough. After four years of, well, of nothing, all that seemed riches unimaginable.

His master, though much richer than he was, still had debts to settle, debts from the days before he sailed with Pánfilo de Narváez. One of those debts was to Antonio de Mendoza, the viceroy of New Spain: not a man on whose bad side anyone with a grain of sense would want to stay. To settle that score, Andrés Dorantes sold Estevánico to the viceroy. Dorantes told Estevánico to leave the eyewear behind, but the Moor took it with him anyhow. He was sure his old master wouldn't tell his new master—or anyone else—about it.

Antonio de Mendoza studied Estevánico with cold, hooded eyes. "I've heard that you and your comrades came close to seven cities filled with gold," he said, steepling his long, thin fingers. "Is this true, or is it not?"

If it wasn't, Estevánico figured he was in for a lifetime of the hardest, shittiest work the viceroy could find for him. He wasn't a cook or a majordomo or a pretty woman. He was just a Moor . . . unless he was a Moor who knew how to find seven cities full of gold. Picking his words with care, he replied, "Your Excellency, I cannot say for sure, because we did not see them ourselves, but all the natives in those parts seem sure they are there." That stretched things a bit. Unduly? Estevánico didn't think so. It might get him off the hook if the cities turned out not to be there after all. A slave, especially a slave with a new master, needed as many ways off the hook as he could find.

The Viceroy of New Spain went on studying him. "If these seven cities *are* there, can you lead an expedition to them?"

"Absolutely, your Excellency." Now Estevánico spoke with perfect confidence. And why not? The eyewear would take him wherever he wanted to go.

Antonio de Mendoza must have heard that confidence and known it for what it was. A man didn't get to be viceroy—a man couldn't come close to such a rank—without recognizing such things. "*Bueno*," Mendoza said. "Such an expedition is fitting out. Francisco Vásquez de Coronado will command it. You—you and Father Marcos of Nice, who has also traveled in those parts—will guide him to another triumph for Christendom and for good King Carlos."

"It would be an honor, your Excellency," Estevánico said, as he had to.

"No doubt." His new master's voice was dry as dust. No doubt he recognized garbage when he heard it, too. He jerked a thumb toward the doorway to his chamber. "Now get out of here."

Estevánico got. He wondered whether Esperanza/Amal would reappear now that he'd got new orders. He even made a point of going off by himself to give the white-haired man the chance to do it. And, sure enough, the man who walked through years did. "So, you're chasing the Seven Cities, are you?" he said without preamble.

"That's right. What about it?" Estevánico wasn't so overawed now as he had been when Esperanza/Amal first showed up. You could start taking even miracles for granted. "When I do, I'll be a big man. I bet the viceroy frees me."

"I could tell you . . . " Esperanza/Amal shook his head like a man bedeviled by mosquitoes. "No, I probably couldn't, not unless I felt like winking out. But you'd better keep your eyes—and your eyewear—peeled for Aztecs. They haven't improved in seven hundred years, believe me."

"What are you going on about now?" Estevánico asked peevishly.

"Just that they're even better at cutting the—" Faster than a castanet click, Esperanza/Amal *did* wink out. He didn't come back, either. But he didn't need to finish *that* sentence. Estevánico knew about the Aztecs' delight in human sacrifice, and about their delight in the fresh meat they got from the sacrifices. The seven hundred years? He could worry about that some other time.

Worrying at it—which was not the same thing—made him keep the eyewear on as he walked through Mexico City's nighttime streets. Only occasional torches lit them. Even so, the eyewear kept him from stepping in anything nasty and let him evade the noisy, half-drunken patrol parties the viceroy used to keep order.

Then the eyewear showed him doing something out of the ordinary: jumping into one of the canals that survived from the days when this had been Aztec Tenochtitlan. He didn't want to. The canal was full of stinking sewage. Remembering all he'd seen, remembering Esperanza/Amal's advice, he jumped anyhow.

The eyewear said he could stick his head up. Gasping and spluttering, he did. But he stifled the splutters, because soft, determined footsteps were coming up the street.

Two men paused, not six feet from him. They wore coveralls of a style he'd never seen before and carried weapons that looked something like arquebuses. Without needing the eyewear to tell him, Estevánico was sure those guns would be deadlier than any arquebus ever made.

"Where'd he go?" one of them said, not in Spanish but in a clipped, sharp dialect of Nahuatl, the Aztecs' tongue. Estevánico understood just enough to follow.

Pointing down the street, the other fellow answered, "Has to be that way." Off they went. He spoke Nahuatl, too, or what Nahuatl might turn into in . . . seven hundred years?

Estevánico clambered out of the canal, shivering and dripping. Without the eyewear, he *would* have gone that way—but probably not for long. He waited for Esperanza/Amal to reappear and say *I told you so*. He would have taken it without a murmur. But the white-haired man didn't come back.

Slowly, following the roundabout route the eyewear gave him, Estevánico returned to Antonio de Mendoza's residence. A senior servant chewed him out for getting drunk and falling into the canal. Estevánico didn't deny it—he apologized again and again. The soft answer turned away some wrath, anyhow. The servant gave him water to wash with and a blanket to wrap himself in, then took his clothes to the laundresses.

It could have been worse. All the same, with those bastards hunting him here, Estevánico could hardly wait to get out of Mexico City.

Coronado seemed a capable man, maybe not ready for anything like Cabeza de Vaca but certainly better than Pánfilo de Narváez. But Estevánico quickly discovered he couldn't stand Father Marcos. The man never shut up. He even talked in his sleep. And he had a shrill, grating voice that reminded the Moor of nothing so much as fingernails scraping across a slate.

Going up into the country through which he'd wandered with Cabeza de Vaca, Dorantes, and Del Castillo was a relief. Coronado commanded two hundred fifty riders, seventy arquubusiers on foot, and a thousand natives and Negroes in charge of spare horses, wagons, and meat animals. It was a real army, the first ever seen in these parts.

Along with Father Marcos, Estevánico rode ahead to scout the way. And then he took a few servants and started riding ahead of the padre. It was that or kill him, and the eyewear didn't show Estevánico that he could get away with murder. *A pity*, he thought.

Some of the natives remembered him from his earlier trek through these lands. Others had heard about him from people who'd seen him then. He made the most of it. No matter what the Spaniards thought, the locals had next to no gold. Maybe things would be better up at the cities they talked about, maybe not. He'd worry about that when he got there.

In the meantime . . . In the meantime, they did have turquoise. The eyewear showed they'd give him some if he asked. Ask he did. The eyewear also showed they'd give him women. You couldn't load screwing onto a donkey and haul it back to Mexico City, which didn't make it any less a treasure.

Because Father Marcos and Coronado and the army followed in his wake, Estevánico spoke of the white men and their god. The Spaniards *were* going to convert the natives. The villagers and wandering hunters needed to get used to the idea.

Get used to it? They thought it was funny. "Here you're so dark, and you're telling us about white men? You expect us to believe that?" one of them said.

"You'd better. It's true," Estevánico answered, not for the first time. He'd heard the joke often enough to get sick of it. The natives thought it was new every time.

One evening, as they camped in a little stretch of flat ground next to a narrow trail set into a mountainside, the eyewear showed Estevánico he needed to talk to his cook. "I need a . . . a pot of lard, José," he said. The eyewear showed him what to ask for, but he had to figure out what to call it.

"What for, *señor*?" José was a native, but spoke better Spanish than Estevánico did. He couldn't have been more than five when Cortés conquered Montezuma, and he'd grown up serving Spaniards. Estevánico wondered how much Nahuatl he remembered.

"Never you mind," the Moor said. He didn't know, either. The eyewear hadn't shown him yet. He saw the intrigued look on José's face as the cook gave him the pot. How widespread were the rumors that he wasn't a proper Christian? Muslims didn't eat pork or have anything to do with stuff that came from pigs. If he wanted lard, he couldn't be a Muslim, could he?

He'd have to work that out for himself later on. Now? Now he had to see what the eyewear told him to do with the lard. It waited till after nightfall before showing images of him smearing the stuff on a couple of rocks right where the trail was narrowest, about fifty yards farther on than the wide spot that made a campground.

He wondered if he should stand watch after that. But the spectacles showed him wrapping himself in his blanket and looking like a man asleep. He found a lawyer's loophole: that didn't have to mean he actually *was* asleep. And so he lay there, yawning, wondering what would happen next.

The moon was getting close to full. Pearly light spilled down from the sky. Even through half-closed eyes, he had no trouble spotting the man sneaking along the trail toward the camp. If that wasn't one of the Aztecs who'd hunted him in Mexico City . . . Estevánico didn't have to worry about what he'd do then, because it damn well was. He could even see the fancy arquebus the son of a dog carried.

But that fancy weapon couldn't match the eyewear's foresight. The grim stalker's left foot came down on one of the stones Estevánico had greased. The Aztec slipped. As he flailed for balance, his right foot landed on the other greased stone. Coincidence? By now, Estevánico doubted there was any such thing.

With a despairing shriek, the Aztec slid off the trail. The shriek went on for some little while. It was a devil of a long way down.

Estevánico rolled over and pulled the blanket tighter around him. Before long, he really did sleep.

A few days later, he got his first glimpse of Hawikuh, the so-called city toward which he was advancing—Father Marcos called it Cibola, for reasons Estevánico never fathomed. He'd seen cities in Morocco and Spain and Mexico. He knew how they were supposed to look. These dwellings stacked on a cliffside seemed distinctly unimpressive.

Some of the natives at the last place he'd stopped had sent him resentful looks when he demanded turquoise and a pretty girl from them. They'd given him what he wanted, but they hadn't liked it. He wondered how the people at Hawikuh would like it. *I'll ask the eyewear*, he thought, and then, *I'll ask it tomorrow*. He was sleepy. The air in this high country was so thin, everybody was sleepy all the time.

Once sunrise pried his eyelids apart, he reached for the leather wallet where he put the eyewear when he went to sleep. His hand closed on . . . nothing. His eyes opened wide. He looked all around. The wallet wasn't there. That meant the eyewear wasn't there, either.

"*¡Madre de Dios!*" he exclaimed. When that didn't come within leagues of venting his spleen, he swore in Arabic. He felt better, but he didn't feel good. Nowhere near.

He didn't need to be brilliant to figure out what had happened to the wallet. One of José's helpers, a native called Manuel, was also missing. The stony ground wouldn't begin to hold his spoor, and he had a long start.

José stated the obvious: "I am very sorry, *señor*, but we will never catch him. I hope the coyotes"—his name for the little yellow wolves—"and the pumas fight over his bones." Pumas wanted to be lions, but didn't quite have what it took.

"To the Devil with his bones," Estevánico snarled. "I want the eyewear back."

José spread his hands. "I am very sorry, *señor*," he repeated.

Estevánico was very sorry, too. What would he do if he couldn't use the eyewear? The question answered itself: he'd damned well do *without*, that was what.

On to Hawikuh, then. It was a bigger assemblage of stacked houses than he'd seen before, anyhow. A city full of gold? That seemed most unlikely. The tribe that dwelt there—they called themselves Zuñis—let down a ladder so he could come up to them and tell his story.

Tell it he did. As other natives had, they laughed at him. "You, a dark brown man, talk about white men behind you?" one of them asked. "And you expect us to believe that?" The assembled Zuñis laughed some more. To Estevánico's ear, the laughter had an uncommonly nasty edge. He wished he could see what the eyewear thought he should do. But he had to go ahead without it. "You'd better believe me," he said. "They *are* coming, and they're bringing their god with them. He is a stronger god than any of yours. If you give me turquoise and let me sleep with a pretty girl, I will talk them into going easy on you."

"I do not think any of this is so," the Zuñi leader said. "Even if it is, I am sure we can deal with these white men." He laughed that unpleasant laugh again.

"You are wrong," Estevánico told him. "You have no idea how wrong you are."

The native chieftain gestured. The eyewear would have warned Estevánico what kind of gesture it was, but he didn't have the eyewear anymore. As things were, the spear that went into his back came as a complete surprise. He screeched, more in astonishment than in pain. He was still alive when the Zuñis threw him out of Hawikuh, but not once he hit. Oh, no. Not after that.

Po'pay hated the Spaniards and everything they stood for. For two long lifetimes now, they'd oppressed all the tribes of what they called New Mexico. They'd even forced their own religion on people who'd long been happy with what they believed on their own. Po'pay had been baptized into the Christian faith. He'd secretly used soapweed to wash himself clean of the baptism, but he didn't feel it had done a good enough job.

He wandered through the rugged country west of the Spanish settlement of Santa Fé. Drive the invaders out of that fort and they would lose their grip on New Mexico. But how? They were strong. They had armor. They had guns.

Something white on the ground—a bone. Po'pay left the trail to see what kind of bone it was. He wasn't surprised to find it had come from a man. Disease and hunger made skeletons anything but rare in New Mexico in this year the Spaniards called 1679.

This poor dead fellow might have lost his flesh, but a leather wallet—an old, old leather wallet—still lay by his hip bone. The scavengers that ate him hadn't bothered it. Curious, Po'pay reached inside. He pulled out . . . what looked like a pair of the eyeglasses some white men wore.

Curious about white men's magic—for what else could eyeglasses be?—Po'pay put them on. *If only I had some way to get rid of all the invaders*, he thought.

And the eyeglasses started to show him how.

Watching from behind a fat sagebrush, the white-haired man with the big nose sighed. He might have known the eyewear would be tied up with the New Mexico uprising. How else could the Native Americans drive out the Spaniards and keep them away for thirty years?

And what he'd discovered, the Aztecs and the Incas of Tawantin-suyu would also learn—or already know, depending on how you looked at things. Which meant life in these parts would soon get complicated . . . again.

Afterward for "Eyewear"

The story . . .

I've tremendously admired Fred Saberhagen's work ever since I first ran across the Berserker stories going on fifty years ago now. And I've always been fascinated by the Spanish conquest of the Americas; till the little green men in the saucers really do land, it's the closest thing to an encounter with aliens we'll ever see. So it's not surprising that when I saw *Mask of the Sun* in a bookstore back in 1979, I did a scream-and-leap and grabbed it. It was every bit as good as I hoped, which is saying a great deal. Fine writing, interesting characters, a time-travel situation that does its best to tie itself in knots, splendid research (and I was and am in a position to testify about that) . . . *Good* stuff!

So I felt particularly honored when Joan Saberhagen asked me to contribute a story to *Golden Reflections*. I got to play in Fred's sandbox for a little while! A little thought made me wonder how Álvar Núñez Cabeza de Vaca and his three companions could have made it from the Gulf of Mexico to the Gulf of California *without* help from a Mask. They were, after all, wandering across a major chunk of the North American continent, and one completely unknown by Europeans before they went through it. The odds were all in favor of their perishing. Unless, as I say, they had a Mask. And if they did . . . "Eyewear" is the result.

Thinking about this project also gave me another idea, which turned into the novelette "Vilcabamba." It's on the tor.com Web site. One more debt of gratitude to Fred and Joan, and to her co-editor, Bob Vardeman.

Like the Rain
by
Jane Lindskold

A.D. 1675

The lash came down with a singing scream, pulled back spraying gouts of blood.

Bound to the whipping post, Po'pay heard his blood patter to dampen the drought-parched soil of the plaza of the city of Santa Fe de San Francisco.

Let my blood be as the rain, he silently prayed. *Let the ancestors take pity on my people and send the rains. Should I die here, I will become a cloud and rise from this body to join with the ancestors. I will plead with those who are clouds, beg them to no longer withhold the rains.*

Po'pay's prayer was not the only one raised that afternoon in the crowded plaza.

A safe distance from the shower of gore, a tonsured man wearing the brown robes of a Franciscan priest recited words about accepting the mercy of the good lord Jesus and putting away all worship of the Devil and his arts.

Words, Po'pay thought. *Meaningless words.*

Did the *padre* not see the contradiction between his speeches about a god of mercy and justice, and the treatment being meted out before his very eyes?

Words. Words that Po'pay wished with all his heart he did not possess the knowledge of the Spanish language to understand. It was bad enough being beaten as a man would not beat a dog. Worse was having heart and mind lacerated with rage at the pure stupidity of the situation.

The "crime" for which Po'pay and forty-six other men had been "arrested" was that witchcraft had been practiced at the village of Powhogeh, called San Ildefonso by the Castillians. This witchcraft had led to the sickness of Fray Andres Duran, his brother, the brother's wife, and the interpreter, Francisco Guitar. These "witches" were also accused of the deaths of seven friars and three other Castillians.

Po'pay despised witchcraft, abhorred it as any good man should. However, he could not see why he and his fellows had been arrested in addition to the four who were accused.

Po'pay lived in Ohkay, the "pueblo" the Spanish had named San Juan de Los Caballeros. Ohkay was many leagues from Powhogeh. True, both of these pueblos were Tewa speaking, but that did not mean they were friends or even allies. Moreover, among those arrested were Tiwa and Keresan speakers. What could these different peoples have had to do with this?

Nonetheless, following these deaths and the subsequent accusations of witchcraft, Governor Juan de Treviño had ordered Spanish soldiers under the command of Francisco Xavier to make a circuit through the various pueblos. Their guide was the same Francisco Guitar who claimed to have been a victim of witchcraft. Po'pay wondered that none had commented on how opportune Guitar's recovery had been.

Doubtless spurred by anger at how his fellow Tewa now shunned him, Guitar had told Xavier who were the most important men in each pueblo.

The Spanish had entered their houses uninvited. They had stolen holy masks, prayer-sticks, and sacred herbs. Finally, they had "arrested" many of the leading men of each village on a charge of practicing sorcery or witchcraft.

Po'pay, a senior priest, head of one of the religious societies, had been among the forty-seven who were seized.

Cutting through Po'pay's thoughts, the whip again sang its ugly song. The agony of its hitting undamaged flesh flung Po'pay back into the present moment.

Po'pay pressed his lips together, composed his features. He would not scream. He would not argue. Such behavior would be beneath his dignity, as arguing with a small child was beneath the dignity of a grown man.

He was Po'pay, a man of some fifty years, a priest and a leader among the Tewa of Ohkay. He would not fail to act with the dignity and restraint expected of one of his high position.

As Po'pay struggled to keep his features neutral, he overheard one of the observers who sat near Governor Treviño saying, his voice lazy with boredom, "I don't know why we bother with public chastisement. They're like animals. They don't feel pain or shame as men do."

These words fired in Po'pay's heart the rage he would not permit his face to show.

Blood coursed down the naked skin of his back, soaking the rag of a loincloth that had been left to preserve Po'pay's "modesty" when the rest of his clothing had been stripped from him.

"Modesty" was another of the strange Christian gods, a god who insisted that his worshipers wrap themselves in heavy layers of wool and leather so that they stank of sweat and dirt, so that they gathered fleas and lice.

"Modesty" was offended by the skin with which every human was born. If a gentle Jesus who sanctioned torture was puzzling, so was this "modesty" who was offended by the honest realities of what it was to be human: sex, pleasure in eating and drinking, joy in worship, and so many other things that the gods Po'pay knew celebrated side-by-side with humanity.

Another lash fell, crossing the cuts already made. Po'pay felt this new impact as a dim echo of the others, for the feeling parts of his skin were ruined by continued abuse. If he lived, there would be scars, not the honorable trophies of battle, but memories of humiliation.

The Christian gods were nothing if not puzzling. Maria, a Mother Goddess who cradled her murdered son as if he were a baby.

Deus, a Father god who apparently engendered his son so that he might be tortured, then slain.

Sin, a corruption and rot from before birth. Water to wash away sin. Sour wine and flat bread that was also a cannibalistic feast.

Since he had been a child, Po'pay had listened to the sermons, had tried to understand the Christian religious view. Sometimes he came close but, every time he neared understanding, the actions of the men who called themselves followers of this peculiar pantheon drove understanding from him.

The whip ceased its ugly song in mid-scream.

Vaguely, through a haze of pain, Po'pay became aware of voices raised in excited conversation. He felt the leather thongs that had bound him to the whipping post being sawed at by a knife. When the leather parted, he staggered a few steps, refusing to fall into the hands that reached to catch him.

"Just like animals," said the unknown commentator, a man, Po'pay could now see, who was wearing soldier's armor. "Too dull to even feel pain. I'm not sure the Church is right in insisting these savages have souls to save. Far better to accept that they are little more than beasts in human form. It wouldn't even be slavery to use their labor, just taming, as we do with wild horses."

Po'pay wondered if they would kill him now. He would become a cloud, a cloud weeping red rain.

Already, Governor Treviño had sentenced four of the accused *hechiceros*—witches or sorcerers—to be hanged as specifically implicated in the cursing at Powhogeh. Treviño had ignored that these four men lived great distances from each other and belonged to different pueblos.

Three of those sentenced to hang had already been executed, the first at Walatowa, the village deep in the mountains that the Spanish called Jemez. The second had been executed at Kootscha or San Felipe, south of Santa Fe. The third had been hanged at Nambe, north of Santa Fe.

The fourth accused *hechicero* had managed to kill himself before he could be hanged. The Spanish probably thought this was an act of cowardice, but Po'pay knew the suicide for courage, an example that even in captivity a man could choose his fate.

Here and now, his back bloodied, men armed with both guns and swords standing guard over him, Po'pay's choices were few.

Effort enough to breathe in and out, to feel the blood drying on his skin, the slow stiffening of his mutilated flesh.

He was shoved back toward the ranks of his fellow captives. All the survivors had been brought forth to watch the "punishment," probably in the hope of breaking their spirits before their bodies were broken and enslaved.

Respecting his efforts to give their captors no satisfaction, none of the other captives offered Po'pay obvious comfort. They showed their sympathy for him in less obvious ways. Po'pay felt how room was made for him so that none would jostle his torn flesh, saw someone move so that Po'pay could sit on an adobe *banco*.

Po'pay saw a very old man plucked from among the captives, heard a few of the soldiers placing bets on whether the old witch would be conscious when they cut him down.

Po'pay tried to give the old man—he was from Nambe, another Tewa pueblo—the respect of his attention, but he was having trouble focusing. The pain must be affecting his mind, for it seemed that the gathered Castillians on the other side of the Plaza were rippling. He hoped he was not about to faint from pain and blood loss. That would be humiliating.

Then Po'pay realized that the rippling was not his imagination. A messenger was pushing through the packed observers to where Governor Treviño and his advisors sat.

The messenger spoke urgently to the officials. The crowd had grown silent as everyone strained to hear the news. Even the soldiers who were binding the old man from Nambe slowed so that they could listen.

Po'pay only heard a few words. Something about a group of men, Indian men, advancing upon Santa Fe.

"We will conclude another day," Treviño said hastily. "Return the captives to the holding area. I want to speak with Captain Lopez and—"

The governor never finished his commands. Another messenger, this one a soldier, wild-eyed and obviously frightened, came running up.

"My lord, the Indians are demanding entry. Shall we fire upon them?"

"How many are there?"

"At least seventy. There may be others. We have seen movement among the hills in the near distance."

"Are these men armed?"

"Possibly. They carry war clubs and leather shields, but these are heavily adorned with feathers and such, so they might be ornamental. They also carry what look like gifts."

"Gifts?"

Disgusted, Po'pay saw the Spanish governor brighten with interest.

"What sort of gifts?"

"Most are in bundles, but we saw live chickens and some rolled deerskins. The two who came to the gate offered the guards a fine pottery bowl filled with dry beans. He said that there would be other gifts if their message was promptly carried to the governor."

"Perhaps I should see them," Treviño mused. "They seem to be peaceful enough. However, it is hot and dusty out here. Have them brought inside the palace."

Belatedly, Treviño seemed to notice that the captives had not been returned to their holding area.

"Keep those men well-guarded," Treviño ordered grandly. "However, I see no need to delay the delegation while the prisoners are moved. The prisoners will serve as a warning to their fellows as to what happens to those who dare challenge our imperial rule."

While the Castillian rulers moved inside, one of the younger Christian priests brought gourds holding warm, stale water. He made certain that Po'pay and those who had been beaten drank.

"Splash water on your wounds," the Christian priest said, his voice hardly above a whisper. "It will help keep them from stiffening. Later, I will make certain you are given grease to coat them."

The young priest spoke as one who might have known a beating or two. Po'pay reminded himself that, like their god, the Castillians believed that beatings were somehow holy.

The warm water made the lash wounds sting, but drinking helped Po'pay feel a little stronger. He watched with interest as the Indian delegation came through the plaza to the thick-walled adobe palace into which Treviño had retreated.

Po'pay knew that the delegates must have noticed the fresh blood splashed on the dirt, must have seen their fellows packed like sheep before a shearing to one side of the plaza, but they did not react. Their attention was for their destination—and for the guards spaced around the plaza.

The Indian delegation was a large group, especially when considered in combination with the forty-three captives. Po'pay saw several of the guards shifting nervously. Surely they recognized that despite the feathers and bright paint that adorned them, the war clubs the men held were quite dangerous?

The Castillians' flintlocks and swords were frightening in their destructive capacity, but a gun could only fire once before needing to be reloaded. Swords needed more room than war-clubs to be used efficiently. Moreover, the Castillians would be hampered by the need to protect the civilians and unarmed officials. The Indian delegates would be fighting for their lives and for those of the prisoners.

The delegation filed into the palace of the governor, eventually filling two rooms to overflowing. Doors and windows were left open, and so Po'pay and the other captives could easily hear what was going on within.

Tagu, another captive from Po'pay's home of Ohkay, gestured for Po'pay to join him.

"You can see through here," Tagu said, motioning to a window.

If the guards without were nervous, Treviño did not seem aware of his danger. His gaze was fixed greedily on the bundles or pots that each delegate carried in his free hand. The goods within might not be the gold and silver the Castillians had come north from Mexico in search of, but the foreigners had learned to value some of what the Indians made or grew.

From the larger group of delegates, a dozen or so men stepped forward, one from each of the eight Tewa pueblos, the rest representatives of the Tiwa, Towa, and Keresan. Po'pay felt a surge of hope. Only one thing would have brought this group together, for despite the Castillians designating them all as "Indians," the various pueblos were more usually rivals than allies.

Saca, an important man from Teotho, the pueblo which the Spanish called Taos, spoke first. Saca's Spanish was quite good. He began by addressing Governor Treviño and his aides, giving them the ornate titles the Spanish valued. Po'pay's hope began to flicker.

Then Saca ceased to grovel and became grimly serious.

"We are well aware that you believe that *hechiceros* from among the Tewa have cursed you. Four confessed, and those four are now dead. These men you have taken and questioned were in no way involved. However, you have sentenced them to beatings, these to be followed by a period of slavery, for no other reason than that Francisco Guitar indicated they were witches.

"I speak for all of us here gathered and for those who are not present, but who have sent us to be their voices, when I most humbly request that you return to us these men you have arrested. We bring you gifts to represent our goodwill and that of all our peoples."

Saca gave a slight nod. One of the younger men stepped forward, offered a respectful bow after the fashion of the Castillians, then extended the pottery bowl he carried. As eagerly as a child offered a piece of honeycomb, Treviño reached into the bowl.

"Tobacco," he said approvingly, sniffing the aroma as he bruised the dried leaves between his fingers. "This fine gift demonstrates your goodwill. Let me confer with my advisors."

Saca of Teotho stepped back into the ranks. Po'pay noticed how hands now shifted their grip on their war clubs. If the Castillians chose to fire their flintlocks, there would be consequences.

Po'pay wished he was in a position where he could overhear the deliberations, but he had to settle for attempting to read the expressions on the bearded faces. He saw many emotions there in addition to the expected greed. There was fear and calculation.

The young priest who had brought the captives water had joined the group surrounding the governor, uninvited, Po'pay thought, and was arguing passionately. His voice alone carried as he spoke of innocence and justice.

Treviño did not seem impressed by these idealistic words, but Po'pay thought that some of the other arguments, especially those made by Captain Garcia and Captain Lopez, bore some weight with the governor.

Eventually, Treviño signaled an end to deliberation and motioned for the leaders of the Indian delegation to come forward.

"Wait a while, children," Treviño said grandly. "I will give your people to you and pardon them on condition that you forsake idolatry and iniquity."

Saca nodded his agreement. Easy enough to do, for, like Po'pay, Saca did not see the practice of their traditional religion as idolatrous or their way of living as iniquitous.

Treviño looked expectantly at the bowl which the man next to Saca held, but Captain Garcia gave his commander a disapproving frown.

"We have also decided," Garcia said, "not to accept any of these fine gifts you have brought, in order that we might show you how highly we value your repentance."

And, Po'pay thought, *to show that you cannot be bought—at least not so obviously.*

But one of the younger delegates called from the outer room, "Leave the gifts there if he does not want them. We will not be said to go back on our promise."

Treviño was pleased by these words. He spoke quickly, before Captain Garcia could disagree. "Very well. We will have an exchange of gifts. Bring some woolen blankets and give them to the leaders of this delegation to use as they see fit."

As gifts were accepted, prisoners were released into the charge of the departing delegates. This was good, for although all had not been beaten, there were none who were not weak from having been poorly treated for many days.

Po'pay was escorted out by his son-in-law, Bua, husband of his daughter, Oxu'a powi. Po'pay was pleased to see Bua, but he did not lean on Bua's arm as he might have on Oxu'a powi's. Bua had always respected and honored his wife's father, but Po'pay would not show weakness.

Po'pay and Bua were among the last to leave, for Po'pay had refused to be ransomed until he had seen that everyone was being permitted to depart unmolested.

Saca had also remained. When the two crowded rooms were nearly empty, Captain Garcia asked, his jocular tone not hiding his evident relief, "Come and tell me why so many of your people came armed to see the governor?"

Saca responded coolly. "We came determined to kill him if he did not give up the prisoners, and on killing him, to kill the people of the villa as well. You do not think we came alone, do you? We have more armed men waiting in the hills."

There was no laughter in Captain Garcia's tone when he said, "You know we would have come after you and burned every pueblo to the ground. Aren't you afraid of being forced out into the mountains where you would be at the mercy of the Apaches?"

Saca replied with perfect calm. "In order to defend our holy men—these you have defamed by calling *hechiceros*—we would have fled to the mountains, even at the risk of being forced into battle with both you Castillians and the Apaches."

Although Bua pulled at Po'pay's arm and tried to hasten him on, Po'pay waited to see the reaction to Saca's declaration. Governor Treviño had looked up from gloating over the bowls and bundles spread before him, his face suddenly pale. Captain Garcia's face, however, was darkening with fury, his lips pulled white within the dark border of his beard.

Saca gave a bow, mocking in its perfect correctness, and turned his back on the Castillians. Along with the few remaining delegates, he joined Po'pay and Bua.

Only when they were safely out of both flintlock and arrow shot of the walls of Santa Fe did Po'pay believe they were truly, safely away.

The long walk home to Ohkay was purest agony. Even after a healer of great skill had anointed Po'pay's back with ointment, still the lash cuts burned whenever Po'pay moved.

The pain of his wounds made Po'pay's sleep restless. He was seeking a comfortable position to rest when he heard a voice calling his name.

"Po'pay, come to me."

Po'pay rose, noticing an unusual stillness in the air. Around him, the others slept soundly, breathing evenly. No one stirred, not even when Po'pay touched them.

"Po'pay!" The voice was unfamiliar, without any accent Po'pay recognized. *"Come to me."*

Po'pay followed the voice and found a stranger standing near a clump of juniper. Although the stranger was dressed as a Tewa, in kilt and leggings, his upper body bare to the pleasant warmth of the night, he did not seem quite Tewa. His features were somewhat different. He was taller than was common, muscled like a young god. When he smiled in greeting, his teeth were perfect.

"Who are you?" Po'pay asked. "Are you a god or one of the ancestors?"

"I am Tleume. Say, rather, that you and I share ancestors, Po'pay. I have come as a messenger from them, and from Pose-yemu to whom you have raised many prayers. I have come to tell you that your prayers have been heard."

"Prayers?"

"To free the land and its peoples from the Castillian rule."

"That has long been my prayer," Po'pay admitted. He reached as if to touch his wounded back. "More now than ever. The success of the delegation to Governor Treviño has shown that the Castillians will back down if challenged."

Tleume nodded solemn approval.

"Yes. Many among the captives were frightened by their treatment at the hands of the Castillians, but you were not."

Po'pay realized that this was true. He had not been afraid. He had been willing to serve as a sacrifice, but what he had truly desired was to light a fire of continued resistance in the hearts of his people.

"We Tewa alone cannot hope to drive the Castillians away. There are not enough of us."

"Then, as with the delegation to Governor Treviño, you must make allies of the other peoples who belong to these lands," Tleume said calmly.

"Allies of Tiwa and Towa? Of Keresan?"

"Allies of them," Tleume said, "and of others, of Hopi and Zuni, as well."

"But we do not speak the same languages! We do not worship the same gods. Their stories are not our stories. Their heroes are not our heroes. In the days before the Castillians came, we were, if not enemies, certainly not friends."

"But these are not those days," Tleume said. Po'pay could hear a note of laughter. "Have only Tewa suffered abuse from the Castillians?"

"No," Po'pay admitted. "But it will be very difficult to know who to trust, even among the Tewa, much less among these others."

"We know," Tleume said. "That is why my people have come to offer you assistance."

Po'pay nodded. "Even without such assistance, I will try, but I would not reject your aid."

"I would help you. I come from the lake of Copala, where I am one of those who fight across time and space against peoples such as the Castillians, those who destroy as well as conquer."

"If you are sincere in your desire to drive the Castillians from your homelands, go to the hot springs at Posipo and pray for guidance."

Po'pay nodded, not committing himself, but acknowledging the invitation.

"If you go to Posipo," Tleume continued, "you should make masks and prayer sticks to replace those stolen by the Castillians."

Again, Po'pay nodded.

"Finally," Tleume said, "do not speak of this meeting to anyone, not even those you trust most."

He stepped into the darkness and was gone.

Po'pay went back to his bedroll. Balanced against the new fire of hope burning in his heart, the pain in his back seemed nothing. He easily fell asleep.

When they arrived in Ohkay, the returning delegates and freed prisoners were greeted warmly by most of the inhabitants. After another night's rest, Po'pay told his daughter, Oxu'a powi, that he planned to journey to Posipo.

"I will pray for wisdom," he said, "and I will make new masks and prayer sticks to replace those taken by the Castillians."

Oxu'a powi protested. "Father, your back is horribly wounded. You should rest, go to Posipo when you are stronger."

Most would not have spoken so to Po'pay, for he was known to be stern, but there were strong bonds of love and affection between father and daughter. Oxu'a powi was Po'pay's only surviving child, his wife having become sick after the birth of a son who had not survived his third year. The grieving mother had died not long thereafter. Po'pay had never found a woman he liked as much.

Oxu'a powi had been nearly a young woman when her mother had died. Although her aunts had finished her education in women's matters, she remained very much her father's child, drawn like him to religious mysteries and traditional ways.

Po'pay had been a touch surprised when Oxu'a powi had settled on Nicolas Bua as her husband since, even as a young man, Bua had seemed to straddle the worlds of the Tewa and Castillians. Still, Bua was a good provider and well-liked. The pair had produced several healthy children. Most importantly, Oxu'a powi seemed content, even happy.

Like her father, Oxu'a powi was past the first bloom of youth. She was respected among the women, and had led several of their societies. In her younger years, Oxu'a powi had been a Blue Corn Girl—assistant to the female war chief. Now she was the female war chief herself. One of her roles was to advise on appointments to a wide variety of chieftaincies. Po'pay knew she was a good advisor.

This time, however, he was not going to take her advice.

He reached and patted Oxu'a powi's hand. "To you I will say what I will to no other. My wish to pray is sincere, as is my belief we must replace our religious items before the people feel the want. However, I also think the waters of the hot springs will be healing. I will bathe in the hot springs and pray to Pose-yemu, the one who scatters mist before him, for rain and for inspiration. I will also pray to his grandmother, who lives within the hot springs, that courage for right action will well forth in the hearts of our people as her waters do from the earth."

"Right action, Father?"

Po'pay hesitated, but if he could not convince his own daughter, what chance would he have with the others? Moreover, as the female war chief, she would be a strong ally.

Therefore, although he did not mention Tleume, Po'pay told Oxu'a powi how he hoped that the success of the delegates against Governor Treviño would be enough to awaken a full resistance, a resistance strong enough to send the Castillians away forever.

Oxu'a powi was hesitant. "You say the Castillians backed down before nothing more than soft words and a show of force, but they did not hesitate to come right into our homes and take you and the others prisoner. What is to keep them from doing so again?"

"We were too mild," Po'pay said. "They came and we went, like their own stupid sheep. We forgot that they came for us because they feared our magic and curses. If we had held firm, they would have backed down. One or two might have been killed—perhaps Tagu, perhaps me—but that would have warned the others."

Po'pay added, his voice reverberating with passion, "And, despite our good manners in answering the governor's summons, four did die, accused of witchcraft, not only their bodies killed, but their reputations blackened. If I am to die named a witch, I would rather choose to die as a warrior."

"My husband Bua told me," Oxu'a powi said, speaking carefully, as if dreading her father's wrath, "that the only reason Governor Treviño accepted the delegates' gifts and let them leave in peace was that Captain Garcia and Captain Lopez warned him that Indians outnumbered the soldiers present that day in Santa Fe. Many of the soldiers had been sent out to fight the Apaches who have been raiding to steal the early harvest."

Po'pay wondered who had told Bua this. His son-in-law was a bit too friendly with the Castillians for Po'pay's comfort. Sadly, many of the people of Ohkay accepted the Castillians as part of the natural landscape, for when the Castillians had first come to the Tewa lands, they had first settled at Ohkay—a thing that Po'pay had later learned was in violation of their own laws.

Another proof of Castillian hypocrisy.

"So?" Po'pay said with more confidence than he felt. "What does this matter? All to the good if the Castillians realize that they must work with us as equals if they are not to be overwhelmed by both us and the Apaches."

"I understand," Oxu'a powi said, looking pleased. "Yes. The Castillians constantly remind us of the Apache threat, but the Apaches are as much a danger to them as to us."

"More so," Po'pay said confidently, "for the Castillians possess the horses and goods that the Apaches crave."

Eventually Oxu'a powi realized that it would be wise for Po'pay to go to Posipo. The other leaders of Ohkay agreed that the village needed new masks and prayer sticks. They spoke loudly of their admiration for Po'pay, injured as he was, for offering to make them.

One of the priests, Agoyotsire, went so far as to suggest that Po'pay borrow a horse to speed his journey, since Posipo was many leagues from Ohkay.

Po'pay refused. "Even with fresh wounds upon my back I can run as a proper Tewa should. I am not weak enough to need to rely upon a foreign animal."

Agoyotsire was appropriately shamed. As proof of his repentance, he offered to accompany Po'pay. "There will be many masks to carve, many prayer sticks to wrap. I would be honored to assist."

Po'pay graciously accepted the other man's aid. Agoyotsire had also been among Treviño's captives, but had been one of those to come away eager not to threaten Castillian authority. Po'pay hoped to bring Agoyotsire over to his way of thinking.

Two young men, hardly more than boys, who had shown promise for election to some of the minor priesthoods, also volunteered to come to Posipo. Po'pay was pleased to accept.

The group traveled lightly burdened. In addition to a few blankets, all they carried with them were the powdered minerals used for making paints and some especially fine feathers.

They made the journey without interference. For all the Castillians claimed to own the lands, they rarely ventured into this area. Po'pay could imagine that this was the world as it had been before the coming of the Castillians over eighty years before. Only the occasional Spanish word that crept into the young men's talk or the references to wool, melons, and other such things that the Castillians had brought with them ruined his idyll.

When we have eliminated the Castillians, Po'pay thought, *we must eliminate these weakening influences as well. Cotton was good enough for our grandparents, and the plants did not strip the earth as sheep and cattle do. There will be some resistance among the lazy, but surely our men and women would rather prove themselves strong.*

The hot springs were situated in a deep, somewhat narrow valley bordered by high plateaus. Once there had been a large community here, but those people had moved on, and existed only in tales.

The young men who had accompanied Po'pay and Agoyotsire delighted in hunting in these open, unspoiled lands. Both of the priests found the hot springs soothing to their old bones and new wounds.

Several days after their arrival in Posipo, Po'pay woke from a sound sleep. A now familiar voice had been calling his name.

He glanced to where Agoyotsire slept. The other man breathed slowly and evenly, but did not stir.

"Po'pay. Come forth."

Po'pay rose with alacrity. The waters of the hot springs had done much to loosen his muscles and heal his back.

When he emerged from the lean-to, the two young men continued to sleep by the embers of the fire. Although they breathed evenly, they did not stir even when Po'pay walked directly past them.

Not long before, Po'pay would have taken this as an example of how lax the training of the young had become, but tonight he was aware of the touch of miracles in the air.

"Po'pay. I wait at the shrine."

Although there were many holy places in this river valley, Po'pay did not doubt which one the voice meant. On the plateau that fringed the river cut was the shrine where for several days he and Agoyotsire had labored making masks. Immediately, Po'pay gathered up two heavy river cobbles and began the climb.

The earth-navel shrine was the type of sacred place the Castillians did not respect: a large ring of smooth cobbles standing waist-high in some places and as many as eight or ten cobbles wide. The ring was large enough from edge to edge that three grown men could have lain down head to foot and still needed to bridge the distance with outstretched arms.

Perhaps the Castillians did not consider how much labor was needed to carry this many stones to one place and position them.

They use slaves to build their holy places as well as to feed themselves and make their homes. What do they know of honest sweat offered to the gods?

Before Po'pay entered the center of the ring through the opening left at the east side, he set in place the two cobbles he had carried with him, their weight during his climb part of his prayer.

Beneath the shelter of a large piñon in which he and Agoyotsire had hung both finished and unfinished masks, Po'pay saw that Tleume stood. He wore one of the masks Po'pay and Agoyotsire had finished blessing earlier that day. It made him seem more like a god than ever. Tleume held another mask in his hands and was studying it thoughtfully.

Tleume looked up when Po'pay approached. Behind the mask, his eyes glinted bright and human.

"You have decided to come," he said, his voice warm with approval. "This is wise, for the gods have decided to grant you the means for rousing the peoples against their enemies."

Framed as the speaker was by the many masks that hung upon the piñon tree, clad in a mask himself, he spoke with divine authority. Behind him, carved mask faces swayed, nodded, and otherwise indicated their approval.

Tleume extended the mask he held in his hands. "This mask, who in Ohkay will wear it?"

"I will. I am the chief celebrant of the ritual in which it is used."

"Good. That is what I was told. What is your greatest desire?"

"To drive the Castillians from these lands, to return our people to our traditional ways."

"Concentrate upon that goal, Po'pay. Fill your heart and soul with it. When you have done so, raise the mask to your face. Tell me what you see."

Po'pay did as he was directed. The mask was one associated with rituals for healing and for the health of the land. He had lavished much effort when carving the details, carefully painted the mask, and lastly adorned it with two particularly fine turkey feathers.

Po'pay raised the mask to his face and held it there. For a long moment he saw only darkness, as one would expect. Then he realized that there were tiny flickers of color breaking up the blackness. First these were stars, but they transformed into rainbows. Po'pay's hands shook with awe, but he held the mask firmly before his face.

Breathing deeply, Po'pay concentrated on envisioning the land free of the Castillians, of the people living as they had before alien ways intruded. He imagined young men running barefoot to hunt rabbits, maidens gossiping as they carried painted jars filled with water, mothers singing traditional songs as they ground corn or spun cotton, older men solemnly dancing the traditional dances without dread of censure.

The flickering colors resolved into pictures, pictures more perfectly drawn than the elegant prints in the Bible. In these pictures, Po'pay saw more than his own imaginings. He recognized himself talking to a small group, and knew each man and woman in the group by face and bearing.

He saw a few of these going forth and speaking with others. Tagu of Ohkay was shown going to Nambe, where he had kin. Oxu'a powi spoke to some of the women of their village. From these groups, others went forth in a glorious web, complex as that of any spider.

Po'pay knew the Mask was showing him who could be trusted to spread his vision of the land free of the Castillians. The mighty web was spun once, then again. After that, the eyes of the Mask flickered into more usual darkness, and he lowered it from his face.

Tleume asked, "What did you see?"

"I saw how to weave a web that will catch the Castillians in its meshes," Po'pay said.

"Do you think you can follow this pattern?"

"I do."

"Look often into the Mask," Tleume said, "but do so only in the company of those you can trust beyond doubt. There are those who will fear what it tells you. There are those who will desire its power for themselves."

Po'pay nodded.

"Another warning," Tleume said. "The path you have chosen will make you allies, but it will also make you enemies—and not merely among the Castillians. Can you be ruthless?"

"Squash and pumpkins only grow large when the weak fruit are culled from the vine," Po'pay said. "I can be ruthless."

"Here then is a tool. If the need comes, you will be shown how to use it. Otherwise, hide it away."

Tleume handed Po'pay something that resembled a traditional prayer stick bound around with feathers and sage. It was somewhat smaller, and much lighter than such would usually be. At one end, something—perhaps a small rock crystal—caught the light and glittered.

Tleume stepped back. "We may meet again, Po'pay, if the ancestors so ordain. Farewell. Remember my warnings."

Turning, the divine messenger lifted the mask from his face. He hung it on the cottonwood tree with the rest. Then he vanished into the darkness.

Infused with wonder and awe at the promise of divine favor the Mask offered him, Po'pay immediately began weaving his web. The Mask had shown him that those who had accompanied him to the hot springs were to be trusted.

Now feeling free to speak his passion aloud, he infused them with his ardor. When the masks were completed, the young men, Omtua and Catua, did not accompany the rest back to Ohkay. Instead, they carried messages to those the Mask had shown Po'pay must be brought earliest into the conspiracy.

Those messages had been a challenge to word. The Mask helped in that it showed who must be spoken to, and even which of the young men should carry the message, but it did not tell Po'pay what to say. This he must work out for himself. He became quite skilled at doing this, both for these first meetings and thereafter.

An important early ally was an elder of the Towa of Walatowa. Another was a woman from Acoma, the city on the high mesa to the southwest. Po'pay had doubted the Mask's wisdom when it had included this Keresan woman in the inner web, but he had hardly spoken five words with her when he thrilled at the wisdom of the Mask.

By birth, this woman belonged to one important family. By marriage, she was affiliated with another. Moreover, she had grown to womanhood hearing tales of the atrocities the Castillians had committed seventy-five years before when Acoma had been attacked. Hundreds of residents had been killed. Many of the survivors were mutilated or sold into slavery.

Po'pay would have never selected this woman of his own accord, but she was the perfect person to bring many of Acoma to act against the Castillians. Moreover, as a woman, her comings and goings would be overlooked—an important thing, for the Castillians had never ceased to view those of Acoma as troublemakers.

As he wove his web, Po'pay consulted the Mask regularly, as Tleume had instructed him to do. At first the images offered inspiration and encouragement. Later, they began to repeat. In these repetitions, Po'pay found disquiet and discouragement.

One thing the Mask forced Po'pay to realize was that the Castillians would not be sent from the lands quickly. This would be no autumn and winter of planning, followed by a rapid summer campaign.

Po'pay deduced this from an image the Mask showed him repeatedly. In it, Po'pay handed two runners knotted cords and sent them off along routes that would take them to the various pueblos. At each pueblo the runners gave a knotted cord to the chief among Po'pay's allies in that place. When they did so, they motioned to the sun and demonstrated that each day a knot was to be untied.

Po'pay had puzzled over this image until he realized that these knotted cords were a way to coordinate action at each of the scattered pueblos, so that the various groups could strike as one. Those pueblos the runners arrived at first had more knots to untie, those at the end fewer.

This was a simple way to assure the Castillians were not alerted by a snare snapping before the full weight of the prey was in the noose. Po'pay was heartened. Then, studying the images so that he would know who the runners should be—for they looked familiar and yet not—he realized that they were Omtua and Catua. However, these were a changed Omtua and Catua.

Both, now young men hardly beyond boyhood, were clearly several years older. Omtua bore a nasty scar across the left of his face, an old wound, not a new.

Time, therefore, must pass before they could strike.

Po'pay could resign himself to this, even encourage patience in his allies lest they be defeated as the people of Acoma had been defeated. However, another image the Mask showed him offered no guidance, only created disquiet in Po'pay's heart.

This vision was of a man lying facedown in the sand near a stand of junipers, either dead or asleep. The man wore his hair after the fashion of a Castillian, and his clothing was a hybrid of Tewa and Castillian styles. There was a mark on his shirt as if it had been burned.

This image always preceded that of Po'pay speaking to the runners, as if the Mask was telling Po'pay that without this death, the day when the resistance against the Castillians would begin could not come.

Po'pay did not recognize the fallen man. From his attire, he was probably someone like Francisco Guitar, a half-blood who had sided with the Castillians. Even so, it was an ugly image, and Po'pay was not comforted by how often the Mask repeated it, nor by its refusal to show him the man's face, no matter how often he pleaded or even demanded that it do so.

A.D. 1676

Yet even with the Mask's assistance, matters did not progress smoothly. Over and over, Po'pay heard the same concerns: the Castillians had swords and flintlocks; the Castillians had horses; the Castillians did not need to farm or hunt. They took their livelihood from their *encomiendas* and *repartimientos.*

These last were uniquely Castillian customs, ones even those who were resigned to the Castillian presence did not particularly like. *Encomienda* was the Spanish custom of stealing part of any crop for their own use, although they did nothing to help raise it. *Repartimiento* was similar, but here what was being stolen was labor, rather than goods.

The Tewa all contributed to the community in various ways—even if all did not actually plow or hoe or carry water. No one said, "This is mine. I planted this seed. I will keep the corn for myself alone. I will work for myself alone."

Some contributed in ways other than farming, but all contributed. Only the Spanish believed they could behave like small children and say, "This is mine. Your labor is mine. Give it to me." Only the invader's weapons and propensity toward violence—like children indulging in vicious tantrums—had permitted the custom of *encomienda* to become established at all.

But Po'pay found a way to turn even this argument to his advantage.

"After I was tortured in Santa Fe, the ancestors told me that they do not like that the Castillians now take away part of what the earth and rain give us. That is why there has been drought. The ancestors do not wish to feed the Castillians, for the Castillians would have us deny acknowledgment to those who bring us the rain."

Continued drought was feared even more than the Castillian swords and flintlocks, but although many were willing to complain, few were ready to act. Po'pay knew that his people needed reason to hope.

Po'pay longed to show others the visions the Mask shared with him, but he did not. Not only did Tleume's warning remain fresh in his mind, but the Mask itself reinforced the caution. Several times it showed Po'pay a vision of himself hiding the Mask before some co-conspirator arrived—even those such as Tagu and the woman from Acoma, whom Po'pay now trusted as deeply as he did himself and Oxu'a powi.

Seeking further inspiration, Po'pay fasted. He walked pilgrimage between the sacred shrines. He danced beneath the heat of the sun and into the darkest night. At last, when he was beginning to believe that the Mask would offer him no further guidance, it brought him fresh counsel.

Although the Mask had been guide and councilor to Po'pay from the first, Tleume's second gift had served no purpose. Po'pay had studied the prayer stick carefully, but other than ascertaining that at its core was metal, rather than wood, he had learned nothing.

Upon finding this metal core, Po'pay had resisted an urge to throw the prayer stick away. No single thing in his experience was so closely associated with the invaders than iron and its cousin steel. Indeed, when the Castillians had first come into the land, the people had called them "Wearers of Rock-Hard Metal" or "Metal People" because of their strange armor and weapons.

On closer examination, Po'pay had decided that the metal at the heart of the prayer stick was not iron or steel. For one, it was not as heavy and was a great deal more flexible. For another, it did not rust, even after Po'pay was soaked to the skin while carrying it.

Heartened, Po'pay had continued to carry the strange prayer stick, hiding it, as the Mask had guided, in plain sight among his ceremonial attire. Now, in Po'pay's hour of desperation, the Mask showed Po'pay how this prayer stick might be used.

He was in Powhogeh at the time, deeply discouraged by his allies' continued faintheartedness. That night they were to have a final meeting before Po'pay and his escort moved on. Po'pay left the Mask well guarded by young Omtua, but, following the Mask's instructions, he carried the prayer stick.

Memories of the accusations of witchcraft remained acute in Powhogeh. Therefore, meetings were held in an isolated kiva. Oddly, the Castillian military leaders, always rivals for authority with the religious, had given Po'pay and his allies permission to continue to use the kivas for their "social" organizations. The priests would have filled the kivas with sand out of a lingering suspicion that all their converts were not entirely sincere.

As he climbed down the ladder into the kiva, Po'pay thought how the Spanish misunderstanding of the Indian peoples and their religion was reflected even in the word they used for the kiva.

The Spanish called the kivas *estufas*, a word that reflected their belief that the round, underground rooms were used as steam baths. In reality, the kivas represented elements of the sacred landscape, set underground as a reminder that man had emerged from the world before into the world above.

Although the weather outside was hot, the air within the kiva was cool. The thick, adobe-plastered walls, combined with the mud and lattice roofing, provided insulation against the heat. The kiva was sparsely lit by embers of the sacred fire. Today was a day for listening, not for watching.

When the prayers and offerings of fine ground corn meal, tobacco, and pollen had been made to the gods and ancestors, Po'pay began.

"What if I told you," Po'pay asked after the usual complaints had been raised, "that, in addition to our own numbers, the gods and ancestors have blessed me with magic certain to intimidate the Castillians?"

"If I could see such magic," said Francisco El Ollito, a prominent priest, "I would be swayed."

He spoke as one who did not believe such magic existed. Po'pay had not known what El Ollito would say—the Mask never revealed such—but he had been shown El Ollito's speech as the cue upon which to act.

"Then I will show you," Po'pay said.

He already stood in the center of the kiva. Now he nodded to Catua. Catua tapped a measure on the drum he held braced between his knees. The sound reverberated in the close space. Po'pay saw some of the more nervous shift and look about, obviously fearing Castillian interference.

Po'pay did not hesitate, but fell into the steps of a dance, shifting from foot to foot so that the copper bells on his leggings sounded in time with his motion. He began to chant, invoking Pose-yemu, Tinini Povi, along with other gods and culture heroes of the Tewa people. In his heart, Po'pay also invoked Tleume, who had given him the prayer stick, which he now took from where it hung at his waist.

In the dim light within the kiva, it was doubtful that many saw what Po'pay did next, but none could miss what happened when, raising his hands skyward, Po'pay touched a raised knot on the metal shaft of the prayer stick. He slid it to one side, then the other, then down, following the prescribed pattern the Mask had revealed to him.

Lightning shot forth from the prayer stick, lightning so brilliant that afterimages wavered and shimmered before his eyes. Had the Mask failed to warn Po'pay not to point the prayer stick at anyone, someone would have been blinded, but the Mask's guidance was sound.

Still moving in the shuffling dance, Po'pay now directed the tip of the prayer stick around his own feet. Again lightning shot forth, this time accompanied by small stars.

Catua accelerated the pulse of his drumming. Po'pay directed the prayer stick to send lightning into the roof over El Ollito's head. The elder's eyes went wide with awe and terror.

"You said if I showed you the new magic," Po'pay challenged, "that you would be swayed to join our sacred cause. Will you keep your word?"

El Ollito gasped. "I will! I will!"

His eyes streamed with tears, but Po'pay found himself heartened, for the expression on his new ally's face was one of hope and wonder—not of fear.

El Ollito and the people of Powhogeh were his.

A.D. 1677

Despite the Mask's aid and the awe-inspiring power of the prayer stick, the work of creating an alliance against the Castillians remained slow. Po'pay traveled many leagues, always on foot, to visit the various pueblos. When planning who to speak with and in which order, the Mask saved him much trial and error. Without its divine advice, Po'pay first would have sought to build a strong power base among his own Tewa people.

The Mask directed him otherwise. In Welai, the Tiwa settlement that the Castillians called Picuris, Po'pay found an avid ally in Tupatu. In Khe-wa, a Keresan settlement called Santo Domingo, a half-breed called Alonzo Catiti proved to bear more bitterness against the Castillians whose blood he bore than did many of those of purer heritage. In Teotho, Po'pay renewed his association with the Tiwa leader Saca.

Even with the Mask's encouragement, making these contacts was not easy. As Po'pay had told Tleume, there were barriers of language and custom between the peoples the Castillians lumped together as "Indians."

Yet despite these obstacles, the web of alliances grew under Po'pay's skillful handling. Although the Castillians, arrogant in their power, convinced of the docility of their "Indian children," suspected nothing but some individual discontent, within two years of the beatings on the Santa Fe plaza, a majority among the Indians knew there was a new power in the lands.

This awareness of power was in itself a tool for gathering allies, for now, in addition to awing the doubters with miraculous fire, Po'pay could threaten the retribution of his warriors upon those who sided with the Castillians.

Just as his alliance was gaining power, events close to home forced Po'pay to consider the wisdom of continuing.

Returning to Ohkay from one of his recruitment expeditions, he was met outside the pueblo by his daughter, Oxu'a powi.

"Father, I have news for you."

Po'pay wondered if Oxu'a powi might be again with child, but she did not look as happy as such news should make her. Then he wondered if something had happened to Tagu, the man who was coordinating the Tewa of Ohkay.

"News?"

"My husband, Nicolas Bua, has been named governor of the pueblo of San Juan."

She spoke deliberately, stressing both her husband's Christian name and the Castillian name for Ohkay.

"Bua? He has accepted this appointment?"

"He has. He has been governor for over a month now. The Castillians are very pleased with him. So are many of our own people. Nicolas has done many helpful things, such as arranging for oxen to help with turning the fields, and with hauling kegs of water up from the river."

"And you, daughter, do you live with him in the governor's house?"

"He is my husband," came the cryptic reply. "My hearth fires are warm, and my children play with their cousins."

Po'pay was horrified. The position of governor meant little within the traditional structure of Ohkay's daily life, but outside that traditional structure it was of highest importance. The governor was chief among the Castillian's allies. He received many gifts from them. Skillful use of these gifts could earn both favors and prestige among the people.

Spending as much time as he did with those who hated Castillian rule, Po'pay could almost forget that there were those among the people who had come to view the Castillians as friends. First among these were those who had adopted Christianity over traditional rites, rather than merely adding new prayers to the old, as most did.

Next were those who had gained some prominence because of their association with the Castillians—prominence that they would not have otherwise earned. Some of these were younger men, raised by the Castillians' desire for native troops to augment those who had come from the Castillians' far homeland. Others were of mixed blood, barred in most traditional communities from holding chieftainships or priesthoods. Still others were women who had become fond of one or the other of the Castillian men, for the Castillians had few of their own women among them but many of a normal man's needs and desires.

Po'pay had often felt a twinge of uneasiness regarding Bua's devotion to the Tewa, and because of this he had not included Bua in the gatherings where Po'pay spread his vision of a land free from Castillian domination. Now he wondered if he had erred. He had trusted family ties to bring Bua to him when the time came. Now it seemed that Bua had made alliances that would forever sever him from the cause.

Po'pay was far too stunned by this news to question Oxu'a powi further. In any case, he was now uncertain as to where her loyalties rested. A wife had reason to be loyal to the father of her children.

Deciding that she had done nothing to make him distrust her, Po'pay placed a hand on Oxu'a powi's shoulder and gave it a reassuring squeeze.

"Thank you for telling me of Bua's new prominence," Po'pay said. "I shall be certain to treat him with the respect he deserves."

As the sun was westering, Bua came riding to where Po'pay sat leaning against the wall of his house, resting after the day's long walk, enjoying the play of his grandchildren, anticipating a well-cooked meal.

The horse Bua rode was shabby compared to the mounts the Castillians kept for themselves: a sway-backed, sunburnt black gelding whose ears promised a wicked temper if aroused. But nonetheless it was a horse, and any horse was a prize.

Bua rode with only a blanket to cushion his rump from his steed's bony spine and a light bridle. Tied behind him was an irregularly shaped bundle.

The new governor was well-dressed. Below the waist he wore a traditional kilt and leggings, but above the waist he flaunted a Castillian shirt open at the neck to show an ornate silver cross. His hair had been cut shorter, and he seemed to be trying to grow a mustache.

Po'pay did not comment, although he thought that Bua meant the cross in particular to be a goad to prick his father-in-law's temper.

Yet, even as he swallowed his immediate criticism, Po'pay felt a prick of uneasiness, as if he was seeing something he had long-dreaded seeing.

Bua said, "Welcome back from your journeys, father-in-law."

"Congratulations on your new position, Governor," Po'pay replied, but he did not rise. Bua had greeted him as a family member, so this was not an official visit.

"I have brought a treat to sweeten the evening meal," Bua said, handing down the bundle to the tallest of the many children who were dancing around the horse in expectation, keeping well clear of those wicked hind hooves.

Bua has demonstrated his influence this way before, then, Po'pay thought. *The children know the horse's temper. How long before the people grow tired of Bua's arrogance?*

The children had torn open the bundle and were shrieking in delight. "Melons! Melons!"

"From the good *padre*'s own garden," Bua said. "They will be very tasty."

As they should be, Po'pay thought sourly, *since they take more water than even corn to grow, and need much pampering.*

Later, Po'pay saw how Bua watched him when slices of melon were handed around, and thought it prudent to accept a small piece, although it had become his custom to refuse Castillian luxuries.

The melon *was* very good.

But not as sweet as ridding ourselves of the Castillians would be, Po'pay thought, spitting out a stray seed.

Over the next several days, Po'pay watched Bua and felt certain that Bua watched him. He became certain that Bua—Don Nicolas, as he now preferred to be called—planned to betray Po'pay to the Castillians. He was equally certain that Bua was waiting to do so until he had something he could use to secure himself more firmly within the Castillian's trust.

As many times as Po'pay prayed for guidance, the Mask would only repeat certain visions: the web of his allies, the fallen man, the runners with their knotted cords. It was as if the Mask was telling him that until one matter was resolved, nothing new would come.

At last, Po'pay decided that in this matter of Bua his own heart was certain what the right path must be, and that the Mask's lack of advice was confirmation that Po'pay was right.

Nicolas Bua must be removed from the picture.

Po'pay had carefully considered the situation from all angles. Bua might not know the details of the planned action against the Castillians, but he did know that something was being planned. Bua's likely successor as governor under the Castillians was a man so deeply committed to the Christian faith that he probably knew less of the plot than did some of the older children. Remove Bua, remove the threat. Moreover, the Castillians would be further isolated from the truth by their new choice as governor.

As many times as he reviewed the situation, Po'pay could not see a better answer. He felt certain that Bua was simply waiting to betray them when that information would be to his best advantage. Moreover, Po'pay had promised to visit Saca in Teotho, perhaps even to spend the winter there. He felt he must act before he made that journey.

Once Po'pay had made his decision, the Mask became helpful. It showed him a vision of Po'pay meeting Bua at a minor shrine some distance from Ohkay. The vision showed a fingernail crescent of the moon in the sky.

As always, the Mask did not show Po'pay what he must say to get Bua to that place at that time, but Po'pay had watched his son-in-law long enough that he thought he knew how to bait his snare.

Imply that I will give him intimate knowledge of our plans against the Castillians, Po'pay thought, *that I trust him intimately, that I need his assistance as governor of San Juan to make my poor rebellion a success. He will come.*

A few words spoken in private to Bua one evening after dinner, and agreement was reached.

When the chosen day came, the Mask showed Po'pay when to leave Ohkay so that his departure would not excite comment. Po'pay was to carry with him the Mask in a bundle on his back. The prayer stick that shot lightning was shown carried over his left hip. As always, Po'pay was awed by how, when he precisely followed the course displayed in those neatly drawn pictures, nothing would trouble his course.

A nosy neighbor turned away at the precise moment Po'pay was passing. A child who might have asked to come with him was called to fetch water. A contingent of Castillians riding arrogantly by were distracted when a rabbit burst from a clump of thread-leaf sage and ran among the hooves of the horses.

And Po'pay, walking openly as any honest man going about his business, was as unnoticed as the wind.

Following the Mask's directions, Po'pay took a circuitous route to the shrine. Once there, he took shelter within a cluster of piñon.

Pillowing his head upon the still-wrapped Mask, he dozed as the sun moved west.

A coyote's cry from very nearby woke Po'pay. Jumping to his feet with an ease that would have done credit to a much younger man, Po'pay saw that the sky was dark. The moon was a fingernail crescent against the stars, just as it had been in his vision.

Po'pay's heart pounded with a flash of fear. What if he had overslept?

From slightly farther away, the coyote laughed mockery. Po'pay forced himself to relax. The Mask would not have shown him where to wait if it would let mere physical weakness mislead him. He must trust in the Mask and in his destiny.

Unwrapping the Mask from its bundle, Po'pay made a quick check, but the Mask did not add to its earlier vision. It encouraged him with a brief repeat of the vision of himself walking forth to meet Bua. In that vision, Po'pay carried a bundle on his back, so although he longed for the Mask's guidance in the encounter that was to come, he faithfully wrapped it and shouldered the bundle.

Bua did not come to this meeting on his horse, but quietly on foot. Po'pay heard Bua's panting breaths before he saw him.

Too much sitting on a horse. Too much eating fat mutton and sweet melons. Too little honest work. This is what the Castillians admire?

Po'pay waited until Bua had reached the exact place where the Mask had shown them meeting, then stepped forward.

Bua was taking a long drink from a gourd he carried at his belt. Insolently, he did not stop to greet his father-in-law as manners between younger and elder would normally direct. Nor did he offer to share his water, but turned and leaned against the shrine, waiting for Po'pay to join him.

It was doubtful that the Castillians would even have recognized the shrine for what it was. They would have seen a particularly large rock, that was all. But Bua knew this rock marked a sacred location, a place of annual pilgrimage among some of the priesthoods. His action was a statement without words, and Po'pay wondered that he would make it.

I understand! he thought. *Bua is reminding me that although he has come in answer to my request, he is still an important person, one who answers to the Castillians and so has no need to fear a "witch" or that witch's gods.*

"Don Nicolas," Po'pay began, careful to be polite. "I am pleased that we will have an opportunity to speak in private. You have become such a busy man."

That Bua was pleased by the flattery was evident in how he straightened and stood tall. He was still a Tewa at heart. Among the Tewa, prestige meant more than any physical wealth. Having a senior priest speak to him deferentially would be sweeter than any melon.

Po'pay felt a flash of sorrow for this man he had known since he was a boy, for the husband of his daughter, the father of his grandchildren. A Tewa heart still beat beneath the silver cross Bua wore so prominently upon his breast.

Maybe I can win him back to us, Po'pay thought, hope filling his heart with butterfly wings. *Perhaps that is why the Mask sent me to this shrine, so that the gods could assist me in bringing the father of my grandchildren back home.*

"A pleasant night for a run," Bua commented when Po'pay did not speak, "but morning and the resumption of my duties will come all too soon. Still, I am never too busy to remember I also have a duty to the father of my wife. There was something that you wished to speak with me about. I am here to listen."

Careful not to commit himself, Po'pay thought. *Does he fear the Castillians have set spies on him? Or has he himself brought someone to witness what I will say?*

Po'pay looked around, but the crescent moon revealed little. Bua was growing restless, and Po'pay realized he could delay no longer.

"You have worked closely with the Castillians for some time now," Po'pay began. "Are you content with this?"

"Content?" Bua shrugged expressively, broad shoulders rising and falling. "If the Castillians would agree among themselves, perhaps, I would be more content. As it is, I must do one thing to make our *padre* and the other friars content, another to satisfy the needs of the military and governor."

"What if agreement among these Castillian factions was not an issue?" Po'pay asked cautiously.

"Have you a way to make the priests agree with the soldiers?" Bua laughed. "If so, your gods are wiser than theirs."

Po'pay permitted himself a small smile. "Rather, I think we should let them disagree with each other all they wish—and a long way from here."

Bua stilled in mid-chuckle, but he did not look surprised, rather like a stalking coyote who has heard the rabbit stir in the brush.

"Why should they go far from here? The Castillians have ruled since before you were born, since before your father was born."

"Yes. They came in my grandfather's day," Po'pay agreed, trying to sound easy about this. "However, if simply coming and staying was reason to accept rulership, then why do we pick the caterpillars out of the corn?"

"Are you comparing the Castillians to caterpillars?"

"They eat what they do not plant," Po'pay said. "Like the caterpillars, they are parasites upon our labor."

"The Castillians protect us from the Apache raiders," Bua protested.

"Raiders who would not be so dangerous if the Castillians had also not let them steal their horses, while denying the same to us, those they call their 'children.' "

Bua looked shocked at Po'pay's words, but Po'pay thought some of the shock was feigned, that Bua was actually pleased to hear Po'pay speak his mind.

He thinks I am spinning the rope by which I will hang, Po'pay thought sadly. *Still, perhaps I can win his heart by reminding him of our shared heritage.*

"Once this land was ours," Po'pay continued, allowing the passion with which he had spoken so many times rise to color his voice. "We lived here and farmed here and no one but ourselves benefitted from our toil. Then these strangers came from the south and spoke words our ancestors did not understand. We Tewa are accustomed to living side by side with people who worship other gods, who have different customs. How were we to know that these Metal Men were different, that they were not asking to come and live side by side with us, but to make us slaves?"

"I am not a slave," Bua said, his voice rising. "I am governor of San Juan."

"No!" Po'pay retorted. "You are a slave. A slave valued for his smooth tongue and insinuating ways, rather than for his muscle or skill as a warrior, but you are a slave. I am not insulting you—or if I am, I am insulting myself and every other Tewa who walks the land, and every Tiwa, Towa, Keresan, Hopi, and Zuni, every person who permits these aliens with their strange gods and stranger ways to dominate us merely because they are willing to slay us if we do not submit."

"Then you are saying," Bua said, "that we should die rather than live under Castillian rule?"

"I am saying," Po'pay countered, "that we should accept death if death is the price for not being a slave."

"What if I could accept my death," Bua said, "but not the death of my children? What if one came to me and said, 'You are a good man, a Christian and a father of children who could be Christians. We will help you not only to prosperity, but to eternal life. All you must do is be our friend.' "

"For this eternal life you would live as a slave in this one?" Po'pay countered. "Our way offers an eternal life as well. Our spirits continue on, although changed. Some become the ancestors whose counsel we seek through prayer; some join the clouds. A changed life, but an eternal one—and we do not need to live as slaves in this life to merit it."

"You are a rebel, Po'pay," Bua said. "One who has given his word and now goes against it. The Castillians are the law."

"No! I am not a rebel," Po'pay said. "I am a man of this land, born in this land, as my father and my grandfather and my great-grandfather were born. I am not a foreigner who comes like a bully taking away a weaker child's ear of corn and sweetening the theft by saying, 'Look. I have only taken this ear of corn. I offer the withholding of my fist in return.' I am not a rebel, for I do not accept that the Castillians have any rights here."

"The Castillians," Bua said, turning away, the insolence of his smile clearly visible even in the faint light of the crescent moon, "will not see matters as you do. They have flintlocks and steel swords and thousands of fellows in the southlands and across the great sea."

Po'pay shook his head sadly. "And you think I will let you go to tell them?"

Bua stared at him. "And how will you stop me, old man?"

Po'pay touched the prayer stick at his belt. "If the gods of the Castillians have given them steel, our gods have given me lightning."

In the kiva, Po'pay had never used the prayer-stick to make more than light, but the Mask had shown him that if he twisted the shaft further the lightning would sting, further still and the lightning would burn.

Laughing mockery, Bua began to run, clearly intending to out-distance Po'pay in the darkness.

Po'pay twisted the shaft once, twice, then, hesitating for a moment, regret bitter in his mouth, a third time. He leveled the tip of the prayer stick at the fleeing man. A slim hot beam leapt forth, caught Bua between his shoulder blades.

Bua collapsed between one step and the next, landing on his face in the sandy soil. There was a mark on the back of his shirt.

Hastening to Bua's side, Po'pay knelt and turned his son-in-law over. The lightning had burnt through Bua's back and emerged from his chest, melting the silver cross into shapeless slag.

Bua no longer breathed.

Despite his victory, Po'pay felt tears flooding his eyes, tears that fell on the parched earth like the rain.

Afterward to "Like The Rain"

About Fred Saberhagen, Mask of the Sun, and the Pueblo Revolt . . .

Mask of the Sun is not just my favorite of Fred's novels, it is one of my favorite SF novels ever. When Roger Zelazny set up a chance for me to meet Fred, I was in such awe I could hardly walk through the door into the Saberhagen's house. Of course, Fred turned out to be a lovely person. (So did Joan.) I never did get over my awe, though, not even when Fred and I collaborated on the Berserker story "Servant of Death."

The Pueblo Revolt of 1680 is one of the most remarkable events in American history. After five years of meticulous planning, the allied Pueblos under the leadership of the mysterious Po'pay succeeded in routing the Spanish from their territories. The Pueblos would retain their lands for the next twelve years, until the Spanish managed a successful—and no matter what anyone tells you, far from "bloodless"—reconquest.

Unbelievable elements from my fictional account that come straight out of the historical record include the successful alliance of peoples with different languages and cultures, the use of the knotted cord to synchronize attacks across a vast area, reports that Po'pay had mysterious advisors (Tleume was one of these), and, perhaps most remarkably, that Po'pay shot lightning from his fingertips and feet.

In this context, the introduction of help from the far future seemed natural.

Today, the pueblo peoples of New Mexico and Arizona retain their culture, languages, and some of their lands. The legacy of the Revolt, therefore, is a success. I would like to think that in the realm of the Mask, it was even more so.

Remember

by

Dean Wesley Smith

February 23, 1836
Bexar, Republic of Texas

"Incoming!" a voice shouted from behind Dennis Holcomb as the muzzle flash from the Aztec cannon cut through the darkness, followed a moment later by the explosion of sound echoing over the mission. The cannon, one of two, sat on a small rise built in the center of Bexar, which would become the future San Antonio.

Around him men ducked for cover behind the two-foot-thick west wall of the Alamo. Holcomb held his position on the wall, his night glasses allowing him to see clearly the three Aztec warriors already starting to reload the cannon.

Behind them stood another Aztec warrior wearing a thin head-dress and a wide robe. From what Holcomb had learned over the last week of studying the Aztec society, the warrior looked to be a member of the Arrow Clan. That meant he was in charge of the other warriors working the cannons.

The Aztec had less than a second to live. He just didn't know it. Holcomb already had the wind figured, had the distance figured to exactly 865 feet. He was ready, had his target in his sights.

As the shell exploded at the base of the wall of the Alamo mission twenty feet down to the left from his position, he fired under the covering sound, knocking the Aztec leader off the mound.

Holcomb then moved quickly, still covered by the echoing thunder of the cannon shot impact. He moved the gun sight to the second mound with another Aztec cannon twenty yards to the right of the first one. He picked the Arrow Clan warrior clearly in charge standing behind the three working on the cannon and shot, knocking him over backward before his men even had a chance to fire that cannon.

No other person behind the Alamo wall heard his shots because of the explosion of the shell and the silence technology on the gun.

Beside him, Berg DeWitt patted him lightly on the shoulder. "Nice shooting."

"Old skills come back quick," Holcomb said. "Two down, four or five thousand more Aztecs to go."

"Yeah, going to be nothing to it," DeWitt laughed, staring through night-scope binoculars at the cannons. "Just like 'Nam."

"We lost that war, remember?" Holcomb said, watching through the night scope on his glasses as the Aztec warriors scrambled around the cannons, pulling their dead leaders away from the mounds, leaving the cannons unattended.

"So we make up for that here," DeWitt said, focusing over the thick wall into the dark.

Holcomb glanced at the Vietnam vet beside him. DeWitt was a tall guy, maybe six-two, and he had arms on him that could bench-press more than Holcomb wanted to think about. The guy had military short hair and intense green eyes. He was originally from Montana and had served in 'Nam for two terms leading right up to the end of the war.

He and DeWitt were dressed as frontiersmen of the time, in soft deerskin jackets, cloth pants and heavy boots. They both had on a poncho-like gray wool coat against the chill of the night.

Along the top of the Alamo wall, the Texans and other fighters got back into position as the dust from the explosion drifted on the cool evening breeze, rifles poised and aiming into the pitch darkness of the night. Halfway down the west wall, Davy Crockett stood, staring into the blackness.

Holcomb just shook his head and looked away. The real Davy Crockett looked nothing like Fess Parker, the actor who had played him on television when Holcomb was a kid. ·

The real Davy Crockett was short. That had been a real disappointment.

May 18, 1981
Portland, Oregon, USA

Holcomb sat on the park bench staring out over the calm waters of the Willamette River, not really paying any attention to those walking the path behind him or the boats floating past on the river. The day had turned warm and brought hundreds out of their homes and offices to enjoy the afternoon sunshine and beautiful spring day along the waterfront.

Holcomb hadn't noticed any of it. He had just come from a doctor. All he could remember now from the conversation was the word "cancer" and "two months to live."

It didn't seem real, but it had been the third opinion, the third doctor, actually. He hadn't trusted the first two, hadn't believed them. But now it seemed there was no doubt. He was dying, and there wasn't a damn thing anyone could do about it.

A young woman laughed, the sound high and light, floating on the soft breeze. Before learning of the cancer, he would have sat here, watching her, enjoying the sun and the afternoon. He had spent many a warm afternoon on this bench and even knew some of the nearby shop owners by name. This bench, beside this path in the narrow park along the river, had been his favorite place in the city. He called it his spot, and anyone he dated or his few friends at work knew where to find him on nice days. And Portland, in the spring and summer and fall, had a lot of nice days.

Now the sound of someone laughing just annoyed him. How could anyone be enjoying a day like today? He had just been given a death sentence. There was nothing worth laughing about today. He stood and without a look at the beautiful calm river or the park around him, turned and headed back into the center of the city.

His apartment was on the third floor of an old converted hotel six blocks from the river, and he didn't notice the walk, other than the few times he bumped into someone. All he could think about was dying. He had faced enemy fire a lot of times in 'Nam, had killed more than his share of the enemy, but never in all that time had he worried much about dying. Now that death faced him, like a train coming head-on, he didn't know how to deal with it.

It just made him mad, actually.

One thing for certain: he had no intention of going the way the first doctor at the VA had described, sitting in a hospice the last few weeks, medicated so that he wouldn't feel the pain. He had bought a pistol after that little talk just for the occasion, and now, with a solid third opinion, there sure didn't seem to be any reason to put off the end. He would face it just as he had faced most things in his life. Head-on.

He had no family since his parents had died in a car wreck the year after he got back from 'Nam, and even though he was liked for his dry sense of humor at work, he didn't have any real friends to speak of, just a few old buddies from 'Nam. He was just too much of a loner to let anyone close. At least that's what his last girlfriend, Sandra, had told him.

He hadn't argued with her. She had been right. No one would really miss him, and there certainly wasn't anyone to take care of him in the next two months. Only the VA, and he doubted they really wanted to see him at this point either, after the fuss he had made about getting a second and then a third opinion.

He had no real money except the little bit his parents had left him, and his job driving a city bus could be filled in ten minutes.

The pistol would do everyone a favor.

He opened the door to his single-bedroom apartment and tossed the key onto the small kitchen table after kicking the door closed behind him, leaving it unlocked. The place still smelled of the eggs and bacon he had made for himself for breakfast. It had been a good last meal for a condemned man.

The apartment had been a pretty good place to live, so no point in staining it all up with his blood. He'd leave the world in the bathroom, in the tub, with the curtain shut. He just hoped some-one found him quickly so that the smell wouldn't ruin everything.

"Not having a good day, huh?" a voice said from the big chair in his living room to the left of the main door.

Holcomb spun around to face a man sitting in Holcomb's favorite chair in front of the television. The guy had long gray hair combed back, dark eyes, and tan skin. He looked Native American or of Mexican descent. He had on standard Oregon casual, jeans; and a tan button-down dress shirt with his sleeves rolled up.

The guy was clearly not the type of robber that Holcomb would expect going through these apartments. He'd been robbed twice in his four years living here, both times by hippie types looking for drug money.

Two steps and Holcomb had the pistol out of the kitchen drawer and pointed at the guy.

The guy didn't even flinch. "Thought you were going to use that on yourself?"

Now the guy was just pissing Holcomb off. No one knew his plans. And no one but his doctors and a couple people at the VA knew about the cancer. He hadn't told anyone, not even his friends at work. So how could this stranger know what he had been thinking?

"Nice of you to do it in the shower," the guy said, nodding. "Saved a lot of clean-up and they found your body in ten minutes because your neighbor heard the shot, so no real smell issues. A young married couple moves in here next month. Nice folks. You would have liked them, but of course you'll never get the chance to meet them, will you?"

Holcomb couldn't let the guy confuse him. He focused, got his mind clear like he used to do in the service before a mission.

"Who the hell are you, and what are you doing here?"

"Just call me Kontar. I know, strange name, but my father was Egyptian on his father's side." The guy shrugged as if any of that meant something.

Holcomb waved the gun in frustration. The guy was really starting to make him angry. And a soon-to-be-dead man wasn't a good person to piss off.

"What I am doing here?" Kontar asked, smiling. "Actually, I'm here to recruit you to help in a fight for your country."

"Yeah, right," Holcomb said, leveling the gun at the man. "Ten seconds to tell me the truth or they end up cleaning this place after all because of two bodies. As you seem to know, it will make no difference to me."

"You won't believe the truth, but I'll tell you anyway," Kontar said. "I know you are about to kill yourself because of terminal cancer, because I am from the future. Actually, looking back from my time, you killed yourself in that bathroom back there, curtains drawn, that gun in your mouth. Because you have no family or real friends, we figured you to be a perfect candidate to help us out with a mission to save your country."

"And which government agency do you work for?" Holcomb asked, shaking his head. "The nut-ball service?"

Kontar shook his head. "I don't work for *your* government. I work for the Inca Nation. But the survival of your country is wrapped up in the survival of mine, which is why I need your help."

"In the future?" Holcomb said, still not believing a word this nutcase was saying.

"Actually, no," Kontar said. "I need your help in the past. Since you're going to die anyway today, or in a few months from cancer, I have a mission for you first."

"A suicide mission," Holcomb said, disgusted and about ready to shoot the guy. "Right?"

"Of course," Kontar said, smiling, showing perfect, very white teeth. "But considering what you were about to do in your bathtub, I figured you wouldn't have a problem with that."

February 24, 1836
Alamo Mission, Bexar (future San Antonio), Republic of Texas

When the shooting from the other side of the long Alamo compound started, it woke up Holcomb. He had dozed off against the west wall, his gun across his legs.

DeWitt snorted and came awake beside him. They watched as the Texans on the south wall laid down covering fire for someone coming to the gate. A few moments later the large wooden gate was opened in the wall built between the south buildings of the mission and the church itself. Five men came through leading twenty horses loaded down with supplies.

"Looks like we're eating tonight," DeWitt said.

"Yeah," Holcomb said, taking in the scene in front of him. They had come in just after dark last night, and he hadn't gotten much of a chance to look around since they went right to the wall and cut down the cannon fire from the Aztecs.

The Alamo grounds were a lot larger than he had ever imagined from the movies and stories he had been told. He had always thought just the church was the Alamo, but actually it covered about five city blocks of where modern San Antonio would someday stand.

Between the buildings along the west wall and the barrack wall on the east, it was a good half a football field wide, and one and a half football fields long. A cannonade had been constructed right in the middle, large enough to let cannons turn in any direction and high enough to see over the walls in all four directions.

There were also four cannons along the west wall, two on the top of the building on the north wall, four along the south wall, and three in the back of the old church facing east. In the fort there were twenty-one artillery pieces of different caliber, an impressive fortification. A guy by the name of Neill had managed to turn the old mission grounds into a pretty impressive fort in the months before they arrived.

From what Holcomb could tell, there had to be a good hundred and fifty men here already, mostly volunteers. Two names from the history books of Holcomb's time were in charge, and he and DeWitt got to meet them both. Travis led the Texas Regular troops while Bowie seemed to be in charge of all the volunteers. Both men seemed much smaller to Holcomb than their legends led him to believe. And Travis was very, very young.

DeWitt and Holcomb were put under Bowie with the volunteers, but at the moment Bowie seemed to be sick and Travis was doing just about everything. Considering how young the kid was, Holcomb found him impressive. Even Congressman Crockett nodded to Travis as the man in charge.

Supposedly, there were other teams from the future in the mix, but Holcomb hadn't really spotted any in the short time he and DeWitt had been inside, since everyone was dressed for the time period and didn't stand out. The Incas were also supplying much-needed ammunition and food to the fighters inside the Alamo without anyone knowing about it, but both Holcomb and DeWitt had their own supplies in the form of small pills as food. Interestingly enough, the pills were filling. Not much fun to eat, but enough to keep them going.

They both also had their medicine to keep them going long enough to die for the cause. DeWitt had less time left to live than Holcomb and at times coughed so hard he spit up blood.

Holcomb watched, his back against the west wall of the Alamo as four men shut the gate at the other end of the compound and Travis welcomed the new volunteers and the supplies they brought.

Holcomb had to admit that there were some brave men here, fighting for a cause they felt was right. Many of them had families and children at home they would never see again. Even if they lived and became prisoners of the Aztecs, they would be sacrificed and their hearts eaten, as was Aztec custom with war prisoners of this time period.

Death was the only way out of this battle.

Holcomb watched the small celebration around the new arrivals and wondered if he would have had the courage to fight this fight if he wasn't dying anyway. He hoped so. Sometimes, your country and a way of life you believed in were worth fighting and dying for. He had thought that when he joined the army and was sent over to Vietnam.

When he got home, he hadn't been so sure anymore.

He just hoped this time the fight was worth the lives and the blood and the pain. Davy Crockett and all the other men here sure seemed to think so.

Unknown Date, 2300
Cuzco, Inca Nation

Holcomb felt like his brain was about to explode. Kontar had been trying to explain time travel and different universes to him and a guy by the name of DeWitt for the last half hour and none of it seemed to make sense.

They were in what looked like a standard conference room, inside a huge building with no real character, inside the vast city of Cuzco, the capital city of the Incas.

Flying in on some strange plane with porthole-like windows, Holcomb had been stunned by the beauty of the twenty-third-century city spread out below. But as Kontar said, there wouldn't be time to look around. Holcomb, with his cancer, just didn't have that much time left. But he had no doubt at all that he was in a future city from what little he did get to see. No city on his earth in his time looked like Cuzco.

He had been permitted a room to sleep for the night, a change of clothes and shower. After what felt like a short eight hours, he was given a breakfast that tasted a lot like cold Cream of Wheat cereal. He was assured it was good for him and would give him extra strength. Bacon and eggs would have tasted a hell of a lot better.

After breakfast there had been yet another physical that once again confirmed what the doctors in his time had told him. He didn't have long to live.

Great, a fourth opinion confirmed yet again he was going to die, and not even the medicine in the twenty-third century could save him.

After the physical, he had been introduced to another Vietnam vet from the East Coast and put in a plain meeting room with tan walls to get their first briefing. If the first thirty minutes of this briefing were any indication, he and DeWitt might not live long enough to get through the lectures, let alone fight for their country.

"Okay, hold on a second," Holcomb said, holding up both his hands in a show of surrender. "Let me see if I got any of this right."

"Thank you," DeWitt whispered, shaking his head.

"DeWitt and I are from a timeline where the Spanish win over the Incas and the Aztecs and the Mayas. That forms what we know as Mexico and all the Central and South American countries. Right?"

"Correct," Kontar said, nodding.

"Good, got my own history correct then," Holcomb said.

DeWitt actually applauded him.

Holcomb went on. "You say we are sitting in a timeline where the Aztecs and the Incas both win against the Spanish and keep them out of Central America and South America. And you hate each other. Correct?"

"Yes," Kontar said.

"And in this world, the United States still exists in pretty much the same configuration as it does in our timeline."

"It does," Kontar said, clicking something in his hand.

The wall behind him showed an image of North and South America. The Inca Nation was South America, the Aztecs held Central America and Mexico, and the United States looked normal, as did Canada.

"So, why are we fighting at the Alamo again?"

"Because, if the Texans don't hold off the Aztecs at that time and win, this is what the world looks like by 1850, just a short time after the Alamo battle."

The map on the wall changed to one showing the United States cut off below Georgia with a line extending to the Mississippi and then up, with the rest showing the color of the Aztec nation.

"Without the Texans winning against the Aztecs, the Aztec/ American war is never fought," Kontar said

"Like the Mexican/American war in our world," DeWitt said.

"Correct," Kontar said. "When the Aztecs discover gold in California, they wipe out all English and European settlers on the West Coast and cut off all westward expansion with the help of the native tribes. They then buy the Lousiana Purchase from a cash-strapped United States and basically close off the area. In this timeline, the Aztecs take over all of North America in the late 1920s while Europe was still fighting what you call World War One. With the vast resources of North America, the Aztecs become very powerful and we fall to them in 2010."

Holcomb didn't much like the look of that map showing all of North and South America as one bright red Aztec nation. Not one bit.

"How many timelines does that happen in?" DeWitt asked.

"A great number," Kontar said. "See why the battle at the Alamo is so important?"

"Actually, no," Holcomb said. "In my timeline, the Battle of the Alamo was lost, and it made no real difference at all, other than as a rallying cry. If I have my own history correct, that is."

"You do, but it does in these timelines," Kontar said, pointing to the ugly map showing all red, of the Aztec empire covering everything. "If the Aztecs win the Battle of the Alamo easily, they simply sweep across Texas and don't stop. They easily defeat the Texas army under Sam Houston and take Louisiana and Florida easily as well. Only a truce with the United States stops them at that point, but by then it's too late."

"Santa Anna, in our timeline, had thousands of troops," Holcomb asked. "How many are the Aztecs going to bring against the Alamo?"

"The War Chief will lead four to five thousand warriors," Kontar said with a straight face.

DeWitt just snorted.

Holcomb laughed. "You expect less than two hundred men to stop five thousand Aztec warriors?"

"No, I don't, actually. But with a few modern weapons to help out, you can slow them down and do some real damage, enough so that Houston and his men, with a little help as well, can stop them."

DeWitt shrugged and glanced at Holcomb. "We're both dead anyway in a few months. Better to go out fighting for our country, even though this isn't really our country."

Holcomb nodded. DeWitt was right. It was much better than sitting in a hospice drooling on a bib waiting to die, or standing in a bathtub with a gun in his mouth.

Besides, he had always wanted to see the Alamo, ever since he was a kid. Looked like he was going to get a real close look at it.

February 28, 1836
Alamo Compound, Bexar (future San Antonio), Republic
of Texas

The cold night had broken into a warm day, letting the dust and the dry wind swirl through the large compound. In the distance, the sounds of thousands of Aztec warriors chanting and moving equipment echoed over the rolling hills. Travis reported to everyone that the Aztec numbers were still under two thousand, but growing by the day. And the great Aztec War Chief was still a few days from the Rio Grande. He would have thousands of warriors with him.

Kontar had told him and DeWitt the Aztec War Chief's name, but Holcomb had forgotten it at once, since it was long and had more consonants in it than vowels by a margin of five to one. He'd never been that good in school with the English language, so learning Aztec names in a few day's time just didn't seem to be worth the effort in his final weeks alive.

He was just glad that the Spanish had gone into Florida and across into Texas and Southern California when defeated by the Aztec and Inca nations. Otherwise, the Alamo would have had some other strange name as well.

Holcomb was now very sure, after five days in the Alamo, that there were numbers of other teams from the future inside the Alamo. He and DeWitt had been given permission by Travis to fire when a target was clear, since more than enough ammunition and food had somehow managed to be brought to the fort, both from outside supplies coming in from Sam Houston and the Texas government, and also from scavenging missions outside the walls searching surrounding buildings now abandoned by the settlers of the area.

So all night and all day, the sporadic sounds of gunfire cut through the air.

The number of men inside the walls still numbered less than one hundred and sixty, but with enough food and firepower, spirits were high at the moment.

Holcomb and DeWitt had both kept any Aztec warrior from poking his head up within hundreds of yards of the Alamo west wall. The two Aztec cannon placements on the mounds in the town were nothing more than a killing field for the two men. Aztec warriors would rush up onto the platforms to try to load the cannons, or even move the cannons off the platforms, and DeWitt or Holcomb or both of them would make the warriors pay with their lives.

Other teams down the wall and on both end walls had been doing the same to the other Aztec cannon emplacements, so unlike the history that Holcomb had studied of the Alamo in his timeline, this time around the constant cannon bombardment of the walls of the Alamo wasn't happening. That allowed the men inside to be more rested, and, since they had better food and lots of water, they were going to put up one very nasty fight when the time came.

Also, the fort walls were not beaten down by the week of bombardment, meaning that it would be a lot harder for the Aztec warriors to get inside.

One day, while walking the west wall, Travis had noticed Dewitt and Holcomb's accurate shooting and asked them about it. Holcomb had simply said, "Kentucky practice. I can knock the left eye out of a squirrel at two hundred paces."

DeWitt laughed. "And I can knock the right one out at the same time from three hundred."

Travis had just laughed and moved on. The kid was smart enough to not question his good luck. Holcomb wished a few lieutenants back in 'Nam had been that smart. They and a lot of their men would still be alive.

Well, actually, they hadn't been born yet, since this was 1836, and in a different world, where Aztecs were a powerful nation. Holcomb just shook his head at the thought. All of this was just confusing.

Twenty paces to their right, three men laughed, and Holcomb watched as they worked to raise a cannon a precise amount, using some sort of measuring device that didn't look like it belonged to this period of time.

After a moment, they looked pleased and called Travis to watch, having him focus on one of the cannon placements that Holcomb and DeWitt had been guarding.

As one man signaled to fire, Holcomb covered his ears. The old cannons were amazingly loud. The explosion still rocked him and sent dust swirling in all directions.

DeWitt coughed a few times, hard, but then recovered. That cough wasn't sounding good.

Travis didn't seem to mind the sound of the explosion, and neither did Crockett on the other side of the cannon. Both just stood their ground and stared at the intended target.

Holcomb followed their gaze and a moment later one of the Aztec cannons just exploded, flipping over backward and flying into a hundred pieces.

The three men manning Travis's cannon cheered, as did all the men up and down the wall who had been watching.

"I didn't know those old things could be that accurate," DeWitt said, shaking his head in amazement.

"They can't," Holcomb said, laughing.

DeWitt stared at him for a moment, then laughed as well. "Nice to know old Kontar and his people are covering all the bases. Maybe we're going to have a fighting chance here."

"Well, we'll be fighting, that's for sure," Holcomb said. He had no illusion that they had any chance of surviving.

Unknown Date, 2300
Cuzco, Inca Nation

Holcomb stood at a table in an indoor firing range and studied the fake antique gun in his hands. It looked old, right out of the 1800s, modeled after the type of long rifle you saw Davy Crockett carrying. It was a Kentucky rifle with brass inlays on the long butt and along the wood under the barrel. It even had marks and wear making it seem like it had been used a great deal and carried in a saddle holster.

But this rifle, under the disguise, was far, far more.

Even though it looked like it fired the old-style ammunition, it didn't. Hidden in the long stock was a clip that held fifty high-powered rounds. The used shells were stored in the long wood area under the barrel until removed. The rounds looked no bigger than a .22 caliber, but Kontar assured him that the small shells and tips had more length and velocity than a sniper rifle of Holcomb's time.

And even more amazing, when fired, the gun spit out the same smoke and smell that a Kentucky rifle did when fired.

The only problem would be carrying the amount of ammunition they would need, reloading the clips into the butts of the rifle, and hiding the spent shells. That would be hard, at times, but workable, Holcomb was sure.

In the service, both Holcomb and DeWitt had been top marks-men, but Holcomb just couldn't believe he would be able to hit the side of a large building from a hundred yards with the fake old gun, even though it felt a lot lighter than it looked and balanced perfectly in his hands.

"Try it," was all Kontar said, smiling at both DeWitt and Holcomb.

"Too stupid for words," DeWitt said. "We're all going to die, why worry about pretending to be from the time period?"

"Because the Aztecs of this world have time travel as well," Kontar said.

That fact stunned Holcomb right to his core and made his stom-ach twist. It hadn't occurred to him that the two sides would be evenly matched.

"So we're not so worried about hiding your presence from the locals inside the fort," Kontar said, "but from the Aztecs outside the fort who are from our time period. If they can't tell who our plants are, if any, and who are just locals, you'll live longer."

"Super," DeWitt said, shaking his head. "We're not only fighting five thousand Aztec warriors in 1836, but Aztec agents from the future? What's the point? Just shoot us now."

"The point is," Kontar said, looking first at DeWitt, then focus-ing on Holcomb as if he was going to understand more than DeWitt, "that we don't know which way this timeline will fall. We do know that much of the outcome will come down to this one battle, and we're hoping the Aztecs do not know that as firmly as we do, and once they discover that fact, we will already have won the day."

"So, this is the first timeline your two people have fought over?"

"No," Kontar said, shaking his head. "We are fighting across many, many timelines at once, actually. We have turned the tide in other timelines by helping Sam Houston, by winning at the battle of New Orleans against the Aztecs, by driving them back with surprise attacks out of Georgia, but never once have we tried to stop them at the Alamo before."

"How do you keep all this straight?" DeWitt asked a moment before Holcomb could ask the same question.

"It isn't easy," Kontar said. "But this timeline is the one I focus on, the one I am in charge of."

Holcomb was shocked. "You're telling me that the fate of millions of people and your very culture's existence rests on your shoulders alone?"

"No, my culture is right here," Kontar said, indicating the building and the firing range around them. "I'm just trying to help other timelines follow this culture, to get the chance to develop to this point."

Holcomb could feel his head wanting to explode again. "So tell me, how many timelines that you know about developed to this point without outside help?"

"None," Kontar said. "We had help in our past as well in the form of a very special gift from someone far, far into our future. But we're not allowed to talk about that."

Holcomb just shook his head and tried to focus again on the fake antique rifle in his hands. He knew guns. Guns he understood. Time travel just gave him a headache.

"Ahh, well," DeWitt said, picking up the rifle and taking a stance aiming down the range at a human-shaped target one hundred yards away. "I'm going to die soon anyway. This way might just be fun."

He pulled the trigger, and the loud sound filled the range at the same moment as a perfectly shaped hole appeared where the middle of the nose of the target figure would be.

DeWitt turned and smiled. "I'll be go-to-hell, this thing actually works."

Kontar nodded. "Wait until you see what the pistols and the grenades shaped as rifle rounds will do."

Holcomb held the perfectly balanced gun in his hands. At least in this war, he was going in well armed. Outmanned, but with real firepower.

March 1, 1836
Alamo Compound, Bexar (future San Antonio), Republic of Texas

Holcomb watched from his normal spot on the west wall as over thirty troops arrived, riding through the covering fire and into the compound.

"Part of Gonzales's ranging company," DeWitt said. "If I remember my history correctly, those are the last reinforcements we're going to get."

"Unless Kontar changes the history," Holcomb said.

"Oh, yeah, forgot about that part. We can only hope."

At that moment, the boom of an Aztec cannon filled the air.

Holcomb glanced up, waiting and watching for the flaming fireball coming at them. The Aztec had brought in more cannons and were now firing what Kontar, in a briefing, called "Flaming Arrows" from a greater distance and hidden from direct line of sight behind buildings.

It took exactly three shots for the cannon crew down the wall to narrow in on an exact location and destroy the enemy crew every time an Aztec cannon started firing, but in the meantime, when the Flaming Arrows landed, they seemed to catch anything near them on fire. Holcomb figured they were more annoying then damaging, since there wasn't that much besides staircases and window frames made of wood inside the big compound. All the rest was thick rock and mud walls.

This shot landed short of the wall and caused no damage at all in the hard surface.

Very few Aztec cannon shots had hit the thick walls, so the fort didn't look much worse for wear than when Holcomb had arrived.

He and DeWitt had just kept knocking down any warrior out there that moved within range. And the accurate range of the fake rifles they had in their hands was almost frightening. They seldom missed, and it seemed neither did the other few sharpshooting crews from the future placed along the walls. That kept the Aztec warriors a great distance away.

The great War Chief couldn't be very happy about his troops not getting close to the fort. He and the main band of warriors still hadn't arrived yet, even though they had crossed the Rio Grande three days before. Holcomb and DeWitt had talked a lot about what they thought the War Chief would do when he arrived. The only conclusion they had was that he would send his men in a full assault against the walls, just as Santa Anna had done.

It would cost him hundreds and hundreds of lives, but it would get the job done fairly quickly, even against weapons from the future.

DeWitt nudged Holcomb and got him to turn away from staring out over the empty and silent town of Bexar that would be San Antonio in his timeline. "We got company."

A man with a long moustache and carrying a rifle and a large knapsack was coming up the wooden stairs toward them. He looked to be tall, maybe six foot and then some, with large arms and a slight limp on his right side. He had a cowboy hat pulled down low over his eyes to shade from the bright sun.

Both Holcomb and DeWitt started to stand, but the man signaled they stay in position behind the wall and then knelt in front of them, pushing his hat back.

"Stacy," the guy said, sticking out his hand.

"Sergeant Ben Stacy, from California?" DeWitt asked, taking the guy's hand and pumping it like it was old-home week. "I'll be go-to-hell. What are you doing here?"

"Same damn thing you are, it seems," Stacy said, smiling. "Committing suicide by Aztec. I was hoping you were still alive when I got here. Kontar said you most likely would be."

"Fit as a fiddle," DeWitt said, lying.

Stacy laughed. "Yeah, me, too." He glanced around. "So this is what the Alamo looks like. Bigger than I expected. I thought it was just that church part over there in the corner."

"Me, too," DeWitt said, then broke into a coughing fit before he could say another word.

"He gets all choked up seeing old friends," Holcomb said, sticking out his hand. "I'm Holcomb. Snatched right out of 1981. Lung cancer, about a month left if I survive this."

Stacy smiled and took his hand. "1986. Prostrate cancer, don't want to think about spending that much time left. Riding a damn horse was painful enough."

"Yeah, understand that," Holcomb said, trying not to laugh. "Welcome to the fight."

Stacy dropped the leather satchel and waited until DeWitt's coughing fit passed with a little help from an inhaler he kept hidden in his shirt pocket.

"This is from Kontar," Stacy said, indicating the leather pouch. "I told Travis down there it was personal stuff from your family. It's actually more clips, hidden in the shirts, and about fifty small grenades with six-second delays once you twist the caps."

"How is our old friend Kontar?" Holcomb asked. "He have any idea how things are shifting in the fight?"

"Haven't seen him since you have," Stacy said. "I was put in with those men down there three weeks ago so I could get in here and deliver this and help you two in the fight."

"Before he recruited me?" DeWitt asked, looking puzzled.

Holcomb just patted DeWitt's arm. "Time travel, remember? Don't worry about it."

"Gives me a headache just thinking about it," Stacy said.

"Me, too," both Holcomb and DeWitt said at the same time.

All three men laughed, and then Stacy took up a position on the wall beside them.

It felt good to have another fighter with them, another 'Nam vet. Holcomb had no doubt he was going to die in the coming fight. But he didn't mind so much and wasn't afraid of it at all. There were a lot worse ways to go.

May 20, 1981
Portland, Oregon, USA

Kontar had spent the afternoon trying to explain everything, then left, giving Holcomb two days to decide and get his affairs in order if he decided to go.

After the strange man with the white teeth left, Holcomb had gone back to the park, sitting and thinking about how crazy it all seemed, yet how right it was as well. He had watched kids playing in the grass, a couple kissing on another bench, a boat going past with a woman sunning herself in a bikini on the bow.

In other words, a normal spring day in the park.

He had figured, just as his father had said, that this world was worth fighting for. That's why he signed up for Vietnam. But coming back, it had gotten so confusing. Nothing was as black and white as his father had explained it to be.

But now Kontar had given him straight black-and-white talk. He needed Holcomb's help in a fight to help the United States to even exist in a different timeline. The Aztecs were a warrior race that still believed in human sacrifice, even into the twenty-third century when Kontar was from. The United States and the Inca Nation were the beacons of human rights and freedoms in Kontar's time. And the survival of one nation depended on the survival of the other, it seemed.

Holcomb didn't pretend to understand, and Kontar promised to explain even more before the mission started. Kontar had also promised that if Holcomb came along, Kontar's people could help someone or some member of Holcomb's family, if he wanted. But Holcomb had no real family, so he had told Kontar that he would think about that.

Sitting on that park bench, in that park, two hours after Kontar had left, Holcomb had decided to go. He might not have his name in any history books, but if he helped at the Alamo and it made a difference, at least he would be part of a fight that an entire nation would remember.

He gave his notice at the bus garage, talked to a few friends there, and then went back to give notice on his apartment. What surprised him was how many people, both at work and in his building, seemed genuinely sad that he was leaving. He might not have that many good friends, but he clearly had people who liked him, and he liked them back, and some of them would even miss him.

One elderly woman down the hall even brought him a small plate of sugar cookies for a travel snack. He'd only seen her a few times in the hall, and couldn't remember her name, even though she knew his. She told him that he just made the place seem safer. She was going to miss that.

He had never noticed any of it. He just felt he had been walking through the world alone. It seemed he had been far from alone.

This time around, Kontar knocked on the apartment door and Holcomb answered, a small bag on his shoulder that included his pistol and bathroom supplies and a few changes of clothes. Everything else he was leaving with a note on the kitchen table.

"Seems you have decided," Kontar said, smiling as he backed up and let Holcomb step out and pull the door closed.

"Just one favor to ask," Holcomb said as they headed down the wide hallway toward the staircase.

"Ask and I will do what I can do," Kontar said.

"If you can, I would love to have you use what little money I have left in the bank and add some to it and set up a small college scholarship fund for kids of city bus drivers. Put it in my name if you would, even though no one will remember who I am."

Kontar glanced at Holcomb as they went down the stairs to the lobby, clearly puzzled. "We can do that, no problem at all. That's very nice of you."

Holcomb shrugged. "Always thought about going back to school. Just never got around to it."

"What would you have studied?" Kontar asked.

Holcomb laughed. "History. I always loved history."

Kontar laughed. "With luck, for an entire culture in a different timeline, you're going to help make some history."

As they went out the door and into the bright light of the warm spring day, Holcomb said, "That's why I'm doing this."

March 5, 1836
Alamo Compound, Bexar (future San Antonio), Republic of Texas

The sun was easing behind the low hills to the west. Holcomb, Stacy, and DeWitt had been firing consistently all day, picking off any warrior that moved, just as they had done for the past four days.

Travis had reported that the War Chief and the thousands of warriors with him had arrived earlier in the day. And as history in Holcomb's timeline had shown, no more men came to help those inside the Alamo. With around two hundred men , they were going into battle against thousands of Aztec warriors.

But so far, the men inside the walls were in good spirits. No real damage had been done to the walls of the fort thanks to the sharpshooters keeping the cannons at a distance. The fort had stayed a safe little island in a sea of death. Holcomb had no doubt that was about to change. If the Aztec War Chief followed Santa Anna's plan, he would attack tomorrow, on March 6.

But many historians and many of Santa Anna's own officers had thought it stupid to directly attack the fort. But that had been in another timeline, with another commander and a much weaker Mexican army. The Aztec War Chief was known for just taking what he wanted. There didn't seem to be any doubt in anyone's mind he was coming hard and soon. The key would be how much damage the men inside the walls could do to the Aztec force.

DeWitt used an inhaler to stop a coughing fit and Stacy used the time to refill the clip in his rifle, tossing the empty shells over the wall wrapped in a small cloth bag. The bag had a special acid inside it that ate the shells and turned them into dust in a matter of days. The shells themselves were designed to deteriorate quickly. No one in ten years would dig up any shells or signs of anything from the future at this site.

"Incoming," a voice shouted, and all three men went back to staring out over the wall.

Holcomb was shocked at what he saw.

Coming at full run, directly from the center of the city, were about fifty warriors, their war cries filling the air.

"All four sides," Travis shouted from a perch atop the center cannonade. "They're coming at us from four directions."

Firing started up at once, the sounds covering the cries of the warriors. One right after another the cannons of the fort fired, filling the air with smoke, the booming sounds echoing over the countryside.

Holcomb, Stacy, and DeWitt fired as well, Holcomb taking a warrior on the right and killing him. Stacy aimed at the left, and DeWitt the middle.

The cannons sent more warrior bodies into the air, and each of them fired five more times before the firing eased to a stop with no more warriors to kill.

The wave of warriors hadn't even made it to within a hundred yards of the fort on any side.

"That was just a test," Holcomb said, staring at the bodies strung along the field between the fort wall and Bexar's buildings. "The War Chief wanted to know how strong we are."

"He sacrificed two hundred men to test us?" Stacy said, shaking his head.

"Sure seems that way," DeWitt said.

Suddenly Holcomb realized what he had said. With any test, someone had to be looking at the results.

"Watch for movement in the distance," Holcomb said, flipping his glasses to binocular vision and studying the roofs and walls of the city buildings. "Lower War Chiefs had to have been watching so that they could report back."

Beside him, Stacy fired, and a brightly adorned warrior spun and fell about two hundred yards out.

Holcomb caught sight of another warrior staring at the scene from the top of a building and put a shot between his eyes.

A few of the other sharpshooters on the other walls were also firing, taking out anyone who might show their face.

DeWitt laughed. "The great War Chief ain't going to like any of this."

"We just pissed him off is all," Holcomb said.

"So, when do you three think he will attack us?"

Holcomb spun around away from the wall at the same time as DeWitt and Stacy to see Travis kneeling behind them.

Holcomb couldn't think of a thing to say to the leader of the fort. And clearly DeWitt and Stacy were just as shocked.

"Look," Travis said, "I know you three have military experience from some place I am not familiar with, as do a number of others who are volunteers here. And you are the best shots I have ever had the pleasure of watching. I'm just glad you are all here helping Texas in this fight."

"It's our honor, sir," Holcomb managed to say. Stacy nodded, and DeWitt coughed as he nodded his agreement.

In the last days he had only said a passing hello to Travis. He figured he and DeWitt and Stacy were staying under the young officer's notice. Clearly they hadn't been.

History always said that Travis was both smart and very brave. He had just proven history to be correct.

"What just happened was clearly a test," Travis said, "and you sharpshooters cut down the number of reports the War Chief will get about the results. Any theories about what's next? Will it be a full attack tonight or any chance he might just leave us and go around?"

"He won't attack at night," Holcomb said and again both his friends nodded. "From everything I know about the War Chief of the Aztecs, fighting at night has little honor. They will prepare at night, and they have no problem in small skirmishes at night, but if they come in full attack, it will be at first light."

He had learned all that from Kontar in the distant future, but he wasn't about to tell Travis that.

"And he won't go around us, either," Stacy said. "He can't show any weakness to those under him or they will challenge and kill him."

"Agreed," Holcomb said. "They're coming in full force at first light tomorrow."

Travis seemed to think about that for a moment, then nodded. "I agree."

He stood and saluted Holcomb and Stacy and DeWitt. "Thank you, gentlemen, for the honor of fighting and dying beside you."

With that he turned and went down the stairs and back toward the sick room where Bowie was being cared for.

"This is a long damn ways from Vietnam," DeWitt said after a long moment of silence.

Down the wall, Holcomb noticed that Davy Crockett had been watching the exchange. He gave Holcomb a thumbs-up and went back to watching out over the wall.

For the first time, Holcomb knew completely that what he did in this fight really mattered. Dying for this cause was the right thing to do. He knew now what his father had described about fighting in World War II.

"This doesn't even feel like the same world," DeWitt said, shaking his head.

"Actually," Stacy said, "it's not, remember?"

Holcomb glanced once again at Davy Crockett, one of his childhood heroes. "Tough to forget."

March 6, 1836
Alamo Compound, Bexar (future San Antonio), Republic of Texas

The moment the sun tipped an edge over the hills in the east, the Aztec Flaming Arrow cannons filled the sky with streaks of fire, sending rolling thunder over the fort and the peaceful sunrise of a Texas morning.

The night had been long and quiet, with only an occasional shot cutting the stillness from a sharpshooter who picked off a warrior stupid enough to show himself.

About midnight, Travis had sent two men on horses out of the gate, more than likely with his last message to Sam Houston. Holcomb had watched him put on a strange pair of goggles that looked a lot like an old mask, then shake his head, take them off, and tuck them into one of the saddle bags of the riders. Maybe Travis was not only smart, but he also had some help from the future. In this fight, there was just no telling.

"Here we go," DeWitt said as the cannons went off, bracing himself against the wall.

"It's been my honor," Holcomb said, glancing at the two men on either side of him that he now called friends, "to fight with you."

"I will remember these days for as long as I live," Stacy said, smiling.

"That's going to be at least another thirty minutes," DeWitt said. "If we're lucky."

"I'm hoping for more like an hour," Holcomb said, laughing.

A moment later, thousands of Aztec warriors seemed to appear out of nowhere among the buildings of the town and the gullies of the hills around the fort.

Waves and waves and waves of warriors.

"Make that thirty minutes after all," Holcomb said, starting to fire.

The sounds of the exploding cannons and thousands of rifles being fired at once smashed into Holcomb as he fired off one round after another into the ranks, trying to pick off any warrior who looked to be dressed better than any other.

He went through his first clip in twenty seconds, reloaded, and went back to firing, cutting down warriors in the front lines so that others behind them might trip over the bodies.

It was like facing a sea of ants. The Aztecs swarmed everywhere, screaming and firing as they ran.

One bullet nicked the top of the wall near Holcomb and sent sand into his face, but luckily nothing got into his eyes behind his protective glasses given to him by Kontar.

Beside him, DeWitt was grazed by a shot across one arm. He just swore, wrapped the surface wound in a piece of cloth, and went back to firing, his inhaler stuck in his mouth like a bad cigar.

Holcomb just kept firing, through another clip and then another, his shots always dropping a warrior. And every warrior he killed was one less to fight against Sam Houston and the others defending Texas and the rest of the United States.

The cannons of the Alamo kept up a constant bombardment of the rushing warriors, smashing five and ten at a time into the air.

Suddenly, DeWitt tapped his arm and pointed out at the town's buildings. The main wave of the warriors was now only a hundred yards from the bottom of the west wall and closing fast. On the buildings of the town, well decorated and brightly colored Aztec warriors had climbed up to watch the fight.

The one in the center looked to be the top War Chief himself, not more than nine hundred feet away.

The idiot was too arrogant to know he could be killed.

Holcomb tapped Stacy and pointed to what DeWitt had shown him. Stacy glanced up, then smiled and nodded.

Holcomb used the old hand signals from 'Nam to indicate in the intense sound of the battle the way the three of them should fire. Stacy would take the ones on the right side, Holcomb would take the top War Chief in the middle, and DeWitt the chiefs on the left side.

Then on the count of three, they all fired, ignoring the wave of warriors approaching the wall below them.

Holcomb knocked down the War Chief with a shot directly between his well-painted eyes.

Before the others could react around him, Holcomb killed two more of the War Chief's top lieutenants, while DeWitt and Stacy cut down the others on either side.

If nothing else, they had cut the head off of the snake. It would grow a new one quickly enough, but with luck that might give Houston and his Texan army some time and a real fighting chance.

All three of them went back to firing at the rushing warriors below as the remaining brightly dressed war chiefs scattered back into hiding.

When the leading wave of warriors reached the base of the wall and started trying to toss ropes with hooks over the top, Holcomb grabbed a few of the pen-sized grenades, twisted the caps, and dropped them as beside him Stacy cut a rope and then did the same.

Other warriors were bringing ladders at the walls. Others behind the leading waves were moving cannons into position.

There were just too many. But the Aztecs were paying a very, very high price for this attack.

Along the wall, other defenders followed suit, firing over and over and tossing explosive charges into the mass of warriors coming up at them from the base of the twenty-foot wall.

But nothing seemed to slow the warriors down, they just kept pouring at the wall, climbing on their own dead.

Holcomb went back to picking off the warriors trying to set up cannons to fire directly at the wall from close range. Beside him, Stacy leaned forward to drop a few grenades. Suddenly he spun backward, a gaping hole in the back of his head from a shot that blew his skull apart.

He went over backwards and then tumbled down the stairs.

Holcomb gave his friend a quick salute of honor and went back to fighting.

Farther down the wall, Crockett was shoving a ladder away from the wall and butting two warriors with the hard end of his rifle, sending them back into the mass of death below.

Holcomb tossed half a dozen grenades along the base of the wall in front of him and DeWitt and Crockett.

The smoke from the explosions and the gunshots drifted so thickly it felt to Holcomb like trying to fight on a thick foggy night along the ocean. Only this fog smelled of gunpowder and sweat and blood.

Lots of blood.

DeWitt jumped up and moved to Holcomb's right along the wall, firing at a warrior trying to breach over the top of the wall. Then he dropped a grenade at the bottom of the ladder and fired downward into the mass.

Suddenly, he dropped over backward, a bullet hole directly between his eyes.

They had all been wrong. It didn't look like they all were going to last fifteen minutes.

At a half-dozen places along the wall, the warriors were coming over the top.

Holcomb took his last ten grenades and twisted the caps on all of them, tossing them at different places along the wall at the bases of ladders.

A shot ripped through his left arm, spinning him around and sending waves of bright red pain across his eyes.

His vision cleared quickly, and he dropped his rifle and grabbed his pistol, firing as he went.

Crockett moved toward him, firing and butting at warriors reaching the top of the wall.

"Retreat to the church!" he shouted.

"I'll cover you," Holcomb shouted back and Crockett nodded and scrambled down the staircase to the middle of the compound, where dozens of Texans were retreating toward their last stand in the church, the building that most Americans thought was the entire Alamo.

Holcomb kept firing, protecting his childhood hero as much as he could, until a shot ripped through his left shoulder and he went over backward, tumbling down the stairs to the hard dirt at the bottom.

Somehow, he managed to keep the gun in his hand.

A moment later, Crockett appeared in his vision and yanked him to his feet, pulling him across the huge yard toward the church.

Holcomb let the pain clear his mind and he focused one last time, firing at a warrior who was about to attack Crockett.

Then a shot cut through the Tennessee congressman, spinning him away from Holcomb. The shot had caught him in the chest, but he was still alive.

Now it was Holcomb's turn to pull his hero to his feet and stumble onward.

But it wasn't to be.

More fire from the right and more pain cut through Holcomb's legs and back, and he and Crockett went down.

An Aztec warrior with a brightly painted face loomed over Holcomb as he struggled to turn over.

Crockett tried to get up to fight, but the warrior cut off his head with a quick swing of a sword.

All Holcomb could do was smile at the ugly painted face of the Aztec as the warrior raised his sword yet again.

Holcomb knew that they had accomplished what they needed to accomplish. He was sure of that. They had slowed the Aztec army and caused enough damage that Houston could defeat them.

This would be a good world he had helped create.

And maybe in Portland, Oregon, in this timeline, there would be a nice park on the river for people to enjoy. He hoped so. He loved that park, especially on warm spring days.

And as the warrior's sword came down to cut off his head, Holcomb just kept smiling.

It was going to be good to be remembered, after all.

Afterward for "Remember"

How I came up with the idea for "Remember."

When I was rereading Fred's book, I was caught by a scene in the future Cuzco where a map is shown of the world and the main character is happy to see the United States is still looking normal. I couldn't seem to let that go, wondering how that was possible, what an American/Aztec war would be like, and so on. I finally figured that the Spanish, when shoved out of Mexico by the Aztecs went to the northern shores of the gulf and across into California, beyond the reach of the Aztec nation at that point. But the Aztecs would have gotten that land from the Spanish, setting up the same sort of fight Texas and America had with the Mexican government, only with the Aztecs. And that led naturally to the Alamo, with the idea that Vietnam vets dying of cancer would fight there with modern weapons to slow down the Aztecs. The hardest part of writing "Remember" from that point forward was keeping it short enough to fit.

Washington's Rebellion

by

David Weber

.I.

Major Dunstan Carmichael of His Majesty's Own First Carolinas Light Infantry watched moonlit surf roll rhythmically up the tan, sandy beach in intricate curlicues of shadow and foam. He was a man of medium height, broad-shouldered and sinewy, with sandy-brown hair, gray eyes, and a complexion too many suns had turned into bronzed leather. His Shoshone grandmother's strong nose had resurfaced in him, and light from the window behind him gleamed on the bottle as he poured fresh whiskey over the ice.

He set the bottle back on the wicker table, swirling the amber liquor gently, letting just enough ice melt for the water to bring out the full texture of the whiskey. It was an old habit, and he snorted in bitter amusement as he realized what he was doing. The days when he'd properly savored fine whiskey were part of the life that had been so brutally destroyed two months ago, and he raised the glass to pour liquid fire down his throat.

It didn't help.

He'd known it wasn't going to. Whiskey couldn't anesthetize the pain; it could only make him feel even less of a man because he needed the anesthesia it couldn't provide.

If Kate could see you now, she'd kick your ass up between your self-pitying ears, and you'd damn well deserve it, he told himself, watching a distant pleasure boat's lights sweep slowly across the horizon. *But she* can't *see you, can she? And that's the frigging point, isn't it?*

He drank more whiskey and closed his eyes, remembering.

It hadn't been his fault. Everyone told him that. For that matter, *he* knew it hadn't . . . but he'd still been the one driving when the pulp lorry slammed into the back of the van. He'd been the one who hadn't seen it coming in the fog.

Who hadn't been able to avoid it.

And he'd been the one who walked away with scarcely a bruise from the catastrophe, which had killed both his children and left Kate in a coma from which she would probably never awaken.

And even if she does, she'll never walk again. She'll never do anything again with that much spinal damage.

His face tightened as he remembered the anguished moment when he'd realized he didn't truly want her to regain consciousness. Didn't want her to discover she was trapped in an inert body that would never again answer to the sharp, laughing mind he loved so much. Didn't want her to know Brian and Cassie were gone after less than six years of life and love. Better—so much better—for her never to awaken at all.

And what about me? He opened his eyes again, staring out at the boat's lights. *The colonel's not going to be patient forever. He can't be. "Compassionate leave" or not, the unit needs me back. Or else it needs someone else who can still do his damned job.*

He grimaced, set the glass aside, and walked barefoot down the boardwalk. His toughened soles ignored sharp-edged fragments of shell as he waded through the powdery sand above the tide line. Then he was out on the smooth, firm surface with the final ripples sluicing cold across his toes. He waded out a few feet, feeling sand swirl away under his heels on the undertow, then looked north toward the skyglow of the sleepy little town of Myrtle Beach.

He needed to get back to the unit. He needed that distraction from the black pit his life had become, and the unit needed him, too. The Carolinas Light Infantry was one of the Crown's elite special-operations regiments. Simply qualifying for the CLI pushed a man to his limits; surviving the harsh, unending training was even worse, and Carmichael had been in special ops for six years. He knew there'd been times Kate longed for him to get out, transfer to something which would give him more time at home, more time with her and the kids. But she'd understood him too well to do more than wish. She'd told him once that sometimes she hated the unit but that his commitment to it was part of what made him the man she loved.

He'd always figured that eventually age or a training accident would catch up with him, and a part of him had looked forward to it. When that happened, it would be all right for him to give his life fully to his wife and family without that nagging feeling that he'd failed his unit, his country, and his king.

Except, of course, that he no longer *had* a family.

He never knew how long he stood there, but the undertow had buried his feet to well above the ankle and the incoming tide had sent waves lapping to mid-shin before he shook himself and turned back toward the beach house. The dry sand above the tideline glued itself to his feet, and he paused at the foot of the steps to hose it off—Kate had always been particular about that—then climbed to the veranda, the ice bucket . . . and the bottle.

He scooped them up and headed inside. The remaining ice must have melted while he stood in the surf, and he started toward the kitchen refrigerator.

He was halfway across the living room when he realized the bucket didn't feel quite right. He glanced down at it and paused in mid-stride. Instead of the water he'd expected to see, with perhaps a few scraps of not-quite-yet-melted ice, the bucket's interior was bone dry. He could tell it was, because the paper-and-string-wrapped parcel in the bottom wasn't even damp.

The whiskey fumes seemed to dissipate abruptly, and his mind clicked into overdrive.

While he was willing to admit he'd been lost in his thoughts while he stood in the surf, he knew he hadn't been drunk enough for anyone to have crept past him without his even noticing. So how . . . ?

He stood there for several seconds, then shook himself, continued into the kitchen, set the ice bucket on the counter, and parked himself on a bar stool.

He could think of quite a few people who would be delighted if something unpleasant happened to one Dunstan Carmichael.

Most hailed from points south, although there were probably several more scattered around places like Damascus and Teheran. Unfortunately for the purposes of his present analysis, he couldn't think of any who would have settled for depositing a small paper parcel in an empty ice bucket instead of cutting his throat, shooting him, or blowing him into tiny pieces.

He thought about it for several more moments, then shrugged and cautiously— cautiously!—lifted the parcel out of the ice bucket and used a utility knife to cut the plain brown string. He unfolded the paper, and his eyebrows rose as he found himself looking down at a pair of goggles.

That was what they looked like, at least, although why anyone would make goggles with lenses of opaque, quarter-inch-thick quartz was a mystery. If they'd been smoked, he might have thought they were welding goggles, but nothing, not even the sun-bright fierceness of an electric arc welder, was going to get through *those* lenses.

He examined them carefully, noting the elasticized strap that was obviously intended to hold them in place over the eyes . . . which would be unable to see a single damned thing through them. Offhand, he couldn't remember ever seeing anything less useful.

Finally, he shrugged, laid the puzzle aside, and examined its wrapping for clues. Unlike the bizarre goggles, the paper and twine were about as normal and prosaic as they could possibly be. Until, at least, he found the note written on the inside of the wrapping.

"Look through the goggles if you want to live."

He sat staring at the absurd message. Nine words in a perfectly reasonable sentence, which made absolutely no sense. How was he supposed to look through a solid hunk of quartz? And assuming he'd been able to do that, how was it supposed to keep him alive? For that matter, why shouldn't he stay alive quite handily *without* looking through it?

He sat that way for what probably seemed longer than it was, then picked up the goggles once more. He turned them in his hands, wondering if he'd missed something the first time around. But there wasn't much to miss—just two stubbornly opaque hunks of crystal joined by a nosepiece of woven wire and fastened to a perfectly ordinary elastic headband.

Finally, despite the suspicion that he looked almost as silly as he felt, he fitted those quartz lenses gingerly over his eyes.

As expected, he saw absolutely nothing. In fact, he felt something like relief when he didn't. He snorted at his own reaction and started to remove the goggles, then froze. Something was happening. It was like little speckles of light leaking through, wandering across his darkened field of vision like shining motes of dust. But then the lights brightened, grew thicker, solidified, and he stiffened.

It was like looking at a television screen. He saw himself sitting in the living room. There was no sound, but then he saw himself climb out of his armchair, cross the room, and open the door. A man he'd never seen before stepped through it. The stranger was several inches shorter than Carmichael's six feet two inches and slender, without his solid muscularity. His features were dark, his shoulder-length hair was drawn back into a neat ponytail, and he wore a nice suit that looked out of place in the simply furnished living room.

While Carmichael watched, he and the stranger spoke. The conversation seemed to take a while, although it simultaneously flashed past in a handful of seconds. Then he saw himself shaking his head, and the stranger shrugged with a smile. He said something else, then stood and started back toward the door. He paused just inside, turning back, as if he'd thought of one more point . . . and his hand came out of his jacket.

Dunstan Carmichael was familiar with a vast range of firearms, but he'd never seen anything that looked as if it were made out of some sort of silvery wire—a preposterously fragile affair, with a "barrel," if it could be called that, which seemed to be a solid, slender rod of crystal.

He watched himself start to react to the bizarre weapon, but his image never had the chance. However fragile the thing might look, the beam of light which snapped from that solid rod blasted a two-inch hole straight through his chest.

The well-dressed stranger rolled him onto his back, went down on one knee, and touched his throat, clearly checking for a pulse. Then he shrugged, stood back up, and walked calmly out of the room.

Carmichael sat frozen as his vision blanked. He started to snatch the goggles down, then paused as the scene he'd just witnessed started over again. He opened the door to admit the same stranger. Again, they talked, and again he shook his head. The stranger shrugged, smiled, started for the door, then paused. He started to turn . . . at which point, Carmichael's hand emerged from between the cushion and the arm of his chair and he put two .40 caliber slugs from a Vickers automatic through stranger's head.

The well-dressed corpse dropped its own bizarre weapon and slid down the living-room wall in a smear of red, and Carmichael saw himself rise. He crossed to the body, pistol ready, and knelt to check its pulse.

That was when the living-room windows burst inward in a spray of shattered glass, and two men who might have been twins of the dead man came through them with weapons blazing.

Dunstan Carmichael watched himself die a second time. Then the entire scene started over again, a third time. Again he shook his head, again he killed his visitor before his visitor could kill him. This time, he was waiting when the windows shattered, and he killed both of the intruders . . . only to have the door blown in a heartbeat later so that *three* new attackers could cut him down.

Then the scene started yet again. It repeated at least a dozen times, and each time, he shook his head and ended up dead. Well, except for the one in which he was waiting with an assault rifle and simply blew his visitor away without opening the door. He didn't have to shake his head that time, which might have offered some consolation if the entire house hadn't blown up seconds later.

But, finally, the vision changed and, instead of shaking his head, he nodded. Obviously, it was the right thing to do, since instead of shooting him dead, his visitor shook his hand and waved vigorously at the door. He watched himself say something else, and, again his visitor nodded. He saw himself step into his own bedroom and pack a bag—the bag with the hidden side pocket, which he somehow knew contained the goggles—and follow the stranger down the front walk to a waiting car.

And then the goggles' lenses were suddenly chunks of opaque quartz once more.

He lowered them slowly, looking down at them, trying to make some sort of sense of the insanity he'd just seen. Or *thought* he'd seen, since the most reasonable explanation was that it was actually some demented hallucination. But it didn't *feel* that way. He didn't know what it *did* feel like, yet some instinct warned him he'd better take all of this—whatever "this" was—seriously.

Although how he was supposed to do that was something of a puzzle.

He closed his eyes, reviewing the images with all the intensity of a highly trained, highly disciplined memory. From his doppelganger's reaction, it was clear he hadn't been expecting the other's arrival. It was equally clear his visitor had made some sort of proposal . . . and that failing to accept it was what the intelligence pukes called "contraindicated." That much was obvious, but as he studied the memories, he realized something else as well. He could see the coffee-table clock, and, according to it, his visitor would be arriving in another ninety-three minutes.

He opened his eyes, conscious of a strong temptation to go find a bar and stay there for the next few hours. Unfortunately, while he could see the *clock*, there'd been no *calendar* in view. The fact that he was dressed in the vision exactly as he was now wasn't much help, either, since Kate had teased him for years over the lack of variation in his civilian wardrobe. So unless he was prepared to never again sit in his living room at 11:41 p.m., simply going and hiding tonight would guarantee nothing.

He looked at the single, unsigned sentence on the wrapping paper again, then grimaced, drew a deep breath, and pushed himself up off the bar stool. He carried the goggles into his bedroom, found the bag from his . . . vision, and carefully tucked the goggles into the hidden pocket.

Then he went back to the living room, poured another glass of whiskey—this one without ice—and settled back into his armchair.

The doorbell rang at precisely 11:41 p.m.

Carmichael twitched, surprised, despite himself, by the sudden chime. He'd felt the tension coiling steadily tighter inside him, the way it often did when he prepared for a jump or a helicopter insertion, yet he discovered he hadn't really believed the doorbell was going to sound. Not deep down inside, where stubborn rationality insisted magical goggles weren't mysteriously delivered in empty ice buckets.

He sat very still, and the chimes sounded again. That got him out of the chair, although he found himself wishing he'd squirreled away his sidearm after all. None of the visions had shown it doing him any good, but simply knowing it was there would have been good for his morale.

That thought carried him across the room, and he opened the door. The stranger who'd become a familiar presence in his living room stood on the front step.

"Can I help you?" Carmichael was surprised he sounded so normal.

"Dunstan Carmichael? *Major* Dunstan Carmichael?" The stranger's courteous voice carried a hint of unfamiliar accent. Carmichael's training had exposed him to rather more languages and accents than most people encountered, even in the Empire, yet he couldn't place this one.

"Yes," he confirmed, allowing himself to sound a bit cautious, like someone facing what he expected to be an aggressive salesman.

"My name is Jefferson, Major. Tom Jefferson." The man on the steps smiled pleasantly . . . almost as if his name really were Jefferson.

"And what can I do for you, Mr. Jefferson?"

Jefferson's smile grew a bit more reassuring as he heard the more pronounced note of caution in Carmichael's tone.

"I'm not here to sell you anything, Major. I *do* have an offer for you, but I promise it won't cost you a shilling. In fact, I think you'll find it quite profitable."

"That's very kind of you, but I'm not really interested in—"

"I really think you should listen, Major Carmichael." Jefferson's voice and expression were both much more serious. "I realize this is a stressful time for you, and I'm sorry for your recent loss. However, what I have to say to you could be very important to the future of your wife."

Carmichael's mouth closed, and it required no acting talent to tighten his cheek muscles and clench his jaw. Or to put a dangerous glow in his eyes—one that warned Mr. Jefferson any attempt to use Kate Carmichael's injuries for profit would be costly.

He stood for a moment, staring at the man on his porch, then stepped back.

"All right, Mr. Jefferson," he said more than a little grimly, "I'll listen."

Carmichael settled back into his armchair, suppressing a shiver as Jefferson seated himself on the facing couch, exactly where he'd sat in each of the goggles' visions—except the one with the assault rifle. The other man looked around, as if absorbing the comfortable décor, which reflected Kate's touch, then cocked his head.

"What I'm about to say is going to sound bizarre, Major, but there's no way to explain it that doesn't sound at least a little crazy. I hope you'll bear with me. Of course"—he smiled a bit thinly— "I imagine you've heard some fairly preposterous things in intelligence briefings. Perhaps that will help."

"I hope this proposal doesn't infringe any security restrictions," Carmichael said in a steely tone, and Jefferson shook his head quickly.

"I don't intend to ask you a single thing about your duties or any classified information. On the other hand, I can't pretend that the nature of your . . . skill set, let's say, doesn't have quite a lot to do with my presence."

"In what way?" Carmichael settled farther back.

"Oh, you might be surprised about that," Jefferson said with a peculiar smile. "May I show you something?"

"Go ahead."

"Thank you."

Jefferson reached into his jacket, and Carmichael stiffened. But the hand that emerged wasn't wrapped around an outlandish-looking toy gun. Instead, Jefferson produced a featureless, mirror-bright cube, about an inch square, set it on the coffee table, and pressed its top.

He vanished.

Carmichael jerked up out of his chair, staring at the suddenly empty couch.

"Over here, Major," a voice said, and his head whipped around. Jefferson stood just inside the arch into the kitchen, smiling at him. He opened his mouth . . . and Jefferson disappeared again.

"No, over here," he said, and Carmichael's head snapped around in the other direction. Now Jefferson was standing by the door to the veranda! Then he vanished yet again.

Carmichael stood staring at the veranda door then twitched as the doorbell rang again. He crossed to it in three long strides, yanked it open, and discovered—as he'd more than half expected—that Jefferson had somehow magically teleported back to the porch.

"May I come back in?" he asked with a grin.

"How in hell did you do that?" Carmichael demanded.

"That's one of the things I intend to explain, Major. Now that I've got your attention, I mean."

"You can damned well say *that* again." Carmichael stepped back and pointed at the couch. "This time, though, I'd appreciate it if you stayed put," he said grimly, and Jefferson raised both hands shoulder-high in a placating gesture then sat obediently.

"Whatever you wish, Major."

"About that explanation?" Carmichael prompted as he settled back into the chair himself.

"The reason I demonstrated this device," Jefferson said, slipping the cube back into his inner pocket, "was to provide at least a little evidence for the preposterous things I'm about to tell you. You see, it created what we call an achronic field."

"An 'achronic field'?" Carmichael repeated obediently when Jefferson paused.

"Think of it as a field which displaces time. I know it sounds impossible, but what happened was that I stepped out of phase with your time. Then I simply got up and walked around to another position and allowed my own temporal frame of reference to synchronize with yours once more."

He shrugged, as if what he'd just said actually made sense.

"You're saying you can manipulate time?" Despite his best effort, Carmichael sounded less incredulous than he'd intended to.

"Precisely, Major."

"And just when did someone acquire that capability?"

"In your terms of reference, sometime in the . . . oh, late twenty-second century."

Carmichael sat very still, gray eyes narrowed.

"You're telling me you're from the twenty-second century?"

"No," Jefferson replied. "Actually, I'm from a bit farther away from that. You'd think of it as the twenty-*third* century."

"Of course you are." Carmichael leaned back, crossed his legs, and cocked his head. "And you're sitting in my living room because . . . ?"

"Part of that skill set of yours I referred to a moment ago is the fact that you're a science-fiction reader, Major," Jefferson said calmly. "As such, you at least have a frame of reference for the concept of time travel. But I'm not here to ask you to do anything to affect your own past. Or mine, for that matter. I couldn't. If I asked you to do anything to change events . . . upstream, let's say from where you are at this moment, it would create a paradox, and the physics of time travel won't permit that. I could ask you to perform actions which would change your *future*, but even if I did, whatever happened wouldn't be *my* past."

"Excuse me?" Carmichael had no need to feign confusion.

"In a sense, I'm here to offer you what could be thought of as a mercenary assignment. And because of our ability to manipulate time, we'll be able to return you to your own time at effectively the same instant you left it, if you should accept our offer. In other words, no time will pass for anyone who knows you between the time of your departure and the time of your return."

"My departure to *where?*"

"Major Carmichael." Jefferson leaned forward, bracing his forearms on his thighs, his expression very serious. "There's a war being fought to determine the future of all mankind. I realize that sounds like particularly bad dialogue in a low-budget movie. Unfortunately, it's true. Two competing sides—call them cultures or philosophies—are fighting to determine the ultimate fate of every human being, and there are far more human beings than you've ever imagined."

"What are you talking about?"

"I'm sure you're aware of the concept of multiple universes," Jefferson said. "Well, although your current time's grasp of the underlying theory is far from perfect, it's reaching in the proper direction. There really are an effectively infinite number of universes, each resulting from some event, some outcome, unique to that universe. The differences are often so minute that if you could step between this universe and the next one over, let's say, you'd never even realize you'd done it. Other differences are rather more profound, and one of the consequences of time travel and the inability to create paradoxes in one's own past means that if past events are deflected into a different outcome, that act creates a new and unique timestream—a completely new universe, with a completely new planet Earth, a completely new Milky Way galaxy . . . a completely new *everything*."

"Christ," Carmichael murmured, and Jefferson shrugged.

"I realize it's a lot to take in. However, human beings being human beings, once the technology for achronic travel was perfected, crackpots, lunatics, and fanatics began trying to create universes where events suited their own prejudices. Universes where their pet political lunacy was universally accepted, where they were richer than Croesus . . . where they were emperor of the world! As you can imagine, it didn't take long for the situation to get thoroughly out of control, and institutions emerged to deal with the problem. As I say, I was born in what you'd call the twenty-third century; the institutions attempting to police the timestream—call them the Directors, since that's what *we* call them—actually originate substantially farther in the future than that. And, unfortunately, as a result of that meddling with the timestream, there are two *sets* of Directors."

"Who don't agree on how to fix the problems," Carmichael said shrewdly.

"Who don't agree," Jefferson acknowledged. "I represent one set of Directors, and I'm speaking to you as their agent."

"Why? If you're from two hundred years in my future, with the kind of technological gadgets you've just finished demonstrating, what could I possibly do that you couldn't do yourself?"

"Frankly, Major Carmichael, relatively few people possess both the mental flexibility to handle the concept of time travel and the skills required to accomplish anything. And, to be blunt, we've found that those from times earlier than our own tend to have a certain . . . toughness we no longer have. It's not that humans from earlier time periods are any less sophisticated, or any less intelligent, but they're less insulated by their technology. Less protected, I suppose." Jefferson grimaced. "For want of a better term, people of my time tend to be like well-fed family pets, not guard dogs with the attitude and *developed* intestinal fortitude to deal with potentially ugly situations."

"And just what 'ugly situation' brings you to *my* door?"

"As I say, there are two competing ideologies," Jefferson replied. "One believes in providing security, health, material prosperity, and individual freedom to every living human. The other believes in conquest, personal power, brutal repression of those who disagree with those in authority. In many ways, that's a gross oversimplification —one that *understates* the differences between them—but it's suitable as a working model. Trust me, the stakes couldn't possibly be higher."

"Why? If each alteration in the 'timestream' creates its own universe, how can either side control what happens to 'every living human'?"

"Because the resources of each universe in which one side, one faction, wins domination become available to that side. It probably *isn't* possible to ultimately control every universe, but according to the Directors—*both* sets of Directors—it will ultimately be possible to manipulate the timestream so as to *destroy* the losing side's universes. *All* of them. And if that happens, the billions upon billions of humans who will be killed in each of those destroyed universes will be just as real as you yourself are. Which doesn't even consider the fact that each of the Earths involved is only one infinitesimal speck in an entire *universe* which will perish with it."

Despite the lunatic quality of the entire conversation, Carmichael felt an icy shiver run through his bones. He stared at Jefferson, trying—vainly, he knew—to wrap his mind around what the other man had just said.

"I—" He broke off, cleared his throat, and tried again.

"I don't know if I can believe all that," he said. "And even if I could—believe it, I mean—what makes *me* so important?"

"You personally, as an individual, are scarcely vital," Jefferson said in the tone of a man conceding a point, "but you could be very useful to us. In many ways, your background makes you especially well suited for the sorts of operations we have to stage. You're adept with weapons, with small-unit tactics and operational planning, and when it comes to thinking on your feet—improvising and overcoming. And, like most special-operations troops, you have the sort of self-confidence that drives operations through to success. And while I hope you'll agree to assist us with a single mission, I also hope that once you've had a chance to see the nature of the conflict for yourself, you'll agree to undertake additional missions."

He paused, looking earnestly at Carmichael, who tilted his head to one side and smiled quizzically.

"And?" he prompted. Jefferson looked confused, and he snorted. "There's an 'and' in there somewhere. Another reason you're talking to me."

"I suppose there is," Jefferson admitted. "You see, you not only have the skills and personality we require, you also have a need only we can meet. I won't insult you by calling it a price, Major, but it's something we can provide as compensation for the risks we're asking you to assume."

Carmichael's eyes flamed with a sudden, terrible hope, and Jefferson shook his head quickly.

"No," he said softly. "We can't go back and prevent the accident. We can't restore your children to you. If we could, we would certainly offer it, but in this universe, in your personal timestream, they're already gone. The physical laws that prevent paradoxes won't let us change that for you. What we *can* change, though, is your future . . . and your wife's."

"Kate? You can help *Kate*?" Carmichael's voice was hoarse, whipsawed by sudden hope, dreadful disappointment, and hope restored.

"Yes," Jefferson said simply. "If you agree to assist us, your Kate will recover fully."

Carmichael stared at him, stunned. Several seconds passed, and then, finally, he shook himself.

"I'm tempted—God, I'm tempted! But I'm not going to sign any blank checks. Tell me what it is you want me to do."

"Basically, all we want you to do is to help defend the natural course of events in another timeline—one in a family of time-streams which we call the Tawantinsuyu Aberration. For that matter, your own universe is technically known as British Empire/Tawantinsuyu-21, because it's a subset of the Aberration, which split off from the rest of the universe in the sixteenth century. In the universe we're asking you to help defend, however—British Empire/Tawantinsuyu-18–a team of operatives from the other side is attempting to destroy the British Empire. If they accomplish their objective, Washington's Rebellion will rip the entire conti-nent of North America away from the Empire, clearing the way for the Tawantinsuyu Empire to dominate this hemisphere from Antarctica to the Arctic."

"And you don't want that to happen."

"No, Major, we don't."

"What *do* you want to happen, then?"

"We would vastly prefer for the British Empire to survive, instead," Jefferson told him. "At the very least, as a check on Tawantinsuyu's imperialism. To be honest, however, what we *hope* will happen is that our own homeland—what you would call Mexico—will survive as an independent nation. That didn't happen here, in your history, of course, but it *almost* did when Palmerston tried to prevent the collapse of Nueva España during the Terrazan Wars. If he'd succeeded, the Inca couldn't have undermined the local juntas and split Nueva España into such a snakepit of warring factions and narco centers."

"So, you don't much care for Inkies, do you?" Carmichael half jibed.

"No, we don't. And we haven't much cared for them for quite a lot longer than *you* haven't." Jefferson showed his teeth. "The Inca and the Tenocha have been enemies for a very, very long time."

.II.

The view from the window was remarkable, especially for someone who'd spent entirely too much time conducting clandestine operations in what had once upon a time been the *Virreinato de Nueva España*.

The disintegration of the Viceroyalty of New Spain during the Terrazan Wars—and the succeeding century or so of stepped-up Inky subversion—had given the *coup de grâce* to a shambling, ongoing disaster. One "liberation movement" opposed to European rule after another had convulsed Nueva España for centuries, starting as early as 1612, and if one looked closely, there'd almost always been Incan involvement buried in them somewhere. Not that the Inkies could have stirred them up without plenty of help from Spanish ineptitude.

British dislike for Spain was traditional, but Carmichael's own antipathy for most things Spanish had more to do with growing up next door to Nueva España's moldering carcass than with his European fellows' automatic, knee-jerk hostility for the memory of Emperor Alfonzo.

The single remnant of Spain's one-time empire that he considered even partially successful was the Republic of California, and even there he had reservations. Having everything west of the Rockies and south of the Columbia River under moderately stable rule was good, but the "Republic" was considerably less representative than his own New England. On the other hand, British influence had been leaking across the mountains for almost two hundred years. Given *another* fifty years or so, and a few basic human rights reforms, California might actually be a decent place to live.

The same could not be said of anything south of the Province of Oklahoma. The Spanish crown had maintained titular authority in that portion of Nueva España until the Revolution, when the provincial juntas had seized the opportunity to secure their own power. With all of Europe preoccupied by the wave of revolution sweeping the continent after the Storming of the Escorial and general massacre of the Spanish aristocracy in 1851—and Alfonzo Terraza's meteoric career—there'd been no one to rein them in.

Terraza's rise from obscure army officer to emperor of Spain (not to mention king of Italy, France, Holland, Sweden, and Denmark, and protector of Prussia) had produced two decades of war, which had raged back and forth across Europe until the "Catalonian Tyrant" was finally toppled (and killed) at the Battle of Zaragoza in 1874. That had fully occupied most people's—and especially Great Britain's—attention. In fact, without the British Empire, Terraza's dynasty might still be on his throne today. Only Queen Victoria's sheer stubbornness, with Prince Albert's inspired support, had sustained resistance to Terraza after his conquest of France, defeat of Prussia, and marriage to the Austrian emperor's daughter ended the First Coalition in 1862. For that matter, the Empire had faced the Spanish juggernaut completely alone for over seven years before Palmerston and Albert finally managed to bring the Russian Empire into the fray and create the *Second* Coalition in 1870.

Terraza had done his damnedest to turn the Mediterranean into a Spanish lake, and from 1854 to 1870, Victoria's navy had found itself facing a resurgent Spanish Navy, which had been quicker to embrace steam and ironclads as a counter to Britain's crushing superiority in traditional wooden warships. In the end, the Royal Navy had emerged victorious, and Britain's enormous (if belated) advances in naval technology had culminated in HMS *Warrior*, the prototype of the modern all-big-gun battleship. In fact, the Terrazan Wars had been a good thing, overall, for the Empire, since they'd hugely boosted British industrialization and created the naval supremacy that still supported the Pax Britannica. Today, King Edward IX's empire stretched from London to the Rockies, from the Red River to the Yukon, from Gibraltar to Cairo, from Cape Town to the Gulf of Aden, from Ceylon to the Hindu Kush, and from Mandalay to Australia, all supported by the most powerful navy the world had ever known.

But while Britain had been busy building her empire, Tawantin-suyu and Japan had been busy building *theirs*.

Neither the Inca nor the Japanese were fond of the British. In fact, the only thing the Tawantinsuyu-Japanese Axis truly had in common was its members' joint rivalry with Britain. Well, that wasn't entirely accurate; both were governed by emperors who were officially divine beings, and neither was particularly concerned about human rights or civil liberties.

Once upon a time, however little Carmichael liked admitting it, the Inkies had probably been closer to benevolent despots than the mikados, but that benevolence had taken a turn for the worse since Nueva España's collapse. Today, Tawantinsuyu controlled all of South and Central America as far north as the old Captaincy General of Yucatan, but that expansion had come with a heavy price.

Tawantinsuyu had spent four hundred years systematically undermining Nueva España's stability, both to create a buffer against Britain and to ease its own expansion. The result was literally dozens of postage-stamp–sized "republics" and *"altepetl"* (most ruled—more or less—by governments with barely a trace of legitimacy and even less true authority) between its northern frontier and New England.

The Inkies had sown the wind and inherited the whirlwind. The ungodly mess in Nueva España had flowed back into their own territories, and their ruthless suppression of dissent, which they blamed on New English agents provocateurs, had spawned resistance movements throughout their own empire, especially in its northern provinces. Which hadn't made the situation in Nueva España's successor states any better. The popular term was "failed state." As far as Carmichael could see, that was just a fancy way of saying that in a poverty-, disease-, and corruption-riddled hellhole, the fellow with the bullets made the rules, and that suited the Incan resistance movements just fine, since it simplified the transport to New England and California of their only true cash crop: cocaine.

It was a nightmare, and Dunstan Carmichael was one of the majority of officers who believed war against the Axis was inevitable. And a nasty war it would be, too, given the Inkies' control of South America and their newly completed Isthmian Canal and Japan's vast empire in Korea and China. The only factor holding the tenuous balance at this point was uncertainty over which way

Russia would jump. Japan had obvious ambitions in British Indo-china, but the Manchurian frontier was another great potential flashpoint. Unfortunately, Tsar Nikolai wasn't prepared to embrace Britannia, given certain long-standing rivalries in the Baltic and the Black Sea . . . not to mention Russia's own stubborn attempts to expand towards India. On the other hand, Japan was clearly the closer threat, especially to Nikolai's Pacific naval bases and incredibly productive Alaskan oil fields.

But whatever ultimately happened on that front, the Mexico City of Dunstan Carmichael's experience was a huge, crime-ridden, polluted sink of depression and misery huddled around fortified and heavily patrolled enclaves of ostentatious wealth. Which was distinctly not what he saw as he gazed out the window.

Tenochtitlan, his new superiors called it. He wasn't clear on whether this timeline's Aztecs had remained in control of Mexico or if they'd retaken it before Spanish influence became entrenched. He suspected the former, although the Tenocha declined to clarify the matter. That was especially frustrating, since the Tenocha's neural teaching machines *could* have given him all the background he wanted literally overnight. But they'd explained that they had to be very careful about "temporal contamination." According to his instructors, allowing someone to learn too much about someone else's history before he returned home created almost as many unpredictable consequences as allowing that same someone to learn too much about his own *future* before he returned home.

He remained a long way from understanding all the ramifica-tions of paradoxes and temporal contamination. From his instruc-tors' sober expressions, though, it was clearly something to avoid at all costs. Of course, he couldn't be certain how forthcoming—or even honest—they were actually being. They hadn't given him any cause to suspect they were being *dis*honest, but those bizarre visions of what would—or could, or *might*—have happened if he'd declined Jefferson's recruiting pitch were never far from his mind. He had no idea if they'd contained even a trace of accuracy, but he also had no intention of mentioning them to anyone. Because if they *had* been accurate . . .

So even as he'd cooperated fully with his instructors, he'd kept the existence of the goggles—still hidden in the side pocket of his bag—secret. After all, if they weren't going to tell *him* everything, it seemed fair enough not to tell *them* everything.

Even if his opportunities to learn the Tenocha's history were virtually nonexistent, however, what he could see of their twenty-third-century present was a vast improvement on what had overtaken Nueva España's one-time capital in his own past.

The Tenocha had preserved, or possibly re-created, the lakes that had been at the heart of the Aztecs' pre-Columbian empire. They stretched out in a sparkling sheet of blue from Lake Zumpango in the north all the way to Lake Chalco to the south. He wished he'd been able to explore the island in Lake Texcoco, which had been the seat of the ancient capital, but concerns about temporal contamination prevented him from actually visiting it. From his window, he could see its pyramids, greenery, huge temple-like museums, and palaces separated by parks and huge beds of flowers. The island and its white stone structures were a gleaming jewel, a living time capsule like a calm, restful oasis at the heart of the city of soaring, pastel-tinted skyscrapers—of broad avenues and boulevards, green belts, huge towers capped by flowering gardens, and air cars moving with graceful, jaguar-like speed—which had grown up around the lakes.

An opening door turned him back from the windows, and he saw the other members of his team rising respectfully as the dark-skinned, hawk-visaged man they knew only as "the General" entered the room.

"I see we're all here," the General observed in harshly accented English. "Please." He gestured at the conference table. "Be seated."

Carmichael and his team obeyed the polite command and settled into the chairs around the table.

Carmichael hadn't expected to command the team. False modesty was no part of the special-ops personality, yet he'd fully expected to find a Tenochan officer in direct command. Things didn't work that way in the bizarre world of temporal warfare, however. Thanks, in no small part, to that "temporal contamination" everyone was being so careful to avoid.

Every member of Carmichael's team had been drawn from the same timeline and century. The idea was to construct a group with enough common background to avoid culture-based misunderstandings. And given the fact that they were building scratch teams out of very disparate building blocks, it undoubtedly did make sense to avoid unnecessary complications.

Yet the policy injected a few complications of its own. Most notably, the members of the team were prohibited from discussing their own pasts, or exactly what year they might come from, with any of the others. It wouldn't do for, say, someone like Dr. Jennifer Brownell (known as "Shamrock"), from 2022 Dublin, to pick up a hint from someone like Dunstan Carmichael, from 2031 South Carolina, about how the stock market had performed in the intervening eleven years. While it might make Dr. Brownell a wealthy woman, it would also introduce all manner of potential complications into the timelines. And if someone from their own century could have contaminated things, the mind boggled at what a careless word from a *twenty-third*-century team leader might have done!

As *this* team's leader, Carmichael was the only member who'd had access to the dossiers of the entire team. There were limitations— *strict* limitations—on the information available even to him, however, and all of them had been assigned suitably anonymous team names. Carmichael was the only one who knew, for example, that "Bullock" was lieutenant Sherman Adcock, an ex-Royal Marine, recruited in the year 2009. Or that "Frenchy" was Jean-Pierre Lascaux, a survivalist from Alberta and a sergeant in the Territorials, who'd been recruited in 2016. And then there was "Fisherman," Sergeant Geoffrey Fisher of the Twelfth Parachute Regiment, a three-quarter-blood Cherokee recruited in 2037.

All of them had military backgrounds, although Shamrock's had been as a Royal Navy doctor, not in one of the combat arms. Before she left the service, she'd risen to commander and commanded both a field hospital in support of the Marines in Indochina and the surgical department of one of the navy's hospital ships during Operation Desert Warrior in Persia, and at the time of her recruitment, she'd been head of surgery in a major trauma hospital. They'd have to medevac casualties to one of the Tenocha-staffed bases for any "miraculous" medical procedures like the ones that would soon have Kate up and walking again, since Shamrock had been restricted to medical techniques and technology with which she was already familiar. On the other hand, she'd had plenty of experience dealing with combat wounds, and her "sickbay" would be incredibly well equipped by twenty-first-century standards. If they got back to base alive, Shamrock would keep them that way until they could get better medical attention.

By now, after four months of intensive training, they were all familiar with their equipment, with one another, and with the implications of their mission. What they weren't familiar with—yet—was precisely how that mission was to be carried out.

Which was the point of the General's present briefing.

"I'm not going to touch on any technical details at this time," he said. "I've kept track of your training and read your instructors' reports, and I'm confident all of you have mastered those details. What we need to discuss today is precisely where and when you're being sent, what we intend to achieve, and what our latest intelligence reports have to tell us about your potential opposition. And make no mistake—there *will* be opposition."

He looked around the table, meeting their eyes one by one.

"All of you are subjects of the British Empire," he continued then. "All of you, I'm aware, have thoroughly familiarized yourself with the history—your own timeline's history—of Washington's Rebellion. All of that happened over two hundred years in your past, however, and because it's part of what you've 'always known,' the Rebellion's failure may seem inevitable to you. After all, all of you have read histories pointing out the various factors that *made* the outcome 'inevitable.' But nothing is truly 'inevitable' until after it's happened . . . nor can it be *changed* within a timeline once it *has* happened. That's the fundamental basis for this entire temporal war, and you can be certain the Tawantinsuyu have analyzed the Rebellion, seeking opportunities to create a very different outcome.

"Your job is to see to it that they fail. We would prefer for the new history you'll be creating to be as close as possible to your own timeline's, but it won't be *identical*, however hard you strive for that result, and you must not let yourselves be limited by what you 'know' of your own history. It's probable—indeed, a certainty —that the conflict between our efforts and those of the Tawantinsuyu will produce a different outcome. So long as the Rebellion ultimately fails, we'll consider your efforts successful. The earlier and more completely it fails, the better. Is that all understood?"

Again, his eyes circled the table, and this time everyone nodded. Nothing he'd said so far was really new, although his somber manner underscored how seriously the Tenocha took this entire operation.

"Good," he said softly, settling back in his chair. "You'll be leaving this evening for the winter of 1776 to ensure that Washington's attempt on Trenton fails. One of our senior field agents will coordinate your operations, and he'll have your detailed briefing when you arrive in-century."

His tone made it clear he'd finished, and Carmichael nodded.

"Of course, sir," he said, and stood. The other members of his team stood with him, but to his surprise, the General remained seated.

"Was there something else, sir?"

"Not for the rest of your team, Major," the General replied. "I do have one other matter I need to discuss with *you*, however."

"Yes, sir." Carmichael looked at Adcock, his second in command. "Get everyone started on the final equipment check, Bullock. I'll be along as soon as the General's finished."

"Yes, sir," Adcock acknowledged then twitched his head at the others. "Let's go," he said simply.

No salutes were exchanged. The Tenocha didn't go in much for that sort of thing.

"Sit back down, Major," the General said as the door closed behind the others.

"There's been some debate at quite a high level about whether or not you should be told what I'm about to tell you," he continued in a very serious tone. "In the end, our in-century probes have turned up some disturbing indications you need to be made aware of. You are *not* to make the rest of your team privy to what I'm about to tell you. Is that clear, Major?"

"Yes, sir."

"Very good. In that case, look at this."

The General manipulated a control, and a hologram appeared above the table. It was the image of a golden mask, and Carmichael had never seen anything quite like it. It had a definite pre-Columbian feel, with a subtle smile, a powerful hooked nose, and inlaid eyes of white stone. It was realistic enough to be a life-sized portrait, except for the eyes. They were a bit too large, a bit out of proportion to the rest of the face.

"Beautiful, isn't it?" the General said softly. "But don't let its beauty deceive you. I realize this isn't something you expect to see in eighteenth-century New Jersey. Hopefully, you *won't* see it there. If you should, however—if you catch even a glimpse of it—you are to immediately kill whoever has it in his possession. Don't hesitate for even a fraction of a second, or *you'll* be the one who dies."

Despite himself, Carmichael blinked. The other man was clearly in deadly earnest, however, and the major frowned.

"May I ask why, sir?"

He more than half expected the General to tell him no, given how strongly the Tenocha harped on avoiding temporal contamination, but . . .

"I can't fully answer that question," the General said. "In part, because I *literally* can't; we don't fully understand the technology involved ourselves. There are also aspects which have to be held back for reasons of operational security and avoiding temporal contamination. What you need to know, however, is that the person who wears this mask will have a significant, even a decisive, advantage over any opponent. It will allow him to . . . maximize the possibilities in any situation."

"Wears it, sir?" Carmichael repeated, looking back at the opaque eyes.

"Just take my word for it, Major." The General's expression was grim. "In fact, if you get a shot at him, and he doesn't go down immediately, get the hell away. It's vitally important that we know if this"—he twitched his head at the image—"is anywhere in your area of operations. If you don't take him out with the first shot, you *won't* take him out, and the only thing you can do is get out and report back as quickly as possible."

"Yes, sir."

"Now, in the event that you encounter the mask and manage to neutralize whoever has it, do not—I repeat, *do not*—experiment with it yourself." The General showed his teeth. "I'm sure it will occur to you that if it bestows such advantages on the enemy, it should logically offer those same advantages to *us*. Unfortunately, it won't. Or, rather, it will . . . briefly."

Carmichael's confusion was evident, and the General snorted.

"Major, this mask conceals a piece of technology which comes from some point far downstream of my own time. We don't know exactly how far downstream, in fact. What we *do* know is that it appears to have been tossed into the past by what we think of as the 'Rogue Directors.' I know none of your briefings have mentioned them, and this is another piece of information which should be shared with the rest of your team only if it becomes absolutely necessary. However, there are actually more than two sides in this war. In fact, there are—or will be, or were—three."

"*Will* be, sir?"

"I'm afraid English doesn't really have the right tenses," the General said, "but what I mean is that the two primary opponents are ourselves, and the future we represent, and the Tawantinsuyu. Allowing them victory would have the horrendous consequences which have been explained to you, at least in general. For obvious reasons of temporal contamination, we can't explain them in *detail*, of course. However, at some point downstream from where you and I sit at this moment, a third side, a third set of Directors, will emerge, and their goal will be to destroy both Tawantinsuyu *and* Tenocha. Their objectives will be only slightly less crushing than the Tawantinsuyu's, and, at some point, they'll come into conflict with both of us. This mask represents what may well be their most dangerous weapon, and the Tawantinsuyu have been foolish enough, *stupid* enough, to allow it to be used against them by choosing to attempt to use it against *us*."

He paused, obviously considering how much more he could safely say.

"This technology offers enormous tactical advantages," he said finally, slowly. "Unfortunately, it also corrupts whoever uses it. It will, indeed, allow him to accomplish his short-term goals, but without his awareness, it will begin reshaping *his* goals into those of the Rogue Directors, and the process—we've discovered to our cost—doesn't take long. In fact, it begins almost immediately, and once it's underway, the person attempting to use the mask will discover that, instead, *it* is using *him* to sabotage his own team's efforts and shift any situation in the Rogue Directors' favor." The General shrugged. "From their perspective, it's an ideal weapon. Not only does it help their operatives carry out their orders, but handed to someone *else's* operative, it converts him into *their* operative. They don't even have to recruit their own people; they can simply corrupt—brainwash—ours."

Carmichael suppressed a shiver at the bleakness in the other man's tone, and the shiver was deeper and colder as he gazed at the mask's crystal eyes. That mask was just about big enough to . . .

"Don't attempt to destroy it in the field if the opportunity should present itself," the General continued. "Don't even touch it. I mean, don't allow it to come into contact with your skin. Pick it up with something else—a glove, a jacket, anything—and return it immediately to base. Put it in a secure, locked container and send it immediately uptime to my personal attention. There's no way you could destroy it. In fact, it will probably go uptime from Tenochtitlan, to somewhen where the Directors *do* have the capacity to destroy it. All you'll accomplish if *you* attempt to destroy it will be to expose yourself to its influence. Is that perfectly clear, Major?"

"Yes, sir. Clear."

"Very good, Major." The General's expression lightened and he smiled approvingly. "In that case, go catch up with the rest of your team."

.III.

Under normal circumstances, there wouldn't have been much to see outside Dunston Carmichael's window. Sunlight didn't penetrate four hundred feet of water, after all. But his office's light attracted curious fish—including some truly enormous sturgeon —when it streamed through the window. He could have sat for hours watching them through the incredibly tough not-quite-glass, but providing the team's CO with the equivalent of his own private aquarium wasn't something he would have associated with the businesslike Tenochan approach to temporal warfare.

Probably gave it to me to remind me we are four hundred feet underwater, he thought, turning back to the briefing documents on his monitor. *Jefferson would find that worthwhile, I suspect.*

He'd been a little surprised to discover that his recruiter was also the senior field agent assigned to oversee the operation, but it turned out he'd also recruited all the other members of the team. Apparently the Tenocha Directors believed in allowing field agents to select their own personnel.

That suited Carmichael reasonably well in most ways, yet he couldn't quite forget the images of Jefferson blowing holes through his personal anatomy. He was still inclined to take those visions with a grain of salt, especially after the General's revelations, yet he'd also detected a ruthless streak in Jefferson. That didn't surprise him; he'd seen the same thing in enough special operators from his own century. But there was something else, as well, like a sound pitched just too low to identify. Something that warned him Jefferson was more prepared than he wanted to appear to sacrifice personnel if it enhanced the operation's chances, perhaps.

And maybe it's just those "visions" giving you the willies, too, Dunstan! For that matter, if there's anything to that business about "corrupting" people . . .

At any rate, Jefferson had gone to considerable lengths to emphasize the security of Champlain Base's location. Carmichael still found the ability of the lightning bolt–marked Tenochan flyers to configure themselves into submersibles remarkable, but no doubt someone who could build a *time* machine considered building genuine triphibious capability into its flyers a minor technological trick. And Jefferson was obviously correct that no one in eighteenth-century New York or Vermont was going to go looking for anyone on the bottom of Lake Champlain! For that matter, their location was in obvious keeping with both sides' policy of building bases where no one was ever likely to stumble over any embarrassing archaeological remains, he reflected, reading over the operations plan again.

He glanced at the time display in the corner of his monitor. Whatever operating system the Tenocha were using, it ran on standard twenty-first-century computers for his team's benefit, and so far he hadn't gotten Portals's "blue screen of death" even once!

He snorted, but his humor faded quickly as he realized the final briefing was due to begin in less than thirty minutes.

Calm down, he told himself. *Even if everything goes perfectly, tonight's only the first skirmish. If the Inky Directors are even half as determined as the Tenocha, they're not going to give up just because we bloody their nose in their first attempt.*

No, they weren't, yet he knew that wasn't really what made him feel so antsy.

He hesitated for another moment, then shrugged and pushed his chair back from the desk. He crossed the office, stepped through the door into his personal quarters, and opened the closet. No one in Tenochtitlan had objected when he tossed his bag into his personal cargo container for the trip to Champlain Base. None of them were likely to need any of their twenty-first-century possessions, but one thing he'd noticed was that the Tenocha accepted on an almost genetic level that rank had its privileges. They'd probably written it off as one of the foibles to which a field commander was entitled, and he was just as happy they had, since he was still so strongly . . . disinclined to mention the goggles' existence to anyone.

Partly that was because of what those goggles had shown him before Jefferson's arrival. Given the stakes in their war with the Inkies, he couldn't really fault the Tenochan emphasis on preventing temporal contamination in the event a potential recruit turned down their offer. Personally, though, he would have preferred a less . . . permanent solution, and surely, given their neural teaching technology, they could have come up with something else. Something like that amnesia-producing "pen" the senior agent had carried in *Fellows in Black*, perhaps.

Even more to the point, he didn't know if "his" goggles came from the same source as that quartz-eyed mask, but it certainly seemed possible—especially since that business about "maximizing possibilities" struck him as a remarkably good description of *not* getting oneself killed. Given how emphatic the General had been about shooting on sight, he wasn't eager to admit he had them, either. On the other hand, if they did come from the same source and the General was right about the mask's "corrupting" effect, it was possible his "visions" had been false—lies designed to lead him to trust them more than he did the Tenocha. For that matter, they might be a separate piece of technology entirely. Not to mention the possibility that his visions had been accurate . . . and the General had been less than candid.

He hadn't attempted to use them again. He'd been afraid to in Tenochtitlan, because he'd been pretty sure his team's quarters were wired. *He* would have set things up that way, however benign a fellow he might have been, and the entire team had tacitly assumed they were under observation at all times without ever actually discussing the matter.

He wasn't about to assume anything different about Champlain Base, either, so he stood in a casual, natural posture which would just happen to block any hidden camera's direct line of sight into the closet as he slipped the goggles out of the bag and into one of his uniform's cargo pockets.

Goggles in pocket, he crossed to his personal head, closed the door, and seated himself on the toilet lid. He'd examined every inch of the bathroom under the guise of routine housecleaning and decided that if he'd been going to wire the room, the mirror above the lavatory would have been his first choice of where to put a camera. That was why he'd casually arranged a towel this morning to screen his present position from any camera behind the mirror. Assuming he wasn't being unduly paranoid, the Tenocha's technology undoubtedly gave them all sorts of options he couldn't even imagine. But he'd taken every precaution he could, and since there was no point worrying over precautions he *couldn't* take, he drew the goggles back out and, not without a qualm or three, pulled them into place.

They settled over his eyes, opaque lenses cutting off the light, and at first he thought that was all they were going to do. He was wrong about that, though. It took a little longer this time, but eventually those tiny motes of light appeared once more.

He inhaled deeply as the light dots coalesced into a fresh "vision." He watched himself climbing into his assigned flyer. He looked much as he did now, except for the med kit in his left hand and the Ferguson .46 magnum on his hip. Neither of those was on tonight's equipment list. For that matter, the flyers had their own bulkhead-mounted medical kits, which were much more fully equipped than the one he was carrying. No one seemed to have objected, however, and he watched himself hook the med kit to his belt. Then he saw himself draw the revolver, swing out the cylinder, and check the loads. His eyebrows rose behind the goggles as he saw the cartridge headstamps, but the Carmichael he was watching simply reclosed the cylinder, reholstered his weapon, and began the preflight checklist.

At which point the goggles promptly turned opaque again.

The entire "vision" lasted less than ten seconds. He waited twice that long for the next vision then realized there wasn't going to be a "next" this time.

He frowned, stripped the goggles off, and shoved them back into his pocket. He started to rise, then made himself stop and sit patiently for another full minute. Then he stood, deliberately banged the toilet lid, and flushed. He paused at the lavatory long enough to wash his hands—which let him casually remove the obscuring towel—and headed for the door.

"—so watch your air-to-air sensors, too, Bullock," Carmichael finished up. "We may not *expect* them to be up in force, but the last thing we need is for your head to be buried in the weeds if they *do* try to bounce you."

"Yes, sir."

The marine had persistently posted the highest air-to-air combat scores, and he smiled like a lazy, confident tiger. As Carmichael had said, no one really expected the Inkies to use uptime weaponry, but that didn't mean they *wouldn't* use whatever they decided it took—including full-fledged airstrikes. Which was why he'd designated Bullock to provide top cover.

"I think that's everything, then," he said and glanced up at the flatscreen above the conference table. "Do you have anything to add?"

"No, Major," the Tenocha called Jefferson replied. Rather than share their quarters in Champlain Base, the agent teleconferenced via secure satellite link from the main Tenochan base, located in what would one day be the Province of Alberta. It seemed cumbersome, but the Tenocha were determined to minimize temporal contamination, and the command arrangements seemed to be working out reasonably well so far, although Jefferson had overruled his original plan to take along some heavier ground-based firepower of their own.

As the Tenocha had pointed out, tonight was more in the nature of a first skirmish than an all-out assault, and neither side wanted to inject unnecessary contamination by flashing around advanced technology. Inexplicable manifestations of "divine intervention" were acceptable in prehistoric eras; leaving obvious fingerprints where they might find their way into the historical record was not.

Jefferson hadn't said so in so many words, but Carmichael suspected another reason was that the field agent didn't want his team feeling overly aggressive. The peculiar nature of temporal warfare meant there were often significant advantages to playing defense. The iron rule that prevented paradox meant both sides tried to avoid initiating decisive action until circumstances most favored them or they absolutely had to. Once an event had occurred in any given timeline, it could not be changed. No one who'd been party to the original event could subsequently affect it in any way, and even if someone from a third or fourth timeline intervened, it would simply create yet *another* new timeline "downstream" from the event.

Carmichael understood the concept, but while he wasn't prepared to simply disregard Jefferson's argument that the Inkies probably wouldn't be expecting heavy combat either, he'd never been happy planning operations based on what the other side "probably wouldn't" do.

I really wish the intel pukes could keep their damned noses out of operational planning. Just tell us what to do, then get the hell out of the way. He snorted mentally. It wasn't the first time he'd wished that, after all. *And when all's said, I don't suppose there's any reason for Tenochan intel pukes to be better about that than the twenty-first-century variety!*

"I think you covered everything quite thoroughly," the field agent continued now. "Just remember that even if tonight's mission succeeds, the operation as a whole isn't over until the Rebellion fails."

Heads nodded around the conference table.

"Very well, then. Good hunting," he said, and the monitor blanked.

.IV.

Carmichael tapped the control panel on his belt unit, and the flyer whined obediently back up into the icy clouds as he headed across the small field toward the deep ditch leading to his pre-selected position. Fresh snow and sleet made the footing treacherous, but his twenty-third-century uniform maintained a comfortable body temperature, his helmet's clear visor provided better vision than any twenty-first-century low-light vision gear he'd ever used, and at least the miserable precipitation would conceal any tracks.

His initial planning had used a single large flyer to put him, Frenchy, and Fisherman on the ground while Bullock covered them from above and Shamrock monitored their communications from Champlain Base. As he'd studied the maps, however, and reflected on how damned little they knew about the Inkies' possible strategy, he'd changed his mind.

He hated going in with so little intelligence on the other side, but one of the main purposes behind tonight's little soirée was to try to get some feel for how the opposition intended to operate. *Stopping* a river crossing covertly on a night like this would have been far simpler than helping one *succeed*, and although he'd tried to figure out how *he* would have approached the Tawantinsuyu's problem, nothing had really come to him. Despite that, Jefferson remained adamant that the Inkies were going to try *something*. Personally, Carmichael was less sure of that. As he saw it, the real reason he was out here tonight was to observe. If it turned out the Tawantinsuyu did have a team in the area, his people would do their best to frustrate any intervention, but he wanted his own people to remain as covert as possible, and in a best-case scenario, there'd be no contact between them and the Inkies at all.

But with no knowledge of the other side's possible plans, he'd decided they needed better eyes. Tenochan stealth capability was impressive as hell to anyone from the twenty-first century, and he had to assume the other side's equaled it. Despite that, airborne sensors would be the best way to spot ground targets, and the Tenochan flyers were designed to operate as unmanned combat platforms at need. So instead of using a single large transport, each member of the ground team would be individually inserted by his own vehicle, which would then loiter at five thousand feet. Their onboard sensors would network with those aboard Bullock's craft to give far better coverage . . . and they'd also provide him with additional weapons platforms if the Inkies did turn up in strength.

So far, however, there was no evidence of any direct tampering by the Tawantinsuyu. Satellite recon had located two enemy bases—one in Québec and another, for some reason, much farther south, in the Appalachians. In fact, the second base was barely a hundred miles from Carmichael's own South Carolina birthplace. That base seemed oddly placed, given the Rebellion's total failure in South Carolina and Georgia, and he wondered if its location signaled something about the Inkies' ultimate strategy.

If it did, it hadn't had any impact on events to date. Washington's rabble of militia and volunteers, aided by the artillery captured at Ticonderoga, had driven General Howe out of Boston and, in turn, been hammered into retreat on schedule when they tried the same thing at New York City. Little more than a month ago, the rebels had been driven out of Fort Lee, on the west bank of the Hudson, and Cornwallis's hard-marching pursuit had very nearly caught Washington's disintegrating force at New Brunswick on the first of December, only to be stopped there by Howe's orders. Personally, Carmichael thought Cornwallis should have ignored orders and continued the pursuit across the Raritan River, even though the rebels had destroyed the bridge and his own men were exhausted. On the other hand, Washington's "army" was down to barely three thousand men, half of whose enlistments ran out at the end of the month, and General Charles Lee—after conspicuously failing to unite the five thousand men under his command with Washington —had been snapped up by a British patrol on the thirteenth, in White's Tavern.

It had always seemed to Carmichael the Rebellion should have collapsed at this point. Outnumbered, fleeing a professional army, driven from every position, riddled by desertions, battered by miserable weather, short of every imaginable supply, and hampered by "experienced officers" like the feckless Lee, on the one hand, and overenthusiastic amateurs like Nathaniel Greene, on the other hand, even someone as stubborn as New Englanders should have seen the writing on the wall. But since his recruitment, he'd delved far more deeply into the period's history. For example, he'd never bothered much over the "Declaration of Independence" the rebels had issued in Philadelphia the previous July. His high school history classes had skimmed it, but as far as he'd been concerned, it was mainly a catalog of grievances and propaganda put together by an ambitious colonial elite intent on overturning the legitimate government. God knew he'd seen enough of that in Nueva España, where every strongman and dictator invariably proclaimed the nobility of his own intentions!

Intellectually, he'd known Washington's Rebellion had reflected genuine unhappiness with British rule. Certainly the twenty years between 1763 and 1783—from George Grenville's ministry through the younger Pitt's first ministry—had been marred by one misstep after another where the American colonies were concerned. In fact, the lessons George III's ministers had learned the hard way in New England had contributed a great deal to the later Empire's stability.

For all that, though, he'd never really thought of rebels against the king as men of principle. Malcontents, power seekers, even genuinely disgruntled colonials pinched by maladroit ministers, yes, but not the sort of people who produced true revolutions of ideas.

Now, though, he'd been forced to realize that the Americans' discontent was far deeper and more widespread than he'd ever realized. He'd always been willing to accept that their "Declaration" expressed deep-seated anger on the part of its *drafters*; now he was forced to admit that that anger touched far more of the total population than he'd believed. Despite the disintegration of Washington's "army," there was a widespread, genuine belief throughout the colonies that the Rebels were in the right. That they were fighting not against a legitimate authority but rather to preserve the same "Rights of Englishmen" enshrined in the Empire of Carmichael's time.

So, yes, now he understood, at least in part, why the Rebellion had survived—for a while—after Washington's disastrous attempt on Trenton. In fact, he'd actually begun to respect the rebels. Even sympathize, to some extent. And he had to admit that watching Washington in action made it difficult to cling to his schoolboy textbooks' view of Washington the arch traitor and would-be "Second Cromwell." In real life, the difficulties he'd faced were even more overwhelming than Carmichael had ever realized, and his response to them was downright impressive. In fact, it had become evident to Carmichael that most historians' offhand dismissal of the Trenton attack as the feckless blundering of an inept military amateur was simply wrong. Instead, it had been what the military liked to call a "calculated risk" . . . when it worked.

It was clear Washington recognized the danger he was courting—and the doubtful quality of his ragged, freezing troops—yet he had the nerve to order the attack anyway because he judged it was essential to the "Patriots' " morale after such a devastating chain of defeats. More than that, his intelligence on his enemies' deployments and the readiness of the Trenton garrison was more accurate (and that garrison's readiness was lower) than Carmichael had ever suspected.

Few historians had commented on the state of Colonel Johan Rall's troops, since the disaster of the Delaware crossing had preempted Washington's attack upon them, and the handful who *had* looked at Rall's readiness had relied on his correspondence to his superiors. But although he'd expressed worry over an attack, requested reinforcements, and asked to have the town of Maidenhead garrisoned to protect his supply line to Princeton, he'd also rejected his own subordinates' suggestions to fortify the town. And, after all, it was Christmas. As one of Washington's officers had noted, "They make a great deal of Christmas in Germany, and no doubt the Hessians will drink a great deal of beer and have a dance tonight. They'll be sleepy tomorrow morning." They'd done just that, too, and from what Carmichael could see in Trenton, Washington might well have carried the day if he'd been able to get his forces across the river as he'd intended.

The truth was that Dunstan Carmichael found much to admire in the rebel general's battle plan, but that wasn't going to prevent him from doing his level best to make certain it failed on schedule.

It was one o'clock, the snow and sleet were even worse than Carmichael had expected, and Washington was behind schedule. That wasn't surprising. In fact, it would have taken divine intervention for the rebels to get everyone across before midnight as planned. Unfortunately, however, it looked as if they were going to get across in the end, after all. The barges manned by John Glover's 14th Regiment might be hampered and slowed by weather and drifting ice, but they were made of stern stuff, those Marblehead fishermen, and they'd already managed to land the main force's first wave—including Washington—on the New Jersey shore.

Carmichael's position was almost ideal—a deep ditch overlooking the main crossing site—and he was in communication with Frenchy and Fisherman over their encrypted satellite link. From their reports, even Washington's secondary crossings—James Ewing's south of Princeton to seize the bridge over Assunpink Creek and John Cadwallader's diversion at Bristol, still farther south—might get across in the end. That was far better than the rebels had managed in his own history, yet he could see no sign—yet—of Inky interference.

Where the hell are they? he wondered, then grimaced.

They're probably doing exactly what you are. Lying out in this crappy weather—I'm a southern boy, damn it!—and watching. They must know you're in the area, so why give away their own positions as long as Washington's managing just fine on his own?

Which raised the question of why Washington *was* managing on his own. He wasn't supposed to be doing that. . . .

Crap, Carmichael thought. *I'll bet it's us. The Tenochan boffins keep saying* any *change sets off an entirely new universe where* everything—*including, oh, weather changes—can be different. The instant both sides started mucking around, they probably initiated a whole* slew *of changes . . . including whatever's given the rebels a better chance of getting across. And as long as* that's *true, the Inkies don't have to do a damned thing!*

He swore under his breath while he pondered his own response.

The apparent success of Glover's boatmen meant the initiative had shifted dramatically. But if he and his people took more . . . proactive action, the other side was going to object, and he still had no idea where any Inky team was, how big it might be, or how it might be equipped. And while both sides did their best to avoid killing downtimers because of the impossible-to-predict ramifications of such deaths, *Carmichael's* people weren't "local." Killing one of *them* in 1776 was unlikely to have any temporal ramifications worth worrying about.

Except for them, of course.

Well, he told himself grimly, *it's not as if you've got much choice, Dunstan.*

"All Tories, this is the Major," he murmured over the link. "We're going to have to get involved after all. Frenchy, Fisherman, all this snow'll cut our effective range, so if you need to adjust your firing positions, do it now. Bullock, stay on your toes up there."

Acknowledgments came back, and he checked his own rifle-like maser stunner. Despite the weather, he was close enough to the river for his fire to be effective, and he waited patiently for the other two to work closer to their targets. The rebels might be doing better than they were supposed to, but it would take hours yet to get Washington's two thousand-plus infantry and Knox's eighteen field guns across the river. There was time.

"Frenchy, in position," a voice said over his headset.

Fifteen more minutes ticked past, and then Fisherman's familiar Appalachian accent announced the same thing.

"Good," Carmichael acknowledged. "Any sign of the Inkies, Bullock?"

"Negative."

"Let's hope it stays that way." Carmichael flipped up his visor and gazed through the stunner's electronic sight at a daylight-bright target.

"Engage," he said.

The stunner made no sound at all. Anyone who'd ever been in covert ops treasured silence above rubies or gold, and Carmichael smiled as his target crumpled. It was hard to identify the barge's actual commander, but the fellow he'd chosen had been half standing, crouched as he peered forward and pointed out chunks of ice to be fended off by other members of the crew, and the big boat swerved as he collapsed.

Carmichael moved his sights to one of the forward oarsmen, and the man folded over his oar, tangling up the rower beside him. The boat's course became even more erratic, a big ice cake slammed into it, and the barge immediately astern dodged hastily to avoid collision.

The consternation as members of the barge crew began to slump over was evident, and it was all Carmichael could do not to chuckle as he watched them. It was almost like some video game, especially since he knew none of the men he'd put out of action had actually been harmed in any way, and he found himself wishing he could take a dozen stunners on the CLI's next op.

No wonder they're so focused on eliminating every opportunity for "temporal contamination!" a corner of his mind reflected. *I can't be the only person to wish—*

"Bandit! *Multiple* bandits, coming in from the north!"

It was Bullock, and Carmichael swore fervently. So the Inkies *had* put out their own observers, and unlike the barge crew, they knew exactly what was causing the sudden epidemic of unconsciousness. And what a stunner's emission signature looked like.

On the other hand, the sides of his ditch screened him from every angle except directly to his front. They'd play hell finding him without a direct overflight.

"Keep them off us, Bullock," he heard his own voice say calmly as he sent a third oarsman sliding into the barge's floorboards. Another ice cake hammered the boat—this time hard enough to start seams—and the barge turned suddenly back the way it had come.

One down, he thought.

He made himself choose his next victim with care, despite the Inkies' arrival, looking for boats that had already almost collided with someone else. If he could encourage them to run into each other, spread confusion—

"Major, Frenchy," a voice barked over his headset. "I'm taking fire!"

"Inkies or locals?" Carmichael asked, even as he began stunning members of his second barge crew.

"It's silenced automatic weapons in the treeline!" the Canadian survivalist snarled back. "These bastards are playing for keeps!"

Well, that *sucks*, Carmichael reflected.

"Disengage, Frenchy. Get your ass out of the line of fire!"

"You've got *that* right," the other man replied. "Frenchy is *out* of here!"

Carmichael grunted in satisfaction. Frenchy's objective had been Ewing's relatively small force, which wasn't going to accomplish much even if it did get across . . . as long as the main force didn't.

His second target was clearly out of control, wallowing downstream with a quarter of its crew out of action, and he shifted to a third barge.

I should've assigned Frenchy to help me cover this force and left Ewing the hell alone. This is the crossing that matters, and with another stunner—

Something exploded suddenly. It was several miles to the north and so high he could barely hear it. Moments later, a second explosion rumbled, even farther north. Both had been high enough above the cloud cover the locals would probably think they'd been thunder, however unlikely that might seem. Unless, of course, wreckage started raining down on them.

"Bullock, this is Major. You still with us?"

"Yes," the marine's taut voice came back, "but I'm sort of *busy* just now!"

"Cut and run if you have to," Carmichael told him quickly.

"Understood," Bullock replied, and Carmichael grunted sourly.

Confusion was spreading, yet he doubted he'd done much more than delay things a bit. He was confident he *could* stop the crossing, but he'd need more time, and the Inkies were clearly out in force. And operating a lot more openly than anticipated. Shooting down enemy aircraft was all well and good, but only if you could police up the wreckage before any of the locals stumbled across it, so—

He'd just taken down two oarsmen in the third barge when something hissed unpleasantly across his position and buried itself in the frozen mud. Several more somethings followed, and Carmichael dropped prone in the slushy water and ice at the bottom of the ditch.

"Major is taking fire," he announced. Another flurry of slugs thumped into the mud, coming from an entirely different angle, and he grimaced.

"I have multiple hostiles, at least two, and they sure as hell aren't using stunners," he said. "Abort. I say again, all Tories abort and withdraw!"

He wished the Inkies *had* been using stunners, but unless you could control the range of the engagement, it only made sense to choose weapons that let you reach out and touch someone, since sooner or later you'd sure as hell have to do just that. That was the very point he'd made to Jefferson when he'd been overruled.

His own stunner probably matched the effective aimed range of his revolver, the only other ranged weapon he had, however. And while he really would have preferred to be able to return the compliment if someone wanted to kill him, he'd damned well settle for putting them silently to sleep if it let him get out with his own hide intact.

He began crawling down the ditch while more slugs snarled overhead. They were using subsonic rounds—there wasn't much point using *super*sonic ammo in silenced weapons, since the whip-crack of passing bullets tended to draw the ear—and he had no idea where they were. But *they* were still firing at where he'd been, which suggested they'd lost track of him, as well. Which, in turn, suggested that if he could only haul ass fast enough enough . . .

"I'm hit!" Bullock shouted suddenly over the radio. "I'm going d—!"

Shit! Carmichael thought bitterly as he sloshed through the icy ditch. *Smoking wreckage all over the goddamned countryside, Bullock down, Frenchy taking fire, and me with fucking Daniel Boone chasing my ass!*

"Major, Fisherman," a voice said in his ear. "I'm clear to the primary evac point. Can you make it?"

"Not to the primary," he replied, sloshing even more rapidly along. "You and Frenchy get clear. I'll evade and contact Shamrock when it's time to send someone to pick me up."

"We could—" Fisherman began, but Carmichael cut him off.

"We don't know how many there are, and all you've got are stunners. Get the hell out."

There was a moment of silence, then—

"Copy, wilco," Fisherman said. "We'll be waiting for you."

Carmichael flipped his helmet visor back down and poked his head up cautiously. Wearily leaning dried corn stalks stood up out of the empty, wintry field's crusted snow, but there was no sign of anyone else, and he'd always been good in the woods. If he could make the wilderness beyond . . .

He made one last, careful scan, then climbed out of the ditch and crawled cautiously across the field on his belly. Instincts screamed to get up, run, and get the hell out, but he'd seen too many people killed because they'd listened to instinct instead of training.

The small field seemed impossibly wide, but finally he was into the trees and moving in a quick half-crouch. At the moment, he was less concerned about where he was going than simply *going*. The more distance he put between himself and—

A baseball bat slammed into his left calf, and he crashed down. For a moment, all he felt was the shock of the impact—then the pain began, and he grunted in anguish, even as a harsh tone buzzed in his headset. Stunners were more fragile than firearms. His had taken the brunt of his fall, and its onboard computer was telling him it hadn't liked it.

Despite the searing pain, his mind ticked through his limited options with crystal clarity, and he made his decision quickly. He didn't think the leg was broken, but he knew it wasn't going to take him either far or fast. For that matter, if he didn't stop the bleeding pretty damned quickly, he wasn't going anywhere ever again.

The damaged stunner was useless, so he pressed a button on the stock and dropped it where he'd fallen. The visible telltales he'd deactivated before setting out came to life, glowing faintly, and he grinned through pain-clenched teeth as he squirmed into the underbrush.

He didn't try to get far. Instead, he settled into the first half-decent position he found, whipped an improvised tourniquet around his leg, and tightened it. Then he drew the Ferguson, wiggled around to face back the way he'd come, and waited.

The smart thing to do was to keep running, slowed or not. The *last* thing he needed was to let himself be pinned down while multiple pursuers converged. But whoever had shot him would think exactly the same way. For that matter, the shooter couldn't be *certain* he'd actually hit Carmichael, and there was only one way he could find out. Of course it was unlikely the other fellow was out here by himself, which posed its own complications.

You're going to get yourself killed, he told himself calmly. *Unless . . .*

Dunstan Carmichael had never been a "hunch player," but he was pretty certain the goggles' warning about Jefferson's recruiting visit had been accurate. And his leg wound suggested they'd been right to warn him to bring along the med kit, too. So if they'd wanted him to bring the Ferguson, there had to have been a reason, right?

You are so grasping at straws, he thought, trying hard not to groan in pain. *What're you going to do when it turns out—*

A shape emerged from the darkness.

Carmichael had been thoroughly briefed on both standard Tenochan weapons and their Tawantinsuyu counterparts, and he recognized the compact assault rifle. *Forty-round magazine, .28 caliber, length 30.8 inches*, his mind supplied automatically. *Delayed blowback, cyclic rate of fire nine hundred RPM, max effective range six hundred and fifty yards with optical sights. No sign of the grenade launcher, though.*

The newcomer eased cautiously closer, head turning alertly. Then he paused. He stood motionless, then straightened and stepped forward more confidently. Carmichael lay very still as he watched the other man cross to the abandoned stunner; the dim glow of its telltales reflected in Carmichael's own helmet visor.

He was close enough Carmichael could just hear his chuckle through the patter of sleet on dead leaves. He would really have preferred for the bastard to continue his pursuit of the fleeing Tenochan operative without ever noticing the wounded guy in the shrubbery. He didn't think that was going to happen, though. And—

The other man looked up. His head turned, and, for just an instant, Dunstan Carmichael looked into his pursuer's eyes. Their visor systems showed each of them every detail with perfect clarity. Carmichael recognized the other man's typical Incan features: the strong nose, the high cheekbones, the dark eyes. He saw those eyes narrow, then widen in sudden consternation as they saw the massive handgun—the handgun loaded with tungsten-cored ammunition capable of blasting through even the hardshell body armor he wore.

It was the *last* thing they ever saw.

.V.

Things are looking up.

Dunstan Carmichael told himself that rather firmly, since he seemed to be taking some convincing.

He grimaced, panting as he supported his limping weight on a hastily cut staff, but at least the Inky he'd killed had apparently been operating solo after all. He didn't know why, unless the Inkies were as thin on the ground as his own team. In the meantime, he'd appropriated his enemy's assault rifle, and so far he'd seen no sign of any other pursuers.

That was the good news. The *bad* news was that the Inkies had to have a good idea where their man had fallen out of communication. They were going to converge on that spot quickly, and despite the med kit he'd brought along, the ugly leg wound both slowed him and made him easier to track. And for good measure, he couldn't even contact Shamrock, because his radio was down.

That's not supposed to happen, he thought grumpily as he hopped along as quickly as he could. *I landed on the damned* stunner, *not the radio!*

He knew he ought to concentrate on the positive, like continuing to breathe, but human nature was human nature. Besides—

The damned goggles can tell me to bring along a med kit and load the Ferguson with armor-piercing, but they can't tell me to bring along an extra battery—or whatever!—for a frigging radio? Some "super weapon" they are!

He suspected he was concentrating on his sense of ill usage in order to avoid thinking about the proof his goggles did indeed do what the General had warned him the golden mask did.

And about what the mask was supposed to do to anyone who used it.

Carmichael wasn't happy at the thought of being brainwashed. Still, if the goggles planned on turning him into a brainwashed pawn, they also presumably meant to keep him alive to *be* brainwashed. At the moment, that struck Dunstan Carmichael as a very good thing.

One thing at a time. First *stay alive, then—*

"Major Carmichael, I presume?"

Carmichael dropped his staff and spun on his good foot. He almost fell, but he didn't, and the assault rifle snapped magically into firing position.

"Don't do anything hasty," the voice said almost soothingly. "If I'd intended you any harm, I could simply have stunned you—or shot you—instead of talking to you."

Carmichael's eyes swept the cold, icy woods. Despite his visor's magic vision, there was no sign of whoever was doing the talking, and he felt his pulse throbbing in his temples.

"I don't blame you for feeling a bit distrustful," the voice continued, "but I really am a friend."

"A *friend*?" Carmichael snorted harshly.

"Well, that's what I'd *like* to be, at any rate. And despite what you may be thinking, I'm not one of the . . . 'Inkies,' I believe you call them."

Between exhaustion, blood loss, and pain, Carmichael's thoughts were less than clear. Still, he was inclined to believe the voice truly wasn't an ally of the corpse he'd left behind him.

Which didn't mean anything else it might say happened to be true.

"So, if you're not an Inky, who the hell are you? And how are you managing the invisible-man trick?"

"You can call me Esperanza. And the reason you can't see me has something to do with the fact that *my* technology is better than yours. Two or three hundred years better, as a matter of fact."

Carmichael realized he was standing very, very still, and the voice—Esperanza—chuckled softly.

"That's right, Major. I'm the one who sent you the goggles."

"Why?" Carmichael heard himself ask.

"Because you seem a capable sort, and I knew the Tenocha intended to recruit you. It struck me that the best way to show you what's really going on was to let them go ahead and do that, and the goggles were the best way to keep you alive long enough to digest the lesson. Among other things."

"The lesson?" Carmichael repeated.

"Oh, the *real* lesson is only just beginning, Major," Esperanza replied. "Assuming you want to know what's really going on, of course. Do you?"

"Esperanza" might or might not be a real name, Carmichael reflected thirty minutes later, and its owner might or might not be being honest, but he'd obviously told the truth about his technology, at least. It really was considerably in advance of anything the Tenocha had.

At the moment, the major sat in a comfortable bucket seat, gazing through a bubble canopy at pinprick stars above a sea of moonlit cloud. Esperanza's flyer had collected them from the snowy woods with what Carmichael could only think of as a "tractor beam" even before Esperanza deactivated his own stealth systems and materialized out of apparently thin air less than twenty feet from him.

Now he turned from the stars to the man in the seat beside his.

Esperanza wasn't particularly large, yet he seemed somehow bigger than life. He had fierce, dark eyes, and a nose even more lordly than Carmichael's. He was also casually dressed in twenty-first-century denims, hiking boots, a plaid shirt, and a mackinaw that could not have looked less like Carmichael's own "smart fabric" uniform.

"I trust the leg feels better?" Esperanza said, turning his head to return Carmichael's gaze.

"I think you might say that," Carmichael acknowledged dryly, flexing his calf muscle.

The wound had been even worse than he'd thought—a messy wound channel, which had miraculously missed bone but torn a fist-sized exit hole. Without his hasty tourniquet and the med kit, he would have bled out quickly, he thought, and it was no wonder he'd found it so difficult to keep going. But Esperanza's flyer came equipped with a medical unit that had taken all of five minutes to not simply stop the bleeding but heal the wound without leaving even a scar. Nothing. Not even lingering soreness.

"Good." Esperanza smiled. "And now, about those questions . . . ?"

"You might start with that bit about keeping me alive long enough to 'digest the lesson' about what's *really* going on," Carmichael suggested pointedly

"All right," Esperanza said agreeably, then tipped back his seat comfortably and interlaced his fingers across his chest.

"At the risk of undermining my aura of omniscience, I don't know exactly what the Tenocha have told you," he began. "I'm fairly confident about the gist of it, but not of the details. So I'll just give you *my* version. When I'm done, we can compare notes. Does that seem reasonable?"

"Your flyer, your rules," Carmichael replied with a shrug, and Esperanza chuckled.

"In that case, I'll begin by saying I'm certain they lied to you. I base that on my evaluation of your personality—and, yes, I did some research on you once I became aware of their interest in you. If they'd told a man like you the truth, you never would have agreed to serve them, no matter what they promised in return."

"No?" Carmichael's jaw tightened. "What they offered me was pretty damned tempting."

"I know." Esperanza's expression and eyes softened, and his tone was gentle. "And I realize you'd do almost anything to win your wife's recovery, Major Carmichael. But you *wouldn't* have agreed to serve the Tenocha if you knew the truth about them. Not even for her."

Carmichael only looked at him stonily, and Esperanza shrugged.

"I'm not going to try to tell you the complete truth about them right this minute. Frankly, if I did, you'd think I was feeding you lies to get you on my side. But let me ask you this. During your training, did you ever have a genuine opportunity to see their society? To meet anyone except your trainers? Actually spend any time wandering around Tenochtitlan?"

"No," Carmichael replied after a long, thoughtful moment.

"Of course not. They told you they were worried about 'temporal contamination,' didn't they?"

Carmichael's expression answered for him, and Esperanza snorted harshly.

"There really is something to all that claptrap about 'contamination.' Not as much as I'm sure they told you there was, however.

What they *really* wanted was to keep you isolated. Their training facility is what people in another timeline might call a 'Potemkin village'—a façade with no real substance, where everyone plays a role for your benefit. And the object of all of that was to train you as an effective operative while making damned sure you never had the chance to compare what their society's really like to the one they described to you. Trust me, you wouldn't have liked the real one."

"Maybe not, but I'm not especially crazy about the Inkies, either," Carmichael retorted.

"I'd be surprised if you were." Esperanza shrugged. "The tension between Tawantinsuyu and the British Empire in your timeline makes that inevitable. That's one reason the Tenocha decided to recruit you.

"The texture—the . . . geography, if you will—of this transtemporal war is extraordinarily complex, Major. *Your* Tawantinsuyu is scarcely a force for good, although even in your timeline, that wasn't always true. The historical record reflects the viewpoint of the historian, you know, and I think if you considered the 'Inkies'" *actual* history up through, oh, the late eighteenth century, you might discover some significant differences from what everyone in your time 'knows' happened. That's when Tawantinsuyu . . . 'went off the rails,' is the expression I believe. And that, frankly, was the result of Tenochan meddling."

Carmichael frowned, and Esperanza shrugged again.

"The Tenocha refer to your timeline as belonging to the 'Tawantinsuyu Aberration.' That's because in *their* timeline the Inca Empire was destroyed in the sixteenth century. Instead of Tawantinsuyu, it was the *Aztec* Empire that put its stamp on North and South America, and the resulting civilization became a nightmare. I know the Tenocha have told you they're fighting for a future which maximizes human freedom, dignity, and opportunity, but they aren't. However unlikely it may seem in light of your own experience, that's what the *Tawantinsuyu* Directors are doing. And the reason the Tawantinsuyu Empire in your own timeline is a repressive authoritarianism is that the Tenocha succeeded in bringing about the failure of the American Revolution—what you call 'Washington's Rebellion.' "

"Wait a minute!" Carmichael shook his head hard. "Even assuming any of that nonsense about the *Inkies* being on the side of goodness and light is accurate, why the hell would the Tenocha recruit someone from a past they created in order to go back and create it in the first place? Are you trying to tell me everything they had to say about paradoxes was a lie, too?"

"No, it wasn't. For example, I can't tell you anything about the future of your own timeline—not a single thing that happens after the last moment you personally experienced there. Or, rather, I could tell you all sorts of things about it . . . except that by the very fact of telling you, I'd prevent that future history from ever becoming yours. It would still happen somewhere, in another universe, but it would never happen to the Dunstan Carmichael to whom I described it. It couldn't."

"So you're saying . . . what?" Carmichael realized he sounded plaintive.

"I'm sure the Tenocha have pointed out to you that 'historical inevitability' becomes 'inevitable' only after the fact. Having said that, I have to tell you that your own history represents a very low-probability outcome. Washington's Rebellion is—or *was*, depending on your viewpoint—far more likely to succeed than to fail. Which means the timelines and universes in which Washington won greatly outnumber those in which he lost. What they want to do is to create more in which he *didn't* win.

"The reason the Tenocha recruited you and your team was that you come from one of the timelines in which he failed. That naturally predisposes you to assist in making sure the Rebellion doesn't succeed elsewhen, whereas someone from one of the majority timelines would have the opposite inclination. In a sense, that offers a sort of microcosm of how the entire war's being fought. Your timeline provides a natural source of recruits who can be used in *other* timelines to promote the Tenocha's ultimate objectives. Recruits who, because of their own history, will naturally see the failure of the Rebellion as a good thing."

He paused, and Carmichael frowned. It all *sounded* reasonable enough . . . but so had the Tenochan version.

"So why would it be a good thing for the Rebellion to succeed, instead?" he challenged. "I'm not saying the Empire's perfect, because God knows we aren't. But we've done one hell of a lot more good in the world than the Inkies or the Nips or the Russians!"

"Yes, you have. But your present Empire is the result of a history in which the United States of America was aborted. And because the American Revolution failed, France didn't collapse economically after becoming embroiled in a fresh war with Great Britain as an American ally, so something called the French Revolution never happened, either. Instead, you got the *Spanish* Revolution and the Terrazan Wars. Which led to an even more destructive collapse of Spain's New World empire and a completely different complex of tensions *within* the Tawantinsuyu Empire, as well as with its neighbors. While Tawantinsuyu ultimately becomes a force for human greatness in the majority of possible futures, it also contains the seeds of its own destruction. Its tendency to authoritarianism, the degree of deference to *the* Inca, its rigid focus on conformation to a single acceptable, tightly defined societal norm and caste-oriented roles . . . All of those need to be offset by a much . . . messier philosophy which emphasizes individual *freedom*, the right—indeed, the societal value—of an individual to seek his own destiny even at the cost of society's *corporate* efficiency. And to achieve its true potential, Tawantinsuyu needs to be challenged by a neighbor—a rival—with that type of society. Someone with whom they may not always agree, someone they may not always even *like* very much, but someone with whom they will ultimately find a common interest in . . . cultural cross-pollination.

"And, by the same token, the United States which never existed in your own timeline can also become either a power for good or a power for evil. Tawantinsuyu doesn't absolutely *need* the United States in order to achieve its potential, and the United States doesn't absolutely *need* Tawantinsuyu to achieve *its* potential, but both of them are far more likely to achieve their joint potentials when they have each other as a challenge, mirror, and check upon overweening ambition."

Carmichael sat back, thinking hard.

"So why tell me all this?" he asked finally. "Why not simply help the Inkies? Assuming, of course, that the particular batch of Inkies on the other side of this particular Rebellion are from one of the universes of which you approve." He grimaced. "God, I can't believe I just said that!"

"It does get complicated, doesn't it?" Esperanza smiled.

"Damn straight it does," Carmichael said feelingly. "And I'm still waiting for an answer."

"Well, I already admitted the Tenocha have at least some point about avoiding temporal contamination." Esperanza shrugged. "And there's a lot less chance of inadvertently creating a paradox working with someone native to neither your own timeline nor the one in which you're operating. It's always just a *bit* inconvenient when you suddenly blink out of existence in the middle of an operation." He grimaced. "That's the real reason the Tawantinsuyu Directors first started recruiting agents from other timelines rather than run their own operations directly, and it gave them a sufficient advantage the Tenocha decided they had to acquire the same edge, even if they had to lie to their new agents to do it."

"You keep talking about the 'Tawantinsuyu Directors,' " Carmichael said slowly. "And I don't see any sign of you 'blinking out' despite all the information you're busy dropping on me, which means—assuming you're telling me the truth—that it's not producing any paradoxes for you to talk to me about *both* the Inkies and the Tenocha. Which means . . . which means *you're* the Rogue Directors the General was talking about!"

"More or less." Esperanza's smile turned crooked. "It's more than a bit of an oversimplification, though. For that matter, I'm only one of several Esperanzas working the problem. Most of me—probably all of me—started from the same initial decision point several centuries from now, but by this point in my personal life experience there's probably a huge cascade of me in various other timelines and histories. I've actually met me a couple of times, in fact, although I really don't have any idea how many of me—us?—there actually are. Or will be. Or for that matter, *were*." He frowned reflectively. "I imagine quite a few of me have managed to get ourselves killed by now, after all. Don't have any idea how many, though."

"Gaaaah." Carmichael's eyes tried to cross. In many ways, he would have preferred the General's description of the Rogue Directors to what Esperanza was saying. In fact, trying to think about *Esperanza's* version made his brain hurt.

"Wait a minute," he said. "I'm not ready to go there yet—not until I've had a *lot* longer to think about it. But from what you're saying, you—or 'this' you, at least—were, what, monitoring my timeline for Tenochan recruiters?"

"That's pretty much accurate."

"And when they looked like recruiting *me*, you slipped me the goggles?"

"Yes."

"So, what exactly do the damned things do, and how?"

"I don't know," Esperanza said simply.

"What!"

Carmichael glared at the other man, and Esperanza chuckled.

"I can't go into my own future and ask those questions. I can share 'future information' with you because you're not 'upstream' from my own personal history. And in theory, at least, someone could have a similar discussion with *me* under the same circumstances. So far no one's seen fit to do anything of the sort, however. So although I have a fairly good notion of *what* the goggles do, my grasp of *how* they do it is no better than, say, *your* grasp of how to generate an achronic field."

"So where did they come from in the *first* damned place?"

"The *future*, of course." Esperanza shrugged. "Interestingly enough, as far as we—in this case, the people you've referred to as the Rogue Directors, not just however many Esperanzas may be running about—are aware, only a single pair was ever actually made."

"I'm beginning to think the only thing that should really worry me would be discovering that I understand a single damned thing you're saying," Carmichael said tartly.

"I've thought that a time or two myself." This time, Esperanza's tone was frankly sympathetic, and he shook his head. "As I say, we don't know where they came from, but as nearly as we've been able to determine, the goggles' introduction into the past is what created the Tenocha in the first place. Given the multiplicity of timelines, we can't be absolutely certain, but it seems the appearance of a single pair of goggles led to the creation of the original Aztec Empire in a single timeline. Once Europe impinged upon the New World, however, that timeline split into a huge number of subsidiary timelines. In several of them the Aztecs disappeared into the dustbin of history; in most, they became the Tenocha who recruited you, instead. But in every single one of those subsidiary timelines, there was—at least initially—a pair of goggles. Usually concealed inside the golden mask I'm sure 'the General' told you about. That means there are quite a lot of them now, but all of them are really only different iterations of the same pair."

"That's . . . crazy," Carmichael said.

"Of course it is!" Esperanza snorted. "If it were easy, this war would have been over a long time ago, Major!"

"But if the Tenocha only came into existence because they or their ancestors had the goggles, and if the goggles provide the kind of advantage the General suggested, why haven't they used them to kick everyone else's ass?"

"Three reasons, really," Esperanza said promptly. "Well, probably more than three, but three that come most immediately to mind.

"First, they work only for a single individual at a time, and because they work only for the single individual using them, *group* objectives can be accomplished only in so much as they're also *personal* objectives.

"Which, of course, leads to the second factor: human nature. The goggles are very, very powerful, Major. They can help someone accomplish virtually *anything* he truly, deeply desires. Think about that. *Any* ambition. Human nature being what it is, most people succumb to the temptation to use the goggles for their own purposes, and Tenocha being Tenocha, *their* purposes tend to be personal power. And given the nasty sorts of games they play, giving most Tenocha something like this would be rather like giving a twelve-year-old—a poorly *socialized* twelve-year-old—a grenade launcher.

"Even Tenocha are smart enough to recognize the downside of *that* situation! None of them are about to trust any of their fellows with them; no one who actually has a pair would ever admit it to anyone else; and even someone who does have a pair eventually dies. At which point the goggles either find themselves with a new owner or end up lost because their old owner hid them so well no one else can find them. If neither of those things happens, it's usually because they've fallen into official hands, at which point they're placed under extraordinarily strict controls intended to prevent any individual from using them. Certainly no Tenochan authority 's going to trust one of its agents to take them into the field! And, to be honest, the Tawantinsuyu feel pretty much the same way."

Esperanza raised both hands in a there-you-have-it sort of gesture.

"And?" Carmichael prompted after a moment.

"And what?"

"You said there were three reasons the Tenocha don't use them."

"Oh, yes, I did." Esperanza smiled. "Well, you see, the *third* reason is me. I've been sort of . . . collecting them. Partly to keep them out of Tenochan hands, of course. But mostly to use them *against* the Tenocha."

"I thought you just finished saying they're so dangerous not even the Tawantinsuyu trust people with them," Carmichael said slowly. "Wouldn't that apply to *you*, too?"

"What I actually said, Major, is that *most* people eventually succumb to personal ambition. Not everyone does."

"And you, of course, possess sufficiently absolute selflessness and willpower to be immune to that temptation," Carmichael said ironically.

"Not really." Esperanza shook his head cheerfully. "I like to think it might take me a little longer to succumb than some, but I don't really think I'd make the best keeper in the long run. On the other hand, I never said *I* intended to use them, now did I?

.VI.

I feel like a character in a really bad martial-arts movie, Carmichael reflected as Esperanza's flyer headed back for 1776 Pennsylvania. *Me and my mysterious, inscrutable mentor and his obscure pronouncements. Oh, and let's not forget the "mystic weapon" he's provided!*

Not that he really saw Esperanza in that light . . . yet, at least. And he still wasn't *totally* convinced the goggles weren't manipulating his mind. But after two months in Esperanza's company, he was *almost* convinced the Rogue Directors agent had leveled with him, and that was more than he could say about the Tenocha.

Now, at least.

His mouth tightened. Esperanza might have been afraid he'd reject stories of Tenochan depravity as propaganda, but Carmichael had insisted on being shown the truth. Not secondhand stories, not video footage that could be fabricated: the *truth*. And so, genegineered temporarily into a typical Tenocha by Esperanza's technology, he'd finally visited those pyramids and public buildings he'd seen shining jewel-like from his Tenochtitlan window. For the first time, he'd seen them close up, at first hand . . . and discovered that the true heart of Tenochan civilization was beauty, cut flowers, blood, agony, and cruelty.

No wonder they hadn't wanted his team members to mingle with the people who'd recruited them. "Temporal contamination" made a marvelous excuse, but the truth of human sacrifice, cannibalism, slavery, and "sporting events" that would have done Nero proud was the real reason.

And what would they have done if you'd ever found out anyway? he asked himself now. *You're useful to them, yes. Now, at least. But if you'd discovered the truth, you'd have had to go, wouldn't you? And what about Kate? Did they ever really intend to help her at all? And even if they did, what would happen to her if they decided you might have become a threat?*

Carmichael shook himself up out of his thoughts as the flyer went into a silent hover with sleet and snow whispering against the canopy.

You may not fully trust Esperanza, but you do believe him . . . about the Tenocha, at least. Of course, if one set of Directors can lie to you about the virtue of its objectives, there's no reason another set couldn't do the same thing. Which puts you in an interesting quandary, doesn't it?

"Ready?" Esperanza asked quietly.

"Yes."

Carmichael glanced at his left leg. His uniform had been repaired down to the microscopic level, the blood, which had soaked it, had been thoroughly removed, and Esperanza's nanotech had reversed the genegineering that had made him a temporary Tenocha. Even his hair length was precisely what it had been at the moment Esperanza retrieved him. The only real difference between then now—aside from the fact that his mangled leg was no longer leaking blood—was that his radio worked.

"According to my instruments, the nearest Tawantinsuyu operative's over eight miles southeast," Esperanza said. "I'm not picking up any of their flyers, either. You should be clear."

Carmichael nodded, although he really hadn't needed the reassurance.

He'd spent quite a bit of his two months trying to master the goggles' use. As Esperanza had said, they responded to individuals, not groups. To personal desires and ambitions. And he'd also discovered that the *quality* of their response seemed to depend in large part on the clarity with which he could formulate his desires. His previous visions had been . . . obscure in large part because he hadn't really known what he wanted—or feared. The greater clarity of his pre-Trenton vision, and the fact that there'd been only *one* of it, rather than the multiplicity he'd seen the night Jefferson recruited him, had stemmed from the fact that his desire had been very simple and clear: to survive.

But getting full utility out of them required more direction . . . which, conversely, threw its own grit into the gears. In order to give them that direction, he had to figure out what he wanted with much greater clarity, and the more complexity he introduced into his planning, the greater the number of possible paths to his goals the goggles insisted on showing him.

And not being certain he could truly trust even Esperanza's motives didn't help.

Getting back on the ground and reestablishing communications with Shamrock was a blessedly simple proposition, however, and the goggles had shown him exactly where Esperanza needed to drop him.

Of course, they hadn't shown him what would happen to Esperanza on his way out if he happened to run afoul of one of the Inkies who'd shot down Bullock. On the other hand, he seemed capable of looking after himself.

"Good luck," Esperanza said now, opening the hatch, and Carmichael stepped out into several hundred feet of cold, empty air and the waiting grasp of the tractor beam.

A pronounced chill filled the room despite Champlain Base's carefully maintained internal temperature.

Carmichael reminded himself that barely twelve hours had passed for the rest of his team. The others were still grappling with their first op's disastrous outcome . . . and with the fact that Bullock wouldn't be coming home again. At least the Inkies seemed to have done a decent job of policing up the wreckage from the air battle, but all of them had been surprised by the strength and openness of the other side's actions.

The team's other surviving members—and especially Shamrock
—were obviously confused by the *nature* of those actions, as well.
They'd expected the Inkies to be forced to intervene to get Washington across the river. Without the knowledge Carmichael had
acquired, they had no way of knowing the Tawantinsuyu Directors
had anticipated the crossing would *succeed* in the absence of *Tenochan* interference. Looked at from that perspective, the strength
and nature of the forces they'd deployed made a lot of sense. Not
that he was in any position to go raising that point.

Now those survivors sat watching the flatscreen as a grim-faced
Jefferson looked out of it at them.

"Well, *that* didn't work out, did it?" he said without preamble.

"No, it didn't," Carmichael agreed, but there was no apology in
his tone and he held Jefferson's gaze levelly.

Jefferson frowned. The conference room was very still for a
few moments, but then the Tenochan agent grimaced and waved
one hand.

"We're still analyzing the satellite data," he said in a tone that
was much closer to normal. "We've had a few thoughts from this
end, but I'd like your impression of what went wrong, Major. From
your perspective."

"I think that's fairly simple," Carmichael replied. "First, the
Inkies were present in much greater strength than anticipated.
Second, they were prepared to operate far more openly than our
intelligence briefings had suggested. And, third, we were overconfident."

"I see."

Jefferson considered him without expression, and Carmichael
looked back impassively. They both knew his first two points were
indictments of the intelligence Jefferson and the main Tenochan
staff had provided, and the New Englander wondered how the
field agent was going to respond.

"Tell me about the overconfidence," Jefferson said after a
moment. "Whose was it and how could it have been avoided?"

"We were *all* overconfident," Carmichael said. "Even though all
of us—I mean those of us here in Champlain Base, as well as the
support staff—kept telling each other it was only the first skirmish,
I think most of us really figured deep down that it would be decisive. After all, it pretty much *was* decisive according to our own
history. What we forgot was one of the most basic principles you

taught us in training: nothing is inevitable until it's happened. We expected the . . . momentum to be on our side. We were just there to make sure things happened the way they were 'supposed to,' so we were unprepared when they started to work out *differently*."

And they'd certainly done *that*, Carmichael reflected. Neither Ewing nor Cadwallader had gotten across, after all, but the main body, with twenty-four hundred men and eighteen field pieces, had reached Trenton by eight o'clock without anyone in the garrison realizing they were coming.

Major General John Sullivan had moved down River Road, swinging around south of the town into the position Ewing had been supposed to occupy, cutting off any retreat in that direction. Meanwhile, Washington and Nathaniel Greene had marched north from Beatty's Ferry to Pennington Road then east, moving between the garrison and Princeton. And then the Rebels had hit Rall's sleepy, unprepared men from both directions at once, almost simultaneously.

Roused with some difficulty by his subordinates, Major Rall had headed straight into the streets to rally his men . . . and encountered a rebel bullet. The combination of surprise, American numbers (the Hessians were outnumbered by almost sixty percent), and the loss of their commanding officer had turned the battle, which never occurred in Carmichael's history, into a rout. A hundred and five of Rall's fifteen hundred men had been killed or wounded and another nine hundred captured . . . against total rebel losses of only *two* men, both of whom had died during the brutal four-hour march from the river to Trenton. *None* of Washington's men had been killed in the actual engagement. And to add insult to injury, he was already back across the river, taking his boats with him, which neatly denied Cornwallis any chance to follow him up and avenge the Hessian defeat.

With barely four thousand men on both sides, it hadn't been much of a battle, by most standards. But Carmichael had glimpsed the history of a rebellion that had come out rather differently; he knew how important Washington's victory had proven to that other history.

And so does Jefferson, whether he's going to share that with the rest of us or not, he reflected grimly, then shrugged slightly.

"In some ways," he said, "this may actually turn out to be a *good* thing—aside from losing Bullock, at least."

"Really?" Jefferson snorted. "I'd be fascinated to hear the logic behind that conclusion, Major!"

"It's going to help all of us remember we aren't simply going through the motions of our own history. That this is a *new* timeline, where things can work out differently. The *Inkies* are going to remember that, and we need to take this as a wake-up call. Use it to remind us to be more flexible, because this really *was* only the first skirmish . . . and neither side's giving up until we get all the way to the end."

One of Jefferson's eyebrows arched. Then, slowly, he began to nod.

"You're absolutely correct, Major." The Tenocha's voice was much warmer. "And I think your analysis is essentially correct as well. For that matter"—he smiled thinly—"you're also correct—by implication, at least—that we suffered a major intelligence failure before we even sent you out into the field. I'll do my best to see that that doesn't happen again."

"Thank you." Carmichael put an edge of quiet sincerity into his tone.

"Obviously, it'll take a while to see how the consequences play out," Jefferson continued, "but I doubt anything significant's going to happen before spring . . . unless we're lucky enough to have the rebels disintegrate over the winter. Which, unfortunately, is much less likely now that their morale's been strengthened."

"Agreed," Carmichael said with a nod.

"At the same time," Jefferson went on thoughtfully, "the other side's come out of this very well. No doubt they'll want to press their advantage."

"I've been thinking the same thing," Carmichael said, "and it's occurred to me that it might not be a bad idea to try to draw *them* into a bit of overconfidence, if we can."

"How?"

"I think we should lie low," Carmichael replied. "Convince them we're licking our wounds—adopting a defensive stance because we're afraid to run into them head-on again."

"As long as we're actually *doing* something while we lie low," Jefferson said slowly, and Carmichael smiled.

"Well, according to our own history, Trenton was only the beginning of the end for the rebellion. What *finished* it was Burgoyne's Hudson Valley campaign. Under the circumstances, it's even more important to make sure that succeeds, and my thought is that instead of simply concentrating on what the Inkies might do to screw up his invasion, we concentrate on what *we* can do to keep the rebels from *stopping* him. Let the Inkies have a free run in Pennsylvania and New Jersey while we quietly establish conduits into both the Rebels' and Burgoyne's forces and look for ways we can . . . complicate the rebels' lives. If we do it right, we can force the Inkies into intervening openly if they want to stop Burgoyne, and then it'll be *our* turn to cut *them* off at the ankles."

.VII.

Dunstan Carmichael managed not to grimace.

It took some effort. Eighteenth-century American beer ranged from excellent to execrable, and his current mug fell toward the lower end of the scale.

Still, it was better than the local whiskey, and beer went better with his current persona. And taverns were where people tended to discuss current events, which was why he was here in the little village of Skenesboro at the southern end of Lake Champlain.

It was June of 1777, and things were getting . . . interesting.

General John Burgoyne had assembled more than eight thousand men at the other end of the lake, and everyone knew he was going to head south shortly, bound for Albany by way of the Hudson Valley. In Carmichael's history, the ensuing campaign hadn't exactly covered British arms in glory. In fact, Burgoyne had courted catastrophe more than once. But in the end, with help from General Howe, he'd captured Albany and succeeded in splitting the colonies in half. Coupled with the Continental Army's virtual collapse farther south, that had finally convinced the rebels to throw in the towel. Their submission had been sullen, grudging, and probably, in their own eyes, temporary, but London had learned finally from near disaster. Pitt the Younger had adopted a conciliatory policy, and his key reform—offering the colonial assemblies direct Parliamentary representation—had been extended to other imperial possessions, which explained a great deal about the British Empire's subsequent strength and durability.

Washington's Trenton victory meant things had happened a bit differently in this iteration, and one of those differences was the huge change in General Horatio Gates's fortunes. Gates, who'd once been Washington's adjutant, had always thought *he* should have been the Continental Army's commander. After all, unlike Washington, Gates had risen to the rank of major before selling his royal army commission and emigrating to the Shenandoah Valley in 1769. His administrative skills had been vital in the army's original organization, as well, and several influential delegates to the Continental Congress had agreed with him that he would have made a better commander than Washington.

The two men certainly offered a contrast in command styles. Gates was cautious by nature, and the thought of facing European regulars in open battle didn't appeal to him. Nor was he overly blessed with personal courage, in Carmichael's opinion. He'd opposed the Trenton attack, urging Washington to continue retreating instead, and although his troops participated in the attack, Gates himself was mysteriously "ill" the night Washington crossed the Delaware, which hadn't exactly earned him his commander's confidence. In Carmichael's history, however, that had actually helped him when the attempt ended in disaster, and he'd been named to replace Washington, who had retired into obscurity until his date with the executioner in 1779.

Predictably, Gates had conducted himself cautiously, leaving General Howe free to move out of New York and capture Philadelphia in February 1777. But in *this* history, Washington had followed up his victory at Trenton by repeating the process at Princeton in early January, which had further raised American morale, before settling into winter quarters. As a consequence, not only had he retained his command, but his troop strength was greater than anything Gates had enjoyed during the same period. So, instead of capturing Philadelphia that winter, General Howe was still sitting in New York City the following spring, and that had led to a certain confusion in the Crown's strategy for 1777.

Howe's attention remained fixed on Philadelphia. He firmly believed that seizing the rebels' capital would bring out the large loyalist element he was certain existed, and he was determined to prove his point. Lord George Germaine—the American Secretary in London—was aware of that; what he *wasn't* aware of was that Howe had decided to move his troops by sea to the Chesapeake, then up the Delaware, rather than march to Philadelphia overland. Thus, when Burgoyne had suggested that he himself drive down the Hudson and that Colonel Barry St. Leger lead another thrust down the Mohawk River to link up with him where the rivers joined near Albany, Germain had thought it was a wonderful idea. After all, a glance at a map showed Cumberland Head was barely two hundred and thirty miles from Albany—less than the distance from London to Manchester. Admittedly, it was two hundred and thirty miles of howling wilderness, but Lake Champlain and Lake George offered a watery highway all the way to Fort George, a hundred and thirty miles to the south. Since troops and supplies could travel that far by *water*, who cared about the terrain ashore? Even better, General Howe's forces, operating out of New York toward Philadelphia, were bound to draw American troop strength away from Burgoyne's advance. And if that advance prospered, and if Howe turned north to meet Burgoyne at Albany . . .

Unless, of course, General Howe was occupied elsewhere.

Still, Burgoyne's plan had several things going for it. One was the caliber of his subordinate commanders, including General Simon Fraser and Baron Friedrich von Riedesel, both of whom had gone on to distinguished careers after the Rebellion. Another was the confidence of his troops. And yet another, of which he was unaware, was the state of the command arrangements in the rebels' Northern Department.

General Philip Schuyler held that command, but he was scarcely popular with his men, many of whom blamed him for the failure of the rebels' invasion of Canada. He was also a Dutch patroon—a proud man who distrusted "Yankee egalitarianism." His New England troops returned his distrust with interest and resented his aristocratic bearing to boot.

Schuyler's problems were compounded by none other than Horatio Gates, who'd ended up Schuyler's second-in-command . . . and, of course, promptly begun conniving with his friends in Congress. During the winter, Gates had succeeded in having himself named commander in Schuyler's place, but Schuyler had influence of his own, and in May he'd been restored to command. Unfortunately, Gates was once again his *second*-in-command . . . and Schuyler knew perfectly well that he—and his Congressional patrons—were far from reconciled to that, none of which did anything for his command's cohesiveness.

With the crisis point approaching rapidly, Carmichael's team had been spending most of its time in the field, and its male members had all established solid local identities: Fisherman as one of the four hundred Iroquois recruited to serve Burgoyne as irregulars, Frenchy as a French loyalist scout, and Carmichael as a traveling tinker specializing in small repairs to household utensils in towns like Skenesboro.

The little village, founded in 1759 by Captain Phillip Skene, had been captured by Ethan Allen on his way to Fort Ticonderoga in 1775. Later, the vessels—which had clashed on Lake Champlain at Valcour Island in 1776—had been built at Skenesboro, so the townsfolk were scarcely unaware that they lived on the most direct invasion route from Canada. That made Skenesboro a good place to pick up local rumors and news.

That was one of the reasons Carmichael had advanced in his discussions with Jefferson for putting actual boots on the ground. Given what had happened at Trenton and Princeton, Carmichael had argued, their original models for predicting what was going to happen had become suspect, to say the least, which made it more important than ever to know exactly what the people living in the actual area of operations really thought. And if his team members could blend into the local population, any Inky operatives would probably be less inclined to shoot first and identify the bodies later. Besides, if they were going to influence events through anything besides a brute-force approach of their own, they needed access.

That was the second reason for building established identities for him, Fisherman, and Frenchy. The other two men were both inside Burgoyne's forces. Carmichael wasn't . . . but he *was* tapped into the *American* forces, since he was one of Schuyler's spies. His tinker's profession gave him an excuse to travel, and the Tenochan reconnaissance satellites gave him plenty of reliable information to establish his bona fides as a spy. Not that he wanted to make himself *too* valuable. He needed contact and access, but the last thing he wanted was to arouse the suspicion of any Tawantinsuyu operatives who might have been planted on Schuyler or Gates.

"I'm telling you," one of the locals was saying now, "it won't be much longer. Them Redcoats are a'going to come down the lakes just as sure as we're sitting here. Be lucky if them and their damned Indians don't burn the place to the ground!"

"Ah, you're always lookin' on th' dark side!" one of his neighbors retorted. "Didn't happen when Carleton come through."

"Yeah? Well, he headed *home* after Valcour Island," the first speaker pointed out. "Didn't like the thought of winterin' out here in the woods very much. But this other fella—this 'Gentleman Johnny,' they call him—he's got *other* plans. And the year's lots younger this time around, too."

"Reverend Hollis had a letter from his sister up to Québec," someone else put in. "Reverend says this Burgoyne's been talking mighty big. 'Cording to Mistress Letty, he's sayin' as how he's got 'thousands' of Indians workin' for him, and he's ready to turn 'em loose if we don't roll over and play dead!"

"Yeah, and he's got all them Hessians, too," the first man said, his face twisting. "From what I hear, he's real loud 'bout his 'Christian duty' to suppress us rebels an' all, but he don't give much of a damn 'bout how many farms get burned or how many families get butchered along the way!"

Carmichael sighed silently. John Burgoyne had been a successful dramatist in England; it was a pity he hadn't been able to leave the bad dialogue on the stage. Propaganda always tended to exaggerate things, but the truth was that the Skenesboro townsfolk were actually understating what he'd been stupid enough to say in a public proclamation. Including a delightful little sentence about the fate of "hardened enemies of Great Britain" that ended "The Messengers of Justice and Wrath await them in the field; and devastation, famine, and every concomitant horror that a reluctant but indispensable prosecution of military duty must occasion, will bar the way to their return." Adding the incendiary threat that "I have but to give stretch to the Indian forces under my direction, and they amount to thousands, to overtake the hardened enemies of Great Britain and America," he couldn't have come up with anything better calculated to harden resistance if he'd tried. Even Loyalists were infuriated by that!

Well, Carmichael thought, *he did the same stupid things in the history you know, Dunstan, and he still managed to pull it off there. Maybe he can do it here, too.*

Maybe.

.VIII.

"Well, at least they *started* more or less on schedule," Jefferson observed sourly.

Carmichael stood in the Champlain Base conference room. Jefferson was in the main Tenochan HQ in Alberta, but both of them were looking at displays that showed the same information. On June the twentieth, Burgoyne had finally begun his invasion, sailing from Cumberland Head to Crown Point, eight miles north of Fort Ticonderoga.

The old French fort had been in American hands since the first year of the war. The works had been denuded of much of their heavy artillery for the siege of Boston, yet the belief persisted, especially among people who'd never seen the place, that Ticonderoga was "impregnable." In fact, however, it was dominated by high ground, especially Mount Defiance. Defiance lay about a mile to the south-southwest, across the rapid-filled La Chute River connecting Champlain and Lake George, and although Ticonderoga's defenses had been improved since 1775, it remained outside them. Unlike some people, Arthur St. Clair, Ticonderoga's newest commander, recognized his position's weaknesses. Unfortunately, with only two thousand men, he'd been unable to do anything about them, and once Burgoyne managed to get artillery to Mount Defiance's unguarded summit, which took several days, St. Clair had no option but to abandon the fort.

He'd done that on July fifth, beginning a precipitous retreat before the vastly superior invasion force. Two days later, General Fraser, with a column of eight hundred and fifty men, had caught up with St. Clair's rearguard under Colonel Seth Warner, sparking a vicious three-hour fight. Fraser had been getting the worse of it, but Baron von Riedesel had turned up in time to drive Warner back into retreat. Meanwhile, Burgoyne had sailed down the lake to Skenesboro, where he'd almost caught the boats carrying Ticonderoga's sick and wounded. His troops took Fort Anne, but they were unable to catch up with St. Clair, who reached Fort Edward on the Hudson River—with his sick and wounded—on the twelfth.

Meanwhile, Saint Legere's offensive had kicked off on schedule from Lake Ontario and headed for Fort Stanwix on the Mohawk. All things considered, things had gone very much as planned so far, and possession of Ticonderoga gave Burgoyne control of the critical three-and-a-half-mile-wide neck of land between Lake Champlain and Lake George. Hauling supplies overland through dense forest slashed by ravines, rivers, and streams would be a nightmare, but transporting those same supplies by water was a very different matter. That, after all, had been the basic underlying logic behind his entire campaign.

Which made his present inactivity all the more puzzling.

"What the hell is he waiting for?" Jefferson growled now, irritably.

"We're trying to find out," Carmichael replied. "According to his own original planning, he should already be sailing down Lake George."

"Tawantinsuyu, do you think?" Jefferson frowned, obviously unhappy with the possibility he'd just raised. "Has Fisherman or Frenchy seen any sign of tampering in Burgoyne's decisions?"

"Neither one of them's part of Burgoyne's inner circle," Carmichael pointed out. "They're watching for exactly that, but whether or not they'd catch the Inkies at it is problematical, at best."

Jefferson growled under his breath, and Carmichael shrugged.

"I'm heading back out this afternoon myself. I want to check in with Schuyler—I've got enough info from the satellites to tell him where St. Legere is, which ought to make me welcome. At the same time, I'll try to get a feel for what *his* plans are. After that, I'll fly up to Skenesboro, hide the flyer underwater, and sneak in to make contact with our boys. Hopefully they'll be able to give me at least some better idea of what Burgoyne's up to before I carry out my little . . . midnight requisition."

"Good." Jefferson glowered at his HQ display for several more seconds, then looked back out of the conference room flatscreen and made himself smile, albeit a bit sourly. "I know I'm being a pain in the ass," he said. "It's just that this started off so well, despite that business in New Jersey last winter. I don't want to see anything go wrong at this late date—especially with Howe screwing around at Philadelphia."

"No, sir," Carmichael agreed. "Neither do I."

That evening, Dunstan Carmichael sat swatting mosquitoes while he waited at a prearranged rendezvous point outside Schuyler's camp.

After moment, he reached into his tinker's backpack, extracted a peculiar looking pair of goggles, and weighed them in his hand, considering the visions they'd shown him over the past months. His lengthy periods in the field had given him lots of time away from base to work with them unobserved, and he'd found he could change what they showed him by reframing a problem. If he imagined himself approaching it in a specific way, or if he redefined its parameters, the goggles presented different menus of probabilities. He wasn't anything he'd call proficient at directing them even now, but he did appear to be gradually mastering the technique.

Despite which, he still didn't understand everything they showed him. He'd used their visions to put his own strategy in place, yet now that the decisive moment had arrived, he found he still had more than a few nervous butterflies about fully trusting them. So much of what he'd decided was based on those visions —the projected consequences of actions or inactions and what those consequences would mean for innocent bystanders. What if they were lying to him? What if the Rogue Directors were just as manipulative, dishonest, and deceitful as the General claimed? What if he really had been . . . brainwashed by the goggles? If his decisions and his actions were no longer truly his? If—?

Sometimes you just have to pay your shilling and take your chance, he told himself grimly. *I know it goes against the grain to do anything to help the Inkies*—any Inkies!—*but you saw what those bastards in Tenochtitlan were really up to. Whatever else the Tenocha may be doing, they're sure as* hell *lying about being on the side of the angels! And, no, that* doesn't *necessarily mean the Tawantinsuyu* are, *but, damn it . . .*

He made himself draw a deep, steadying breath, then admitted the truth. Whatever the Tawantinsuyu were truly like, he'd take his chances with them instead of the Tenocha. Worrying about *that* choice didn't really terrify him. Nor did the thought that he might be being manipulated by Esperanza or the goggles. Not anymore. No, that was left for something else. That was left for Kate.

The Tenocha assured him she would fully recover, that her treatment was already well underway, yet all the proof of that he had was their word. What if they were lying? Worse, if they decided he'd betrayed them, what would they do to *Kate*? He was willing to take his chances for himself, even after what he'd seen in Tenochtitlan. A man didn't go into special operations if he wasn't prepared for that. But Kate? Did he have the right to risk the restored life *she* might have had? And did he want to risk surviving in a universe where she'd *lost* that because of his actions?

For that matter, what about the rest of his team? If the Tenocha decided he'd turned against them, would they decide the others must have done the same? And if they decided that, what would happen to the *others*' "hostages to fortune"?

So—

"Sorry I'm running late," a voice said, and Esperanza stepped out of thin air in front of him. "Our stealth's a lot better than theirs, but for some reason there seem to be quite a few overflights—Tawantinsuyu and Tenocha, both—in the vicinity at the moment."

He smiled wryly, and Carmichael barked a laugh.

"Now, I wonder why that might be?" the major said dryly, and it was Esperanza's turn to chuckle. Then he sobered.

"Some of my superiors are getting a little concerned over how many balls I have in the air simultaneously," he observed.

"I was under the impression that *I'm* doing the juggling," Carmichael replied, and Esperanza shrugged.

"You are. But I'm the one selling this whole business to my own supervisors, and they are not privy to all the details."

"They aren't?" A hint of alarm edged Carmichael's voice, and Esperanza waved a reassuring hand.

"Let's just say there are a few . . . irregularities in the way I get things done. Overall, I'm successful enough not too many questions get asked, but that doesn't mean there isn't the occasional awkward moment."

"You cheeky bastard." Carmichael shook his head wonderingly. "You haven't even told your own superiors about the goggles, have you?"

"Well, no, if you're going to be picky," Esperanza said. "I do have my weak moments, though, so I'm sure *some* iterations of me have reported fully to their—our?—ultimate superiors. And technically, you know, my immediate supervisors aren't *really* my ultimate superiors, whether they know it or not. 'Rogue Directors,' remember?"

He smiled toothily.

"On the other hand, they do *think* they are, and they probably would be a bit . . . miffed if they were to figure out just how, um, *profligate* I've been with that particular item of equipment. After giving the matter due consideration, I'd really just as soon they don't find out."

His smile was even broader, and Carmichael shook his head.

"But if they don't know about these"—he waved the goggles under Esperanza's nose—"how do they think you keep producing the sort of results you apparently produce?"

"Mostly I've developed a reputation for identifying Tenocha operatives who can be turned. I'm not talking about corrupted people I can corrupt in turn, although there *have* been a few of those. No, what I do is monitor Tenochan recruiters in non-Tenochan timelines and research the people they're recruiting. Some of those recruits are about as vile as you could possibly imagine, but others aren't, so I look for the people they're lying to and tell them the truth. Which, when you come down to it, Major Carmichael, is exactly what I did with you."

Esperanza held Carmichael's eyes levelly for a moment, then shrugged.

"You're far from the first Tenochan agent I've recruited," he said quietly. "And I haven't recruited all of them by handing over the goggles, either. Every time I do that, I risk creating a monster at least as bad as anything the Tenocha might have produced, and I look very carefully at the characters of the people to whom I'm willing to risk giving that sort of power. But even men and women who don't have that advantage can recognize the right thing to do when they see it, and I've turned scores of Tenochan operations inside out that way. Which brings us back to you, doesn't it?"

"Yes, it does." Carmichael gazed back at him, tossing the goggles up into the air and catching them. "Have you made those arrangements?"

"I have . . . though you're going to have to take my word for it, of course." Esperanzas snorted. "This isn't the first time I've had to organize a temporal snatch-and-grab to pull out someone like your Kate or the others. That's at least one thing my supervisors have gotten accustomed to over the years. Trust me, she'll be waiting—they'll *all* be waiting—for you."

"Good." Carmichael inhaled deeply.

"In that case," he said, "I suppose we should get started."

"I'm afraid you may be right, Major," Frenchy said glumly. He and Carmichael sat on opposite sides of a campfire, gnawing on pieces of hardtack. Around them, beyond reach of their quiet voices, the thousands of men in General Burgoyne's encampment provided a surf of background sounds punctuated by occasional shouts, orders, or snatches of song.

"You are?" Carmichael asked calmly, thinking about visions of red-coated infantry struggling through dense forests, rebuilding bridge after burned-out bridge, clearing away trees felled to block their road.

He also made no mention of certain letters he and Esperanza had seen reached General Burgoyne. Some of those letters detailed the movements of other British forces, while others reported the severity of rebel raids on his supply lines. Then there were the ones which promised that vast numbers of loyalists were waiting eagerly to flock to his vanguard's standards. Most of those letters, aside from the promises of loyalist support, were even accurate, as far as they went. In fact, he'd delivered them with Jefferson's blessings as part of their plan to keep Burgoyne fully informed. Was it Carmichael's fault if the way they were phrased pushed the general's conclusions in a somewhat different direction than Jefferson expected?

"Well, it's not like I'm one of his generals." Frenchy snorted. "On the other hand, I do have a hell of a reputation as a scout, thanks to the recon birds." He shrugged. "Some of those generals talk to me, and the questions they ask tell me a lot about what they're thinking. I just find it difficult to believe any *working* brain would be thinking anything of the sort!"

He sounded disgusted, and Carmichael chuckled.

"Actually," he said, "there's at least some logic to it, and I think"—he didn't mention anything about goggles or letters or why he thought anything of the sort—"Burgoyne's probably already halfway to deciding."

"You're joking!"

"No, think about it," Carmichael replied. "He knows now that Howe decided to sail to Philadelphia. That means his entire striking force is bobbing around at sea—hundreds of miles from anywhere useful as far as Burgoyne's concerned—at the very moment they'd have to be marching north if they were going to do him any good. So aside from Clinton's remaining garrison in New York, he's on his own, and he knows it.

"He's also becoming aware he and his army aren't so very popular." Carmichael grimaced. "If he's going to maintain his logistics all the way down the lakes, he'll have to leave detachments to hold the important nodal points. And given the . . . enthusiastic way the locals are ambushing his foragers, they'll have to be fairly hefty forces. But every man he detaches to secure his communications is one less man with his striking force. And by the time he goes back to Ticonderoga and then sails down Lake George, Schuyler and his men will be waiting for him at Fort George. He'll have to fight his way ashore, and I think he's starting to feel the time pressure. All the men he's going to have are already with him, but the other side can still send in reinforcements, especially with Howe out of the picture, so the odds are only going to get worse unless he can smash up some of the opposition pretty damn soon. Don't think that doesn't play a part in his thinking."

"Okay, I can see that." Frenchy nodded. "But you've seen the terrain south of here. And so what if he has to take Fort George when he gets there? For Christ's sake, Major, the fort's only ten miles from the Hudson, and it's got a pretty decent damned road connecting it to the river!"

"I agree." Carmichael shrugged. "But the truth is that the decision's out of our hands."

Carmichael's flyer settled to earth once more, and he grinned. Despite everything, he was actually looking forward to the next little bit. There was something so . . . satisfying about it. It wasn't like the accurate but carefully selected intelligence he'd provided to Burgoyne. This was much more . . . direct. And unlike some of his other activities, Jefferson knew all about this one. He just hadn't known *everything* about it when he authorized it.

Carmichael chuckled at the thought as he sent the flyer back to hide among the clouds again. The night was darker than the inside of a pit, but although Dunstan Carmichael had grown up in a high-tech civilization, he'd also spent more time wandering around the woods in the dark than most of his fellows. The feeble glimmer of the inn's lights were plenty to give him his bearings, and he picked his way toward them.

For want of a nail a shoe was lost, for want of a shoe a horse was lost, for want of a horse a rider was lost . . .

His smile grew broader as he silently recited the childhood rhyme.

One of your better sleight-of-hand moments, Dunstan, he told himself. *Of course, without the goggles, you probably would have fallen for exactly the same argument, now wouldn't you? I mean, look at the man's record.*

He reached a small coppice near the inn and paused in its shadows.

According to the original Tenochan game plan, the Rebellion ought to be on its last legs by now, and General Gates, commanding the remnants of Washington's army far to the south, shouldn't have been able to send reinforcements to General Schuyler. In fact, Schuyler should have been so starved for manpower that even Burgoyne's more questionable decisions ought to have been survivable.

It had been obvious for some months, however, that that wasn't what was going to happen. Which was why Carmichael had argued that since they couldn't prevent the rebels from being reinforced, they ought to concentrate on weakening them internally. From that perspective, having Gates sent north was a good thing from the Tenochan point of view. The man could be relied upon to undermine Schuyler to the very best of his ability, and his lackluster record as Washington's successor in Carmichael's history suggested that having him supplant Schuyler ought to considerably ease Burgoyne's task.

At the moment, it seemed probable Gates *was* going to replace Schuyler. His partisans in Congress were already making noises about the loss of Ticonderoga and Schuyler's retreat before Burgoyne's advance. By Carmichael's official estimate, Schuyler had another two months; according to the goggles' visions, he had no more than another three or four weeks.

But if hamstringing Schuyler's command was worthwhile, then doing the same thing to *Gates* had to be worthwhile, as well. Which was what brought Carmichael to this particular inn on this particular night.

He made his cautious way toward the stable at the back of the inn, heading for a specific stall.

The horse in that stall belonged to a rebel officer whose career had been . . . checkered, at best. He'd begun by leading a desperate expedition from Cambridge, Massachusetts, to Québec City in September 1775. He'd started out with eleven hundred men, but by the time he reached Québec in November, two hundred of them had died en route, and three hundred more had turned back. Then he'd played a major role in assaulting the city—in atrocious weather in the middle of December—when the American force was actually outnumbered by the defenders and had no siege artillery. After that, he'd traveled to Montréal, where he'd served as the city's military commander until forced into ignominious retreat by British reinforcements in May. And after that, he'd overseen the building of the fleet at Skenesboro . . . and been soundly defeated at Valcour Island, leaving Sir Guy Carleton in command of Lake Champlain. Only the lateness of the year and the approach of winter had prevented Carleton from carrying out Burgoyne's present expedition a year earlier.

The man who'd lost at Québec and Valcour Island had made quite a few enemies in the army hierarchy and the Continental Congress, although if anyone looked closely, he'd always been popular with the men he commanded, despite the desperate circumstances he kept getting himself (and them) into. There'd been several courts-martial and investigations—most of them instigated by those enemies—and then he'd discovered he'd been passed over for promotion to major general by Congress.

He'd tried to resign at that point, but Washington had refused his resignation, and he'd ended up promoted to major general after all following his instrumental role in the defeat of a major British raid using a force of hastily organized militia. But Congress had refused to restore his seniority over those who'd been promoted before him. At which point, he'd written a formal letter of resignation.

He'd written that resignation on July the eleventh . . . the very day Philadelphia learned Fort Ticonderoga had fallen, and Washington, refusing his resignation yet again, had ordered him north instead.

In Carmichael's history, of course, it had been Gates who ordered him north to assist Schuyler, rather than Washington sending him north to assist *Gates*. Not that it mattered, since he'd never gotten there, thanks to an accident en route. His falling horse had rolled over on him, crushing and permanently crippling his left leg, which had ended his military career.

Not exactly the resume of a military asset, Carmichael had pointed out. On top of that, the man was fond of the bottle and had obvious issues with authority—not to mention a temper best described as "tempestuous," and "a history" with Gates, whom he cordially disliked. He was clearly an impetuous, undisciplined loose

cannon who could be counted upon to create even more divisive-
ness in the American command structure. And since he held major
general's rank, he would automatically become one of Gates' senior
officers, while his resentment over the seniority issue guaranteed
he would be driven by a desire to prove Congress had been wrong,
which seemed unlikely to produce coolly reasoned decisions on
the field of battle.

He might not make the rebels' situation any worse, but it was
unlikely he'd make it any *better*, and inserting him into the mix
wouldn't require anything exotic enough to attract Inky attention.
It had taken Jefferson all of five minutes to decide Carmichael had
a point, which explained his current mission. After all, the man's
horse couldn't very well break his leg if someone *stole* the horse
the night before the accident.

Sorry about that, he thought now to the horse's owner. *It's a
good horse, too. I don't imagine you're going to be very happy
when you find out it's gone. And it's not like I can leave you a note
explaining I stole it for your own good.* He chuckled. *I don't know
what they'll find you for a replacement, but, trust me, you'll be
better off with it whatever it is, General Arnold.*

.IX.

Dunstan Carmichael took one last look around his quarters and
patted his pockets reflexively. Paper crackled in his breast pocket,
and the rectangular lump in his hip pocket was hard and reassuring. He didn't pat the cargo pocket on his right thigh, and he felt
his lips twitch when he didn't.

*Superstition, Dunstan? Afraid somebody's watching even now?
Or maybe you're still a little more nervous about trusting them
than you're prepared to admit?*

He shrugged. It was too late for second thoughts, and so he
squared his shoulders, opened the door, and walked down the
hallway.

The others were waiting when he arrived. Frenchy, Fisherman,
and Shamrock sat in their regular seats, but Carmichael's normal
place wasn't available. His chair—the one in the horseshoe bend
where the team leader usually sat—was already occupied.

The Tenocha field agent who called himself Jefferson looked up
with a basilisk stare as Carmichael entered the room. No one had

mentioned any change in seating arrangements, and Carmichael felt an eyebrow quirk. The field agent's expression never even flickered, but he flipped one curt hand at an unoccupied seat, well away from the others.

Carmichael shrugged, then crossed to the indicated chair, sat, and folded his hands on the table with an expression of polite attentiveness.

Silence hovered.

This was the first time Jefferson had physically visited Champlain Base. The rest of the team didn't know the real reason for the rigid separation between Champlain and the local Tenochan HQ had nothing to do with "temporal contamination" or that it was really maintained to minimize contact which might have led them to realize what Carmichael had discovered courtesy of Esperanza and the goggles. Yet even for the others, Jefferson's presence, coupled with his expression and overcontrolled body language, confirmed he'd descended from Mount Olympus to smite the sinners.

Of course, he had other motives, as well. Such as covering his own posterior. From what Carmichael had seen in Tenochtitlan, the consequences of failure, Tenochan-style, were probably . . . unpleasant.

"Well," Jefferson said finally, his accent harsher than usual, "when you decide to fuck up, you don't screw around, do you, Major?"

The team's other members seemed to tighten internally, but the major only shrugged.

"I have to admit the outcome is . . . suboptimal in terms of our mission parameters," he said calmly. "On the other hand, sir, I don't think I can claim full responsibility for that."

"The hell you can't! You're the team leader, I believe?"

"Yes. But I'm not"—his eyes locked with Jefferson's—"the team *commander*. The General made that clear in our final briefing, and you've emphasized that same point to me more than once since, *sir*."

Jefferson's dark eyes glittered, but Carmichael refused to flinch. He simply sat there, gazing back at the furious Tenocha.

"This entire bitched-up debacle is the direct result of your operational recommendations!" the field agent snapped. "You proposed the strategy, *you* were responsible for executing it, and it sure as *hell* hasn't produced what it was supposed to produce!"

He glared at Carmichael, daring him to dispute that final sentence. Which, Carmichael admitted, he couldn't. Or, rather, he couldn't dispute that the operation's results bore very little resemblance to the ones he'd told Jefferson it was going to produce.

Fair enough, he thought coldly behind his calm expression. *One good lie deserves another, after all.*

Of course, as he'd just told Jefferson, he couldn't take total credit. In fact, the real trick had been convincing Jefferson he was carefully and covertly nudging things along—and, of course, keeping an eagle eye peeled for any Inky interference—while actually doing very little. Although, he was forced to concede, making certain Benedict Arnold arrived with unbroken legs *had* turned out quite well . . . from certain perspectives, at least.

Burgoyne had done much of the damage himself, when he had, indeed, decided to move overland to the Hudson rather than return to the lakes. His chosen route had lain along Wood Creek—a stream that twisted sinuously down a steep valley choked with enormous hemlocks and pines. The single primitive road had crossed the stream in no fewer than forty places, many of them deep ravines spanned by long wooden bridges.

General Schuyler, with only forty-five hundred men and plagued by desertions, had no intention of meeting Burgoyne head-on while he could let the terrain do his fighting for him. By the time Burgoyne's army set out, trees had been felled across the road, bridges had been burned, and boulders had been dumped into Wood Creek. No opportunity had been neglected while Schuyler retreated steadily and deliberately southward. By the third day of August, he'd reached the Hudson at Stillwater, twelve miles below Saratoga . . . and on the fourth, he'd been relieved in Horatio Gates's favor.

On the face of it, things had still been pretty much on course, as far as Jefferson knew. True, Burgoyne had taken three weeks to cover only thirty-five straight-line miles. But the unpopular Schuyler had seen his forces steadily dwindle during the same time period, then been relieved by Gates, whose "historical" record as a combat commander was dismal, at best.

Yet all had not been well under the surface. Burgoyne's men and draft animals were exhausted. Supplies of everything except ammunition were short. Worse, as anyone but an idiot or General John Burgoyne should have realized must happen, attaching so many Iroquois to the British force had proved disastrous. When two of them scalped Jane MacCrae, the twenty-five-year-old daughter of a clergyman who'd been engaged to a Loyalist, it provoked enormous outrage . . . and that was only one of several incidents. The nature of the long, bitter conflict between the colonists and the Six Nations had made that inevitable, and the locals' response had been predictable. Raids on Burgoyne's communications, ambushes of foraging parties, and general freelance harassment had skyrocketed.

Short of cavalry mounts, Burgoyne had dispatched a column under Colonel Friedrich Baum into the New Hampshire Grants to forage for horses and food. Unfortunately, Baum's eight hundred men had encountered two thousand New Hampshire militia under General John Stark near Bennington, Vermont. Stark, who'd distinguished himself at Bunker Hill, wiped out Baum's column, then killed or captured a quarter of the six hundred men Burgoyne had belatedly sent to reinforce him. All told, that fiasco had cost Burgoyne a thousand men, and two weeks later, he'd learned Colonel Saint Legere had been turned back at Fort Stanwix . . . largely as the result of a ruse by one Major General Benedict Arnold, dispatched by Schuyler to deal with the Mohawk River drive.

Burgoyne was in trouble, although his plight remained far from desperate. He still outnumbered the defenders, now under Gates's command, and he had a month's rations and plenty of ammunition. But neither Howe nor St. Legere were coming, time was passing, and winter was coming on. His choices were to retreat on Ticonderoga or continue his drive to Albany . . . and pulling back would have been an admission of defeat.

He could have marched to Albany unopposed on the Hudson's east side, but the river was far broader there. It would have been difficult to cross at that point, so he'd decided to advance down the *west* bank and thrown a pontoon bridge across to Saratoga on September thirteenth. Two days later, he had his entire army safely across.

Meanwhile, American reinforcements had arrived steadily. Gates was more popular with his men than Schuyler had been—he could scarcely have been *less*—and the change in command, stories of Indian atrocities, and the morale lift of the Battle of Bennington both brought in more volunteers and hardened his troops' determination. His forces had grown to around seven thousand men, Arnold had returned from Fort Stanwix, and he'd decided, on Arnold's advice, to fortify Bemis Heights, ten miles downstream from Saratoga. The river flowed through a gorge between steep bluffs there, and he'd assigned the fortifications' construction to Arnold and Colonel Thaddeus Kosciuszko, one of the Continental Army's better engineers.

Arnold might have had a problem with authority. He might have disliked Horatio Gates, and he might have been both overly impetuous and prickly about seniority and perceived slights. There might even have been some truth to the rumors that he liked the bottle. But he also had an enormous store of energy, and he seemed to be one of those men who came fully to life only in battle.

General Burgoyne's army discovered that on the nineteenth.

Gates had assigned the more exposed American left to Arnold, while he himself commanded the right. Arnold knew his position could be flanked by someone willing to swing even farther from the river, and he wanted to advance from his fortifications in order to meet that attempt where he could best take advantage of his frontiersmen's woodcraft. Gates, predictably, preferred to sit and await the enemy, but Arnold was persistent. In fact, he was *maddeningly* persistent, and in the end, Gates allowed him to send forward Daniel Morgan's light infantry, which ran into Burgoyne's right-hand column under Simon Fraser at John Freeman's farm at midday.

The savage, confused struggle lasted until evening, with the momentum shifting back and forth again and again. The center of the British line was very nearly broken at one point, but the day was saved for Burgoyne by Riedesel, who coolly took the calculated risk of leaving only five hundred men to protect the vital supply train and marched all the rest of his men straight into battle. What had been on the edge of an American victory turned into a withdrawal, which left Burgoyne in possession of the battlefield . . . at the cost of another six hundred casualties.

Arnold, who'd pled repeatedly with Gates to reinforce his forward troops, believed he could have completely destroyed the enemy that day. He might well have been right, and whether he was or not, Gates's refusal to commit the additional men did nothing to improve their relationship.

Both sides paused to lick their wounds, but Burgoyne's food was growing short and his enemies' fortified position prevented any advance down the river.

Yet all was not serene for the Americans, either. Arnold, already angry over Gates's refusal to reinforce him, had discovered that Gates's dispatches to Congress had claimed credit for the battle . . . and somehow failed to mention the name Benedict Arnold even once. Gates's own officers and men, on the other hand, universally credited Arnold with the victory, and it was indisputably Arnold who'd directed the battle. When he confronted Gates over the dispatch, their mutual, festering resentment broke out into an open shouting match, which ended with Gates relieving Arnold of command.

Meanwhile, Burgoyne's position steadily worsened even as more and more men arrived to swell Gates's command. By early October, he had over twelve thousand men while Burgoyne was down to under seven thousand, only five thousand of whom were fit for combat. Food was running out, morale was sagging, and Riedesel advised him to cut his losses and retreat, but Burgoyne decided to make one more attempt to break through the American position.

When scouts brought news of Burgoyne's movement, Gates used Morgan's riflemen to cover the western end of the American position, then deployed the remainder of the left flank's eight thousand men to receive the British attack. After one hour of combat, Burgoyne had lost another four hundred men, General Fraser had been mortally wounded, and the entire British force was in retreat toward its own entrenchments.

That was when Benedict Arnold arrived on the scene. Relieved of command or not, the sound of gunfire drew him like a magnet, and he plunged headlong into the fight. A furious Gates sent one of his officers after him with peremptory orders to return to his tent, but Major Armstrong didn't catch up with him until evening.

By then, Arnold had seized control of the battle and personally led the American pursuit into the British fortifications. Repulsed in his assault on one of the two key redoubts, he rode through heavy fire to lead a driving attack on the second one. This time, he succeeded. A furious, hand-to-hand fight carried the position, opening up the entire British right and exposing their camp, but night was setting in and Arnold, badly wounded in his left leg, had been carried from the field.

Combat tapered off with his departure and the arrival of darkness, but the Battle of Bemis Heights had been decisive. Coupled with his earlier casualties at Freeman's Farm, Burgoyne had lost over a thousand men in the two battles, and his demoralized army had retreated. By October eighth he'd been back in the positions he'd held a month earlier; now, on the thirteenth, he was surrounded in Saratoga by an army that outnumbered him three to one.

No, Carmichael thought. *Not the result Jefferson wanted at all. Pity about that.*

"Sir," he said out loud, "I presented the analysis behind every one of my suggestions to you. You saw the same data everyone else saw. You read the reports from Fisherman and Frenchy, not to mention my own. And you had access to every bit of satellite reconnaissance. You knew exactly what I was proposing at every stage, and you agreed with and approved my recommendations." He shook his head. "We knew all our models of Burgoyne's campaign had been changed by what happened at Trenton and Princeton, and I still think we did as good a job of adjusting for those changes as we could have. Unfortunately, we couldn't exactly explain to Burgoyne what we were doing." He grimaced. "And before we actually saw him in action, I don't think anyone could have predicted the degree of . . . ineptitude he'd bring to things after Ticonderoga."

Jefferson's expression had grown harder with every word. In fact, Carmichael was a little surprised he couldn't actually hear the Tenocha's teeth grinding together.

"It sounds to *me*, Major," he grated after a moment, "like you're trying to cover your ass by spreading the blame as widely as possible."

"I'm sorry if it sounds that way to you, sir." There was a certain lack of sincerity in Carmichael's cool tone, and Jefferson's eyes flashed. "Nonetheless, I believe the record will demonstrate that every step I took—that any member of my team took—was approved—by *you*—in advance."

"I'm sure we'll see whether or not you're right about that, Major," Jefferson said unpleasantly, and Carmichael saw Shamrock stir in her chair. Obviously it had occurred to her that Jefferson probably had override access to any electronic records of discussions between him and Carmichael.

"In the meantime, however," Jefferson continued, "we have to decide what to do about the present . . . situation."

"With all due respect, sir, I don't see much we *can* do," Carmichael responded. "Burgoyne's surrounded, his troops are starving, he's got hundreds of sick and wounded, and the rebels outnumber him three to one. Alexander the Great couldn't fight his way out of that situation."

"Alexander the Great didn't have *us* on his side," Jefferson said flatly. "The Tawantinsuyu intervened directly at Trenton; now it's *our* turn."

The rest of Carmichael's team stiffened visibly. Carmichael didn't, but that was because he'd already known where this was going to go.

"Sir, again with all due respect, I don't think that's a good idea," he said. "If we act openly, the Inkies are bound to respond, and there's no way either side could conceal the evidence in a situation like this. There are way too many witnesses, and those witnesses would leave way too many written accounts of whatever happened." He shook his head. "I don't think the General would approve of throwing good money after bad that way."

"You don't, eh?" Jefferson snorted contemptuously. "Well, *you're* the one who's left me the mess that needs to be cleaned up. I don't think he's going to approve of *that*, either, Major!"

"Possibly not," Carmichael conceded. "But just what sort of intervention did you have in mind, sir?"

"I think that's actually fairly simple." Jefferson bared his teeth in an ugly grin. "You'll take your flyers out, you'll set their masers to lethal levels, and you'll kill enough rebels that Burgoyne can clean up what's left. It won't leave a mark on them, so *let* them leave their 'written accounts.' Having a mystery they can't explain will be a hell of a lot better than watching Burgoyne's entire campaign go down the drain. Besides, when rumors about what happened get out, it'll knock the bottom out of the Rebellion's morale!"

The other team members stared at the field agent, but Carmichael only cocked his head thoughtfully.

"I can see several things wrong with that notion, sir," he said. "For one thing, I doubt anyone could possibly predict what sort of ramifications killing that many people who aren't supposed to die would have on the timestream. But even setting that aside, I'm sure the Inkies are watching for some sort of desperation move. I doubt we'd be able to kill anything close to enough of Gates's troops before Inky flyers swarmed all over us. Unless, of course, you want to bring down supporting flyers from the main HQ and add a major dogfight to the mix, and I really don't think that would be a good idea." He smiled unpleasantly. "We were lucky the Inkies managed to clean up after Trenton without any of the locals stumbling across something they shouldn't have seen. A dogfight on that kind of scale would dump wreckage all over the landscape. I'd rather not be part of that wreckage, if it's all the same to you, and the potential for temporal contamination would be off the scale."

"I don't really care whether or not *you* approve," Jefferson snapped.

"No, that's becoming apparent." Carmichael's tone was no longer cool; it was *cold*, with a cutting edge. "On the other hand, why do I think that after the Inkies shoot Frenchy, Fisherman, and me out of the sky, you'll tell the General it was all *my* idea? That when I saw the wheels coming off—solely because of my own incompetence, of course—*I* decided, completely without your authorization, to order my team to start killing Gates's troops?"

Jefferson's eyes flickered, and Carmichael could almost physically taste the rest of his team's spiking tension.

"So you're getting paranoid on top of everything else!" The field agent snorted.

"Maybe I am. And maybe I'm not, either." Carmichael's gray eyes narrowed coldly. "Of course, there's still the problem of Shamrock, isn't there? Unless you're planning on sending her up to get shot down with the rest of us, you'll have to figure out some other way to get rid of her."

"That's ridiculous!"

"Really?"

Jefferson had started out furious enough, but Carmichael's cool, biting defiance was fanning that fury still higher. And that edge of desperation was growing steadily stronger, as well. Obviously he had a pretty unhappy notion about the long-term consequences of Burgoyne's defeat . . . and of how his own superiors would react to those consequences.

Doesn't want any of his body parts ending up on the General's smorgasbord at his next formal dinner, Carmichael thought coldly.

One of the problems of the Tenocha system, isn't it, Mr. Jefferson? When the penalties for failure are that extreme, it doesn't leave people a lot to lose.

Which, of course, was the basis for his own strategy.

"I may be wrong," he said now, in a tone that made it clear both of them knew he wasn't. "Maybe you aren't really trying to figure out a way to cover your own backside and dispose of inconvenient witnesses in the process. If not, I apologize for suggesting you were." The irony in that apology could have withered the Amazon Basin. "But I still think what you're proposing would only make the situation even worse, and I *don't* think the General would approve. And because I don't, sir, I must respectfully decline to carry out any such mission without orders from higher authority."

Jefferson darkened thunderously and leaned forward across the table.

"*I* am your 'higher authority,'" he hissed. "You will obey my orders, or face the consequences!"

"Sir, respectfully, not without orders from higher authority," Carmichael said flatly, meeting the Tenocha's eyes glare for glare. "And, still with respect, I also insist that the electronic record of this entire meeting be forwarded to that same higher authority."

"You *insist*?" Jefferson's mouth twitched with rage. "*You* insist? Who the *hell* are you to 'insist' about anything to me?"

"The leader of this team." Carmichael's voice was hammered iron. "And no member of this team is going anywhere without orders from someone with higher command authority than *you*, sir!"

"Are you really stupid enough to think that's going to *happen*?" Jefferson sneered. "Understand this, Major—*all* of you."—His eyes swept the rest of the team. "*I* command this operation. *I* will give the orders, and *I* will determine what electronic records—if any—go to 'higher authority' for review!"

"Should I assume from that, sir," Carmichael said icily, "that you intend to edit, destroy, or somehow 'lose' the record of this meeting?"

"Assume anything you damned well want!" Jefferson barked. "But no one's going to see anything *I* don't want them to see, so you'd better get your ass in gear and carry out my orders—*now!*"

"If that's the way you feel about it," Carmichael said calmly, reaching into his left hip pocket, "it's probably just as well I brought *this* along."

He withdrew the recorder and placed it on the table. Jefferson's eyes widened, then bulged furiously, and Carmichael's smile was thin.

"I'm afraid I anticipated your probable reaction, sir. And since I had my doubts about the . . . security of the base recordings, I thought it might be wiser to be sure we had an independent record. I think the General's likely to be just a little irritated when he hears how you rejected my advice. And I doubt he's going to be thrilled by the notion that you're prepared to doctor the official record to cover up your own mistakes."

Jefferson glared across the table. Then his right hand darted into his tunic and came out with the toy gun that had killed Carmichael in so many outcomes of their very first meeting.

"Give that to me," the Tenocha said coldly. "Now."

"What makes you think this is the only . . . independent recorder in this conference room?" Carmichael was a bit surprised to discover he actually was almost as calm as he sounded. Of course, it helped that the goggles had shown him Jefferson doing exactly this. "Do you really think I'd be stupid enough to bring only one? Why don't you put down that gun before you make things even worse, sir? So far all you've done is make some bad suggestions and throw around some threats, but you're about to step across the line into something a hell of a lot worse."

"You let me worry about that. As for other recorders"—his gun hand moved, tracking from Carmichael's head to Shamrock's—"I think you'll tell me where they are to keep anything from happening to the rest of your team." His smile was ugly. "And if I were you, I'd be worrying about your precious *Kate*, too."

"I don't think so." Carmichael shook his head. "You can kill me—you can kill *all* of us. But after you do it, how do you come up with some kind of explanation to keep the General happy? I don't think he's going to be all that pleased if you wipe out an entire team just to cover your own ass."

Jefferson's barking laugh was even uglier than his smile had been, and his lip curled.

"For somebody who thinks he's so smart, you really are stupid," he sneered. "Wipe out an entire team? That's going to happen *anyway*, you arrogant bastard! Idiots like you are cheaper than dirt—we can always find more when we need them, and nobody in Tenochtitlan's going to lose a single night's sleep over what happens to the lot of you! Now give me that fucking recorder before I start squeezing this trigger!"

Carmichael allowed his expression to crumple. He stared at Jefferson in obvious disbelief for three heartbeats. Then he slumped back in his chair, his right hand dropping into his lap.

"You mean . . . you've been lying to us all along?" he said hoarsely. "All of you. *All* of you have been lying to us? About what you're trying to do? About the Inkies? About *everything*?"

"Why not?" Jefferson's lips worked as if he was about to spit. "It works, doesn't it? Except, of course, when the people we recruit are too damned stupid to get the job done in the first place!"

"I see," Carmichael said . . . and squeezed the trigger of the Vickers semi-automatic pistol he'd taped to the underside of the table in front of this particular chair two weeks earlier.

Jefferson's eyes flared as two hollow nosed .40 slugs hammered him in the belly, and his chair flipped over backward. He was still in midair, falling toward the floor, when Carmichael came to his feet. The pistol in the major's hand was an old, old friend. It knew exactly what he wanted, and the crown of Thomas Jefferson's head spread itself across the floor in a gory fan of red, gray, and ivory splinters of skull.

"I never did like you very much," Dunstan Carmichael told the sudden corpse conversationally in the thunder's wake.

.X.

"Are you sure you know what you're doing, Major—I mean, Dunstan?" Jennifer Brownell asked. She sat in the large transport's pilot's seat, watching the instrument panel, and her expression was anxious.

"Yes," Carmichael replied, extracting the sheaf of handwritten notes from his breast pocket. He sat in the copilot's seat, and he turned to the computer console, unfolded the notes, and laid them where he could see them.

"I don't want to sound anxious or anything," Brownell—Shamrock—said. "And I'm impressed by what you've already managed, don't get me wrong. But somehow I don't think the Inkies are going to be all that delighted to see a Tenochan flyer headed their way."

"And speaking of Tenochan flyers," a voice said from behind them, "I'm picking up three of them coming after us. They don't seem to want to talk to us, either."

"Probably buddies of Jefferson's, Frenchy," Carmichael said. "I don't imagine they want us talking to the Inkies."

He grinned and began keyboarding the complicated code he'd seen through the goggles. Even through the electronic interface, he could feel the incredulity of the startled challenge, which came up on his monitor as the Tawantinsuyu received one of their highest-level security authorizations from a *Tenochan* flyer. But he'd known what they were going to ask him even before they did, and he typed quickly and smoothly, responding flawlessly to each fresh challenge.

"I'm getting a voice transmission from the Inkies!" Fisherman announced disbelievingly from the com section. "They're directing us to a secondary base!"

"Good." Carmichael went on typing.

"I've got Inky flyers heading out to meet the Tenocha!" Frenchy said suddenly. "Christ! There's at least a *dozen* of them!"

"The more the merrier," Carmichael said, and turned his head long enough to smile at Brownell.

"See? I *did* know what I was doing."

"So, how much longer is this debriefing going to take? I've got an appointment this afternoon, you know."

"Oh, we're done, as far as that goes." Esperanza shrugged and poured fresh beer into Carmichael's stein. "I already know what's going into my report. All I'm really doing is spending enough time with you to satisfy the local Tawantinsuyu. I don't think they'd be delighted if they realized I didn't even have to ask the questions ahead of time."

"Yes," Carmichael smiled crookedly. "I can see where that might start them thinking about things you'd prefer didn't cross their minds. Like, oh, mysterious pairs of goggles. Speaking of which . . ."

He reached into his pocket and extracted the goggles. He looked at them for a moment, and felt a flicker of surprise when he realized he truly was ready to hand them back. He understood—now

—what Esperanza had meant about the risk involved in trusting someone with them, and Dunstan Carmichael had never thought of himself as a candidate for sainthood. Yet despite that, despite the fact that he realized he held in his hand the ability to achieve literally any ambition, he felt no temptation to keep them.

They're too *powerful*, he realized, laying them down on the small table between him and Esperanza. *I don't trust anyone—even me; maybe* especially *me—with that sort of power.*

"Don't be in such a hurry," Esperanza chided and left them there as he leaned back in his own chair.

They sat on a twenty-fourth-century deck looking out across the Pacific. The air was crisp and a little thin this high in the Andean foothills, but an invisible field surrounded them in a bubble of comfortable warmth, and the spacious house behind them was a wonderland of advanced technology. Carmichael wasn't sure who it actually belonged to—if, in fact, it "belonged" to *anyone*—but the "local Tawantinsuyu" had made it clear it was his for as long as he wanted it. Or as long as *Esperanza* wanted him to have it, if there was a difference. Either way, it was quite an upgrade on any safe house he'd ever encountered, and he was still a little bemused by it.

For that matter, he was a lot more than bemused by how readily the Tawantinsuyu had accepted Esperanza's guarantee that he and his surviving teammates were actually on the side of light.

From what he could figure out, the local Tawantinsuyu regarded Esperanza as a messenger from their own Directors farther uptime. In fact, Carmichael still wasn't positive Esperanza's Rogue Directors *weren't* the uptime Tawantinsuyu Directors. Whoever they actually were, it was evident Esperanza and the Tawantinsuyu were after basically the same thing anyway. And given what Carmichael had seen so far of Tawantinsuyu-24, so was he. At least this time he and his twenty-first-century fellows had been allowed to see their hosts' real culture. They'd been on the lookout for possible deceptions this time, too, and he'd seen no sign of anything of the sort. And whatever his own Inkies might be like back home, *these* Inkies were everything Esperanza had said they were.

Which was why, later this afternoon, a young woman named Kate Carmichael would be walking—*walking*—out of a twenty-fourth-century hospital room into her husband's arms.

He blinked suspiciously damp eyes, then cleared his throat and washed down the lump of emotion with another swallow of beer.

"I'd think you'd want to put them back under lock and key—or whatever the hell you do with them—ASAP," he said after a moment, lowering the beer stein to twitch his head at the goggles.

"I can see why you'd think that." Esperanza smiled lazily. "Frankly, the fact that you do is one of the reasons I gave them to you in the first place."

"I beg your pardon?" Carmichael quirked an eyebrow.

"Have you thought about what you're going to do next?" Esperanza asked instead of answering his question.

"According to the people I've been talking to around here, that's pretty cut and dried," Carmichael said. "They'll get me and Kate—and the other three—back to our own times. And they'll make good on everything the Tenocha promised us. For that matter, they're going to keep an eye on us to discourage the General and his friends from coming after us."

"I know that's what *they're* going to do. My question was what *you're* going to do?"

Carmichael looked him thoughtfully, eyes narrowing.

"Why do I have the feeling you're about to suggest something to me?" he said after a moment.

"Well, you did do quite well," Esperanza pointed out. "The Tenocha may as well concede that entire timeline to us for at least the next couple of centuries. Burgoyne surrendered four days after Jefferson's . . . untimely demise." He shrugged. "French recognition of the United States is almost certain to follow, and if it does, American independence is virtually guaranteed. The Tenocha may be able to drag things out by interfering in the southern campaigns, but the writing's on the wall.

"On a more personal level, you maneuvered Jefferson into confirming the truth to your surviving teammates first, which convinced them to trust you and let you get all three of *them* out alive, as well. And with my own modest assistance, you got Brownell's brother, Lascaux's fiancée, and Fisher's daughter—not to mention his wife and both their other kids—out of the Tenocha's grasp before you put the blocks to their entire operation. That's pretty impressive."

"Well, maybe," Carmichael agreed. Then he snorted and tapped the goggles. "On the other hand, you did slip me just a bit of an advantage."

"An advantage is only as good as the use someone makes of it," Esperanza said, and his tone was suddenly deadly serious. He looked into Carmichael's eyes. "You could have used those goggles to get just you and your Kate out of the line of fire. You didn't. You got out all of your surviving teammates as well. Not only that, but despite all the excellent reasons you have not to be particularly fond of your own Tawantinsuyu, you put together a plan that shot the Tenocha's objectives in the head and handed *my* Tawantinsuyu that timeline on a platter." He shook his head. "I've seen several people use those goggles, Dunstan. I've never seen anyone use them better, or more effectively. In fact, I want to offer you a job."

"You mean your Directors want me to come to work for *them*?"

"That's not what I said." Esperanza's expression segued into a familiar crooked smile. "I said *I* want to offer you a job. It's occurred to me that you and I—well, this iteration of you and this iteration of me—work pretty well together, and I've been flying solo for quite a while now. It might be nice to have someone to watch my back. Especially someone who can . . . see the options so clearly."

He glanced down at the goggles.

"You don't need me for them," Carmichael said slowly.

"Oh, but I do." Esperanza shook his head. "There's a reason I gave the goggles to *you*, Dunstan. I don't trust myself with them. Not because I think I'm an evil person, but . . . I've got too much of Coyote, too much of the trickster god, in my makeup. Sooner or later I'd succumb to the temptation to *play* God, and then one of my other iterations would have to track me down to stop me."

Carmichael frowned, and Esperanza snorted.

"Trust me, I speak from a certain degree of experience," he said dryly. "No, it's a lot simpler—and safer—to leave them with someone else. Besides, unless I'm mistaken, convincing you to sign up with me would be something of a four-for-one sale." White teeth flashed in a grin. "I'm pretty sure the rest of your team would like the opportunity to kick the Tenocha somewhere sensitive . . . hard. And from what I've seen of them, they've developed quite a lot of faith in your leadership." His grin turned into an almost dreamy smile. "When I think of what the lot of us could accomplish if I can only keep you and the goggles off the books . . . "

Carmichael gazed at him for several seconds, then looked back down at the opaque lenses. They still scared him, and he wasn't as convinced as Esperanza that Dunstan Carmichael was immune to the temptations of godlike power. On the other hand, *Dunstan* Carmichael had *Kate* Carmichael to kick him in the ass when such temptations arose . . . and he *wouldn't* have had her without Esperanza's intervention.

The endless dark blue water of the Pacific Ocean stretched out before him, but there was a storm moving in and out of the west, and there was a metaphor in that, he decided. A man could do worse than spend the rest of his life fighting to protect entire universes from a storm like the Tenocha.

Especially when he had the right people to help him do it.

He looked back at the goggles for a moment, then across at Esperanza.

"I'm going to want a minimum of a full month's paid leave every year, you understand," he said.

Afterward for 'Washington's Rebellion'

I met Fred Saberhagen—in the flesh, I mean—one New Mexico summer that stands out in my memory for a lot of reasons. I was visiting Roger Zelazny and Jane Lindskold, and one evening they asked me if I'd like to visit the Saberhagens. Of course I said yes. I'd read a lot of Fred's stuff over the years and liked all of it (to this day, my favorites are his Vlad stories), and of course I wanted to meet the guy who'd invented the Berserkers! What reader or purveyor of space opera could pass that up?

Roger and Fred were great friends, and he warned me Fred could be a little shy at first and that I shouldn't take it wrongly if he didn't say a lot that evening. Can't imagine why he told me that. What actually happened was that after Fred and Joan graciously welcomed me into their Albuquerque home, and after Fred had brought out the brandy, we sat and talked for hours. Over the years, I came to realize that Fred really was, if not exactly shy, one of those people my mom was referring to when she told me "still waters run deep."

They were *very* deep, those waters. The waters of a quiet gentleman, in every sense of the word. A man with a marvelous, dry wit. A writer with a broad sweep of imagination. A husband and a father whose love for family was right there on his sleeve for anyone with eyes to see. A human being—a man, in the very best sense of the word—who I was glad I met and proud I could call a friend.

Despite the distance between us and how seldom we actually met face-to-face, my wife, Sharon, and I came to regard Fred and Joan Saberhagen as two of our closest friends. And when we lost him, in the same way we'd already lost Roger, it was a hard thing. Hard for us, and hard—we knew—for our friend Joan.

So when the possibility of this anthology came up, I knew I wanted to be in it. I never got to play in any of Fred's worlds when he was alive, but I always loved them, and this is sort of like a final chance to shake his hand, maybe give him a hug.

So long, Fred. God bless.

Biographies of contributors to
GOLDEN REFLECTIONS

DANIEL ABRAHAM

Daniel Abraham is the author of the critically acclaimed *Long Price Quartet* and co-author with George R.R. Martin and Gardner Dozois of *Hunter's Run*. Daniel also writes as M. L. N. Hanover. His short fiction has been nominated for the Hugo, Nebula, and World Fantasy awards, and he has been awarded the International Horror Guild Award. He is presently working on a new epic fantasy series called *The Dagger and the Coin*, among other projects. He lives in New Mexico with his family.
www.danielabraham.com

JANE LINDSKOLD

Jane Lindskold's twenty or so novels include the six volumes of the Wolf series and the three volume Breaking the Wall series. Additionally, she has published over sixty short stories and various works of non-fiction. She lives in New Mexico with her husband, archeologist Jim Moore, and an assortment of small animals.
www.janelindskold.com

JOHN MADDOX ROBERTS

John Maddox Roberts is the author of more than fifty books and numerous short works in the SF, Mystery and Historical fields, including the Edgar Award—nominated SPQR series of Roman mysteries. John and his wife, Beth, live in tiny Estancia, New Mexico, with an ever-varying number of cats.

en.wikipedia.org/wiki/John_Maddox_Roberts

FRED SABERHAGEN

Fred Saberhagen authored over fifty-five novels, published several story collections, and edited a few anthologies. He created four series : Berserker®, stories of killer machines; the high fantasy *Empire Of The East* and the twelve Books of Swords/Lost Swords; the Dracula novels; and the retelling of classic myths in the Book of the Gods. Fred authored over twenty non-series books of fantasy and science fiction featuring Hitler and Lincoln, Daedalus and the pharaohs, Merlin and Were-bears, he explored his imaginings of a mysterious mask, veils of time, aliens in the basement, and more.

Before abandoning himself to imagination, Fred served in the US Air Force, worked as an electronics technician, and wrote and edited articles for the *Encyclopedia Britannica*. Fred was born and raised in Chicago. In 1975, he moved his young family to New Mexico. He left this planet in 2007, hopefully to explore even stranger universes than those he imagined.

www.berserker.com/www.fredsaberhagen.com

DEAN WESLEY SMITH

Dean Wesley Smith is the bestselling author of around one hundred novels under varied names and a few more short stories than that. Not only has he written original novels, but also a large number of Star Trek books, plus two original Men in Black novels, a number of Spider-Man novels and X-Men novels. His latest books are a fantasy novel *All Eve's Hallows* and a thriller under the name D. W. Smith called *The Hunted*. He is also currently writing thrillers under another name.

www.deanwesleysmith.com

HARRY TURTLEDOVE

Harry Turtledove trained as a Byzantine historian thanks to discovering Sprague de Camp's *Lest Darkness Fall* at a tender age. He worked for eleven and a half years as a technical writer because there weren't enough jobs teaching Byzantine history to go around. He has published many novels of science fiction (especially alternate history), fantasy, and historical fiction. Among his titles are

The Guns Of The South, *Ruled Britannia*, *Every Inch A King*, and *Give Me Back My Legions!* He and his wife, writer Laura Frankos, live in Los Angeles. They have three daughters.
www.harry-turtledove.com/

DAVID WEBER

New York Times best-selling author David Weber has forty-seven published titles. He is known for the Honor Harrington series, the Hell's Gate series, and most recently the Safehold series. Before coming to novel writing by way of the gaming world, David worked at a variety of commercial writing jobs. He has stated that he thinks of himself *primarily* as a storyteller, as a writer rather than an author. Writing is the medium through which he communicates the story. David and his family live in South Carolina.
www.davidweber.net

WALTER JON WILLIAMS

Walter Jon Williams was born in Minnesota in 1953, and now lives in New Mexico with his wife, Kathy Hedges. He is the author of twenty-seven novels and three collections of short fiction.

His first novel to attract serious public attention was *Hardwired* (1986), described by Roger Zelazny as "a tough, sleek juggernaut of a story, punctuated by strobe-light movements, coursing to the wail of jets and the twang of steel guitars." In 2001 he won a Nebula Award for his novelette "Daddy's World," and won again in 2005 for "The Green Leopard Plague."

His latest work is *Deep State*, a near-future thriller set in the world of alternate reality gaming.

Walter has also written for the screen and for television, and has worked in the gaming field. He was a writer for the alternate-reality game *Last Call Poker* and has scripted the recent mega-hit *Spore*.
www.walterjonwilliams.net